~ The Parliament House Books ~

Book One

The Trial

by

John Mayer

Second Edition : March 2015

Parliament House

The Trial

Second Edition : March 2015

Copyright © 2015 John Mayer

for Franz

When Glaswegian Brogan McLane completes many years of university education and legal training he crosses that great divide from Glasgow to Edinburgh. 'Called' to the Bar of the Scottish Supreme Court, he becomes a member of the most prestigious club in Scotland; The Faculty of Advocates in Parliament House. With expectations of justice for all and learning from the best, instead what he finds is Low Life in High Places in the Old Town.

About the Author

John Mayer would love to be a top-flight blues guitar player and have dated Jennifer Aniston. But all he ever did in life was to be a 1970s Indie Record Producer before becoming a top-flight Advocate in the Supreme Court of Scotland where he specialised in international child abduction: rescuing the children, not abducting them, of course.

In his youth, John was shot! Twice! Once in Glasgow, Scotland and once in New York City. John attacks everything he does with an intellectual passion as hot as the fires of Hell. And that's what he brings to his first novel in the Parliament House Books. It's called The Trial.

Glossary of Terms

Parliament House: The King himself dispensed justice in Scotland until 1532 when Parliament House (**PH**) was completed. The **Faculty of Advocates** pre-dates Parliament House; because long before Parliament House was built, a body of learned Advocates existed to represent cases personally before the King. Nowadays, Parliament House contains both the **Advocates' Library** and the **Supreme Courts of Scotland** which are separated by **Parliament Hall**; one of the grandest spaces in Scotland. Parliament House sits behind St Giles' Cathedral on Edinburgh's Royal Mile.

Crown Office: The grand old marble building in Chambers Street, Edinburgh, which houses the Scottish Crown Prosecution Service.

Advocate: A Scottish Advocate is equivalent to an English Barrister. He or she wears a 'wig and gown' in court. Advocates are admitted to the **Faculty of Advocates** by being '**Called to the Bar** of the Court'. The top Advocate is called 'The Dean of Faculty'. Most Advocates practice law by writing their legal documents in the **Advocates' Library** and appearing in court.

Lord Advocate: The Lord Advocate of Scotland is the head of the Scottish Crown Prosecution Service. He has a team of '**Advocate Deputes**' who are Advocates who prosecute the Crown case in court. The Lord Advocate and his Deputes are usually members of the Faculty of Advocates.

Solicitor General: The '**Sol Gen**' is Deputy Head of the Scottish CPS. Usually an Advocate, (s)he performs the same role as his or her English counterpart; giving legal advice to the **Lord Advocate** and any Depute who has a difficulty. The Sol Gen is also an Advocate and may occasionally prosecute a difficult Crown case in court.

Home Advocate Depute: An old term for the Senior Advocate Depute. The title 'Home Depute' arose during WW11 when 'Deputes' would go around Scotland prosecuting cases while the 'Home Depute' remained in Edinburgh dealing with the most serious cases.

Crown Agent: The old Scottish phrase for a solicitor is 'Law Agent'. The Crown Agent acts as the **solicitor** (for all business affairs) to the **Lord Advocate.**

Often deals with new procedures being brought in by government. A valued counsellor to the **Lord Advocate.**

Procurator Fiscal: Authorised by the **Lord Advocate** to prosecute in the lower 'Sheriff' courts spread around Scotland. In each region of Scotland the **'PF'** has deputies called 'Fiscal Deputes' who operate from different buildings around Scotland, usually adjacent to a Sheriff Court.

Lord Justice General: Scotland's top Judge who sits in Parliament House. Head of everything legal; criminal and civil, supervising the government, police, etc.

Lord Justice Clerk: Scotland's second top Judge who also sits in Parliament House.

Macer: As in the Houses of Parliament in London, one who carries the shoulder-mounted silver or golden 'Mace' into court to signify that the Sovereign's authority is vested in the judge who sits below the Mace. In the Sheriff court, the Sovereign's authority is signified only by a Coat of Arms above the judge. The Macers in Parliament House are often more than mere labourers; sometimes trusted with secrets, they know a lot about the judges they serve.

Calton Bar: There is, or perhaps was, a Calton Bar in Glasgow but the one in the Parliament House books is fictional. It is an amalgam of many pubs and other places known to the author as a young man in Glasgow. No connection with any such real bar or place is intended or implied.

The Tranny Hotel: Like the 'Gersman' hotel mentioned in this book, this place is also fictional and again, no connection with any such real bar or place is intended or implied.

Table of Contents

Prologue : Et In Arcadia Ego

EDINBURGH : PARLIAMENT HOUSE : 10 YEARS AGO : Around the perimeter of Parliament Hall, pencil-thin night lights cast their ghostly glow down through the high Gothic arches onto the heads of white marble statues. Along her cold stone corridors in the judges' chambers, bundles of orders and interlocutors lay signed and sealed; bound in red tape and awaiting delivery. Parliament House had settled down for the night.

In the darkness of the Advocates' library the King's clock struck 1am. As the final chime came to rest, Brogan McLane flung open the high double-doors and stepped into Parliament Hall. Marching to dead centre, with the smell of the night's celebration on his breath, McLane allowed his eyes to adjust.

In the stillness he could feel the power of those old judges. Immortalised in white Italian marble, there they were; pronouncing verdicts that resonated through the centuries. Regardless of the pace of change outside, in Parliament House their tiny tight-knit world endured intact.

The handing down from father to son of high judicial offices was timed to perfection. From pre-school to university and as young men dining in each other's country estates, they expected power over others as a birth-right. Some got there on merit and lived up to their judicial oath. But others schemed their way to the top and once installed, immediately ignored their sworn duty. Living according to their own casual moral code, theirs was a case of 'low life in high places in the old town'.

That much McLane had learned in his year of training. He also knew that having been born poor, far away from this centre of legal power, he could never rise to be 'one of them'. But for all that, he bore them no ill will. In Parliament House, that was just the price of admission.

The following morning at precisely 10.30 in the forenoon, the Dean's Procession arrived at the old oak door to Court 12 in Parliament House. After striking the door three times with the Golden Mace, those leading their latest Member to the Bar of the Court filed in. Taking the nod from Lord Aldounhill on the bench, the Dean bellowed: 'My Lord, upon this fine day Mr Brogan McLane has been approved as suitably qualified and trained to become a Member of the Faculty of Advocates in these Supreme Courts. Indeed, one of us. It is therefore my pleasure to invite your Lordship to administer the Oath.'

Looking down on this unknown newcomer, Lord Aldounhill began: 'Mr McLane, you will see the Roll of Advocates on the Clerk's table there and you will by now, know of its significance. It contains the signatures of every Advocate who ever practised before these courts since 1532.

In a moment I will invite you to sign the Roll but before I do, tradition demands that I offer you a few words of advice. Always respect the court and your fellow Advocates. Get to know the ways of the macers, the messengers, the jailers and the clerks of court. They will be invaluable to you in years to come. One more thing is very important. Always be yourself. Never be anyone else's man. That is a route to obscurity and we, the judges, don't like it. We prefer men of independent mind. Now with that I invite you to step forward and take the Oath of Allegiance.'

Lord Aldounhill stood and raised his right hand. As he did so, the wide ermine-trimmed sleeve of his judicial robe dropped almost to his waist. Stepping proudly forward and turning his open right hand slightly away from the judge, Brogan McLane hoped no-one would spot the fading red X-scar on his palm; where as a boy he'd cut it before pressing it into the bleeding palm of his closest friend and swearing to be blood-brothers.

Looking the judge right in the eye, he swore the oath. 'I, Brogan McLane do solemnly swear that I will be faithful; And bear true allegiance to Her Majesty Queen Elizabeth; Her heirs and successors; According to law.'

Out of court, in the grand Parliament Hall amongst family and friends, in clothes that would have cost his father a year's wages, Brogan McLane wore the proudest smile of his life. Standing slightly over six feet tall, a few strands of his jet-black wavy hair contrasted with his new legal wig. But what gave his face its most distinctive mark were his thick eyebrows over those steely blue eyes. They looked like a barrier between his head and his chiselled face. They said to the world that while under that legal wig was a prize-winning mind, the face belonged to someone from tougher stock than the usual Parliament House pack. Marked like an animal, everything about him was more like the prisoners being led through the stone corridors underneath Parliament Hall than the refined faces of those sitting in the Advocates' Library.

One or two passing Advocates shook his hand and Joanne McLane flung her arms around her husband's neck. As they kissed, her wide hat pushed back almost to tipping point and the outline of the girdle shaping her waist for the day, pressed through her scarlet two-piece suit.

As she pushed her husband away for another look at him in his legal wig and gown, her eyes fell on the slip of paper peeking out of his waistcoat pocket. The night before, whilst waiting for Brogan to come home, she'd heard a motorcycle arrive and drive away. But it was only when they were leaving for Parliament House in the morning that she noticed this note lying in the wire basket behind the door.

Before leaving the house, Brogan read it before silently handing it over. It read: *'Brogie my brother - there's too many people in Parliament House I've maybe met before. So have a great day big man an' I'll see ye fur a few drams in the Calton Bar when ye'r done schmoozin' wi' the high an' mighty - BJM.'*

~~~0~~~

Part One

Chapter 1

GLASGOW : PRESENT DAY. Glinting and dripping, the carbonated steel demanded to be wiped clean. Once more. Shoving it back in, up to the hilt, then twisting, turning, tightening. Level? Check. Three hooky plates secure? Check. Ready? Yeah. Ready.

With one pulse to her solenoid, she purred, the oil pressure gauge soaring immediately. And as her temperature rose, the exhaust note settled. Clicking-in to the wired waiting dock, the GPS lit up, filling the garage with her scary-bright electronic glow. Crack. The rising electric doors gathered speed, up, up till her throbbing engine filled the silent night with her tune. Then, away! Up through second into third. Watching her speed in the city streets, she passed the motorway sign to 'The West: Glasgow Airport and Greenock' on the other side. Whistling like the wind down the on-ramp and up in to fourth, man and machine slipped effortlessly as one through the damp night air. Between her rider's legs she throbbed more like an animal than a motorcycle. Right trusty and well beloved. Right enough.

Under the bridge proclaiming 'The East: M8

Edinburgh Newcastle' she galloped; effortlessly, quietly and infinitely responsive.

The GPS pages revolved slowly. Edinburgh city centre – wide view. Old Town – wide view. Parliament House – pinpoint. Then the fourth location – pinpoint.

'Gotcha.'

Desperate and with the helplessness of a new-born child, the dying eyes of Lord Aldounhill stared up from the floor into the 18th century chandelier, pleading their silent case. The thick globules of bright red blood spurting from his neck slowed as the old oak grandfather clock ticked at the wall. Then a shadow fell over his face. Towering over the dying Parliament House Judge the rider watched the last light of life ignominiously ebbing away. As the last rattle of breath left Lord Aldounhill, the man crumpled a bundle of legal papers in his fist.

The man stared down, kept his calm and exhaled long and slow before cramming the papers into his jacket pocket and scuffing away the outline of his heavy footprints in the plush Persian rug. Instinct told him to get out as fast as he could. But he couldn't resist the powerful waves of hatred emotionally flinging him around. Spinning on his heel, he took his revenge.

'Lord Aldounhill. Your final appeal is refused.
Case dismissed. How do you *like* it?'

The electric doors rose, stopped, paused and began their creaky descent. Turning the key to 'Off' she breathed her last. Kicking down the stand, pulling off his helmet and stepping out of his boots, a deep sense of relief flooded through him. Job done. No! One last thing. Before lifting the GPS out, the rider touched a button.

'Are you sure you want to delete your last 4 locations?' it asked.

With a broad smile all over his face, he touched the YES box.

'Yeah. Happy to.'

There in the garage of his old friend five doors down, sadly recently departed in an oil rig accident, he looked around. They'd moved to the neighbourhood roughly at the same time. The late 80s and through the 90s business had been good. But now his widow would be one of those women who didn't live, but just ... coped. That was no life. Sitting in relatives' living rooms with everyone feeling sorry for you. Better to get in while you can. Don't live in regret. That was the honourable course. The right honourable course.

The Trial

Pulling off his damp leathers, the rider patted the cooling chrome and steel, and whispered 'Rest in peace.'

In the darkness he quietly walked in his big woollen socks, up the garden and along the pattern-imprinted concrete lane at the back of the gardens which all the neighbours had contributed to laying just the year before. Once inside the back door, the quietness of the house did not betray the big old key turning in the iron lock.

Slumped well down into his big leather chair, his old friend Mr Johnnie Walker by his side, he toasted the night; downing three-in-a-row big drams. But tiredness now began to tell and after another deep yawn he let his head fall back into the chair. Only a few deep breaths and a few mental checks later, with eyes closed and his hand still around the glass, he re-lived those last few gurgling moments before saying to the heavens:

'Thank you, Thank you, Thank you. There is some justice in the world. At least tonight there is.'

As he rose for bed, to sleep the sleep of the well contented, his eyes turned to the shadowy photo hanging in the hallway. Lifting it off its hook, he kissed the glass.

With the familiar glow of the whisky in his chest, and satisfied that all had gone to the plan he'd shared with no other living soul, he pushed on the bedroom door; and was shit out of luck. She was awake.

'Where did *you* go?'

'Just for a run. I couldn't sleep.'

'I heard you leavin'. Nearly three hours ago.'

'I know. Ah just went down the West coast. To our wee honeymoon place.'

Sitting up on her elbow, his wife asked 'The West Coast? What in God's name made you go down there?'

Well prepared for the question he parried using the oldest rule in the book: never tell your wife the truth when she might one day have to give sworn testimony about the answer.

'Ah just wanted tae sort of, you know…visit him.'

'The wee man? Ye went to where the wee man was conceived?'

'Yeah. Ssh. I'm tired. Anybody phone me?'

'Phone you? At this time of night?'

'Yeah. Sshh. Night ma love.'

'Uh huh. Night.'

~~~0~~~

Chapter 2

Lifeless, fat and grotesque, his short legs unnaturally twisted, Lord Aldounhill lay where he'd fallen. The broad brown oak floorboards now masked his dark coagulated blood, most of which had seeped through and been absorbed by the dirt soundproofing between floors.

Out on the tree-lined road, a tall blonde-haired boy of 17 wearing a smart Italian cream suit, open shirt collar and very expensive shoes glanced up at the big house. Pulling out a bundle of £20 notes, Darren Walker paid his taxi driver without looking at the meter.

At the end of the wide stone driveway he let himself in with a set of keys. All was quiet, which was unusual. Skipping down the old worn stone stairs to the basement bathroom he slapped his monogrammed stashbox onto the polished marble washstand and sat on the toilet. Awkwardly unzipping, he peed. Finishing as quickly as he could, he nimbly chopped out a thick line on the wide washstand and snorted. Zipping up, he checked his nose and breath then took the stairs up into the wide square public hall two at a time. There he paused. Still all was quiet.

He let a few moments pass, absorbing the

atmosphere of the judge's house he knew so well. He listened at the morning room door, but heard nothing. Quietly tiptoeing upstairs he peeked into the Grand Reception room. Nothing. But he knew only too well, that in this house, things could be very different from what they seemed. Remembering that the judge's 'six-decanters' were always kept full, Darren figured he'd help himself to a big drink before leaving. But just as he gingerly stepped towards the dining room, his phone vibrated in his shirt pocket. Taking the call with both hands around the phone, he stood rigid on the landing staring down at the narrow door to the basement where his lordship kept 'the equipment'.

'Yeah.'

'Hi Darren, its Giles. Listen mate, I'm still in London. Last night's gig only wants to take me to Paris on the train with him. Can you believe it? Do you really need me tonight? Cos, did I mention I'm actually *from* up there? So I don't really want to … Can you handle the old guys by yourself?'

'Yeah OK. I'm not even there myself yet. I'll maybe not even go.'

'Ok thanks Darren, Byeee.'

As Darren pushed both handles of his lordship's

tall double dining-room doors, his squeal filled the house. Clamping his hands over his face, he tried to force the panic to the back of his mind. One leg shook involuntarily, rattling his entire body. Peeking out through his fingers he spied, childlike, at his surroundings. The chandelier lights were on and the brandy decanter lay tilted against the cheese board, nearly empty. On the dining table, the prongs of the cheese knife lay stuck in some stinking blue.

Drawn by the drag of the dead, dropping his hands across his chest, Darren fixed his eyes on the body; steeling himself from vomiting.

Shit. ***Shit.*** *Shit.*

Light from the chandelier sent tiny reflections around the room, but seemed to sparkle most brightly in the broken crystal champagne flute protruding from the judge's neck. Dazzled, Darren's gaze stopped abruptly at the wide pool of blood, now black and solid. Taking a cautious step towards the body, his ballet teacher's voice resounded. 'Better Darren. Neck long, shoulders back, buttocks clenched, toes pointing'. Inching towards the body, his heart racing but shielded by the 'old training' he stared at the judge.

With the cocaine's icy power swirling around his brain, he breathed in short pants. His nerves jangled.

Visions flashed before his eyes of police and TV cameras. Then his father's disembodied voice rang out.

*'**Do something!** For fuck sake you vain little poof, **do something!**'*

First Aid? ABC Airway Breathing Chest. Save a life – Do It Now. That's what the poster on the school drill hall said. Do it NOW.

Falling to his knees, Darren reached for a thick linen napkin discarded over the arm of a chair. Being careful not to touch the body, collecting every shard of glass, he delicately dropped each piece into the napkin. Grimacing and only half looking, he took hold of the thick base of the glass between finger and thumb and pulled; very slowly. Gritting his teeth, his hand still shaking, the champagne flute began to slide its slippery way out of Lord Aldounhill's neck. Turning away from the expected spray, the moment of release surprised him: no blood spurted out. Carefully laying the flute in the napkin he noticed something coloured on the rim. Staring at it for a second, he remembered. It would be lipstick. Purple lipstick.

With shaking hands and taking shallow breaths Darren tied the little bundle. Around and around in his coked icy mind, spun the Eleventh Commandment: Don't

The Trial

Get Caught Darren.

Lying there: dead. The man who'd promised on the night they met, to turn his life around. And done it. Done it to the point where he was now in a spin. Very carefully backing away, with his jacket sleeve, Darren switched out the chandelier light. Snorting shallow sniffs of air, he crept downstairs; scrubbing the last yard of banister with his sleeve.

With the tip of his toe Darren closed the heavy front door and without turning round, strode down the driveway; the linen napkin bundle inside his jacket.

Quarter of a mile later he saw his chance. Skipping down some slimy stone steps, Darren hid under the old cobbled-stone road bridge over the Forth and Clyde canal, hoping no-one would arrive for business.

Scanning the overgrown pathways on both sides, he was in luck. No-one was daft enough to be walking their dog along here and business for the night hadn't started. Looking around, a few yards out from under the bridge lay a stolen child's bicycle, discarded in pieces. Bolted to the wall, a rusty old iron rail - once used as a convenient tying-up point for canal horses - ran the full width of the arch. Now the only clean parts of it were the marks where young boys' sweating, gripping hands kept the rust from forming. Dead-centre under the arch, a carefully-stacked pile of bricks stood waiting. Each boy could be made exactly the right height demanded by the client.

In a moment of private silence, Darren lowered his head and clasped his hands in front of himself, staring at the bricks.

'Oh Christ help you. You poor little bastards.'

Quickly slipping the bike chain through the rough holes in two bricks he made a heavy weight. Getting chain oil under his delicate fingernails he spat out in anger 'Fuck. Fucking oil. Bastard. Old fuck.' Undoing a lace from a discarded training shoe, he bound it several times around the heavy linen napkin. Joining the napkin to the weight he flung the lot into the middle of the canal.

'Oh Christ, his keys!'

Clutching the evening air as though pulling his words back, Darren fumbled the keys off his belt-loop and threw them into the canal.

Now well out on the busy Gorgie Road waving frantically at every passing taxi and jabbing at his spare iPhone, Darren didn't even see the patrol car slow down in the line of heavy traffic on the opposite side of the road. A taxi stopped, blocking their view and the police drove on.

Darren pulled out a thick bundle of £20 notes for the driver to see.

'Can you take me over to Glasgow airport? Please!'

'Sure. No problem son.'

Chapter 3

Clasping his hands behind his back and squeezing the life out of the rolled-up Thursday Proclamation, Jimmy Robertson, the oldest Queen's Macer in Parliament House resumed pacing nervously up and down the full length of Parliament Hall. It had been many years since Jimmy had even looked at the King's clock; needing only the angle and colour of the light falling onto the parquet floor to know the time exactly.

With every pace corresponding to the Tap-Tap Tap-Tap of the proclamation in his hand, precious seconds ticked away. As 9.30 in the forenoon raced towards him, Jimmy could only hope that no 'Call Over in Court' would be necessary.

Tap-Tap. Tap-Tap. Reaching the bottom of the Hall he acted on a decision.

Half-a-dozen pleading Advocates waiting to appear in the High Court vied for his attention, but Jimmy ignored them. He pinned the Proclamation to the Board outside Court 3, leaving blank the names of every prisoner.

'Jimmy. Jimmy for God's sake man. Am I on first? Their lordships will … Jimmy. Please.'

The Trial

Turning and scanning the corridor for Press, Jimmy clutched the gowns of the two most experienced counsel: 'I'm missing … someone. It could be a Call Over.'

'We haven't had a Call Over for donkey's years. Jimmy! What are you …?'

'Just bide yer time. Ah'm no' bringin' them on till they're a quorum. And that's that.'

Spinning on his heel Jimmy Robertson made straight for the Judges' Robing Room. But just as he got to the stone stairway, his phone rang. The number was unknown and he nearly ignored it; but in the circumstances, thought better of it and took the call.

A little out of breath, he leaned against the curved stone wall. For several seconds there was silence on the other end. Then a woman's voice croaked a few garbled words.

With her words resounding in his head, Jimmy drew a deep breath before climbing the stone stairs to the Chambers of Lord Jamieson, the Lord Justice General of Scotland.

Turning the lions-head brass door handle he stepped inside the windowless oak-lined room where, in hundreds of years, only the Judges of the High Court of Scotland and their Macers had ever set foot. The Macers cleaned the room. Their wives combed the judges' ermine robes, washed their shirts, polished their shoes and starched their winged collars. The Macers also drove their judge home or anywhere else he wanted to go after court and, just as in the British army, they always exchanged pleasantries. But only *very* occasionally did the Macers gave advice – man to man.

When Lord Jamieson was on the phone, Jimmy always kept his eyes of the floor. As befits the top judge in Scotland, Lord Jamieson never got angry, but on this occasion his voice was louder than Jimmy had ever heard it. He positively bawled into the phone: 'Damn it man. You know as well as I do he's lost the confidence of the public and most of us up here too. He eats alone in our dining room. He reads alone in our library. Most of us won't even confer with him on the bloody Bench.'

Pausing for the reply, he retorted: 'I will *not* have the good office of High Court Judge in Scotland dragged through any more mud. This is as much your problem as mine. Just a minute. Someone's arrived. I'll call you back'

Trying to stand at attention, his face pale and with his phone in his hand, Jimmy Robertson was an obvious bearer of bad news.

'Well?'

'Its serious news my Lord.'

'Yes. Then out with it Jimmy.'

'It's Lord Aldounhill my lord. He's been found dead by his housekeeper.'

Chapter 4

In the rear of the crowded Elephant House coffee shop around the corner from the Crown Office, the well-dressed Procurator Fiscal for Edinburgh waited; stiff and awkward. A gang of scummy boys from the west of the city jostling with under-age girls who ought to have been at school were making too much noise for her liking. Every one would come her way in due course. Madam Fiscal knew how to wait.

'9.30 a.m.' he'd said and that meant on the dot. A fastidious man. Always had been. Even as a boy at Sunday school and later in Law school. He had to be top dog. He led. She followed.

Peeking out of her handbag the pay-as-you-go phone she'd used only once before said 9.28 am.

Untouched, the frothy cappuccino cup sitting invitingly in front of her would be the last thing to clean for fingerprints before leaving. After the call. When the coffee was cooler. And a napkin. Yes. A napkin to hold the elephant's-ear handle would be the thing to do.

9.29 am. Beginning to fidget nervously, a thing she never did, Madam Fiscal had always known a day like this would come. Hers wasn't the top job, by several ranks. But being the first woman to be PF in Edinburgh came at a price and Marjorie Millbank was about to pay it.

Startled by the vibration, she jabbed the little green phone icon.

'Hello.'

'It's me. I said 9.30 didn't I?'

'Yes.'

The elephant's face clock touched the half-hour precisely.

'You've heard of course.'

'Yes. On the News. The radio on my way in. The police issued a …'

'We have a suspect.'

'What? *Already*?'

'Yes. It's that ruffian, Brogan McLane. You know who I ...'

'Him? Of course I know … But … Why isn't this in a formal …'

'It won't be in one. This is 'close-hold' for the time being. I want you to sit-in on Morning Prayers.

'*Me*? Is this absolutely necessary? I'm certain the European law on …'

'You! And no-one but you. The officer leading is Commander Imrie. You must leave him to me.'

'Well … I know you're top floor and all that …

but what if I think otherwise?'

'In this case, there is no otherwise. This is *it* Mar … I need this handled well. McLane is our man. He fits so well because he doesn't fit at all. But, ... shall we say ... he does have a certain *history* with this judge. So all will be well. Understand?'

'Yes. But …'

'I'll be in touch. Toodle–ooh.'

With the price of a lifetime of loyalty and old debts swirling in her mind, Madam Fiscal's Christian conscience dragged like a ship's chain all the way back to the office. Yes, she'd known this day would come. Yes, she knew there would be a price to pay. But what her conscience could not bear, was that a certain Advocate round in Parliament House, was about to pay a price more burdensome than all her years of silent loyalty. All the way up in the lift, she prayed: Dear Lord, for what we are about to do to Brogan McLane, may you in your infinite compassion forgive us. For we are your children. Born in your image and ...

As the lift doors opened a polite recorded voice announced: 'Third floor. Procurator Fiscal for Edinburgh and personal staff only. Keycard pass required.'

The Trial

Out on 'Her' floor Marjorie Millbank stopped, ran her hair behind her ears and took a deep breath. Holding her abdomen and drawing her guts up as far as she could, she knew she just wouldn't make it past the staff; to the far end of the floor and into her private facility.

Slamming the door of the staff lavatory, relief came. All stalls lay empty. Forcing the cubicle lock round to 'closed' and only half-turning, Madam Fiscal dropped to her knees and vomited into the bowl.

Chapter 5

No-one knows how it happens, nor who starts them, but in Parliament House rumours spread faster than fire in a haybarn. Because every procedure is so well known, the merest change of detail - although invisible to the lay passer-by - is instantly noticed by the Advocates and the Macers, the underlying reasons are soon calculated and the effects easily foreseen. Hence, like the shimmering Savannah, the salivating pack often begin to stalk their prey long before the prey knows of their existence.

And so it was, as Brogan McLane strode down the flagstone corridor pulling his wheeled red box carrier piled high with books and papers on his way to the Commercial Court, the pack huddled around the Thursday Morning Proclamation with its empty column had noticed the tall grass moving, then the hovering of the first bird of prey, to be followed by the final sign of certainty. Prisoners were still locked up. Guards were nowhere to be seen, and Jimmy hadn't even turned the big lock in the door leading up to the Bench.

Slowing, McLane nodded and spoke to an acquaintance: 'You look worried Nick. Have you double booked yourself again? You know the Dean doesn't like that.'

The Trial

Shaking his head and exhaling breath from the bottom of his lungs, Nicholas Fairweather-Holboyd looked genuinely worried about the timing of his court appearances; conscious that if his duties overlapped in an attempt to maximise his fees for the day, there would be trouble – Dean of Faculty trouble.

As though trying to squeeze more time out of them, he wrung his rolls of papers and explained in a whisper: 'It's a call-over. One of the judges. Missing we're told. The others' robers have been spotted, so we assume it's Aldounhill who's missing. He's been out before but only as a single judge, so replacements have been drummed in p.d.q. But this is a three-judge court - and they all have to confer - so we're wondering if today's appeals will be …'

Tapering off his speculations, NFH and the whole gaggle turned as one. Emerging from the judges' central staircase, old Jimmy Robertson's face was as white as a sheet. But it was his next move that told the story of how the day was about to pan out. With a crooked finger he summoned the Senior Jailer from the prison platoon and, whispering into his ear, sent those Advocates about to appear in the Criminal Appeal Court into a spin.

With a nod the Senior Jailer acknowledged what he'd just been told, spun on his heel, grabbed his ring of keys and got onto his walkie-talkie. Old Jimmy's message was clear: there would be no Criminal Appeal Court this morning.

McLane let the throng split into their usual cliques and deftly weaved through towards old Jimmy.

The look on McLane's face asked his question without words. The answer came in equally oblique form. With his mouth tight shut, old Jimmy widened his eyes and nodded. Had it been any other judge, McLane would have let it pass with a sorrowful expression and made his way to the front of the queue for the Commercial Court. But Nick had mentioned a name, and that name touched a deep nerve in McLane. Unable to let it pass, McLane whispered into old Jimmy's ear. 'Really Jimmy? Dead? Is that right?'

'Yes sir. Found by his housekeeper this morning. We're in an an awfy flap aboot it. The Justice General is on the phone to the First Minister. The Lord Advocate's office is trying to get these appeals heard before the time limit snaps. Och it's aw just ... Look, sir, I know he was no friend of yours ...'

Raising his hand, McLane stopped the old Macer. 'Say no more Jimmy. I'm grateful for you telling me.'

Easily six or seven Advocates had witnessed their

conversation and McLane mentally noted all of their names. Plus, Jimmy never forgot anything and this passing encounter might need to be recounted, if in the days ahead, things took a turn the wrong way.

As they parted under the crossroads clock, McLane checked his time. If he put off preparing the Opinion till tomorrow, he could slip down to the Commercial Court in half an hour and still have plenty of time to seek the Orders he needed to save a factory in the Highlands from closure.

Now unsure of quite how to play the rest of the morning, McLane parked his papers just inside the Advocates' Library door and turned back out into Parliament Hall. Not wanting to catch anyone's eye directly, he bowed his head, clasped his hands behind his back and began pacing the Hall. With too many possibilities filling his mind, he tried to block them out by acknowledging in turn each of the old white marble judges, and occasionally looking up to their Coats of Arms high above in the stained glass.

Under the massive portrait of the Great John Inglis, the best ever Lord Justice General, McLane paused to gather himself.

'Yes. No friend indeed. And everyone knows it. But

he'd sit there uninterested to the point of falling asleep. He'd tell juries more with his eyes that he ever put on the voice recording. He put away men who plainly were just scooped up by the police ... for ... well, probably for statistical reasons. Judicial Oath? No. He forgot about that five minutes after he took it. But of course, he was so off the wall that they'll have a bucket load of suspects. Now that's a fact. There must be plenty of guys who've just come out, or who've just gone in – and their relatives – and their pals – and their ... There must be ... and of course his private life. Yes. Very private that was. Hmmm. I wonder.'

It was an old habit; but one he'd not practised for many years. Letting his scattered thoughts tumble out as though onto the ground below him, McLane recalled the face of a hippy girl he'd been seeing at university. What was it she called it? Transcendental Meditation. That was it. Let all your thoughts flood out until the head is a quiet empty vessel, to be filled with love and affection. Yeah, right. Try that in Parliament House.

Folding his hands tightly together, McLane unconsciously hid away the X scar on his right palm. The scar matched by his blood brother, Big Joe Mularkey; whose son that evil bastard Aldounhill had put away on evidence so skimpy and obviously so …

With one eye on the clock, McLane began slowly to perambulate. With even pace and carefully measured steps, up and down Parliament Hall. With his wig tilted ever so slightly and ankle length gown touching his heels with every step, he was just another Advocate in the Supreme Court of Scotland deep in thought. And, as for five centuries before, no-one gave him a second look.

'Could they? Of course. Their resources are …. Yes. Would they? Well, yes again. But the finger might point east, to Edinburgh, and they wouldn't …. No. They wouldn't let that … yeah, amateur hour that would be. But if Big Joe Mularkey has snapped or somehow lost command … but there's been no word … and there would be. Immediately. No. There's no way. No way.'

Two hours later, back in the Library, with his written Opinion in the forefront on his mind, McLane blinked, recalling the blue sheet of paper pinned to the wall outside the Criminal Appeal Court: which read 'Hear ye' all who have business this day herein. By Order of the Lord Justice General there will be a Special Appeal Hearing each lasting no more that ten minutes beginning at 2 O'clock in the afternoon. The court will sit until all have been heard.'

His breathing was just about settled and McLane dropped his head. Dipping his pen into the inkwell, the scraping of nib across parchment began to form his considered legal Opinion. Soothing and even relaxing in its formation, McLane sensed that Parliament House had been restored to balance. Glancing out of the window now and then to consider some point of syntax and how more elegantly to express himself, Mr Brogan McLane, Advocate, gave no hint of moving the tall grass; no birds hovered overhead, nor any pack assembled. Well, none that he could see.

Chapter 6

In Edinburgh's old cobbled Causewayside on the third floor of 'A' Division Police HQ 'Morning Prayers' were about to kick off this unique murder investigation. Every officer in the station knew the name of the deceased; always a good start. But as was often the case at this stage, there was more likelihood of progress from prayer than evidence.

With the usual buzz of rough loud conversations and outbursts of laughter the Murder Investigation Squad revved up to full whack. The important factors being hotly discussed filled the room: Football scores at the weekend, a newly born child and the prospect of this case being a 'right good overtime earner'. Some had been pulled from other investigations. Others arrived fresh out of their own beds. One or two had slipped unseen from beds they would never see again. And the remainder came in bleary after a hard night's drinking in their Old Town haunts.

Studiously and instinctively ignoring it all, Commander Terry Imrie began circulating interim reports to his team. Three bolted-on uniforms at computer stations sat ready to collate data and liaise with other police forces in the UK and abroad, if necessary.

Arriving alone and aloof, in immaculate blue

striped trouser suit and buttoned-up white blouse, Marjorie Millbank slipped into the squad room a nervous and awkward figure. Avoiding catching the eye of the officer in command she leaned into a corner, clutching to her breast in plain manilla folders a hurriedly printed selection of Human Rights law on 'Disclosure of information to the defence'.

Around the squad room several computer screens blinked silently, bearing only two words: Lord Aldounhill.

Flinging open the squad room door a scruffy young man with long straggling hair dressed in faded black jeans and a Rolling Stones' Tongue T shirt gave Commander Imrie a 'thumbs-up'. His sweep of the building for listening devices had found nothing he couldn't handle.

'Right. **Right**. Settle down.' was as polite an opening as Commander Imrie ever gave. The buzz diminished but only slightly.

'Hey, shit-for-brains Morrison, shut up when I tell ye.' was his second and final time of asking. The banter stopped immediately.

'Right. From the opening hymns you'll have gathered that we understand a total of bugger all about this case. So what facts *do* we have? For the record this is

The Trial

Thursday 12th November at 9.56 a.m. Lord Aldounhill was found dead at home a little under two hours ago. That is ehm … number 13 Mansionplace Road … by his Housekeeper a *Miss* Mary McCracken. She's aged … let me see … 61. She hasn't worked for the judge for very long. Less than a year. She previously worked as private secretary to *two* Scottish Secretaries of State. One up here and the other in London. She's now semi-retired … lives alone … and of course, there's no Sheet.

A hand went up at the back. 'Sir, do we have a …'

'Shut up. No. It's too early for a forensic path report but the Prof is telling us – off the record for now of course – that the judge has been dead for about two days. So that puts our time of death at some time on Tuesday 10th November. He was found in his dining room. On the table there were grapes, French cheese and a cheese knife lying on a wooden board. We already know for sure the cheese knife wasn't the murder weapon. What does that tell us?

'He was posh Sir'

'Aye, he was posh, that's right. But I was thinkin' more …'

'He probably died after dinner Sir' offered a young female officer, fresh back from Tullieallan fast track police school.

'Woooooh. Put her to the top of the class boys!'

'**Shut up** – she's right. Yes, maybe after dinner on the night of the 10th. So, was anybody else there? He was found naked but we don't know what that means for now.'

'Ah know whit it means.' whispered a few officers under their breath.

Imrie's quiet acknowledgement of that crack came only with a nod and turning his page, he continued: 'Right cracking on. Cause of death was most likely intrusion of the left-hand-side Carotid Artery – internal branch. So that's a stabbing in the side of the neck to you lot. Miss McCracken seems clean. She finished work on Monday. She shops and cooks on Thursdays and Fridays and cleans again on the Monday. So she was starting her cycle today. That all fits Jim Dandy.

The blood spray pattern initially indicates that the victim was on or near the floor when something entered his neck. So he was possibly falling when that occurred. So, did somebody trip him? That sets us up with two obvious problems. One is, we have no witness. Two is, we have no murder weapon; though a quick field report shows tiny shards of glass around him. So it's a puzzle.

There's another Field Report just in; so this'll be

crap as evidence in court. And the early word is that's it's a no-hoper anyway. Too many variables. It's a partial left boot print from the garden near the front door. *Possibly* more worn on the outside. So that maybe means a lean to the left. Big. Maybe a work boot ... let's make sure we quiz the gardener but he's a wee guy about 70, so it's probably not his. Let me see. What do they say? Oh yeah, possibly a hiking boot or a motorcycle boot. Something like that. Now what would a motorcyclist be doing outside Lord Aldounhill's house? Delivering? Picking up?

Bzzzz Bzzzz. His buzzing phone brought howls from the squad.

'Is that yer snitch boss? Who Dun It Boss? Please! Don't tell me boss – ah need the overtime.'

Fumbling his papers and his phone, squinting without his close-up glasses Imrie just made out 'MMcC md 1 fn cll b4 us 2 QM in PH.'

Raising his hand brought instant silence.

'OK, it seems right out of the gate our *Miss* McCracken hasn't told us the whole story. Her phone records show that one minute *before* calling 999 she made another call to? - Parliament House, no less. That was maybe just instinct from too many years of serving top toffs. But let's get to the bottom of that.

Lord Aldounhill was due to sit in court today so he'd be missed. I want his Macer interviewed. He now goes by the title of The Queen's Macer in Parliament House but he was 30 years a polis before he got that job. Auld Jimmy Robertson. He'll know more than most.

Now. Who had keys to his house? Is there a family? Well you can probably guess the answer to that one.'

'Oh aye. Sure. His hoose'll be packed wi' mourners. They'll be linin' up Sir, eh?'

The allusion to all the rumours and newspaper articles knocked Commander Imrie momentarily off his stride: 'That's enough out of you. Keep this professional. You never know – so ask, ok? Check the phone records but stay away from the banks for now. Keep an eye on the Scene reports as they come in. Forensics are trying that new infra-red technique looking for footprints in the stones leading up to the house, but that's a long shot. They're also onto fingerprints outside and inside, DNA from the vacuum sweepings, the Judge's correspondence might help; we haven't found a computer yet. Most of the mail is rubbish. Seems he was chairman of a charity sending water in plastic tanks to Malawi. And another one feeding weans in … Africa somewhere.

Oh and the CCTV cameras from Morningside

Road leading off to Mansionplace Road for as far back as they have are coming in. Right. This is going to be a very high-profile case. We might do a TV appeal for witnesses. I'll let you know.'

'Can I do the telly wi' that Presenter, Sir? The one wi' the big tits and …'

'No! Shut-it. *If* we do it, it'll be the Deputy Chief Constable – not scruffy bastards like you. Right, we'll get a ton of pomp and circumstance from Parliament House when we go tramping all over Parliament Hall and the Advocates' Library in our size 12s; but I don't give a flying one about that. OK, this particular judge put away his fair share of bad guys so we won't be short of suspects.

I want two on the Parliament House 'tick-tock'. I want to know about every second for every entry. Two on phone records and finding that computer. Two on the judge's movements for the last week. And court cases. Who he's just put away, who's just come out – all that, right? Also, I need to find out if that phone call to Jimmy Robertson was logged or did it just reach auld Jimmy privately.

I want two of you on personal items. Was his car serviced in the last month? Where? Did he buy anything with a credit card or on the internet? We know Miss

McCracken did the food shopping. Did he buy any presents? If so, what and for whom? All of that stuff, right?

'Coutts? Are you still studying for the next Sergeant's exam?'

'Yes Sir. Don't tell me I'm on door-to …'

'No. You're with me.'

The rest of you are on door-to-door. So brush your teeth – ok? It honks like a brewery in here. Right, anything else?

'Yes Sir' cried out Tam McKay, nick-named 'The Foreigner' because he came from 40 miles away in Glasgow. Throughout this briefing he'd been more admiring the female talent in running shorts sweating around Arthur's Seat Hill than listening to Commander Imrie.

'There was all that carry-on a few years ago when Aldounhill convicted that Advocate without a trial an' it was a right stooshie.'

'I remember that. So what?'

'Well Sir, Ah was waitin' to gie evidence when it a' happened. It was that murder trial in Court 3 in Parliament Hoose. The one where they fund that Bulgarian immigrant lassie buried in the crypt o' the church in Glasga, Sir. The defence Advocate was cross-examinin'

The Trial

D.C. Collins in the witness box when the Advocate suddenly stopped an' said tae Lord Aldounhill that he wisnae listenin' to the evidence an that it was a disgrace. He said Aldounhill was passin' wee notes tae the prosecutor an' laughin' an' that. Aldounhill went ballistic an' screamed at 'im. Ye know whit he's like Sir, eh? Ah mean, was like, eh? But the Advocate was well able for him. He stood right up to 'im and they were yellin' at each ither. That's when Lord Aldounhill just right off the bat, convicted the Advocate o' Contempt o' Court and slung 'im in the jail for 30 days. It was amazin' like. Imagine getting convicted withoot a trial. Ah mean, we gie' even the most evil bastards a trial. But that Advocate goat none. Nothin'. Just flung in the jail. Ah mean, it was right no' oan like. Well he appealed a' the way to the European Court a' Human Rights an' he won. The UK government hid to pay him aboot hawf a million ah think, Sir. It wasn't sweetie money. They were askin' questions aboot it in the Scottish Parliament an' aw that. How many nurses wid that pay for and how many doctors could they get tae do operations fur that kinda money an aw that. So I wid say we've got a suspect on day number wan. No' bad, eh Sir? Ah canny just quite remember that Advocate's name noo, Sir.'

Smiling at the Foreigner and elbowing each other, no-one even noted this eloquent soliloquy. Pop up suspects being well known dead-ends.

'*Anybody* know that name?' called out Commander Imrie.

Calling back in unison the squad room rang with the name 'Brogan McLane'.

The Trial

Chapter 7

Over the magnificent 'Office in Scotland of Her Majesty The Queen', known simply as the 'Crown Office' darkness falls in the morning. Handed down by Royal and Divine Right in 1494 that darkness is jealous, starless and devoutly bible black. Within its doors, light and its known associates, kindness and forgiveness, are forbidden from working their healing powers. Inside in their warren of rooms, an army does daily battle against the dangerous despicable masses outside. Every statement, every report, everything is given its darkest interpretation.

At 5:01 p.m. as her procession of purse-lipped prosecutors began leaving for the night, a dark blue Jaguar Sovereign whispered to a halt across the street, parking half up on the pavement. Looking like just one more car seeking that elusive parking place in central Edinburgh, only the sheer bulk of the driver and the darkened rear windows gave it an uncommon air.

To passers-by on the street below the grey stone building only seems to have five floors but, like much of what happens in those Chambers, that is a purposeful illusion. Up on the sixth floor in the palatial private Chamber of Lord Caruthers, Her Majesty's Advocate, all lamps blazed.

Tonight, sitting surrounded by statutes of the Great and even the Godly, HMA could not have cared less about keeping the ancient Queen's peace. Tonight, a modern trouble clouded his mind: public perception.

Down in the car the driver's phone rang. 'Send him up' was the short command. Opening the rear kerbside door the driver saluted a tall fit man filling an old suit to best advantage. Crossing the street no-one took a second look at Police Commander Imrie.

Waiting just inside the revolving door, a middle-aged woman in an immaculate blue striped trouser suit and buttoned-up white blouse put out her hand.

'Good evening Commander, we've never actually …'

'No. Hello Madam Fiscal. Where are we going?'

'Over here Commander.'

In the lift the PF inserted a code. As the doors opened on the sixth floor, Imrie held out his arm allowing the PF out first. Stepping out, he noticed a red blinking number on the panel above the buttons. Pausing for only half a second, he watched as the code silently deleted itself.

Should there ever be an enquiry under the Freedom of Information statute, none would be found. This meeting never happened.

At the end of a marble-floored corridor two Special Branch policemen stood solidly on guard. Approaching the Lord Advocate's Chambers, Imrie mentally noted the titles etched into brass plates on each door; Solicitor General for Scotland, Crown Office Solicitor and Home Advocate Depute. Only the wide carved-oak double-doors at the end bore no name.

With a cold smile to Imrie, the PF knocked and waited.

'Enter.'

Sitting at the octagonal table in front of his wide polished desk, the few case papers roughly spread out and his fountain pen in hand, Lord Caruthers was demonstrating that he had not yet reached any decisions.

Silently and slightly awkwardly the two guests stood making no eye contact either with each other or the others now drifting in, blowing into china cups and chatting to each other in familiar if careful tones.

'Do sit' was Her Majesty's Advocate's only

recognition that there were strangers in his Chamber.

Feeling into his inside ticket pocket, Commander Imrie pressed hard on the power button of his phone. The only woman in the room immediately reached into her handbag and did the same. Nervously glancing around, she buried her pay-as-you-go phone.

None of the places were set with helpful notepads or pens. No-one took notes and curiously, no-one but the Lord Advocate touched the table. With a forced smile but in a tone as soft as any priest would envy The Lord Advocate began.

'Gentlemen, where are we?'

Taking that as his cue Commander Imrie drew breath but the Sol-Gen beat him to the mark.

'No real damage, Sir. Forgive me but you knew him, I think'

'I did. Not at school of course. Not one of mine. At the Bar. He Called two years after me. Pushy little shit of a man. I don't know how he got into The Lochies. Shagging someone I expect. Oh well. We are where we are.'

Feeling a tingle of thrill at the mere mention out

loud of 'The Lochies' the only woman at the table gripped her handbag tighter. Here they were: Convened.

Far back through the mists of time, annually the Lords of the Scottish Isles met in secret Council on the tiny island in the centre of Loch Finlaggan, on the island of Islay. Not a soul lived on Finlaggan though many of the dead rested there. Each Lord brought only his eldest son both for advice and protection. As the last boat crunched to rest on the shingle beach, the Lords were a quorum. The outstanding feature of their meetings was that their discussions were frequently heated but their Final Decrees were always unanimous. By the 19th century The Lochies were a perfectly respectable educated young men's debating society. But in the 20th century two world wars decimated its best men and the club deteriorated into a secretive self-help group for *certain* Edinburgh lawyers and politicians.

The Procurator Fiscal had never been asked for 'Maiden Help' but she knew others who had. Casting her eyes around the table, she couldn't be certain of who was a Lochie. But one certainly was. And, she supposed, with the obvious exception of Imrie, that the others were too. Wishing with all her heart that this would be the case to bring her 'inside' she kept her powder dry.

With one eye closed and lifting the other towards Imrie the Lord Advocate asked.

'Well gentlemen, it's the end of the first day, is there a-n-y-thing of *any* interest?'

'Well my Lord, only one name came up at my Morning Prayers but in my opinion he's very unlikely; though others, I know, disagree. I mean, he's actually an Advocate.'

'Really? You do surprise me. Which one?'

'Brogan McLane, Sir.'

'Him? Surely not. He beats us in court a lot … but no. Don't you have anyone else in the frame? Is that all you have? A pop-up? Surely you know better … No. It won't be him. Let me know when you have something else.'

Leaning forward and pressing his palms into the table was Her Majesty's Advocate's sign that this meeting was over. The Law Officers of State began to rise, finishing teas and reviving earlier conversations. But still seated, the PF coughed in the way that brought her own staff to a halt. It had the desired effect.

'Oh. You have something to add?'

The Trial

'I do my Lord.'

'Do go on.'

'My Lord, I beg to differ. McLane is not a man of … well Sir, he's not a gentleman. He's a very heavy drinker. Frequents quite unsavoury places in Glasgow after Celtic football matches and he has admitted, even bragged of, very serious assaults in his youth. Nothing anyone can prove nowadays, of course. My Lord he has reportedly been shot twice. It is said that the man who shot him the first time – when McLane was only 14 – died on McLane's orders. That man went by the unsavoury sobriquet 'Shuggy o' Paradise'. He was lured to a card game in the East of Glasgow and there 'someone' cut him into pieces and threw him into the Drumbrae Canal. I should say Sir, that the body was encased in crushed metal – a car in fact. It was only discovered when the canal was recently dredged. We know that car-crusher belonged to a quite villainous associate of McLane. We are analysing DNA Sir. McLane *is* our man, Sir. I feel very sure of it.'

'What's your name again?'

'I'm sorry Sir … do you mean my …?'

'Never mind. My good woman, there are Junior Counsel galore round in Parliament House who could slice into that … For God's sake, woman. Evidence. I need bloody … something a lot more recent than fights as a boy. I'm taking you off…'

'If your Lordship would allow me? There is something else.'

'Oh all right. Get on with it. I have … other things to …'

'Traffic, Sir. Traffic camera reports.'

Producing a bundle of enlarged photographs Madam Fiscal held the meeting: 'My Lord, I got these only an hour ago from my counterpart in Glasgow.'

Laying them out like a royal flush, her hands trembled only slightly.

'This first one was taken about two miles from McLane's house. They form a series between McLane's house and the home of Lord Aldounhill. Not pinpoint exactly, but …Sir, a motorcycle, a big motorcycle bearing a false plate was first spotted – though not photographed – less than a mile from McLane's home in Glasgow. On the M8, going *east*, at just after midnight on the evening of Lord Aldounhill's unfortunate murder. McLane has been known to ride such a thing; though it has to be said, not for some years. Sir, the same motorcycle was seen returning *westbound* slightly under three hours later, but bearing a different number plate. An operator noticed the resemblance. He recorded images from every camera along the motorway, but lost it in the streets of Glasgow. Sir, the last record we have for that motorcycle is 2:48 a.m. I feel sure that forensics will …'

'Oh that's a very different matter. Yes. Very different. Send my compliments to the operator please. Now then. Hmmm. Alright. Early votes please everyone.'

Flicking his eyes between the Lord Advocate and the PF, the Sol-Gen slapped his right hand on the polished wooden table. Darting her eyes towards him, she noticed his shirt collar beginning to stain with sweat. Being first out of the trap wasn't his style. All his life Andrew Spiggot had waited. A master of never making his move too soon.

The Home Depute and The Crown Office Solicitor silently followed.

'We have three from five. But I want one more.'

Slowly unclasping her hands Madam Fiscal brought her right hand onto the surface of the table. Though sweating a little and slightly ashamed that her palm was marking the polish, nothing could destroy her absolute elation at being asked to vote in what was, in all but name, a Lochie meeting.

'Gentlemen. There we have it. Haul in Mr McLane.'

~~~0~~~

The Trial

Chapter 8

Lifting his eyes from the loose handcuffs, acknowledging the tiny act of kindness, Brogan McLane and the fat turnkey began their slow journey downstairs and along the drab corridor to the cells in Edinburgh's 'A' Division HQ.

'Ah coodn'ie lock them Sir. No' with you an' me havin' been doon these stairs together that many times. Goad-in-Heaven, Ah coodn'ie coont how many times.'

'Ye'r a good man Jackie. I'm always obliged. You know that.'

'Och sir. Ah'm that sorry, Sir. Sorry aboot this.'

Turning the big iron key in the thick steel door, Fat Jackie hesitated. With the door still closed both men could nevertheless see inside. Fat Jackie saw a body. Any body. McLane saw a client. Any client. Every time was the same. Before the door opened, those who daily dealt in death, injury and general destruction of lives could see it. Tangible and horrible. Packing the small cell. More powerful than the downward pull of junk, more pungent than drink oozing from dirty pores. Inside there was fear. Fear of someone being told the wrong thing or something evidential getting out, into the wrong hands. And always

67

alongside fear was its twin. The odourless, colourless, pervasive one. The slightly older one, that outlasts fear and goes the distance every time: Trouble.

On the concrete slab euphemistically called a bed, McLane shifted uncomfortably. His suit was now crumpled and itchy, his belt and shoes had been removed. On his back staring at the ceiling, he pictured the squad room upstairs. Up there it was all laugh-a-minute, but down here was a very different story.

Case upon case, punter after punter flashed by. The guilty, the innocent and the merely stupid. Right now, feeling the sum of all their fears, troubling his mind was the known, rather than the unknown. Fear rising in his guts choked his throat.

*This isn't trouble Brogan. Trouble usually begins with certainty. You **know** that. This isn't certain. Not by a long chalk. Remember that Brogan. This is only danger.*

Looking at the Section Notice in his hand, McLane read out loud that he would 'Pass with all legal speed through the due process of law?'

'Yeah right. Speed and due process. That's a laugh.'

McLane tried to exhale the stench of other

people's stale sweat and dug his nails into his palms. To himself he swore an oath: 'I *will not* go down for this.'

With one downward glance he again checked the scribble at the bottom of the page. A grim half-smile betrayed his thinking: *'No name. No department. No chance.'*

Through the thick narrow plexi-glass and four external iron bars which at 7 feet high passed for a window, McLane drew comfort from the dark night sky. Up there in the inky darkness he saw: A damp back room in a run-down concrete block of flats in the East End of Glasgow 30 years before. Five hard men gathering round a card table; their dealer, a teenage boy. Young but trusted. Smart and kept his mouth shut. With a lot more money than usual on the table, the atmosphere began to tighten. Davie Hume was winning with Ricky Anson losing to him. And as the money piled up, all eyes narrowed. Dealing more slowly, the boy called each falling card and its prospects. Then, that moment; when nobody breathed. Ricky Anson drew an old gun from his suit jacket, but before he could aim it straight at anybody, Big Jake Devine did the business. Flash! Ricky Anson's free hand was staked to the table; the blade entering so cleanly that the cards were undisturbed. As his blood soaked through the green baize, not a word was said. Jake's house. So Jake's rules. With a look of defeat in his eyes, Anson put the gun away. Jake pulled out his knife and Davie dragged his winnings towards his upturned hat. Game over.

As Big Jake left the room he turned to the boy, who'd never even blinked, and asked: 'Same time next week Brogan?'

'Aye sure. Nae bother.'

Right now, when the rest of his life depended on it, 'nerve' was needed and Brogan McLane had plenty of it.

~~~0~~~

End of Part One

~ The Trial ~

Part Two

Chapter 9

In the deepening darkness McLane's cell became as cold as a grave; the grey corridor outside began to hang with the unmistakable smell of junkies' breath and their leftover vomit. And now with the last of them settling in for the night the stale air honked with something even worse; despair. Not the kind of despair that arises from emotional worry or financial loss, but the kind that oozes unconsciously out of every half-shut-down body orifice of those resigned to life in a cell.

McLane lay straight and stiff, trying to exhale more than inhale, desperately fighting back the horrors of that prospect from tightening their grip on his mind.

'Maybe the DNA will be arguable. It often is. Who's doing the Forensic Pathology Report? Jesus this'll be killing Joanne. Were the hell is Big Joe Mularkey?'

Like a little plastic monkey twirling up and down, up and down, up and down a little plastic stick of possibilities, Brogan McLane passed the time. Time that couldn't be counted; it could only be felt, crushing and constant, punctuated by screams and the slamming of steel doors.

Inhabiting a half-world where reason slipped through holes into tunnels of worry, a few faces flashed by. The hardest of men, in the deepest of trouble, who'd surprise him across a table by coming out with something that melted the heart. But after their trial that all seeped away. After trial, daily life becomes about dealing with approaching dangers. Dangers in the doorways, dangers on the duty roster, dangers in the shower-rooms and landings. But most of all, dangers in the Appeal Court. Dealing with the dangers, McLane passed the night.

The clattering tin plate landing close to his ear woke McLane. Bleary and out of focus, the image of Fat Jackie almost filled the cell.

'Breakfast Mr McLane?'

'What?'

'Breakfast Sir? I'm sorry it's just the usual shite. Actually it's yesterday's shite. The sausage guy didnae turn up.'

'Oh, thanks Jackie.'

'If ye ask me Sir, there's something wrang wi' this. I mean, a man like you. Mind when you first cross-examined me in court - when ah wiz still wi' the drugs squad?

'I do. I do. It was the Scott Duncanson case, right? Died in police custody if I remember rightly.'

'He did. Noo ahm ballooned up like this. But ah still know a wrang'un when ah see wan, an you're jist no' a wrang ... well, Sir, the PF's oaffice waants us tae wind doon the investigation. Ah mean! Jist like that? Naw Sir, there's somethin' wrang wi' this an' it's no' you. Sorry, Ah've got tae go. Ah just thought ah wid say, the boys up the stair, we don't think you're getting' a fair crack o' the whip Sir'.

'That's kind of you. But you and I know Jackie, criminal procedure's got nothing to do with fairness. Right? Now that I'm in here, it's about them against me.'

Fat Jackie sloped away, unable to look his prisoner in the eye and was sorry when he slammed the door, purely out of habit.

Looking at the breakfast McLane could hardly recognise anything on the plate. Curling up at the edges a bright pink, square, cold sausage slab about the size of a child's palm was daring him to eat it. The potato scone underneath it had soaked up the white hard grease the sausage had once produced. Something that had once been egg-powder sat half re-hydrated beside the bright pink slab. Shoving it away, McLane preferred to live on memories of dinners eaten at his mother's table.

With aching bones, his head pounding out a marching tune, his right ear throbbing and his clothes crawling around his dirty body in a vain attempt to find a resting place, McLane stood up. Stretching as high as he could, he could touch the walls on either side of the cell and when up on the balls of his feet, he could put his palms on the ceiling.

'These aren't called Dog Boxes for nothing. I'm goin' for a run.'

Through Glasgow's Green Park, round into The Meadows in Edinburgh and waving to the girl in the California Coffee Company kiosk near the Vet College. Nodding hello to the passing police officers; they always slowed their chariot for a look at her. But the sheer exhaustion of the night before soon took its toll.

Slowing and feeling a deep sadness rise from not far below his surface, demanding now to be heard,

The Trial

McLane began to picture his gentle Joanne lying in their big bed alone. She would be washed out. She wasn't used to this. She would be coping, but slowly and nervously; unable to deal with the harsh, cold-hearted police procedures, the prison visits and publicity. The publicity would drain her. With anger rising and replacing reason, McLane cried out to no-one and everyone.

'Ya Bastards.'

With his eyes tight shut, filling his lungs, picking up his knees, he ran. A ghostly figure, down the street and through The Meadows past middle-aged people going to work and younger people going home. Out through Middle Meadow Walk and down Forest Road past Sandy Bell's Bar. Out into the traffic and across the road past Chambers Street, glancing askance at the Crown Office, then down King George the Fourth Bridge and round into the Royal Mile, picking up speed, and into Parliament House.

In the centre of Parliament Hall with fists clenched, arms raised high, his back arching like a man victorious, McLane let out an unholy silent scream.

Fat Jackie's unmistakable voice returned McLane to his four walls: 'Court bus. **Court bus!'**

Ka-chunk-a-clung.   Ka-chunk-a-clung.   Each turning key freed another sad soul pleading innocence, while others tried to straighten stories before meeting again in court.

'You're a dead man. D'you hear me? Dead.' brought a whish-thuck from Fat Jackie's ebony stick into another thigh. That sparked the usual mayhem. But with the slamming of Dog-Cage doors and more whacks on thighs, order was soon restored. With every prisoner except one inside the court bus, its big diesel engine revved up. As it pulled out of the tall steel gates for the short ride through the city centre to Edinburgh High Court, Fat Jackie sat down and wiped his brow. Another lot shunted out.

Pressing his ear to the cold steel door, McLane listened. Nothing. Silence had befallen the station. The cops would be having their tea and reading the morning paper. They'd be chatting about who was playing for their police football team against whoever-it-was this week and maybe venturing into what was happening in the Scottish Parliament. On Friday mornings only those unlucky enough to be 'lifted' just after midnight were left cooling in their cells until Monday; usually retching and craving their fix for the day.

The Trial

Only they remained, moaning but unheard. Those sad souls and one other prisoner. The man sitting alone in cell No3.

John Mayer

Chapter 10

High above Queen Street the river views from Edinburgh's Old Club began to fade in the Saturday morning cigar smoke. As servitors in black swallow-tail coats, scarlet waistcoats, starched wing collars and white bow ties glided silently around placing drinks beside members, only the expert whip-folding of broadsheet newspapers and the occasional tinkling of spoons against the inside of hand-painted antique bone china cups punctuated the birdsong outside their high windows.

The high bay windows of the smoking room had for centuries afforded members a spectacular view from South Queensferry in the west to Bass Rock in the east and over the river Forth to the hills of the ancient kingdom of Fife. Albeit that this was the second best club in Edinburgh, it undoubtedly had the best view in the city; though members rarely gave it a second glance. Everyone accepted that the oldest and *very* best club in the country was up The Mound, in the Royal Mile behind St Giles' Cathedral and membership was restricted. Very restricted.

Sitting uncomfortably in one of the stiff new high-back winged chairs on trial for members' approval, Sir Aubrey Winstanley was keeping an eye on the street below.

The Trial

Refusing more tea with a half-hearted wave, Sir Aubrey's grumpiness left not a trace of offence and the servitor floated away. That morning, on the way to the Club, he'd thought 10 a.m. was the arranged time. But the text message, received after he'd retired for the night, was purposely vague. So he couldn't be sure. Sir Aubrey had slept badly.

As a dark blue Daimler Continental glided around the corner, parking opposite the club, Sir Aubrey's discreet hand signal indicated his change of mind about the tea.

Stepping out of the lift and making straight for the bay window to his left came a portly gentleman in an open-neck check shirt, ancient tweed jacket, thick green corduroy trousers and a pair of brogues that made far too much noise on the parquet floor.

Once slumped down next to Sir Aubrey, the gentleman patted the servitor on the forearm as thanks for welcome tea.

'Morning and all that. How are you?'

Sir Aubrey tightened his mouth; his reply almost inaudible: 'Hello Marchie. I heard yesterday. I was in London with my Minister on Thursday. We flew up late and I didn't see any news until I got home. I only just caught the cricket from South Africa.'

'Well, the thing is Aubrey, now there's more. I've been speaking to the maiden help. I told her this man McLane is nothing but a bloody pop-up. There's really nothing much on him. It's pure speculation, if you ask me. But early reports from the science bods seems to have thrown up whole bucketfuls of things. Fingerprints galore, including yours old boy.'

'Christ! I thought there would be. One is careful but of course one never really expects *this*.'

'Precisely. However, something interesting has just popped out in the last hour or so. It's a DNA sample. From nothing less than poor old Aldounhill's neck. It's what is called a 'Low Count … something'. They're not sure, but they say it's likely to be from a *woman* because it was extracted from some purple lipstick.'

Tilting their heads to almost touching point, the two men trusted no-one. Sir Aubrey raised his eyebrows. The other man simply nodded once. The mention of purple lipstick brought it all back. When still below 10 years old Marchie and Aubrey were climbing trees near their school in Perthshire and came upon a clearing by a bend in a river; stopping only because of what they saw below. The oldest Pillbard brother and Mr Riley-Davis the history master. He wasn't naked but he looked like he was riding Pillbard the way people ride horses. Up and down, up and down. Frozen, the two boys were sure they hadn't been seen. That brief moment as they watched and listened from up in their tree seemed like a very long time. With only some idea of what was happening, they were puzzled as to why both Master and boy were wearing purple lipstick.

That image stayed with both boys; with no lasting effect on Marchie. But that first erotic sight caught root and grew into an indispensable fetish for Aubrey Winstanley.

~~~0~~~

John Mayer

Chapter 11

Over in the ancient village of Duddingston on the edge of Edinburgh, the cackling ducks on Duddingston Loch took flight, soaring between the village's 12th century church spire and the low winter sun peeping over a cloud. In the solid old stone house behind the oldest pub in Scotland, Commander Imrie lay beside his sleeping wife on an equally sleepy Sunday morning.

Awake for the last half hour, his mind was racing and he couldn't make sense of anything. Getting up and shuffling into the en-suite he peed away the last of the night before's whisky. Getting back into bed he slipped one arm around the love of his life. They'd come so close to breaking point after the investigation. But they'd recovered: just. Half-chattering, occasionally snoring, she was still out for the count.

Slipping away, he turned over and over that spectacle of being treated like an imbecile child. As he threw back the duvet, his wife stirred: 'What time is it? Where are you …?

'Och I don't know. Sorry. Sorry love. It's this …'
'I know. Why are you …? Are you going in?'
Her loving face said she understood the usual

82

pressures of a big investigation and knew this one was special. He wasn't himself. He hadn't been himself since the investigation … well, she wasn't going there. Not today.

'No. I want to do this away from the station. I'll make you some tea. Stay where you are.'

Tramping heavily down the stairs in his pyjamas and slippers, barking into his phone, he was already in Commander mode: 'Coutts, it's me. Get round here. I've got a job for you'.

On a cane chair in the cold conservatory, young constable Coutts was the very definition of uncomfortable. He kept flipping and turning over some flash-cards, trying to memorise entire parts of the Scottish Criminal Procedure Act 2005 while his boss took tea upstairs. He was reciting 'Powers of the Lord Advocate and Law Officers of State' when his boss returned, tucking his shirt into a pair of gaudy golf trousers.

'When's your exam? I've whacked the heating on. Here, drink this. African bloody tea we have now.'

'It's next …'

'Never mind. Put those away. I've just promoted

you to the rank of Chief Inspector.'

'Sorry Sir?'

'Just for this morning Coutts. It's what my old Inspector used to do. Grab a bright young officer and see if he has the balls to disagree with you.'

Constable Coutts' face went pale.

'Oh for God's sake. Not literally. I speak. You think and you criticise. See if I'm missing something obvious. Get it?'

'Oh. Yes Sir.'

'Right. What do we know? Well we know that the murder of Lord Aldounhill is about as big a case as one career gets, Right?'

'I imagine so Sir.'

'No Coutts believe me. This is tops. There is no bigger, except maybe ... Never mind. A conviction will probably mean another promotion. Divisional Commander, maybe even higher for me and ... well, there *might* be something in it for you. It's a big responsibility. Correction. A huge responsibility. More pay. Higher pension. Happy days. But Coutts ...'

'Yes Sir?'

The Trial

'I am not happy Coutts. Far from happy.'

'Yes Sir.'

'Coutts. This isn't really working for me. Will you stop saying Yes Sir No Sir and just tackle me like you would on that bloody rugby field you play on?'

'Yes Si... Sure, Terry.'

The look he got back told young Coutts that 'Terry' was stepping a little over the mark, but the ice was broken and they could begin in earnest.

'I'm puzzled Coutts. Puzzled. Firstly, we have a High Court Judge who's been lying dead in his own house for days before anybody finds him. So far as we know, the neighbours have seen and heard nothing. But then his house *is* tucked away from sight of the road at an angle so that the driveway looks out to trees and not another house. That's typical Aldounhill. Secondly, we have his housekeeper, who finds him. Can we rule her out as a murderer Coutts?

'I would Sir.'

'Why?'

'No known motive. Not enough physical strength to fight him. She's posh but not posh enough to be in his circle of friends. Plus…'

'What?'

'She just doesn't strike me as the type. She was too shaky, genuinely falling to bits when we lifted her in to the station and …'

'That's plenty. Me neither. Where was I? Oh yes. Thirdly, no murder weapon, though that may change. Fourth, he's naked when found. Correction, he's naked and rigor mortis had begun to advance when found. Fifth, there may have been a party on the night, or day, he died.'

'Party is sort of euphemistic, Sir. Isn't it?'

'You're right. But we don't know enough to be more precise. Though we can guess. Sixth, he's been stabbed in the neck. The blood was coagulated in the floorboards. The science labs will tell us more about that. There is little or no spray pattern, meaning that if he was stabbed while standing, then the artery was covered. Which means there is, or rather there was, something that stopped the spray and soaked all that blood. Where is it? On the other hand, if he was stabbed lying down, or kneeling down - which is quite likely - then maybe the insertion was slow, deliberate and maybe even expected.'

The Trial

'A sex game Sir? We've all heard the rumours, but he's been successful – twice I heard – stopping newspaper articles.'

'No. No. Coutts. He has *friends* who are very influential in London. But you're on the right track.'

'He may have played it before. We'll have to be circumspect when we question his K/A's.'

'Circumspect? Put that in your exam and you've passed. But you're right again. People know about his parties. Somebody knows.'

Relaxing and downing the remains of his African tea, Constable Coutts got into his stride: 'There wasn't a drop of *anything* on the carpets covering the staircase down to the front door. The back door was locked and bolted from the inside. One bolt from half way down the blank door into the stone floor, another up into the lintel and lock-latched over. The bolt on the locking door was right over; well into the blank door.'

'Ah you noticed the bolts. So did I. But where the bloody hell is that weapon?'

'Sir, we now know there were traces of purple lipstick contained *in* that wound, though not around it. Did somebody pretend to kiss him but stab him instead? Did blood spurt up a sleeve?'

'Good Coutts. Good. A wide sleeve maybe?'

'Yes Sir. Like a Judge's robe or an Advocate's gown?'

Waiting for a response and to be offered more tea, neither came.

'Did I say something wrong Sir?'

'No. That idea. The sleeve. Have you mentioned it to anyone else?'

'Of course not Sir. I've just thought of it. Why do you ask?'

Hesitating, Imrie's concern was clear.

'It's the kind of evidence that makes a big impression on a jury. That's all. Anyway, where were we? Yes. If the killer *was* kissing him, or was even about to, then Aldounhill might have had his eyes shut. But that probably means he knew his killer. Though not necessarily.

'He may only have been an acquaintance; you know Sir, sort of referred by someone else.'

'Even better Coutts. Better. I like this.'

'Sir, I counted four empty champagne bottles in the bin and a corresponding number of corks and ties.'

'Yes, and the one in the …'

'Yes Sir. Two corks were found in the kitchen bin, plus one on the counter. But one was found in a cup *inside* a glass-fronted cupboard. The glass door was closed so the champagne cork must have been popped when the door was open, but from a few yards away, flew into the cupboard and landed in the cup. Then the glass-fronted door was closed.'

'Right. Good lad. So it was 'Party Over' for some. But maybe someone else hung back to drink the unopened bottle in the fridge. Who was meticulous enough to care if the cupboard door was open or not? Did the same person put the other corks in the bin? Moreover, remember that the bottle in the fridge looked like a very different quality champagne from the others. I don't remember now ...'

'Dominique Neuville Brut Reserve Particuliere, a Fontaine.' £90 or more a bottle I'm told – *if* you can find it in this country. Very nice stuff.'

'Bloody hell. Did you remember all that?'

'I've had it, in France, when we played ...'

'Yes. Alright, alright. Follow that line Coutts. Was he about to share a present given on the night, or day, he died? Or was he keeping the good gear for himself? Were there two parties? Or two sets of guests? One set early and the other, possibly a single person, later?'

'Maybe Sir. No main course food was found anywhere. What was scattered around in the kitchen could have been there for a week.'

'Nah. Mary McCracken wouldn't have left that. No way. Maybe though, from the night following her last day there. Yeah, quite possibly.'

'Sir, I noted that the dishwasher was fairly full; and it had completed a cycle. In it there were 8 plates, 4 cups, 4 saucers, 4 bowls and silverware cutlery for four people. Mary McCracken said she *never* put silverware through the dishwasher.'

'By God Coutts. If you can memorise the '05 Act like that, you'll have no problem. But why eight plates?'

'It's 4 ovals under 4 rounds, soup bowls on top, cleared away, main course on round and cheese, grapes and biscuits on the oval. Ovals cleared away as a signal that the party is over; Sir.'

'Jeez! Yes. That's the way the Edinburgh Chief Constable has dinner served. Brilliant.'

'Thank you Sir. The cheeses were mostly French but the whisky-smoked Cheddar is from the Isles of Bute. Possibly bought in a supermarket, but if we're lucky, on the internet.'

'Good. Follow that up Coutts. Mary McCracken

said in interview that she didn't buy his champagne and can't remember buying any such cheeses. Though she did buy several more ordinary cheeses. That squares with what we have. Were either the French stuff or whisky-smoked Cheddar on any receipt amongst her house accounts?'

'No Sir.'

'And those accounts were detailed. By God they were. Did she think he didn't trust her? Where can we go with that?'

'The problem there Sir, is that there were probably plenty of parties. Guests might have brought drink, or food. Mary McCracken's house, car, handbag, fingernails, kitchen and bathroom waste bins and anything and everything else connected to her have all been infra-red scoped and tested. Absolutely no sign of purple lipstick. The type we're looking for Sir, is made by Rimmel. Their 1000 kisses Range. Ordinary and everywhere. About a year old according to the sample we sent.'

'Ah but that's not quite accurate Coutts. Think man. It wasn't really a sample. It was only a *trace*. No more than that. So that's unreliable. Anyway, her schedule checked out and, as we agreed, she doesn't seem the type. No, somebody else was cleaning up Lord Aldounhill's house. Somebody who, during or after a party, a wee party, began to clear up. Who was that? Why did that person stop, leaving champagne corks and ties lying around, crumbs on the counter, cheese and grapes on the table? What happened? What was said? Who else was there?'

Letting the question hang in the air, Constable Coutts thought hard. Nothing they knew, nothing they recovered and bagged at the scene, nothing from anywhere pointed to answering the question he knew his boss was about to ask: 'One thing I am sure of Coutts, is that Brogan McLane probably wasn't there. My first Guv'nor told me something you'll learn as your career develops Coutts. Murder suspects don't pop straight out of the box and bite you on the arse.'

'Of course not Sir. Are we done, Sir?'

'No Coutts. We're not. One thing you won't learn for your Sergeant's exam is this; You are a police officer. Never – and I mean *never* – allow anyone to undermine your authority. I don't care if he's the bloody Lord Advocate. Think for yourself Coutts. Think for yourself.

'I will Sir. Thank you Sir.'

The Trial

Chapter 12

Turning in circles around the tiny 'visitor cell' with his head in his hands, McLane searched through the latest European Law and Supreme Court judgements; hoping that memory would serve him well. Fat Jackie's squeaking boots on the shiny floor and the clink of his big bunch of keys announced the arrival of his lawyer at the door.

Fat Jackie left the door unlocked, winked at the prisoner and squeaked away.

'Where in the name of the Holy Mother of God have you been? I asked for you days ago.'

Garrad Fitzgerald, solicitor, looked more like an unshaven tramp who'd been given a suit by a charity than the most experienced criminal lawyer in Glasgow.

'Sorry. Yi' know how it is Brogan. Ah was attendin' a client arrested fur attempted mass murder at Glasgow Airport. He tried to smash intae the Departchur buildin' wi' a Jeep filled wi' gas cylinders an' a lot o' crazy blow-up stuff. Ah swear to ye Brogan, they only phoned me last night.'

'Alright. OK. God in all the years I've been coming here, I never knew just how hard it would be to do time in one of these cells. I'm about demented.'

Flinging his dishevelled frame onto the concrete

bed and leaning forward onto his elbows, Fitzgerald looked up at McLane.

'Brogan, just tell me wan thing man. Are ye guilty? Don't answer if ye' are!'

'Oh Christ. Why did I pick you? Don't be stupid. Of course I'm no' guilty.'

As two old hands at the game played only in police cells called 'Ask me no questions and I'll tell you no lies' both men had heard this question and a lying answer, hundreds of times. But this time the dynamic was different. Both were experts. They had known each other over 20 years. And on this occasion, neither really wanted to play. After a silent few seconds, Fitzgerald picked up the leather rag held together by a big paper clip which he called his Brief Bag, looked McLane square in the eye and said: 'Right. Let's dae this. The sooner the better.'

Banging on the wide-open door Garrad yelled 'Legal oot'.

Fat Jackie arrived, wheezing and with a half-eaten sandwich in his mouth: 'If you'd like to follie' me gentlemen?'

Raising whoops and skirls from other inmates, the shambling trio made its way along the cells corridor, past the Cell Sergeant and stopped outside a ten feet square interview room with no windows and nothing on the walls.

Snapping down the door handle, Fitzgerald stuck his head into the room: 'Aw hullo Commander. Ah'm just doin' the needful.'

'You're all right. Come in Garrad. You'll find the top brass have complied with the new rules.'

Garrad's eyes flashed around the room. Two video cameras and three microphones were carefully positioned so that, if the defence lawyer and client turned away from the Interview desk to confer, they couldn't be heard or lip-read. New rules indeed. 'Aye. So ah see. Thanks Commander.'

'Please sit down gentlemen. For the purposes of the recordings, I am Commander Imrie. Being interviewed is Mr Brogan McLane, Advocate. He has with him his lawyer Mr Garrad Fitzgerald, from Glasgow. The date is Sunday 16th November and the time by the clock that can be seen in the videotape is 13.31 hours. The subject of the interview is the death of Lord Aldounhill. I'll be conducting the interview gentlemen. I'm now issuing the formal caution to you Mr McLane. "By law you are not obliged to say anything but anything you do say will be video and audio tape recorded and may be used in evidence against you at any future trial. Do you understand the legal caution Mr McLane?"

'Of course I do'

'Can I take it that you are Mr Brogan McLane, Advocate in the Scottish High Court and that your professional address is Parliament House here in Edinburgh? I don't need your home address. Not at this time, maybe later.'

'Again ... Of course you can Commander.'

'Then let's start with your movements over the last few days, Mr McLane.'

'OK.'

'Brogan. Whit ur' ye' daein' ma man? Ye' know better than that.'

'No Garrad. Ah want to.'

Jumping to his feet, McLane let fly. 'For the last two days I've been fuckin' banged up in here as you bastards well know an' if I could get my hands on ...'

Garrad Fitzgerald grabbed McLane in a head-lock, pressing him first against the wall, then down into his seat at the tiny table. Turning to his client, he ended the interview. 'Brogan. Brogan. Shut up. **Shut UP!**

'Right Commander. My client won't be answering any more questions.'

The Trial

There was no need for the duty constables to intervene. The prosecution had all they needed from the initial police interview: the suspect shouting, swearing and making threats into the cameras.

Sitting motionless, Imrie continued: 'OK. Well … So. No answers at all?'

'Correct.'

'Oh well there's no point in me dragging this out. I mean, you two, of all people, know your rights. I am suspending this interview with Mr Brogan McLane at 13.35 hours.'

Holding up his hand for silence, the tape machine clicked off.

'We may need to do a little more of this you understand.'

'You can ask, Commander but I'll be advising my client to say nothing at all, at any time, to anyone, about the death of Lord Aldounhill.'

Giving the prisoner a look of sympathy, Fat Jackie clicked his handcuffs around McLane's wrist and led him along the cells corridor. Garrad called after his client: 'I'll see you at the Bail Hearing in the morning big man. Right?'

At mention of the morning, McLane dropped his head and just nodded.

Pausing at the cell door, Fat Jackie whispered into his prisoner's ear: 'Ah'm off shift at 8. Ah could bring ye in somethin'. A Chinkie or an Indian. Ah'll square it wi' the …'

'Don't be daft Jackie. Ye've done plenty man. Don't piss yer pension away on this.'

'Och Sir. It's just that …'

'Ah know. Jackie. Ah know man.'

Up in his office overlooking the beautiful heather-covered Arthur's Seat Hill, while signing the first weekend overtime sheet, Commander Imrie's phone rang. 'Caller Unknown' read the screen. His high rank afforded him an untraceable phone with an initial 5-digit sequence, different from all civilian phones.

Imrie took it anyway. The woman caller was obviously the Procurator Fiscal for Edinburgh: 'I hear the good Mr McLane is saying nothing.'

'How did you get my number?'

'It was given to me. I heard he threatened you. Did you charge him with that? And I hear he's instructed that thug Fitzgerald. Typical. What a pair.'

'Erm … excuse *me* Madam Fiscal but McLane didn't make a specific threat. And he's entitled to any lawyer of his …'

'Oh *please*, Commander. It's obvious that …'

'No I'm sorry. At this stage nothing is obvious to me. In fact things are …'

'Commander. These decisions have been made. Don't you see? These people are nothing but … Dirt with Degrees … that's what they are!'

'I'm opening a new line of enquiry.'

'What? New line? What new line? That's a waste of police time and my resources and you know it.'

'I'll keep you informed Ma'am.'

'But it was agreed that … in the *Crown* …'

Hanging up, Imrie scribbled his signature deep into every remaining overtime sheet and spun around. Looking out over the Hill, every muscle in his face dropped.

'Bastards. Brought to the Crown Office to be a messenger boy. Don't walk. Take this car. Wait here. Right hands on oak tables. Say nothing. Oh no. Not this time.'

Chapter 13

On shiny old Glasgow street cobbles, the tiny squeak from the broad deep tyres of an unmarked blue Jaguar Sovereign effortlessly fitting between the lines of a parking bay was inaudible in the Laboratory high above.

Stepping out, carefully placing his hat in the crook of his elbow, a crisply uniformed Chief Inspector wearing the epaulettes of Edinburgh 'A' Division nodded his thanks to the driver. Marching in slow time towards the heavy double doors and a bright steel sign covered in student graffiti, he was in no doubt. He'd found the entrance to Glasgow University's Royal Forensic Institute for Advanced DNA Testing.

Inside, the hallways were deathly quiet and both lift doors looked locked tight; leaving only the uninviting prospect of five flights of weary stone stairs.

Fussing and tapping test tubes, tinkering with electronic controls, sometimes over and sometimes under his pince-nez spectacles, Professor Sir Isaac Neuberger checked the work of his brand new Lab Assistant.

'That's fine. These numbers used to be enormous of course. Ridiculous really. Is that ready for bagging?'

The Trial

'Yes Professor. As I said, I didn't mind coming in on a Sunday afternoon. But I really still don't know why they want to use us. I mean they have their own …'

The Professor paused, holding up the Lab Bag containing the tiny Trace Sample of purple lipstick found in Lord Aldounhill's neck: 'My dear girl. The reason Edinburgh 'A' Division sent this sample through here last night has nothing to do with science. This sample was sent for one purpose and one purpose only.'

'What's that?'

'Oh it's much more fun if you guess. Go on.'

'For peer comparison?'

'No. No. Too obvious. You're miles away. No. Try again.'

'I can't think why they …'

'Wait. We're about to be interrupted.'

The policeman knocking on the interior glass door and holding a snow-white handkerchief to his mouth looked an unlikely figure amongst the old brown wooden benches and hi-tech equipment.

'Do come in. It's all quite harmless.'

'Good afternoon Sir. Chief Inspector …'

'Yes. Yes. I've got your name here. It's on my formal instructions from the Fiscal in Edinburgh. Sent to me at home. Last night. Hmm. Yes. Do come in.'

'Thank you Sir. Is your report ready Sir?'

'No. But I can tell you what will be in it.'

'The Fisc … I mean we … I was perhaps hoping for …'

'If you're hoping for numbers like 1,000,000,000/1 whilst I point to the accused person on trial in the dock of the court, then you shall be disappointed dear boy. Disappointed, I say. We don't do that any more.'

Fussing with a mouse, sneezing into his sleeve and shoving his long white wavy hair away from his eyes, the Professor gave the sullen policeman an exaggerated smile. 'Have you heard of that idiot Beacham? Have you? Hmmm?'

'Professor Sir Gregory Beacham? Yes Sir. He's the expert on 'Unexplained Cot Death Syndrome'

'Expert! Expert, you say! Nonsense. The man's a charlatan. And now a well known one too. Hee Hee Hee.

He's the idiot who trots out little stories to juries, as though people are simpletons. Simpletons I say.'

'Well, Sir. He is the world's leading authorit …'

'Simpletons Chief Inspector. People are not simple. Nor is science.'

'Sir, the report I've come to *collect* is …'

'Scaremongering. Scaremongering I say! According to him the chances of one family having one cot death are extremely high. In the thousands-to-one. Which is true. So, he says, extrapolating wildly, wildly I say, having *two* babies die in the same unexplained circumstances whilst sleeping in their cots during the night, though *years* apart, was exactly – *exactly* he says - the same as betting on an 80/1 'outsider' and winning. And not winning once at those odds, but dozens of times in one year. So a £1 bet on those two events would make the gambler – not a millionaire. No Chief Inspector. A billionaire. According to him, *all* such cases had to be murder. Or at least murder of the second child. There was no other explanation. But it's all bogus. Bogus I say!'

'Sir. If I could just see your report, I'll be on my …'

Handing over the Lab Bag containing the sample, the Professor delighted in pressing an old clipboard into the policeman's crisply ironed shirt: 'Sign here please.'

'But there's no report? When can I say it will be …'

'Fret not, dear boy. We use the new methods. And the Report will be available tonight. It's on my computer here. I'll have to go home now. To eat, you know. But I'll email it over. Tonight, perhaps. Timing will depend on the science, you see. The science, I say. That alright? Sorry you've come all this way.'

'But I really do need to know …'

'Oh yes. Yes. Yes. Yes. Sorry. I'm afraid there's not even a hint-of-a-trace of your suspect Mr McLane in the lipstick. The DNA saliva sample you took from him on admission to the police station was of excellent quality. So I have an excellent comparator. Sorry dear boy. But there was one thing though. Curious. Curious I say. I was a little concerned about the age of the sample. It is definitely a day older than I was told it was. There's nothing on the Presentation Form which helps me with that, but I'm sure there's some simple explanation; isn't there? Now I know I wasn't asked to go further than finding Mr McLane –

he's not there – did I say that? oh yes - but I did find a strand of someone else in the trace. It's what we call LCN - a low count number – low. Quite low I'm afraid, but it is there. It will take us a few hours, perhaps a day or two depending upon results, to let you have anything further. Sorry.'

Saluting stiffly the policeman wasn't waiting for another lecture from this nutty Professor: 'Many thanks Professor. I may be back.'

'Oh I have no doubt of that.'

Spinning on one heel the police officer marched out of the Lab as though leaving a police academy parade ground.

'Oh Chief Inspector. One last thing. Why the hurry? I mean why did you need this on a Sunday morning?'

'McLane has a Bail Hearing in Court tomorrow morning at 10 a.m. Sir.'

'But why should you need …' was all the Professor got out before the Chief Inspector let the Lab door swing closed.

With widening eyes the young assistant looked the professor full in the eye: 'Bail Hearing? Ah ha! Is *that* why they wanted this done so …'

'No. No. Dear girl. They wanted *us* to examine their precious sample so that McLane's lawyers *can't* now ask us to examine it. You'll pick these things up as …'

The young Lab Assistant let her esteemed Professor's words drift into the ether. She couldn't take her eyes off the blue Jaguar Sovereign swishing its way up onto the Glasgow motorway and under the sign marked 'The East – Edinburgh'.

~~~0~~~

The Trial

Chapter 14

Climbing the wide steps to his front door, assisted by his Man but slower than ever before, his Grace The 14th Earl of Marchion, now 93 years old, rested under the family's Latin legend. 'Gras Charteris Marciamontis MCCCMLIV Nemo Me Impune Lacessit' (*By Royal Charter the Seat of The Earl of Marchion; No-one Hurts Him With Impunity, He is Protected by Royalty : 1754*)

The legend being now, like himself, rather weather-worn and rounded at the edges, his Grace considered that he was still twice the man who would be the 15th Earl. Holding on to the wide top capstone he could just pick out his eldest son: over in the woods, going for a shoot, with someone, both carrying 12 bores; and thought they were up to something – again.

'Who's that with mi' eldest there Mason?'

'Sir Aubrey Winstanley, Your Grace.'

'Him! Never liked him you know Mason. Never. Light's no damn good for a shoot. What're they doing in there?'

Resting his sight on a 'Boundary marker stane' Boy Marchion locked an old tired stag in his cross hairs but Winstanley was quicker and, firing from the shoulder, he shot the old thing clean through the eye.

'Spot on, old man. You've still got the best eye in the British Army.'

Marchion took out his phone to call his man with the tractor and looked forward to feasting on this old boy; but before he could make the call, his phone rang: 'Sshh. This is him. Aubrey! It's my nephew.'

Breaking his gun and dropping the spent cartridges at his feet, Sir Aubrey Winstanley tramped over the heather to take a look at his kill. Approaching, Marchie's face gave him away.

'Well, what's the word from the dearly beloved nephew?'

'There's something I have to…'

'Oh Christ. I knew it. Out with it Marchie.'

'I'm sorry old man, but as your oldest friend Aubrey, I'm always chosen to bring you messages.'

'Oh shit, Marchie. Not resignation. My bloody pension isn't fully matured until next year.'

'No, it's not that. Not yet. But it's bad Aubrey. Quite bad. The boffins have been checking. It seems the DNA analysis boys in Glasgow have a wider database than our plodders in Edinburgh.'

'But surely that's not legal. The Data Protection

Act ...'

'They pay *money* for it Aubrey. They also picked a
lot of it up free. It's all in the name of science and it is
absolutely kosher; I do assure you. A Professor Sir Isaac
Neuberger is behind it all. Have you heard of him?'

'I bloody well have heard of him. He's the top
banana in that field. Absolutely ruined poor old Gregory
Beacham. I hope he doesn't have me in his sights.'

'Well old boy, only in a manner of speaking.
We're not sure. My people say they'll have to wait until he
leaves his Lab for the day to be sure. They know he's been
looking at the sample provided from inside old
Aldounhill's neck. He's got about 27 million DNA
signatures in his database.'

'Oh fuck. I don't like this already.'

'Yes. My nephew ... the one in the Crown Office,
he tells me Neuberger has all the military people plus odd
bods like diplomats, students and even bloody tourists
from art galleries, cafes, buses, trains; in fact his worker-
bees have even gathered samples of urine and bloody
faeces from un-flushed toilets.'

'Get to the bloody point please Marchie.'

'Sorry old man. Neuberger's very keen. The word
is he's isolated the sample from Aldounhill but he won't

tell anyone whose it is. But you're among the suspects old man. It seems you gave a sample as part of a help-out programme years ago. Before they had much width in the system. Over the years millions of samples were added to his database …'

'But if he's using mine without permission …?'

'No joy I'm afraid. Provision of the sample was implied consent for scientific use. And this is scientific use, is it not?

'Oh shit. Is there *nothing* you can do?'

'Of course there is dear boy. Calm down Aubrey. We're on it. He's just about to leave his Lab. Shouldn't be more than a couple of minutes.'

Tramping back over the East Moor in silence the would-be 15th Earl and his boyhood friend gave no hint of a successful shoot. Marchie's phone rang again. Speaking through his handkerchief, Marchie asked: 'Hello. Any news?'

The voice on the other end gave no hint of involvement, saying only: 'Yes. Your purple friend is one in a million.'

Ending the call, Marchie took the SIM card out of the phone, dropped it on the ground and rolled a large stone over it with his foot. Looking each other in the eyes, to Marchie's surprise it was Sir Aubrey who blinked first.

'Oh Christ Marchie. This looks bad. Don't you think?'

'Couldn't say, old boy.'

'Marchie, for God's sake man! If that bastard McLane incriminates me …'

'Look old boy. Best you stop right there. Remember I've only just been elevated.'

'But Marchie! We go back to …'

'Look. As a Parliament House Judge I will do what I can on the inside. And I'm not alone, as you know. But it's best if I don't *know* … well, the whole truth … you do know what I mean?'

'The truth? Jesus Christ man since when did *we* tell the fucking truth? I know what you want to hear and I'll tell you right now. I didn't kill the little bastard. It wasn't me. Do you hear me? Not Guilty Marchie. I'm not fucking guilty.'

Laying a hand on his old friend's shoulder, the would-be 15th Earl distanced himself even further from trouble.

'Don't worry old boy. We won't let that … and

anyway, even if he does and it goes belly-up, you'll beat him at your trial.'

'My trial! For fuck sake Marchie. There can't *be* a trial. I can't stand … Anything can happen in a fucking trial.'

~~~0~~~

The Trial

Chapter 15

Rock steady on Jimmy Robertson's shoulder, The Queen's Golden Mace gleamed as the whole council of Her Majesty's Judiciary processed into the Judges' Robing Room at the very centre of Parliament House. As the last judge stepped through the oak and iron door, Jimmy lock-barred entry, calling **Cou-ou-rt**.

Old Jimmy allowed a moment for their Lordships to be seated 'in the round' before coughing loudly as a signal to come to order. It didn't work, so he dunted the ancient floor three times with the bottom of his heavy silver-capped ebony rod.

Nodding once in thanks to Jimmy, Lord Jamieson began: 'Gentlemen I have assembled you because, as you know, this morning we have the delicate matter of the Bail Hearing for Mr Brogan McLane. I gather he is to be represented by Duncan McIntyre QC. My main concern is that justice is both done and seen to be done. We can afford no more appeals under the European Convention on Human Rights. So the question arises whether to send him to a sheriff court judge in the normal way, or come before one of us. My Lords, I have given the matter considerable thought, but I will of course take your counsel. Does anyone have strong views?'

Lord Strathcarrington pummelled in, spitting feathers: 'I do. Aldounhill was the Best Man at my wedding over 30 years ago. I want this, this … *person* …'

'Enough Bertie! That's precisely what I want to avoid. Do you think the baying wolves out there don't have that information? Of course they do. Anyone else?

To the left of Lord Jamieson, Lord Marchion, the most junior of their Lordships drew a loud breath indicating his wish to be heard: 'I am the most junior of your Lordships but I think I have the right approach to this problem. It should either be me, or the Justice General. That way we leave the gate open for an experienced member of your Lordships' house to hear the trial and others to hear any appeal. This stage of the case is important. But I do believe it to be quite easy to judge.'

Before Lord Jamieson could say anything in reply there came the ancient sign of universal approval to the suggestion: every judge's toe tapped once on the parquet floor. Twisting one side of his waxed white handlebar moustache, the Lord Justice General took the initiative.

'Good. Thank you Marchie. Then I'll do it. Well, that is all my Lords.'

The Lochies flashed askance from one to another.

The Trial

They'd never been so easily outsmarted. As they visibly deflated, Lord Jamieson stood as a sign that the meeting was over.

Flinging on his legal wig and giving Jimmy the nod, no meeting of their lordships had ever ended so abruptly. Striding along the narrow stone corridor from the judges' sanctum towards Court 3, Jimmy could hear the old fox chuckling to himself.

Jimmy was about to open the door when Lord Jamieson tugged his arm and they stopped. There in the privacy of the narrow stone corridor his lordship and Jimmy exchanged a few whispered words, before Jimmy flung open the high oak door to the Bench, calling '**Cou-ou-rt**'.

The noise of over 100 people rising to their feet on the flagstone floor took more than a few seconds to subside. As Jimmy carefully placed the Queen's Mace in its silver cup-clasp it caught the morning light streaming through the high stained-glass windows. With his Lordship comfortably seated, Jimmy laid out the daily notebook, Lord Jamieson's favourite Mont Blanc pen and two sharpened red pencils. The night before, he'd headed the first page with the stamped insignia of the High Court, the date and the name of the case.

Listening to Jimmy's footsteps walk to the end of the Bench and descend the five wooden steps, the Clerk of Court stood up, turned and bowed to Lord Jamieson, then faced the assembly.

'The prisoner in the dock will stand.'

Not being able to look at the prisoner he kept his eyes on the First Order of Business.

'Are you Brogan McLane, Advocate in the High Court of Scotland?'

'Of course I am.'

'Please be seated'

Picking up his pen then confidently twisting the left side of his moustache, Lord Jamieson asked quietly: 'Who appears?'

Duncan McIntyre QC rose noisily so as to take the eyes of the public away from his client: 'I do.'

'Ah yes. Good morning Mr McIntyre.'

Keeping to formal, neutral language, McIntyre adhered to the old rule that an Advocate never says anything in court that might have the slightest connotation of personal remark: 'I am obliged to your Lordship. My Lord, my motion on behalf of the accused this morning is for bail without special conditions.'

'Thank you Mr McIntyre. I will firstly hear The

Crown', smiled Lord Jamieson, referring to the prosecution by its shortened title. 'Then you will have the last word.'

The Home Advocate Depute rose but didn't even acknowledge McLane. Swallowing and squaring his small bundle of papers, the Home AD's neck and face turned red.

Leaning forward as a father would towards a son, Lord Jamieson asked: 'Mr Depute, are you feeling alright? If there's a medical reason why we can't continue, then I can …'

The Home Advocate Depute coughed more in embarrassment than discomfort, and couldn't give a truthful answer. Before leaving the Crown Office for court he'd put his head round the Solicitor General's door and was *assured* that this Bail Hearing would be sent to the lower sheriff court. A carefully chosen sheriff court judge had been nominated and the lower court staff informed that they would be getting the case. None of *this* was supposed to happen.

'I'm … I'm actually surp … My lord I oppose bail.'

'Really! Would you please enlighten me as to *why* you oppose bail, Mr Depute?

'Well my Lord, the most serious charge is that of

murder, my Lord. Indeed murder of Lord Aldounhill, one of your Lordship's fellow ...'

'I'm well aware of who Lord Aldounhill was, Mr Depute. Do you have anything substantial at this stage?

'Well, my Lord, certain DNA evidence has been examined and, whilst no *direct* connection can be made to the erm, ahherm, Mr ... McLane ...'

'Can *any* connection be made to Mr McLane at this stage?'

'Well he has been charged, as I say, with the erm, murder, erm of Lord Aldounhill but ...'

'Mr Depute. Does Mr McLane pose any flight risk or danger to witnesses? A simple yes or no answer will suffice.'

'Well none that I know of at present, my Lord'

'What kind of answer is *that*, Mr Depute?'

'Well, I'm doing my best to assist your Lordship.'

'Well you're not doing it very well, Mr Depute. Really! Someone of your rank should not be fumbling about like this in what is, by any standards, an important matter.'

'Yes my Lord'

'You know that bail is now competent in murder cases. This court has now granted such bail on several occasions. Now, do you or don't you have any good factual reason or legal argument why I should *not* grant bail to this accused person?'

In a fruitless attempt to gain another minute's grace the Home Advocate Depute flicked through his papers.

'I take it from your actions Mr Depute that you have nothing.'

'Well I *may* have my Lord'

'Well then you should have it at your fingertips, Mr Depute. If this were any other accused, and I have to say any other Depute, then this matter would have been well researched and equally well presented to me. Now do you or don't you have a fact or an argument upon which you rely in opposing Bail?'

'Nothing I can reveal, my Lord'

'Oh for goodness … Once again, what is *that* supposed to mean?

With the Home Advocate Depute in his sights, Lord Jamieson leaned forward again. He locked and fired his missile: 'Mr Depute, there may amongst some Judges be a culture of simply refusing Bail whenever the Crown says so. I have never agreed with that, as you should well know.'

Defeat oozed out of the Home Advocate Depute. Scribbling and flicking their pages, the press in the front gallery got the heated exchange; verbatim. Even the 'old ghouls' just there for regular entertainment, could tell that the Crown had lost the day.

Pushing at an open door, Duncan McIntyre QC rose to his feet: 'My Lord, I had the disgusting experience of interviewing my client in the cells here at Parliament House this morning. It is hardly necessary for me to say that he is a man of honour, a Member of Faculty: one of us. He is married, ordinarily lives with his wife in their house here in Edinburgh, and has a flat in Glasgow. He has, or rather did have, a substantial law practice here in Parliament House. In my submission he poses no flight risk at all and is certainly no danger to witnesses. Accordingly, in the face of absolutely no evidence emanating from my learned friend the Home Advocate Depute, I formally Move the court for Bail.'

Nodding more than bowing, McIntyre sat down, turned to his client and winked.

Carefully noting the remarks and twisting his handlebar moustache, a habit left over from his service in the Royal Air Force, Lord Jamieson, to everyone's surprise casually leaned back in his enormous chair to think for a few seconds. The only sound came from the ticking of the 200 year-old clock hanging in the centre of the top gallery. Holding pens at the ready for noting the Judgement, both counsel stared down into their papers. The clerk of court gently rested two fingers on the keyboard in front of him. One over a key which would automatically fill out the Form for 'Granted' the other for 'Refused'.

In delicate matters involving the liberty of a respectable person who finds themselves accused of serious crime, Lord Jamieson liked to have the counsel of one person in particular. Someone whose judgement of character he trusted. Someone who had, over many years, made instant decisions about people in extremely serious circumstances. So out in the corridor Lord Jamieson had asked the Queen's Macer Jimmy Robertson for his view. As Lord Jamieson pondered on the Bench, he caught Jimmy's eye; both men recalling their conversation:

'Oh my Lord, I would grant Bail without a second's hesitation. I know Brogan McLane, Sir. I can't imagine for a second he is guilty. As a matter of fact I think maybe there is a hint of …'

'You can smell The Lochies, can you Jimmy'

'Frankly, I can my Lord'

'You're right Jimmy. This prosecution honks of them. That's why I convened the whole council this morning. I'm a member of the Lochies of course, but a reluctant one. My father insisted I be nominated. I have never been comfortable with it Jimmy. Never.'

And with that Jimmy Robertson had flung open the door to the Bench.

Sitting upright Lord Jamieson pronounced: 'Bail is Granted. That is all.' then rose, catching everyone unawares. Nipping up onto the Bench as quickly as two heart attacks allowed, Jimmy deftly released the Golden Mace and led the Lord Justice General back to his Chambers.

As he poured two four-finger afternoon stiffeners, the Justice General asked: 'Well? Do you think I did the right thing, Jimmy?'

Sure that this would be one of those days for his memoirs, Old Jimmy lifted his glass. Chuckling, man to man, the servitor looked the Lord Justice General in the eye: 'Oh aye. I'm certain of it my Lord.'

End of Part 2

The Trial

~ The Trial ~

Part 3

Chapter 16

The sight of Jimmy Robertson leading Brogan McLane and his wife Joanne, arm in arm, from the direction of Court 3 sent the howling media wolves into a frenzy. With frozen faces the couple squeezed through their scrum into Parliament Hall. Trying to keep the couple cocooned, Jimmy Robertson and five of his men plus three delivery boys and some big student interns linked arms forming a human corridor between the Advocates' Library and the door out into Parliament Square.

At the door, shaking and unsure of what would happen next, Joanne McLane paused momentarily. Dabbing her eyes and drawing a deep breath, she looked scared. Brogan pulled her close and whispered: 'C'm'ere. Let me see you wee one.'

Wrapping his hands around her face, he kissed her forehead: 'We'll be fine. That's the hardest bit done. I'm out. Come on. Garrad's intern has a car waiting for us.'

McLane shaped her hair with his fingers and kissed her lightly on the mouth, trying to be a rock in a storm. But it was an act and she knew it.

The Trial

Out in West Parliament Square, even more paparazzi bayed for a few words for the lunchtime News. Smiling nervously, a little dishevelled and obviously exhausted, Brogan and Joanne McLane, arms entwined, remained silent. Pushing out in front of the couple and holding up a piece of paper, Garrad Fitzgerald took the focus away from his client, indicating that a statement would now be read.

'Mah .. My client Brogan McLane is innocent of these charges. He's a man of honour and integrity. He'll defend himsel to the bitter end. We're confident of his *ultimate* acquittal, even if we have to go to the European Court of Human Rights. We are not naïve. We don't know *why* Brogan McLane has been charged with the murder of Lord Aldounhill, so for legal reasons we're saying nuthin' more than that at this stage. Thanks.'

All at once, shouting for more, they tried again: 'How's it been in police custody?' 'Will you be resigning from the Faculty of Advocates?' 'What're your chances at trial Mr McLane?'

Out on the Royal Mile a big black 4x4 crept through the crowd allowing the McLanes and Garrad Fitzgerald to clamber in. At the first break in the pack, the intern floored the accelerator sending the big vehicle

125

shooting up the Royal Mile towards Edinburgh Castle. The TV crews followed using long lenses. The Press scribbled even longer rumours.

When the spreading sprawl between Edinburgh and Glasgow eventually gave way to fields of green and a horizon, McLane leaned his head on the rear passenger's window, counting the tiny fields in the distance.

Powering up his phone, he immediately received dozens of text and voicemail messages. While holding down the 'Delete' key he spotted one welcome name. His face widening to a smile, he read: 'Standin' in Defence HQ watchin' you on TV. Get here a.s.a.p.'

McLane turned to his wife, licked his lips and hesitated in the way he always did when gathering his thoughts: 'Jo. You go the flat and I'll be home as soon as I can. OK? I need to see a guy.'

Looking her husband in the eyes, Joanne McLane saw that he'd slid down a tunnel. Back to those days when he lived every day in mortal fear of his life in old gangland Glasgow:

'Oh please Brogan. You're just out. Don't do anything that would ...'

'Don't worry my darlin'. I won't.'

The Trial

McLane squeezed his wife's hand and laid his other hand on the young intern's shoulder. Very quietly he asked: 'Son, do you know how to get to the Calton Bar?'

Chapter 17

The tiny door at the back of the stinking toilet in the Calton Bar in Glasgow is unknown to the city planning authorities although it is known to the police, who nowadays don't really care about it. Few women ever drink in the Calton Bar so, despite hygiene regulations, there is no women's toilet. Those women who do need, just step into the lane and pee directly down the drain that carries sewage from the tenement houses above. Anything else is done in the fish and chip restaurant down the street. The 'wee door' at the back of the toilet is now rarely used. But when opened, it hits a rusty iron ladder. Fixed precariously now, it still rises four floors up to the back bedroom window of Ma Gordon's old brothel. From inside, the skylight window is just a jump onto her old dresser and a pull out onto the roof. The whole system is designed so that some who enter the Calton Bar are never recorded on any police log as having left.

The old apartment is boarded up now but the ladder is left over from the old days before Ma went to jail for brothel-keeping and her wee sideline, supplying guns to the boys downstairs in the Calton Bar. The regulars used to enjoy watching young police officers make a good chase up the ladder; but times have changed. Back then she was protected by the hardest man in the city; the man now standing alone in the freezing-cold brick toilet.

Even with his slight left lean, filling the brick shit-house, Big Joe Mularkey stood six feet four inches and 275 pounds. His three day growth, the same length as his cropped hair, masked a once broken cheek bone that have never been allowed to heal properly. And his bushy eyebrows masked the mark where a ship's crane hook had accidentally caught him in a high swell one night down in the Eastern Mediterranean.

Pressing out the last drops and farting, Big Joe broke into laughter at the efforts of some wag; probably one of the Young Calton Team, who'd spray painted a tombstone on the steel urinal that wasn't there the day before. A nice big tombstone with scrolls and even a failed attempt at Roman numerals. In marker pen he'd written: 'Here lies a Right Bastard of the First Order of Bastards. Hated in life and in death. Here lies Lord Aldounhill.'

With a shake Big Joe finished and buttoned up before checking over his shoulder. From his jacket pocket he pulled an envelope half-way out, but instantly slotted it back into place. What was the point? Every word was indelibly ingrained on his mind.

The pain was hard to bear. Every day now, the pain became harder and harder to bear. Joe's life had been a series of breakages, some into very small pieces. But now? Now there was only dust. This was the worst.

Worried that his wife could hardly bear any more pain and might crack, he'd even thought of calling a Helpline number he'd seen on the subway. Anonymously, of course. As she coped, he saw her die a little more every time there was mention of her boy. About a week before, dealing with this in his own way, Big Joe had flown into his latest rage. But she'd stopped him. Flinging her arms around her giant, she'd pleaded: 'No Joe. No. *Ah* need you *here* tonight. Wait. Please. Stop. The legal thing might be over. But for us? Joe we've got to get used to the idea: this will *never* be over.'

Walking back into the Bar, a voice like broken beer bottles in a blender growled from behind a cloud of cigar smoke: 'Another pint, Joe?'

The kindness being offered came from a man known only as 'The Arab'. He'd come from the South side of the city as a boy of only seven to live with an aunt, but he was clever enough never to tell anyone his real name. One night a girl bragging about her first sexual encounter with him, called him an Arab stallion. When several others also testified to the same extent, the name stuck.

'Aye, on ye go Arab. Ah'll have one wi' ye.'

Behind the bar pulling the beers, Lenny, the new owner - who'd won the Calton Bar in the biggest hand of cards the East End had seen in years - flashed his eyes between Joe, the Arab and outside; where a guy had crossed the street twice in under five minutes.

Big Joe stood alone in silence. Just in case, he took a look around checking for soldiers. He knew every one of the twenty two men in the place. Not just to say hello to, or to have the odd drink with, but the insides of their lives. In some cases he'd lived in their clothes and eaten from their earnings; no questions asked. Every birth, death, arrest, occasional gambling win and who'd had the pleasure of their wives before, and sometimes after marriage, was known to all. To these men the Calton Bar wasn't a second home. It was their first. Sitting behind a newspaper he couldn't read, was 'Sailor', so-called because he'd never left Glasgow. 'Wee Wheelie' so-called because his father was 'Wheelie' and both were expert car thieves before the days of electronic door locking and satellite tracking. Their car business had collapsed but there was always scrap metal. 'Clarino' was, as usual, dealing cards and calculating odds as he dropped each card. He got his nickname because he had a beautiful hand-made Clarinet. He couldn't play it. The instrument had been an inheritance from his grandfather; the spoils of war in '44.

In a quiet corner that could only be seen from the back of the Bar was the wee man Joe had specifically come to see. Invisible behind his newspaper open at the day's runners and riders, in his jacket pocket were yesterday's winnings; but on his mind was tomorrow's message. There sat Tucker Queen. A civilian. Absolutely neutral. Each big district of the city has one and Tucker knows them all. Essentially Tucker is a messenger, but not the kind who runs errands for a few bob here and there. Tucker is more in the way of a Herald. An Envoy McLane had once called him, because Tucker deals only with important messages between the city's top men. A short slim man of about 55, Tucker's birth was never recorded, so his exact age is unknown; but equally irrelevant. His father was unknown and his mother died in his childbirth. He was therefore exactly what the impoverished East End of Glasgow community needed; he had been passed around as a 'money bairn'. Taken as a baby to various government Social Security offices by several women who all claimed payment for the same extra child, each one knowing perfectly well that neither Tucker nor his mother could be prosecuted for compliance. He'd been fed by the whole community and always tucked-in heartily to the scraps of food left for him, wherever he might spend the night. Too small to fight his way to security, he'd quickly adapted; learning a skill. The skill of rat-catching. Big black water rats from the dockside on the river Clyde. Tucker always has a few in stock because he never knows when a message will be required. He always deals in cash, with only one exception; the big man now drinking with the Arab at the bar. Messages could nowadays be sent *to* Tucker by text but he always transposed them for delivery in the same way. Tucker writes the message out by hand, ties the paper to a rat's tail and, in the wee small hours, slips the rat through the letter box of the recipient's house so that it will be there to read in the morning. Usually on the kitchen worktop.

Every man in the bar had been in since just before 10.30 a.m. so that they could watch the TV News from Edinburgh together. Keeping their celebrations until later; right now they were waiting for one of their own.

Chapter 18

Crunching up the tree-lined gravel drive in her scarlet coat and black court shoes, carrying a tiny bunch of white daisies picked in the garden of remembrance, Joanne McLane dropped her head, letting her thick blonde hair shield her tears. Ignoring a car full of mourners, each carrying their own new grief, Joanne walked on. Up the steep rise; stopping at the little gravestone where twelve years before she'd buried the life she thought they would have for ever. That unexpected little gift from God, wee Matthew, who lived only seven weeks and two days.

She didn't even feel the pain in her knees as small stones cut through her stockings, into her flesh.

'Oh son. My precious wee boy. I'm so sorry. I've been busy my darling. With your Daddy. He's in … He's in a spot of … He's coming soon. I promise.'

Carefully filling the little vase with daisies, she pressed her palm down into the wet earth. Firmly for Five. One, two, three, four, five. Right over his heart. The way the doctor said over the phone.

'These are for you son. From Mummy. I'll be back soon. Very soon. With Daddy. I promise. Now I have to go and see him. He's in … He's coming soon.'

The Trial

Emerging from the bathroom in a thick towel, dripping onto the bare floorboards, Brogan immediately regretted his tone. 'Where the hell have you been? I asked you to come here. Your coat's all dirty. And your shoes … What's happened?'

'Don't. I'm fine. Sorry. I mean …'

'It's alright. Where *have* you been?'

Her face etched in grief, Joanne welled up: 'To see … to the … I went to the cemetery.'

'What? ... I was worried.'

'Well. That's where I was. I'm sorry, I just had to …'

'Darling. Don't be. It's OK. You sure you're …'

'I'm fine. You?'

Not too bad, considerin'.

Wiping her coat with tissues and washing graveyard dirt out of her fingernails, Joanne busied herself in the way she always did when she got home from the cemetery.

'Darling. For God's sake. You don't have to tidy every ...'

Turning, Joanne burst into a flood of tears, and let fly: 'Brogan, do you think this is *easy*?'

'What? No! Of course not. What gave you that

…?'

'You *do* Brogan. You do. You think it's all a game. You talk about 'my guy' 'your guy' 'the Crown' 'the body' 'the Legal Aid' when what you really mean is *our lives* Brogan. Last week the police tore our house apart, searching for God knows what.'

He tried, but through her tears with both flat palms she pushed him away: 'Brogan you haven't got it yet. You're up for murder. Not *any* old murder of some scumbag in a knife fight or a drug deal. Brogan, this is about a High Court Judge. Whoever 'they' are, they're not going to treat this like any other case. Brogan I'm scared. *Really* scared.'

Unsure how she would react, McLane calmly tried to console her. 'You know I'll never let the bastards beat me, don't you?'

'*What*? Brogan! You're blind. You're not seeing what I see. What is it you told me? The world is full of people who get convicted because the judge is a bastard, or weak and can't even handle the witnesses in the case, never mind the counsel.'

'Jo, they're …'

'Or they're under pressure from the prosecution. There's a million ways for the innocent to get convicted.

That's what you always say.'

'Yeah, but Jo …'

'It *is* a joke to you. You've said a million times – what's the difference between a surgeon and defence counsel? Both operate to save their client's life, but the defence counsel, while he works, has the prosecution *and* a Judge on the other side of the table stabbing the client to death.'

'Ah but Jo, you're not …'

'I *am. That's* what they're trying to do to you! Brogan, what will we *do* if you have to spend the rest of your … ? Brogan this is not just the usual 'Lost the case. Never mind. Stick in the legal aid fee anyway and go out for a drink.'

Crying and falling into his arms, Joanne McLane dug her nails into his bare back for longer than he thought good for her. Holding her tightly-wound body close McLane let her sobbing subside.

Then, just as he thought she was over it, McLane felt a tiny pressure just under his shoulder blade: One, two, three, four, five. One, two, three, four, five.

Chapter 19

Tiptoeing past a cleaner's bucket Sheila McManus strode across the Crown Office's marble floor and got into the lift. She'd never been in the office so early. But equally, her boss had never called her at home before.

Up on the third floor she flung her coat across the back of her chair, straightened her cardigan and knocked on her boss's door.

'Thanks for coming in like this Sheila. I'm going to need some help on the McLane case. Would you have time to …?'

'Of course. I mean, I'll make the time. Of course.'

Madam Fiscal opened a drawer, brought out a thick prosecution file and dropped it loudly onto her pristine desk. Swallowing hard, Sheila McManus had only ever seen one red file before.

Laying only one palm flat on the file the Fiscal paused, looking for any sign that Miss McManus had recognised her tiny act. But the PF saw nothing. Touching both buttons at the neck of her blouse were only acts of slight nervousness. Relaxing, the Fiscal felt certain that her Senior Assistant had never given maiden help and accordingly, would in every sense be subordinate.

'Well Sheila. As you can see, this meeting is about

a 6th Floor case. The Lord Advocate and I think, … well, let's just say that I have been given complete control of the prosecution case against Mr McLane. It's very high profile of course. As I say, The Lord Advocate and I think we need someone at Senior Assistant level. I've already asked Interpol and MI6 to do a few little things for me, so I need someone who is bound by the Official Secrets Act. I've issued orders to our police that nothing is to be created or kept on file without my say-so. But as you know, I have the whole city to deal with and I cannot allow this case to dominate my entire time. That will be your job.'

'Absolutely Ma'am. Of course.'

'So Sheila. Are we clear? You report directly to me and no-one but me. I report to the Lord Advocate himself, so it's a short line. I needn't say how important it is for you to be thoroughly … Well, you know, of course. Thank you Sheila.'

'Thank *you* Ma'am.'

Clutching the thick red file to her chest, Sheila McManus lingered while closing the Fiscal's door before walking slowly between her colleagues and dropping her latest case loudly onto her desk.

By 2.30 pm, ignoring offers of coffee and lunch, Sheila McManus finished her last scan and allowed the clerks back into the Tech room.

Back at her desk, having turned it around away from any jealous eyes, Sheila cross checked everything. The Edinburgh police with the Scottish Central Criminal Records Office; the names and, if possible, the current locations of all McLane's Known Associates. With the help of a friend from Thursday Prayer Group who worked in the Admin Office of the Faculty of Advocates, Sheila cross checked every name, nickname, charge, verdict and sentence from every case ever conducted by Brogan McLane, Advocate; nicknamed 'Maverick'.

Sheila McManus felt light-headed having eaten nothing since her mother's porridge at 6 o'clock that morning. Through a big yawn, she opened her 'What I Know' file. She hesitated for a second then added a subheading 'What I Think I Know'.

Getting up from her desk for the first time in five hours she slipped her cardigan around her shoulders. Knocking lightly and opening the Fiscal's door, she was rewarded with a friendly wave to come in while the Fiscal finished a call.

'Pardon me Ma'am. I'm just going for a sandwich and a walk to clear my head.'

'Good idea. Getting anywhere?'

'Yes. I am. But he's an odd bod. I mean, I find it odd that someone who's an Advocate has such little history. Did you know, every house he's lived in since childhood, with the exception of his current house, has been demolished? Both schools he attended have also been demolished. Obviously he couldn't have arranged that, it involves too many variables, but it's rather convenient for him now, wouldn't you say?'

'Perhaps. He is from ..'

'And he has some very unsavoury friends. I went to the same school as my mother and grandmother. And he's not a member of anything. Except a couple of things in Glasgow. He just seems to hang around with unsavoury characters trying to pick up criminal defence work.'

'Sheila.'

'He's never even …'

'Sheila. I think you should go for that walk. Don't let this case … Well, I need you sharp and focused. Look at the KA's. That's where you'll find the dirt.'

'Yes Ma'am. I will. I'll just …'

'Do that Sheila. Let me know when anything

substantive comes up, will you?'

'Of course Ma'am.'

Within an hour Sheila McManus strode through the office with her old Girl Guide purposefulness, sensing all eyes following her all the way to her desk. Clicking her Inbox, her heart leapt. Subject: INTERPOL LONDON. SHIPPING SEARCH. Heading: STRICTLY PRIVATE to Crown Prosecution Point of Contact ~ Miss Sheila McManus, Senior Assistant to the Procurator Fiscal for Edinburgh. HMA v Brogan McLane.

She excitedly opened the message but just as quickly dropped her chin into her hands. No secret was revealed. No new information for the 'Prosecution Evidence File' was included. The only content was a computer-generated message saying 'No Result'.

Hoping no-one could detect her disappointment, opening the next email sent her into confusion. Subject : PHONE INTERCEPT. Heading : HMA v Brogan McLane. Sender : MI5 to PF Edinburgh (Sheila McManus) : INFORMATION re BOAT named NERAIDA 2.

To Miss McManus,

The Trial

Having received the usual instructions from London we contacted MI6 (Counter Intelligence - Europe) for any information on a boat named Neraida 2. A witness protection contact on the Costa del Sol in Spain knows this ship to belong to one Joseph Thomas Mularkey, a Glasgow hard man. Mularkey (a.k.a. Big Joe Mularkey / BJM) came up recently in a phone transcript between Edinburgh and Glasgow within an hour of Brogan McLane getting Bail in Edinburgh High Court. This conversation was computer-matched and combined information was sent to us. Neraida 2 is more of a ship than a boat (900 gross tonnes), which plies its trade along the Mediterranean Sea carrying used spare parts for French cars to other Mediterranean countries. The ship first came to attention because it contains a car-crushing machine. See satellite pictures of splashes at night off her port side which cannot be 'sailing generated'. It is believed that, after being stripped for parts, crushed stolen cars are dumped in the Mediterranean Sea to avoid tax duties. MI6 had the ship's name but some confusion arose in Greece with another ship of the same name. We are passing along this information in case it was of use in the prosecution against Brogan McLane.

SECRET : 30 YEAR TERMINUS. See Official

Secrets Act 1949 S3 as amended.

OUT.

'Look at the KA's' the Fiscal had said, and she was right. As always.

Breathing very deeply and checking for reflections in the window pane in front of her that no-one was anywhere near her desk, Sheila opened the 'Known Associates File'.

KA1 : Joanne McLane. Born Devonshire, England. No children. No SCCRO Report.

KA2 : Joseph Thomas Mularkey.

Under her pulsing breath, Sheila McManus felt the thrill of discovery from the safest of vantage points: 'Oh hello Mr Mularkey. Let's have a look at you.'

JOINT UK POLICE / INTERPOL : SECRET.

Born 10 January 1964 in Govan, Glasgow. Juvenile offences 'assault x 2, robbery x 1, theft x 3 and perverting the course of justice x 1' [DO NOT USE – Prevention of Identifying a Juvenile Act 1934].

Flicking open the next page, she was amazed. Since becoming an adult – Nothing!

The Trial

'Nothing? That's impossible. There's something wrong with this.'

Clicking over 'Recent Convictions' she immediately got a hit, causing her to slump down into her chair.

'Convicted of murder in the High Court? How could he be convicted of murder just a year ago? That's impossible. He's not in jail. There was no appeal. This is weird.'

Behind her at their desks, others were closing computers, brushing hair and putting on walking-home shoes.

Struggling to make sense of this confused and conflicting information, Sheila McManus took a blank piece of paper and started to draw a chart. The dates. The time line. The courts. The names. Everything was Glasgow. The East End of Glasgow. And the dates. The dates. Maybe.

She looked up at the ceiling for a second, then something hit her as possible. Lifting the sealed red file from the floor, she dropped it onto her lap. Cutting the tape she dumped it on her desk and flipped it open. Holding two sheets side-by-side, she had it.

145

'Born a day apart and lived in the same tenement building. Hah!'

A check of the trial court's file confirmed her suspicion. The date of birth of the convicted man made him almost 25 years younger.

She could hardly believe it. Punching the darkness, she double-checked before tapping on the Fiscal's door: 'Ma'am. I think I may have something.'

Following her Assistant's finger, as Sheila McManus pointed out the salient details, the Fiscal had never been prouder of her decision to promote young Miss McManus.

'So it's a filing error.'

'Yes. Simple as that. Mularkey has a son who was convicted of murder just over a year ago.'

'Oh and a nasty one too. Oh Father in Heaven. An elderly lady in her own home.'

'Is that a letter from the Scottish Prison Records Office?'

'Yes. There he is. Languishing in Her Majesty's Prison Barlinnie. In Glasgow. Best place for him.'

'There must be a …'

'Yes. In the Correspondence File. Here it is. I didn't scan all of this.'

'That's alright.'

Both women followed Sheila McManus' finger as they carefully read one of the first letters sent under the new 'Scottish Courts Family Information Scheme'.

'Dear Mr and Mrs Mularkey,

As you know, a little over a year ago your son Joseph was convicted after trial in Glasgow High Court of murder and sentenced to mandatory life imprisonment. The trial judge decided that, in view of the horrendous nature of the facts of the case and the terrible way in which his elderly victim died, your son should serve a minimum of 30 years before being eligible for parole. He appealed to the Criminal Appeal Court and was almost immediately refused. Because of your persistence, his case was recently referred back to the Criminal Appeal Court by the Scottish Criminal Cases Review Commission. I now write to inform you that his second and final appeal has also been refused. That will be publicly announced shortly.

I am afraid that this is now the end of the matter. Should you have anything further to say, then may I suggest that you contact your Member of Parliament or other trusted family friend.

I remain, yours sincerely,

J Pringle. Senior Assistant to the Procurator Fiscal for Glasgow.'

'Well well Ma'am. An Advocate with a close friend whose son murdered a defenceless old lady. I wonder if the Dean of Faculty knows about *that*.'

'Yes Sheila. But that's not all. Look.'

On the clerk of court's Minute of Proceedings, there was the name of the Trial Judge: Lord Aldounhill.

'Oh Ma'am. What if …'

'Over the page. Turn over and see if …'

'Dash. Dash it all. It's not him.'

Disappointment filled the space between them but the PF was an older hand at this than her Assistant.

'Don't you find that odd Sheila? I do. Here is this Mularkey person's son on trial for murder and, if convicted, certainly looking at a long recommendation before parole. And McLane is *not* the defence counsel? Why not?'

'Ah ha! Oh Ma'am. Here. Here it is. The Clerk

notes it on day 2 of the trial.'

In all the years they'd been Prosecutor and Apprentice, Section Chief and Team Leader, Assistant PF and Deputy and now PF and Senior Assistant, they had never touched beyond shaking hands in court and sharing communion in church. Sensing a new partnership the two women silently read the Court Note.

'IN THE HIGH COURT OF JUSTICIARY IN EDINBURGH:

Case Name: HMA v Joseph Mularkey. Place: Trial Court No 2.

Trial Judge : Lord Aldounhill. Stage of Procedure: Day 2 of trial. Trial continues.

First Note of the Day: Change of Defence Counsel (Mr John Tannahill retiring in favour of Mr Brogan McLane).'

Their faces glowing in satisfaction, Sheila McManus closed the file and switched off her computer.

Buttoning coats and collecting handbags, the pair strode along the dim corridor towards the lift. Looking up at the numbers slowly changing from 2 to 1 the Fiscal asked: 'Sheila. Do you remember the very first time you assisted me in court? The Brannigan case which was …'

'Circumstantial. Yes of course. You told me that juries like circumstantial evidence cases because the noose tightens slowly. I've never forgotten.'

Tapping her on the arm, the PF's broad smile came to her Assistant as a sign that God's work was done for the day: 'I have every faith in you Sheila. Excellent work.'

Proud as Punch and with a spring in her step, the Assistant PF bowed as she walked: 'And I in you Ma'am.'

Chapter 20

Marjorie Millbank quietly closed the tall double front doors and listened as the daily-help drove away. In her slippers she made no sound climbing the stairs. She pushed on her mother's bedroom door, knowing that the squeaky old hinge her father had often tried to mend might announce her arrival.

'Mother? Mother darling. Are you …?'

Leaning over the bed she carefully removed her mother's spectacles and lifted the tray, noticing that her food was untouched again. Silently descending the stairs to the old Maid's Scullery in the basement, she put the bowl of cold food under foil and absent-mindedly washed the cutlery. Round and round. Round and round in the suds.

Up in the library, she paced round and round, keeping within the borders of the carpet laid in her father's time. Keeping her gaze away from his old leather club chair she picked the telephone out of its cradle, gripping it in both hands. But she couldn't dial that number. Not in this room.

Down in the basement the gas boiler ignited with a loud puuff, sending a shiver straight to her conscience.

Shaking, she pulled out her pay-as-you-go phone and the top of her thumb went white as she jabbed the green button.

Waiting. Ringing. Ringing. Waiting.

'Hello? It's me.'

'So I bloody well see. I told you *never* to ...'

'Did you know that Brogan McLane defended the young Mularkey at his murder trial last year? I've just found out and ...'

'Of course I bloody knew. Don't *ever* call this number again. Got that?'

The Trial

Chapter 21

A soft blanket of Spanish cigarette smoke swirling from ceiling height to below their heads veiled the afternoon drinkers in the Calton Bar. Just inside and to the left of the door, sitting wheezing into the pearl embossed harmonica he'd won as a child in his first card game, old Davie Hume kept sentry duty. To his left, always to his left, his oldest pal Big Jake Devine, over 80 now, shuffled cards showing three young 'strangers' some old tricks.

With their loud London accents, the strangers split the still quiet air and continued to drink heavily. They had been on some long con and were obviously now celebrating a successful job while waiting for their lift back to London.

'All right there mate? You comin' in for a little 'and at poker?'

Folding his racing paper and glancing with a well-worn understanding at Big Jake who'd marked out these boys as his hit for the day, Tucker refused: 'Naw. Ye'r all right boys. Ah'm workin'. '

Tucker thought of himself as a delivery man, pure and simple. He didn't like showing his face to strangers, even if they did come recommended. He did a service for which he got paid. His fee was whatever the service was worth: no more, but definitely no less. Tucker liked things to be predictable. Uncertainty in his line of work, he left to amateurs. Well schooled in the old days, the lesson drummed into him as a boy was 'No surprises means no second prizes'.

From out of his personal cloud of smoke, the Arab emerged, putting two whiskies on the table and sitting down next to Tucker.

'Trouble wee man?'

'Naw. No' yet.'

'They guys?'

'Naw. Naw. It's this.'

Pulling a glossy printed advert from his paper, Tucker carefully laid it on the table, shielding it with his hand.

'What's that? An advert for ... whit is it? Kitchens? Are ye' getting' your kitchen done?'

'Don't be stupid Arab. Ah've no' even got a kitchen.'

'Ah don't get it Tucker. Whit's your problem?'

'To *you* this is just a glossy advert. But to me, it's a message. A good yin. Expertly delivered. I mean, full respect to the guy. Whoever sent this, he's good. An' ah mean *very* good.'

'Who was he?'

'Arab. Fir fuck sake man. This is no' Messenger School. Ah'm tryin' to work oot who he was an how he got it tae me.'

'Ye didnae see him?'

'Naw. An' that's botherin' me. See, ah live alone. Ah get up, feed ma rats, feed mysel', sometimes ah shave, sometimes ah don't. But ah *always* go doon to wee Matt McConachie's corner shoap for ma racing paper and ma two packs o' ciggies. Ten in the mornin'. On the dot. Sharp as sharp can be. An' then ah come here. If I've goat a message to deliver, that would *always* be done later. Sometimes even at night, but that's mair if a threat's involved.'

'Aye. So? What's different aboot the day?'

'Well, see this advert? It was inside ma paper.'

'They usually are. Ur they no'?'

'Naw. That's ... That's no' the point. Ah've checked wi' wee Matt. There's nae advert in this paper the day. Wee Matt says he defo didnae see anybody doin' it. An' he's no' lyin'. No' to me. Whoever pit this in ma paper must've timed it to perfection. No' the paper before mine. No' the paper effter mine. *Ma* paper. If he's no' local he would've stood oot like a dug's baw's. An wee

Matt's no mug.'

'Ye'r right there man. Bit somebody must've seen somethin' surely.'

'Nup. This guy must've knew ma' movements. That's no' easy fur a stranger aboot here. Ah'm no' kiddin' Arab. Ah think this guy might be special. Army maybe. Or polis but Special Branch. Whoever he was, he was affy well trained. Ah know. Ah'm affy well trained masel' an' he's goat me beat.'

'How come? You've goat us. Plus you're a civilian. Ev'rybuddy knows that.'

'That's no' ma point Arab. Ah mean, he can get to me - any time he likes.'

'Tucker man. You'v loast me. It's just an advert fur kitchens an' bathroom shite. Let me take a wee look ootside.'

The Arab moved closer to the card school and leant on the bar. Winking at the Barman, he panned the street outside reflected in the big Dewar's whisky mirror. Every window that overlooked the Bar, their roofs and stairway closes up and down the street.

Arab could read a street as well as Brogan McLane could read a law book. Nobody could measure the speed of a street like the Arab. But he saw no sign; no evidence of anything unusual. Nothing.

Turning to look at the wee man sitting there biting his lip, Tucker looked troubled by this mystery ad in the paper. Tucker knew his stuff. Better than anyone. And he'd read this right. The advert was for kitchen and bathroom re-styling and the prices were way out of the range affordable by the locals around the East End. The place in the advert was in Barrack Street. In the South Side. So the advert had been *brought* to wee Matt's shop. For a purpose. But what?

A few pals coming into the bar got a passing nod, but Arab gave away nothing of what his instincts told him: They were now *all* under surveillance.

Shuffling back into his seat beside Tucker, no words were needed to convey the result of his survey. Tucker seemed lost in his thoughts: '*See the whole board Tucker. The whole board.*' That's what old Danny McGuire used to say. And he was the best. One side the printed advert, the other blank. Hmm. Nothing. Then it hit him.

'Oh ya wee darlin'. Ah see you noo.'

Arab looked into Tucker's eyes for the answer to the mystery but Tucker said no more. There would be no finger-prints on this ad, other than his own. There was no handwriting on it, so no expert could tie it to a particular person who would be a prosecution witness against Brogan McLane. Just pictures of fancy kitchens and bathroom gear. And the print? Just the name and address for this Sale and the opening and closing hours of business. To Tucker's expert eye the message was now as clear as day.

But who?

Tucker tried closing his eyes and tapping his forehead for inspiration. This wasn't within the grasp of the usual city messengers. He'd heard of a few young civilians coming up through the ranks on the north side of the city, and others he'd occasionally met from London, but Tucker quickly judges that none of them had the wit for this. This was the simplest of messages sent in the most sophisticated way.

A full minute later, Tucker tapped the back of his old friend's hand and leaned in to the Arab's ear. 'Ah've goat it Arab. But this'll need to be handled wi' extreme caution. Two back-ups. Maybe even three.'

Impressed, the Arab dipped his head by way of recognition for a job well done. 'Dae yi' think it's maybe thae Russian guys that were in here last week The wuns that bring the lassies and the kids fae Russia under the trucks?'

'Naw. Naw. It's no' them. This is too subtle fur them.'

'So who's the message frae, Tucker?'

Tucker raised his eyebrows but said nothing. He folded the glossy advert in two. Getting up he pushed through a crowd of guys who'd come in just to watch the match and stood at the end of the Bar. Shaking his head to stop the barman coming any closer, he remained otherwise perfectly still.

When he caught the eyes of the two men he needed, they downed their whiskies and slipped over.

'What is it Tucker?'

Sandwiched between McLane and Big Joe Mularkey, a full head and shoulders smaller, Tucker looked more like a lost child than the man chosen to deliver news that could be pivotal to the defence of Brogan McLane. To the casual observer the three gave not a hint of the importance of this meeting. But to the regulars, such a pow-wow meant only one thing: get ready.

McLane and Big Joe didn't need to look at each other to know what was in their respective minds. They'd been doing that since birth. So they waited. Tucker's hesitation was a sure sign that something unusual had happened; so they gave him all the time he needed.

Stroking his chin, Tucker turned and pressed his back into the Bar. Although sure that no-one could lip read him, he put three fingers in front of his mouth for good measure.

To McLane, what was about to be revealed could be good stuff for his defence. But it might be inadmissible. Or maybe just inadvisable to lead in court. To Big Joe, it almost certainly signalled the putting together of a team which was gathering at the other end of the Bar, awaiting instructions.

To Tucker's surprise, it was McLane who broke first: 'Tuck! Out with it man! What ...?'

Stuttering, Tucker began with a flash of his eyes straight into McLane's: 'Well Brogan, at this stage the message disnae say *why* he wants the meetin' or *what* he has to say. But somebody *very very* good has just made contact. An' Joe. Ah think we'll need a team for this.'

The Trial

Chapter 22

In Edinburgh's old Cowgate the low hum of carefully calibrated motors running the fridges and air conditioning system were the only sounds emanating from behind the bland door where a sign reads 'University of Edinburgh Centre for Forensic Pathology.' The dark brick two-storey building sits a little back from the road so that it may discreetly receive unmarked vans bringing cling-wrapped bodies and police cars bringing senior officers.

These silent guests, so varied in life, are in death stacked in individually sealed refrigerated compartments at exactly 1° Celsius in order that one forensic pathology examination doesn't just resemble others in different parts of the country; they are identical.

Inside, under computer-controlled neon lighting, the medical staff moved around in their white head-to-toe coveralls, their own clothing sealed in air-tight lockers.

Waiting in her office, Professor Nadia Suilleman let the noisy medical students file clumsily into the three rows of seats behind plate glass in the observation gallery of her Examination room.

On her orders, all requests from the press and media to attend were refused. But as the 30 or so students made their way to the Cowgate, they were joined unnoticed by a pretty young women reporter from the Glasgow Daily Tribune carrying a Mickey Mouse notebook.

Professor Suilleman satisfied herself that the paperwork was in order and glanced up to the Gallery. A pretty young woman was just taking the seat next to Commander Imrie. In the back row, the primly dressed woman from the PF's office, who'd arrived far too early, seemed to have the air of parasite about her. Professor Suilleman had seen it before. She wouldn't be interested in the anatomic pathology ensuing over the next hour or so. Far less the work of Nadia Suilleman's brilliant Cytologist, who'd be examining individual and clusters of cells looking for benign or malignant conditions at the time of death. The Fiscal's office is interested in only one thing: would Professor Suilleman certify the cause of death as murder?

Clipping on her tiny radio microphone, Professor Suilleman rolled her volume control to maximum. The sudden screech of feedback silenced most of the students. Adjusting her volume control and tapping the steel tray with the metal end of the hose brought the remainder to silence.

The Trial

A simple nod was her permission to begin. Her clinical assistant began making the usual incisions across the mid-line of the chest and abdomen and three others along the top and sides of the head. Walking slowly round the tray, pointing to the naked body lying on the cold steel, Nadia Suilleman went into teaching mode.

'Ladies and gentlemen … this is a person, a human being, now sadly deceased. Let us remember that at all times during this teaching session.'

'De De De Deedle De, De De De Dee' went someone's phone.

One look from the Prof's narrowed eyes sent the student responsible diving into her bag; and several others into their pockets. Allowing only a few seconds for the shuffling of bags and rummaging into pockets to subside, she continued.

'Some of you are post-graduate students, but in your first year at medical school, indeed your first week, you are taught two things. Firstly, to disguise your handwriting for use in later medical practice. Secondly, you were taught to observe the patient; correct?'

To a wave of nodding heads, the Professor quickened her step around the tray.

'So what do you see?'

Waiting for an answer she looked straight at the woman from the PF's office who dropped her head into a notebook. No student braved an answer.

'Alright. What is the first requirement of a forensic pathology examination?.'

Once more the students disappointed.

'The *identification* of the person before you.'

The nodding resumed.

'In this case there is no ID100 Form. Why not? You may ask. Well, because no family member has yet formally identified the body. However, I need no authorisation from the Crown Office because I feel confident that we can continue. Why? Because I know this man. Others who work in this department know him and indeed Commander Imrie up there also knows him. He was Lord Aldounhill, a judge of the High Court in Scotland. I say 'was' because now, he is mine. In the law of Scotland there is neither personality nor right of property in a dead body. Another part of the law allows dissection without fear of criminal prosecution or civil suit because neither a crime nor a tort can be done in the course of this examination. Is everybody clear so far?'

Professor Suilleman noticed more scribbling than nodding, but continued. Walking around the body holding a microscopic camera sending everything it saw to the central recording suite, she asked:

'What else do we see?'

Heads shook.

'Correct. Very little. No smashed skull, no broken bones, no bullet holes, just an injury in the neck. A cursory inspection reveals that the deceased was a practising homosexual; but that didn't kill him. At least, not directly, you understand. In any event, we cannot say whether the damaged condition of the anus was self-imposed or not. It does appear that such intrusions were voluntary because of the destroyed elasticity of the muscle. That would take some considerable time. Perhaps years. But although this condition may be interesting to others, such as the police or the defence, it is largely uninteresting to us because it seems to have no *clinical* bearing on the cause of death.'

Professor Suilleman let that fact sink in to the students' heads. At the top end of the steel tray was a waterproof notepad into which she typed her first official finding: "In the matter of Lord Aldounhill's examination, I certify that death was unnatural."

Holding the camera so that the injury to Lord Aldounhill's neck was enlarged on three screens around the room, she verbally recorded her next finding:

'I am now showing the slash to the Carotid Artery, particularly the internal branch. Damage of this severity, if untreated, would have caused death within a few minutes.'

With a look back up into the gallery, her lecture resumed: 'Now. Timing. Time from point of intrusion of sharp instrument until death? Anyone?'

Pausing for an answer, pursing her lips and relaxing into her own authority, she answered herself. 'Impossible to say. Why? Because he could have tried to stem the flow himself or he could've had assistance. In either case death came quite quickly. Important if you have any family asking whether their loved one suffered before death. But did he have any assistance? Of course, we don't know. Why not? Because there is no marking to the neck that would indicate that anyone else either tried to stem the flow with their hands or with a tourniquet. Observe his left hand. Blood-staining to the fingers and palm extending to the left wrist but, except for a single trickle, no further. What does that tell us?'

Bravery and post graduate confidence in their own abilities brought two answers simultaneously: 'He was horizontal when he tried to stem the flow.'

'Correct. So he probably died alone, though that is uncertain.'

The Trial

Up in the gallery, looking out of the corner of his eye, Commander Imrie took two mental notes. His first being what Professor Suilleman had just said. But the second was much more interesting. Next to him, her hair cascading all over her Mickey Mouse notebook, the young woman thickened the words 'Unpopular Judge Dies Alone'.

'Now people. Circumstances of death. Observe the photographs going across the screen taken by the Scenes of Crime Officers at the time of police discovery of the body. Alone, naked, right arm under body showing clotted blood in the veins of the forearm - Type AB Rhesus Negative – what does that tell us?

'Very rare in Scotland' called an African student.

Correcting him, the Professor gave a nod of approval: 'Very rare everywhere. I can tell you that there was a little of the so-called date-rape drug Rohypnol in the blood. Not much. Just enough to show up in our screening. Now can anyone tell me what happened to Rohypnol post-January 1998?'

The Professor moved her stylus to the Opinion Section of the Report; her precursor to patching their scattered responses together into the proposition: 'Proprietary Rohypnol from the Roche company *should* turn the host drink blue immediately alerting the target and leaving a residue on the surface.'

Turning back to the gallery she asked: 'But what if, as in this case, the drug is not proprietary?'

No-one dared an answer.

'Counterfeit products present much more difficulty. A report in the Emergency Medicine journal offers little hope for methods of detection before consumption. The problem, people, is that the Flunitrazepam readily dissolves and, once in solution, is colourless, odourless, and tasteless. You should already know that the predominant clinical manifestations are drowsiness, impaired motor skills, and anteretrograde amnesia.'

With youthful enthusiasm, Nadia Suilleman turned back to her body.

'Now observe people. *Observe*. We know that the deceased was naked when found by the police. He shows obvious signs of repeated, long-term anal intrusion. One of the effects of non-proprietary Rohypnol is that the inhibitions often drop away. So, did this subject take the drug himself, or was it administered by someone else? Look at the *angle* of cutting of the Carotid Artery. Does that tell us anything? You can see from *this* photograph that the angle is approximately parallel with the floor. The floor is old. Solid oak floorboards. So there would be no spring in them. Also, notice the depth of the incision. No more than two centimetres. So, thinking like an Etiologist, would it be fair to say that he probably did not fall with all his weight on the instrument that killed him, because if he had fallen in that way, then the instrument would have penetrated much deeper. Conclusion? *Any*one?'

'Inconclusive' called an impulsive student.

'Maybe. Not so fast. We don't have the thing which intruded the artery. So we don't know its shape, sharpness or whether it is fixed or flexible. Well, not yet we don't. And you won't be told if and when Commander Imrie up there ever finds it.'

Racing through the Liver Mortis tests; searching obscure nooks and crannies for the settling of blood; calculating blood pressure from the Body Mass Index, scrawling a Greek mathematical symbol equating to the energy given by the amount of food in the stomach; the condition of the tiny blood vessels behind the eyes and the position of the body when discovered by the police (which could be different from the moment of death) Professor Suilleman was a woman at the top of her game.

Only one peculiarity was noted. Lord Aldounhill

had broken his right ankle some years ago.

'The Algor Mortis tests are of little assistance since the central heating in the house where the body was found was left on. So people. So? What do we tell Commander Imrie?'

Silence.

Looking straight up at Commander Imrie, Professor Nadia Suilleman announced confidently: 'Time of Death was between 40 and 50 hours before discovery by police. There being nothing of any significance in the Toxicology analysis I pronounce that the cause of death was the intrusion of a sharp instrument into the Carotid Artery, particularly the internal branch.'

Walking round the body one last time - looking straight up at the woman from the PF's office then flashing across to Commander Imrie - the Professor pursed her lips: 'What the Lord Advocate and others in the Crown Office want to know is whether my Report will corroborate other evidence of murder. They want to narrow their focus. Well, unless and until the instrument which caused these injuries is found, I cannot go that far. Ladies and gentlemen, for the moment, the cause of Lord Aldounhill's death is undetermined.'

Chapter 23

As the small black cortège approached Mount Hall Cemetery the rear two police motorcycles peeled off, silently responding to a call; being closest, they would attend to a fatal accident on the M8 Motorway.

Outside the cemetery's high iron gate, a crowd of about 50 people, men and women, old and young, parted to let the two lead police motorcyclists ease through.

Instantly the bikes picked up a little speed the crowd took its chance, surrounding the hearse. Two strong men heaved the heavy iron gates shut and quickly snapped a padlock into place.

Spinning around, the police motorcyclists were too late. Locked inside the cemetery the officers dismounted, shouting to the men who'd locked the gate to open it immediately or be arrested. But no-one seemed to care about that.

From the back of the crowd, an elderly white-haired woman pushed and shoved her way through until she stood right in front of the hearse. Peering at her, the bewildered driver could only watch as she produced from under her coat a bright blue thermos flask. From a plastic container a girl of about 15 began smearing something that stank to high heaven onto the gate; causing the police

171

officers to recoil.

'Right you bastards! Whatever this is, forget it. We're calling for back-up. You're all going to the jail. Open this *fucking* gate. Do you *hear* me? Open this …'

The crowd just ignored the police, remaining strangely quiet. Jostling and then linking arms, five people who bore a striking family resemblance to the old woman, watched her open her flask and pour a thick heavy fluid onto the front of the hearse. Hitting the hot polished metal, the thick lumpy substance oozed across the surface, the steam carrying the unwelcome stink of human excrement and urine.

Running to the side, one officer tried to climb the high iron railings but he was too late. Several others also produced flasks, pouring their stinking contents all over the hearse. One of the men flung open the back door, flung the flowers onto the street and tried to urinate onto the coffin. A sobbing young woman beat on the coffin with her fists and two youths slashed and scored it with blades.

Shocked and a little terrified that the same treatment might coming his way, the driver in the rear car slammed the gear lever into R and stepped on the accelerator. With traffic behind him braking hard and the sound of squealing tyres, passers-by clung to each other in fear.

In the back, the solitary mourner, Lady Aldounhill tumbled violently around; falling to the floor as the car screeched away.

High on the cemetery hill, alone and looking again at his watch, the Reverend Tom Strang closed his bible and turned this way and that, looking for what he expected, would be a long line of cars filled with the great and the good from Edinburgh. But nothing and no-one could be seen only two police officers in motorbike kit and big boots marching up the hill gave any sign of things being untoward.

Then, overtaking the officers, and coming up the gravelled hill road at an ungodly speed, an unaccompanied hearse streaked with stinking excrement gave the Rev Strang a clue as to why his 11 a.m. was late.

Getting out, the driver flung open the tailgate and hauled the unadorned coffin out onto the gravel. Losing composure the Rev Strang demanded: 'For God's sake man. What in the name of all that's holy are you …'

A young couple who seemed to be the only mourners, came forward asking: 'Can we help? We could lift it. If that would …'

'Oh. Bless you. Yes. The poor man. Yes.'

The Rev Strang opened his bible, and taking his place a few steps back from the head of the grave, he began: 'Lord God we gather today to give thanks for the life of Lord Aldounhill.'

But then, whether by accident or design – the horrified Rev. Strang wasn't sure – one end of the coffin slipped out of the woman's hand, hit a stone and lurched head first down into the grave. Turning, the man grabbed a bag. Pulling out a shoulder-mounted TV camera, to the Rev Strang's unsurpassed horror, the man began filming the brown hearse.

'What in Heaven's name? Stop that immediately. You're in the sight of God and …'

But to the good Reverend's dismay, his words fell on deaf ears as the man panned the camera round.

'Get into bloody shot woman.'

Kneeling by the angled coffin, the young woman went into presentation mode: 'I'm at the graveside of the notorious Lord Aldounhill where the most extraordinary scenes have occurred. Lord Aldounhill, a widely hated

Scottish High Court Judge, was to be buried here today but as you can see, that hasn't quite happened. Though expected, His widow has not attended …'

In the malaise, no-one took the slightest notice of the group of mourners standing a dozen graves away. While the two police officers dragged Lord Aldounhill's broken upright coffin out of the grave, the mourners departed; eager to get back to the Calton Bar to watch the coverage on TV.

~~~0~~~

End of Part 3

John Mayer

~ The Trial ~

Part 4

Chapter 24

High in the bleak Pentland Hills to the south of Edinburgh, cosseted in the warmth of the deep leather interior of his mighty black Range Rover, the old soldier waited. Sitting staring at the floodlit skiers slamming down the dry slope on the north side and, in the distance, the car lights on the Edinburgh city ring-road, Major Sir Aubrey Winstanley (Scots Guards, Retd) silently tapped out an old pipe tune.

There had been a time when the only permanent residents on these hills were the Scottish soldiers from nearby Redford Barracks who, under his command, used them for full-on energy-draining, gut-wrenching week-on-week outdoor training. But all that had changed.

The car's bright green digital clock turned 9.22 p.m. A good time for an impromptu operational check.

Checking the engine temperature, it was still warm, well within optimum operating range, so no steam would emit from the Range Rover's exhaust pipe that could be caught in a stray headlight. If a tyre flicked a stone off the rocky hill and fell causing someone to wonder what moved it in the first place: that would just be unlucky.

Through the pitch darkness, Sir Aubrey checked for any last-minute vehicle coming up before slipping the gear lever into D. Looking over his shoulder, he drove dead-slow turning left, around the hill. The rocky ground held no trace of his steel-walled tyres. Once over the rock and away from the dimly lit car park, a few twists and turns over the deep heather soon put him in total darkness. Slipping on his old night goggles, he let the vehicle climb.

'*What a difference from the old clattering army Land Rovers.*'

Keeping in very low gear, Sir Aubrey ploughed on; occasionally looking over his shoulder at the city lights below. Higher and higher the big black 4x4 splashed easily across the hills' only rocky stream. Confirming his exact position on the GPS, Sir Aubrey braked. Inch by inch, dead slow ahead he counted down the GPS expecting the hit. Dead on position the underside engine protection plate scraped the broad flat rock in the stream; Ah, if that rock could speak it would scream out the number of squaddie boots that have hit it dead centre. Finally, seeing the silhouette of a familiar cliff overhang, he arrived.

In a natural theatre caused by a split in the rock millions of years before, he stopped the Range Rover. It had been more than 30 years since, as a newly promoted army captain, he first rested his men there. Digging into the deep snow for shelter. Huddling, sometimes for days.

With the appointment set for 9.30 Sir Aubrey sat quietly in the car, there being no point in looking around. His man wouldn't be seen. He'd probably leave his vehicle or bicycle in a car park in the nearby town of Penicuik. He'd then cross the fields, keeping to their perimeter for the two miles down past the new shopping mall and turn into the dirt road going west into the woods. He'd climb out of the woods on the northern slopes and begin his yomp up the Pentland Hills. He'd be armed but not obviously so. He'd have hand-held GPS kit, but he could climb these hills with his eyes closed.

Never having met this shadowy figure, Sir Aubrey nevertheless remained relaxed, having trained hundreds like him in his army days. His muscle groups would be developed to perfection. His only meaningful relationships would be only with anything that delivered three hundred rounds a minute. And there would be his unquestioning loyalty. He would obey the last order and happily die crying out 'God Save Her Majesty The Queen'. *Nothing* else in this world matter to this man. If an officer chose him for a special assignment, then his task was not to reason why. The officer would know and that was good enough for him.

Sir Aubrey tinkered with the MP3 player, not entirely sure of its menus and language. After a minute or so of pressing up arrows and looking again for the 'Set' button, Sir Aubrey sat bolt upright. From the corner of his eye, about a yard from the driver's window, a shadow even darker than the night had materialised: there stood his man. At attention. Saluting.

Taking a moment to breathe, Sir Aubrey lowered the window and casually gave his order: 'At ease'.

Softly placing his left boot into the wet heather, snapping his hands behind his back, left on top of right, the shadow came to rest in what passes for 'Standing Easy' in the Scottish Regiment of the British Army. In a whisper which not even a passing mouse could hear, it spoke: 'Yes sir.'

'Do you know what you've been chosen to do?'

'No sir.'

'I need you to retrieve something and bring it here, to me, when you're told. Do you understand?'

'Yes Sir. Might I be permitted to know what this thing is Sir, and where it might be, Sir?'

'It's a few pieces of paper. A Forensic Science

Report about the DNA contained in a sample of purple lipstick. It will be signed by a Professor Sir Isaac Neuberger.'

'Yes Sir. Where is it Sir?'

'It's in 'A' Division Police HQ. In the office of a Commander Imrie.'

'Yes Sir.'

'Don't hurry this. Take your time and do it any way you want. There will be only one shot at this.'

Saluting and turning on his right heel, in less than a second the shadow disappeared, seeming to leave a hole in the darkness.

Now, with the order given, Sir Aubrey breathed easy letting the cold night air fill the Range Rover. Taking his hands off the wheel, he let the cold bite, though just a little – a reminder of those glory days when he trained the toughest soldiers in the world to beat the shit out of bedraggled Paddies who dared to bomb Her Majesty's subjects on sovereign soil.

Involuntarily, a tiny wry smile crossed his face and he reached out into the cold darkness. The biting wind immediately began to freeze his fingers, but Major Winstanley cared nothing for that. Leaving his arm stretched out, he softly tapped the right trusty and well beloved shadow on the shoulder. He'd get that fucking report. Of that, there was no doubt.

At the turning circle two hundred yards from the bottom of the hill, Sir Aubrey paused the mighty Range Rover, looking for movement; but sensed none. Good.

Slipping the drive lever into 'D' he jabbed at the icon on the Media Centre sending a pipe tune swirling around the four corners of leather and wood.

At a steady 60 mph Sir Aubrey was careful to head west under the nearest overhead camera before slipping off the Ring Road and taking the B road which connected at a five-way junction a mile ahead. With his shoulders moving in time to the Pipe Major's tune, Sir Aubrey breathed more deeply now; confident of two things. His meeting had never happened and the case against Brogan McLane looked even stronger.

Chapter 25

Through the misted-up windscreen, filthy December night rain thundered down so hard it seemed to machine-gun the high mossy Victorian wall supporting the Paisley to Glasgow railway bridge. On the girders under the bridge, rats ran back and forth feeding their young. Flapping wildly in the wind, netting designed to catch bird droppings over Bridge Street had long since torn away from its fixings and floods of mucky rainwater surged down through long cracks in the old ironwork.

Standing alone fifty yards south of the bridge, a concrete barn of a shop protected by welded iron bars and a thick steel shutter defied the city's many hovering developers. The railway embankment and the wide, windowless back of the building made a natural haunt for small-time drug dealers. But not tonight; the drenching rain and biting cold having dulled the market.

The shop's washed-out sign read 'Harper's Kitchen and Bathroom Design'. Its owner, trying his honest best to keep business alive, had even gone to the expense of putting hand bills in some daily city newspapers.

A big old blue BMW slowed so the driver could

182

read the sign, and parked in the dark street opposite the store.

Squinting to see through the lashing rain on the windscreen, McLane spoke first.

'It can't be here. There's nothing here.'

'Tucker's sure. Ah think he's read this right. Anyway, we'll see. Worst case scenario is we get done for parkin' on the wrong side o' the street after dark. How bad can that be?'

'I don't need charged with anything else, thanks very much Joe. I think this is a bad idea.'

'Naw it's no'. I think this could be good. Who wants to meet *us* at this time o' the night round about here?'

Slapping the hip flask into his best friend's belly, Big Joe had never seen McLane so unsure of himself. Since getting out on Bail he'd looked gaunt and drawn. And now he was indecisive and jittery. Others had noticed and Tucker had even mentioned that taking McLane to this meeting could be a bad idea. In a tight corner he might be a liability. He might be recognised. Or worse, he might … But Big Joe had over-ruled all objections. It was his trial, so he was going.

'Here. Want a swig? It's Bowmore.'

'No. I *don't* want a swig. Joe, Ah don't like this. It's too risky and we …'

'Shut up ya wummin. Here. Drink.'

Big Joe started the engine, leaned back and put on the windscreen blower.

'Are you cold?' asked McLane.

'Naw. It's just … ye know.'

'What? You might need a few seconds, an' I might be the liability?'

'Shurrup. Ye'r a' right. Arab's doon the street, tooled-up wi' three guys on motorbikes. Any bother an' they're right oan us. Plus ah've got ma new …'

'Aye. An' I wish you hadn't brought that. *That's* all I need.'

'Look, Tucker wiz sure. Ah took him through it time and time again. Go through your morning. When did ye get up? Did ye feed the rats? Whit did you feed them? Did ye feel ok? Whit were ye drinkin' the night before? Could yir drink have been spiked? How did ye discover this advert in yir paper? Dae yi owe anybody Tucker? A Russian maybe? No? Are you *sure* Tucker? It a' sounds a wee bit far-fetched Tucker. You have to agree?'

But Tucker was sure. The Ad was in the wrong paper, so as to be in the right paper. There was nothing added to the printing so the information needed for the meeting was already there, in the printing. The meet wouldn't be at opening time as people were arriving, so it was at closing time when they were leaving. The location was the South Side and there was a time limit. The Sale was to end on Christmas Eve at 10 p.m. but that was weeks away. Nobody would be in that neck of the woods at 10 p.m. Who wasn't looking for kitchen and bathroom fittings. The store would close, at the latest, at 10 p.m. That would take a minute or so. A wee while after that somebody would appear. Somebody with something to say that couldn't be said anywhere else. Something that would cost him dearly if it got out. But he was prepared to risk that. Why? Who was he?

'Wait, somethin's ….'

'Where?'

'That guy. Shuttin' the shop. See. It's exactly 10 o'clock.'

When the shop owner switched out his coloured shop lights, Bridge Street plunged into complete darkness.

185

Watching the front, Big Joe Mularkey laid one hand on the wheel, his other on the gear lever. Keeping his eye on the rear window he grimaced. The lashing rain was distorting every image.

'Anythin'?'

'It's hopeless. Ah can't see a thing. Ah hope Arab's still there.' whined McLane.

'He's there. For Christ's sake stop worryin' Brogan.'

Sitting in silence, a minute passed. Then another. Nothing.

'Maybe he's round the back of the shop.'

'Naw. Yi'd need tae be a crazy man, or a frogman, tae be waitin' back there in this. Naw. Ah think it'll be a wee while yet.'

McLane rubbed his neck now sore from twisting around so many times and pulled his coat around his ears. Big Joe, pressing his hand onto the glass, demisted a tiny hole. An uneasy silence reigned.

'Oh my *Jesus* Christ!'

Rapping his knuckles on the passenger window, a big man wearing a hip-length green waxed jacket with the

186

hood up had stepped out of nowhere.

Big Joe Mularkey reached into his waistband and flashed his eyes around, looking for others.

Rap Rap Rap.

McLane hadn't a clue what was happening: 'Joe! Joe! What the FUCK?'

'Naw Naw Naw. Brogan. Ye'r a' right. It's no' a hit. Calm doon.'

Opening the back door, into the big BMW stepped Commander Terry Imrie.

'By fuck it's cauld out there, man.' shivered the man from Edinburgh A Division.

All his planning had failed and Big Joe felt a sense of defeat and hoped the word wouldn't spread too widely. *'How long has he been standin' there for fuck sake?'* This job had been top priority. Two days before, in Sandbach M6 Motorway Services in the north of England, two teenagers who'd never met before occupied adjacent toilet cubicles. One from Edinburgh, the other from London. On the signal known only to the teenagers and their bosses an absolutely untraceable fully loaded .38 Smith and Wesson passed silently between the cubicles. Gripping the butt of that gun, Big Joe's finger rested on the trigger.

'Mr Imrie! What the *fuck* dae *you* want?'

McLane, never more relieved to see anyone, calmed the tension. His life-long best mate could happily end Imrie's career in the Edinburgh police. Right here. Right now. But McLane sensed that Imrie was carrying his own, even more powerful weapon; a reason for arranging this meeting.

'Easy Joe. Easy man. JESUS H – OK. Let's hear him out.'

Slowly raising his hands, his sleeves dripping puddles onto the floor, Commander Imrie paid Big Joe Mularkey all due respect. 'I swear I'm on my own. Joe. Would you please take your hand off that thing and tell the Arab and his boys to back off?'

Tranquil as Sunday afternoon tea at the vicarage, Imrie put his palms on the seats in front. Big Joe Mularkey remained stony faced.

Calm as calm could be, Commander Imrie tried an obvious question: 'Do you *really* think I'm here to turn you over Joe? Or McLane? If I wanted to do that, I'd be here officially. Right?'

The Trial

Nodding, but still staring him down, Big Joe Mularkey recognised immediately that was true.

'Let's hear him Joe. An' put that away man. A'right?' demanded McLane.

Never more relieved to hear an Advocate of the High Court make his case, Imrie breathed out. Big Joe Mularkey brought his empty right hand into view, cooling the atmosphere; if only a degree or two. Looking into McLane's eyes, Imrie was all business.

'I've got a couple of things to tell you. I don't imagine the first will surprise you. But the second is going to blow your socks off Brogan. Is it OK if I call you Brogan?'

Chapter 26

Only a few feet apart, the three faces breathed in, and out, each other's contributions to the atmosphere filling the BMW; honking whisky breath, wet clothes, cigar smoke and a whiff of something very rare. Mortal danger. Unsure of where this might go, McLane ran through the legal possibilities – for the umpteenth time. But the basics were all there. The first move had been made by someone other than him. The meeting was obviously not a hit – unless of course, Commander Imrie was in so much trouble that he was suicidal – which wasn't unknown in the police. But his demeanour didn't betray that. He'd asked, politely, to use his first name. He'd been standing in a freezing cold dangerous place, probably for hours before they got there. And there was something else; he looked like a man who needed help. So this could be a win-win. With an almost imperceptible nod, McLane acceded to this seemingly innocuous request.

'OK. We've been in a few cases over the years and I've seen you around Parliament House. You can call me Brogan.'

While Imrie ran his hand through his wet hair and pulled at the bottom of his coat, McLane again took a race through the legal possibilities. If Imrie was on a fishing trip, setting them up for confession, then he ultimately risked a motion in the trial court that McLane and Mularkey were victims of illegal entrapment. That might cause the trial to collapse. Or, if the trial carried on, the jury would hear about the entrapment and smell a rat. It could all be severely damaging to Imrie's career and, maybe also to his pension. If he was found by a discipline tribunal to have brought the name of the Edinburgh police into disrepute – in Glasgow! – there would be hell to pay.

'So what is this?'

But Big Joe Mularkey, his face the colour of a hard punch on a fresh bruise, and his heart pumping, didn't trust this situation as far as he could throw Commander Imrie.

McLane imagined all this coming out in a court and laid out the legal position. The bare knuckle truth was, and it could be proved, that Imrie had come to them. Not the other way around. He and Joe could string Imrie along. Play his game. Say nothing incriminating and walk away. So they were OK.

McLane opened by establishing a negative: 'Mr Imrie, you said you had a few things to tell us. Well, first

of all, there is no 'us'. Joe isn't in this. He's just here to
…'

Interrupting, Imrie was back in police Commander
mode: 'That's crap and you know it. He's here. He's
listening to me in the back of your car late at night. He's
probably armed; probably somethin' from London - right
Joe? He's a first-class accomplice. You know it. I know it.
He knows it.'

McLane conceded with a flicker of his eyelids.
The juvenile mistake he wouldn't have made back in the
East End of Glasgow was passed over with no harm done.
McLane had implied that he knew the purpose of this
meeting and that would be enough in a court of law to
prove guilt in conspiracy to pervert the course of justice.
He knew it. Joe knew it and Imrie knew it.

Cold and staring. Carefully laying his hand again
on the .38 and looking for other officers beyond Imrie's
head, Big Joe showed no fear; because he had none, and
got right down to business.

'You mentioned a couple of things. OK. Tell us
the somethin' that *won't* surprise us.'

'OK. First. Did you see the funeral?'

It was an obvious question to which McLane took no objection. Joe eased things forward.

'On TV.'

'From a police point of view, that gave us dozens of suspects. All of them with a great deal more motive than you, Brogan.'

Sensing Big Joe's finger was back around the trigger, Imrie checked his position: 'It's still OK to call you Brogan?'

'Sure'

'But Joe here ... Well, he's in a different ... sorry Joe, I was going to say 'boat'. Still doin' the business with the boat Joe?'

Unflapped, McLane saw the mistake coming. Leading towards entrapment would read equally seriously on an Indictment as the entrapment itself. With the score even in his head, McLane flashed a look at Big Joe; who kept a stony silence.

'Anyway ...We've recently developed the investigation and come up with a few things. Firstly, we've found Lord Aldounhill's laptop. Not the one issued by the office of Scottish Courts Administration. His personal one. Brogan, I imagine you've been to Abbotsford?'

'I have, but it was only for a dinner when Lord Ballacory ...'

Interrupting, Big Joe was surprised at McLane's casual answer. He'd seen enough mistakes for one night: 'Just you tell *us* about Abbotford. You speak. We listen. OK?'

'It's not Abbotford, Joe. It's *Abbotsford*. Brogan knows where I mean. The home of Sir Walter Scott. 19th Century guy. Advocate and Writer. Big statue on Princes' Street in Edinburgh. Right Brogan?'

Taking his cue from Big Joe, McLane kept his silence; flashing back to his two Faculty nosebags in the best private dining room in Scotland.

'Well, Scott was an Advocate in Parliament House. His home in the Border Country is called Abbotsford. The house and his famous library are now owned by the Faculty of Advocates. Bequeathed by Sir Walter to his beloved Faculty in perpetuity. It's quite touching really. Brogan here has dined in Scott's dining room. The last occasion was just over two years ago, when he dined with Lord Justice General Jamieson, the newly installed Lord Ballacory and 9 other Judges and Advocates. The centre-piece of the house is of course Scott's study. Scott wrote some of the world's best loved books from his desk in that wee study.'

Devoid of reverence for one of Scotland's proudest sons, Big Joe tried to keep this train on the track.

'So what?'

'Well. See, that's the thing. My uniformed assistant in this investigation is a great Scott fan. Constable Coutts. Can't get enough of Sir Walter's books. He's been to Abbotsford six or seven times. Only the public tours, you understand. Knows the place inside out. I think he should get himself a life. But hey …'

Taking a slow deep breath, Big Joe asked: 'Could ye' get to the point Commander Imrie?'

'Sure. When we were searching Lord Aldounhill's house it was Constable Coutts who drove me there. I would usually leave my driver in the car but I'm glad I brought him in. You see, when he walked into Lord Aldounhill's study, the first thing he noticed was the desk. A big old thing it is. Leather covered. Drawers down the sides. You know the kind.'

'Yeah yeah …' Joe had had quite enough of Sir Walter Scott.

'The point Joe is, that Lord Aldounhill's desk is an exact copy of Sir Walter Scott's. Complete with secret compartment. You have to remove three pieces to get to that compartment. I mean in the 19th century they really knew how to make craftsman-built …'

Almost at the end of his patience, Big Joe demanded more than asked: 'Yeah! And?'

'*That's* where we found his laptop and the pictures.'

The point seeped into the two Glaswegians faster than the dank damp air. The reason Lord Aldounhill would hide a personal laptop in such a place while having ready access to it any time he wanted, was not obvious, but it was obviously nefarious.

'We found a DVD in the laptop. Aldounhill's fingerprints and DNA are on it.'

Big Joe yelled so loudly that Imrie's hair moved: 'For FUCK sake! I repeat Commander - And?'

'There were two movies on one disc. All we know at the moment is that the disc itself was made in the USA.

We don't know where the filming took place. The first movie shows quite explicit exploitation of two children. A boy about 12 and a girl aged no more than 8. There's even an address in Holland, should you have any wee stars to put on the silver screen. The other movie is a home-made thing. Maybe made in some sort of a TV club, but maybe made in a big private house. Oh, that's not the telly, Joe. TV means Transvestite.'

'Ah know.'

Big Joe's matter-of-fact manner hid a growing unease. Important information was now in police hands and therefore, given the amount this defence was costing, that information should have found its way to the Calton Bar; but hadn't.

'So? You're asking me that? So … it's not your style Brogan. It's definitely not yours Joe. Wee kids and poofie sex.'

Shaking his head and closing his eyes, Commander Imrie shed droplets of rain further than they'd dripped before. The information was unexpected. The messenger was equally unexpected. And the meaning was even more unexpected than that. With those words now out in the air, a new atmosphere pervaded the car. One lighter than McLane could have hoped for. One that shed important new light on the background of a Parliament House Judge everyone knew to be rotten to the core. And now there was proof; but it was hardly surprising proof.

Plus, before Imrie came to his bombshell, something remained unsaid that would require to be aired before McLane would sleep easily that night and Commander Imrie knew it. Looking McLane straight in the face, he said as softly as though he was petting a kitten: 'I'm not buying it. I'm just simply not buyin' it guys. And I don't think a jury would buy it either. Not when presented with your specialism in international child abduction law and your unblemished record.'

With his blood pressure lowering and light dawning in his mind McLane was settling into his new found state when Big Joe had something else to add: 'Hold it. Just a sec. Why are you …? Commander you've just revealed a private police communication to us. Why would …?'

Putting up both hands, Imrie surrendered the point: 'I'm takin' a risk. I know that. But I think it's a risk worth taking. I'm not here on a whim. You see, everything I learn about this case points further and further *away* from you two. And what I'm learning drives me in another direction. I don't mean I can charge anyone yet; or you'd be the first to know. Suffice to say I'm looking at a few people. All very posh. Private educations, private incomes and private clubs. Now there's plenty of them around Parliament House but I'm looking through the PH crowd to include others. Not really your sort of playmates Brogan, you'll agree? '

'MmmHmm. And?'

Desperate to hear Imrie's second piece of news, McLane held his breath, watching Imrie prepare to deliver: 'I said there was something that would blow your socks off, and here it is. We've just pulled something interesting out of the canal in Edinburgh. A set of keys and a broken champagne flute, wrapped in what we now know was a posh linen napkin. What's the odds the keys fit Aldounhill's house? And the napkin is forensically matched to the others lying on his dining table? The thing is, there was something on the champagne glass that is extremely helpful to you Brogan.'

McLane lit up like a child on Christmas Eve: 'Oh thank Christ. Good news at last. What?

'It was lipstick. Purple lipstick.'

The words fell on the men in the front of the car like news of a lost loved-one who'd been found. Open-mouthed, McLane leaned in.

'You see Brogan, if I'm right, that someone wearing purple lipstick may have been the last person to see Aldounhill alive. That person may even have murdered Aldounhill. Or watched as he was murdered by somebody else.'

Cool as the proverbial mountain stream Big Joe asked: 'Do you know who this person is?'

'Oh yes. I do.'

McLane felt like a sack of coal which he'd carried up a mountain had just been lifted from his shoulders. He'd only known this feeling once before, but it was instantly recognisable. When one hears the sound of back-crushing, marriage crushing, mind crushing trouble begin to crack and the possibility dawns that the trouble will fall away and end; there is a feeling called 'Expectation' and it ran round McLane's bloodstream like no rush any addict ever had.

Staring across the darkness at this crossroads in the investigation, Big Joe allowed McLane to blurt out: 'Jesus. I need to know. My defence will … *How* do you know?'

Imrie dropped his hand onto McLane's sleeve. 'Easy Brogan. The scientist, a Professor Isaac Neuberger right here in Glasgow, is absolutely certain he's identified the right person. And this person's world couldn't be further from the two men I'm looking at right now. Are you beginning to get the picture Brogan?

'I don't really … I'm not …' stumbled McLane, whose ability to form rational thought had departed.

But Big Joe still had his: 'Wow! Well, that's a sledgehammer tae the heid aw' right. But Commander, it looks like ye want tae say somethin' else.'

Happy to have been the bearer of glad tidings in this time of peace and goodwill, Imrie raised his right index finger and with that brought the two men in front of him back to earth. 'Oh I do. And it's this. Brogan. It's now clear to me that you're *not* being prosecuted. You're being *persecuted*.

Chapter 27

Shafts of morning sunlight through the stained glass window bounced off the worn wooden bar and up into the smoke, forming the only division between Big Jake Devine's card school near the door and the little war council, huddled head to head in the back of the Calton Bar. No 'Do Not Disturb' sign hung, nor did anyone inquire about this parley. This meeting wasn't a secret; it was a public Declaration of War.

As Chairman of this council, Brogan McLane sat with his back to the door in full-on Advocate mode. Sitting first to his right came Big Joe Mularkey. Next around sat Paddy the Turk from the South Side, trusted because of many previous sterling efforts, some of them delivering sensitive 'messages' to the Med late at night. Tiger Allison, invited for his photographic memory, brought the best wishes of his father; and Tucker Queen for everything else.

The council toasted itself then McLane began: 'OK. It may be nobody's fault. But Joe and I met a guy last night who's pretty sure I'm not being prosecuted. I'm being *persecuted*. So all of this … this trouble … it's personal to somebody. The police don't believe I'm into kiddie sex and ...'

The Trial

'Huh! Ev'rybuddy knows that a'ready Brogan. Ah think ye might have been …'

Big Joe silenced Tiger with a sideways glance. But respect was due, so McLane eased things forward: 'Sorry Tiger. I don't mean it's a trust issue … like with you guys. This guy has *reason* to think that. Now, as I was saying. We need to go over everything. This meeting will be the first of many. But today, I want to look at Wee Joe's trial. See if there's a link to mine. Something *is* there. Maybe pretty deep down. *Something* is the cause we're looking for. Do you catch my drift? We see the *effect*, on me, guys. What we need is the *cause* of that effect.'

Speaking up and with a hint of hurt, Tucker leaned in: 'Well, Brogan, all enquiries *were* made at the time. Joe made some. Ah made plenty and Tiger there kept that father *and* his two sons tied up in their own hoose. Ah think Ah'm right Tiger, ye' wer ready to feed them to they hungry Rotweillers o' yours?'

Pulling his squint face, Tiger Allison confirmed that indeed was the position at the time of Wee Joe's trial.

'Plus, Big Joe had put the word oot that a nice wee holiday in the boattom o' his boat was waiting for anybody who told us lies. Ah forget how many punters we pulled in here. Right here Brogan. Ah mean, how *could* we have missed anythin'?'

No-one responded. Two years before, almost to the day, Tucker had been certain. Tiger was certain and Big Joe Mularkey was certain. The entire community of the Calton Bar was satisfied that Wee Joe Mularkey had been set up for trial in the High Court in Edinburgh.

An understandable tension had arisen and McLane felt the need to relieve it: 'I *know* Tuck. But we see things differently from the way they see things in the Crown Office. Believe me. It's a question of morality. Their ideas of what's right and what's wrong are nothing like ours. Somebody had it in for Wee Joe, or maybe just wanted to get at Big Joe for something. We don't know. We've just got to look back. For instance, is there anything to be gained from looking again at Big Joe's trial?'

'Which waan?' asked Tiger, who was forgiven his ignorance due to absence for several years.

'Sorry Tiger. The one that collapsed ten years ago.' confirmed McLane.

'Bit *why* Brogan? asked the Tiger opening his hands.

Acknowledging his point, McLane conceded: 'Tiger's right. We not only need items of interest, we need *reasons* why these things are interesting to whoever is …'

Poking the table with his finger, Big Joe hit the spot: 'Settin' ye' up Brogan. Jist tell it like it is.'

To nods of approval Tucker opened his hands and looked his old friend in the eye.

'Well Brogan, that's gonnie make things a wee bit difficult for us. Right? Ah mean, you're the oanly wan i' us that can think like them. Know what a mean?'

'I do Tuck. You're right. Too many years in Parliament House I suppose. But back to the business in hand. We all knew he was set up in desperation because they've never convicted Big Joe here. They saw the name Mularkey and jumped at their chance. But we never knew *who* it was in the Crown Office who spun it that way. That's what I'm really after. Now, let's go back to the facts. Basics guys. Nothing is too stupid or embarrassing to mention. Right? It's an old technique we use in Consultations. Right, now correct me if I'm wrong, but I don't think so.

Wee Joe went to a club in Edinburgh. He'd heard some girl's Glasgow accent on the dance floor and got off with her. His mate had a car and they gave the girl *and* her pal a lift back to Glasgow. So four in the car. Correct Joe?'

'Aye.'

'But the girl Wee Joe fancied lived in enemy territory - Maryhill. So they dropped her short in the Cowcaddens. Right?

'Correct.'

'Yes. However, the following night he stupidly spent the only money … Sorry Joe … the only money he had, on a taxi to her address and slipped … unseen? …

'Correct again?'

'Up the stairs to her flat.'

Every head nodded silent approval of the facts so far.

'Shortly after 1 o'clock in the morning he was *walking* home through a back 'dunny' garden … which was sensible enough … He was passing a back close mouth when he was crashed to the ground by two guys running at full pelt out of the back close. Wee Joe hit his head … the forensics evidence said … on the handle of a garbage bin and passed out. The old lady … Peggy Anderson … who lived alone up the close he was passing, had been badly assaulted and robbed. Her last voluntary act in this life was to call the police. The two guys who barged into Wee Joe ran away, but they were seen running in a street a few hundred yards from the back close and were picked up by a uniformed unit. As they were giving statements … at 2.46 a.m. if I remember correctly … the whole thing kicked off. Why? Because the police radio message was sent at 2. 45 a.m. from the Royal Infirmary saying that the old lady was DoA. Joe, am I right? She died of a brain haemorrhage?

'A complication of the pulmonary arterial effect.'

'Right. And naturally the Glasgow police immediately elevated the case from robbery to murder. By the time Wee Joe regained consciousness, had been seen by the doctor and interviewed it was too late – the other guys had got their story in first. They told the police they heard a cry for help, ran through the close and caught the robber; but he passed out in a struggle. At Wee Joe's trial, the witness who lived across the street, whose name I can't remember, said she saw only one young man, roughly fitting the description of the accused – Wee Joe, entering the close from the front. In cross-examination, she accepted from me that one or more men *could* have entered the close before the man she saw; but I clearly remember the judge crushing our attempts to make any more of that point. The word was everywhere around Parliament House, not for the first time of course, that after these two main prosecution witnesses had told their tall tales, the judge made the Lord Advocate's Deputy speed through the rest of the prosecution evidence.'

'Aye. 'cause the bastard waanted away to play golf.'

Laying his hand over his friend's, McLane understood the unnecessary interjection.

'Easy Joe. Let's crack on. Now. Wee Joe stated his defence but the Lord Advocate's Deputy just called him an obvious liar.'

Paddy the Turk spoke for the first time since sitting down; demonstrating his inside knowledge of the police and prosecution forces.

'Aye. That Advocate Depute owed his promotion three months later to 'im.'

'He did. Aye. To Aldounhill. He did. He even ordered the prison van to arrive early. It's an old court trick – don't give the defence enough oxygen to survive.

I remember in his speech to the jury, Aldounhill

specifically praised the two guys for their courage in doing their civic duty in dangerous circumstances. Plus he gave the jury as many non-verbal signals as he could that Wee Joe was definitely guilty. We all saw that. The audio recording of his speech of course sounded just balanced enough to make sure that any appeal on those grounds would fail. Again, that trick's as old as the hills. And, … sorry Joe … Sure enough, two appeals have now failed. So where are we? Is *anything* missing?'

Every head shook. Arriving in crisp white apron and rolled up sleeves, Lenny, the latest owner of the Calton Bar, still revelling in his new capacity as Landlord, delivered another five very large Lagavulin 16 year-olds and five more beers.

'Ah goat they pickchurs scanned in tae ma computer an' printeed oot, Brogan. Wid ye like tae see them? They're up behind the bar.'

'Aye go on Lenny. We're taking a break.'

Hanging up behind the bar, a relic from a bygone age had been carefully restored. Anyone coming in by chance, not that that happened often, couldn't know the significance of the two youngish faces in the picture. Wearing unkempt beards and black woolly hats, there were just two young men embracing.

Now leaning on the bar, as those two blood brothers drank and ate their pies in silence, the volume in the pub came up to its usual Saturday night level. Everyone was letting go of their week. A few second-hand cars had been sold. A few more had disappeared to sunnier climes. A few of the men had just been released and, like the inevitable tide, a few more had gone in for a while. Just the normal ebb and flow of the Calton Bar.

Standing at the Bar like two volcanoes who'd erupted long ago and merged into a single island, Brogan McLane and Big Joe Mularkey were the strongest team in the city. McLane the smartest. Big Joe the toughest. Every man in the bar felt they'd make it. Whatever Edinburgh threw at them.

McLane turned his head, laughing and raising his voice above betting numbers and orders for plates of stew or more beer, and called: 'So, has anybody got a master plan?'

Nobody had any kind of plan. But that light moment eased the pressure. As their two best men stood side by side at the bar looking at every trusted face, every man Jack felt a rare moment arrive. Spontaneous and emotional, proud and hopeful. The type that gets talked about from father to son. Lenny clanged a single toll of the bar bell and silence fell. Standing for the toast, every man proudly raised his glass and waited for McLane to raise his. Lifting his glass and looking slowly around, he acknowledged every man in the place.

'To us!'

Drinking straight down, every man in Defence HQ stood rock solid. No word was beyond utterance to each other. No secret would leave their lips to a stranger. No testimony would ever be given and betrayal wasn't even worthy of contemplation.

With McLane and Big Joe once again shoulder to shoulder, leaning on the old oak bar, McLane whispered into Big Joe's ear. 'Tell me. Tell me now big man. Was it you?'

Pouring in another large Lagavulin, Big Joe Mularkey savoured his smoky dram around and around at the back of his throat; as though it might be his last. Waiting, hoping and half-praying that he wouldn't have to do jail time for his blood brother, McLane pressed the question.

'Joe. I asked you …'

'No Brogan. It Wiznae me. But Ah'll tell ye somethin'. Ah wish wi' all ma' hart, everythin' Ah've got, that it hud been. But Ah'm tellin' ye right now … ma man … ah didn'ae murder the wee bastard. As God is ma witness Brogan, He knows Ah wish Ah hud.'

McLane nodded knowing only too well that Big Joe Mularkey would never lie to him. Not to protect him. Not to deceive him. Not for money. Not if he was tortured. Never. But he got a surprise when Joe turned, asking softly: 'Waz it *you* Brogan?'

'Me? Nope. It definitely wasn't me. I would've been at home at the time. But God in Heaven man, Joanne's a wreck wi' this. And - alibi or no alibi - I'm not making it worse by letting her give evidence for me. If the jury didn't accept her evidence and I went down for life … Man, that would break her.'

'Tell me aboot it Brogan. Molly's the same.'

'Aye Joe. Ah know. What a mess.'

Lapsing into silence, acknowledging occasional slaps on the back and refusing more drink than they could handle, both men stared into the big Dewars' mirror behind the bar.

Tucker Queen approached, pointing at his wrist. He had other business to attend to: 'Are we eh … getting' back to this?'

Pulling McLane by the sleeve, Big Joe Mularkey

answered: 'No Tucker. Give's a minute. Ah need a word wi' Brogan.'

Big Joe leaned in till their faces touched. While giving himself time to think through his idea, their dark suits merged. Standing like one huge man Big Joe whispered: 'I've got a wee idea. See whit ye' think o' this.'

Chapter 28

Around the council table in the Calton Bar, while Tucker argued that he could do the whole job himself, McLane was insistent: put three guys on the job; out of town, the best available. Money is no object.

Operational security demanded that those chosen would *not* be close to the Calton Bar. They were to be told nothing beyond what was already public knowledge. Anything they learned on the job, they would swear to keep to themselves or end up at the bottom of the Med. That's the deal.

Tucker pleaded that the Glasgow wheel guys would be insulted by not being asked. 'Are you listening to me Tucker?'

'Aye, but Brogan …'

'Clean and tidy. No scruff. Right? Suits. Fresh breath an' get this into your head because this is the most important thing, right? No drugs for at least a week before.'

'Whit? Aw … That's gonnie narrow the field a bit Brogan.'

Pursing his lips and his eyes bulging, McLane

poked Tucker in the chest: 'Look at my face. I want a variety of ages. If there's an accident, first impressions could be important.'

'OK Brogan. The local boys won't like it. But you're the boss.'

'And one last thing. I want *nobody* with an outstanding arrest warrant pinned up in some police station.'

At the sound of this impossibility, Tucker threw his arms in the air, protesting his last: 'Aw Christ man, noo ye'r askin' the impossible.'

'Tucker, that's my worst nightmare on this. If this goes wrong, it could turn and bite us. I mean not us, '*me*'. It might even be used in the trial. Right? So it's ***that*** important.'

A week later, sitting astride a new, English registered motorcycle in the car park on Belgrove Street, the tall fit young man reading a city road map and drinking take-away tea, Number 1 looked like any other biker on holiday.

In the Atrium of the 30 storey Scottish Global Media Group Building in a suit, tie and polished shoes reading that day's London Times, the tanned balding middle-aged Number 2 blended seamlessly into the business crowd coming and going.

Outside the steel and glass skyscraper, Number 3, a young hoodie spitting into the gutter kept a clear line of sight to Number 2. Jangling the coins in his jeans' pocket he was ready to follow on foot and, if required, have the exact change to pay bus fares.

The only legal proof that all three were connected was the contact list in their phones. Each contact list looked perfectly normal; but for the next few hours only, each one's speed dial showed Tucker as number 1, each other as 2, 3 and 4 but only Tucker had Brogan as Number 5.

Up on the 25th floor at her corner desk in the News Room of the Glasgow Daily Tribune, her two-year-old Scottish Young Reporter of the Year Award in pride of place, the mark sat squarely in the cross hairs of the binoculars held by Number 1 more than three hundred metres away.

Checking his watch against the clock in the car, it read 6.49 p.m. According to Tucker's best information, she wouldn't be long. The word was that although she used to party late into the night, she did that less and less nowadays.

At the background meeting, something new had come up. Tucker's guy from the North Side reported that the mark had recently begun to change her ways. After work she sometimes took an evening meal to her arthritic mother who lived alone and they visited for two to three hours.

Laughing and chatting into her phone, Louise Bishop - her bright red mane of hair unmistakable - stepped out of the Atrium's revolving doors, leaving work for the night. Walking briskly along Ingram Street, she made two more calls and got out her car keys. Only when she was inside her brand new black Audi TT, did Number 2 relay the description and Registration details of her car to Number 1. Seeing the motorcycle's headlight dip 50 yards in front of him, Number 2 crossed the street and disappeared.

Staying close, snaking through the Glasgow traffic and crossing the River Clyde into the south side of the city was easy enough but the tree-lined suburban streets were quieter with more chance of No1 being seen. Following at 400 yards, Tucker's Mercedes blended-in perfectly with the other vehicles parked up and down the adjoining streets. Stopped at a light, he heard: 'Target just turned right into cul-de-sac 300 yards.'

'Copy that.'

As Louise Bishop pulled into her short driveway, her garage door opened automatically.

Picking up a pair of binoculars, Tucker watched her open the front door of No 35 Orchard View. As the door swung open, the hallway, staircase and living room were dark. She did live alone.

When she lowered the blind, Tucker picked up his phone: 'Baby's in the cradle. Let the wind blow.'

~~~0~~~

The Trial

Chapter 29

A single puny shaft of moonlight lit the rippling waters of Dunsapie Loch but otherwise Arthur's Seat Hill lay in total darkness. On the east side of the Hill, in the 14th century village of Duddingston the only lights burning came from Bonnie Prince Charlie's 'Sheep's Heid Inn' and a candle in the vestry of the ancient church.

In the pub sitting around the bright coal fire under a wide portrait of the Battle of Prestonpans a few regulars sat blethering and drinking in quietness. Standing at the bar a crowd of Scandinavian visitors kept the busty barmaid occupied while making their mark on the pub's long line of single malt whiskies. No-one took the slightest interest in the tall fit man coming in from the cold; his woolly hat pulled down to his eyebrows, his dog on a lead and a newspaper tucked under his arm. Taking his pint to a cranny in the back of the pub, he patted his dog and settled down with his paper.

Mentally the man went through his ingrained Ops Security procedures, taking careful notes. From left to right and back again. He swallowed half his pint in one gulp, lifted the dog's lead and quietly eased open the old wooden back door.

Out in the empty village lane he clipped the lead to his belt and checked around; windows, doorways, parked cars. Nothing. Whispering into the damp Scottish night air, man and dog were a world apart from their meeting place in a scorching Wadi in Northern Kurdistan.

'Come on Saddam. Good lad.'

Sprinting up the steep sturdy wooden steps buried in the earth to make the long climb up Arthur's Seat Hill a little easier for the tourists, Saddam stayed perfectly in pace with his handler.

At the top, tying the lead to a young birch tree and taking some raw rabbit from a plastic bag in his pocket he laid down Saddam's dinner. A few yards away he pulled out the camouflage hold-all bag he'd hidden in the brush the night before. Stepping into a grateful Ops Commander's cover-all suit sent him straight back to an unregistered Nissan hut in Basra. "Guaranteed never to shed fibres. In one of these, you're forensically invisible. God speed guys." the Tactical Commander had said.

He paused, taking a moment to salute the dead, then rolled a black woollen balaclava down over his head and face, adjusting the eye holes for comfort. Lastly, pulling a strong nylon back-pack from the bag he slipped his arms through the straps.

Straightening to attention, his fists clenched, his chest and shoulders granite hard, Colour Sergeant Jim McCauley stood ready.'

Yomping over the wet gorse and heather, trying not to let the letter they'd sent last year cloud his mind, Sgt McCauley focused on the flames it made when he flung that letter on the fire.

He stopped at the end of a tenement building to check his kit. Rubbing his shoulder blades against the back-pack, he felt his trusty crossbow. Tapping around, he touched the Cable - check, Twists and rollers – check. On his hip he touched the safety switch of his 'Leccy pistol' (British Army Electronic Pulse Generating Gun) - check. Diamond tipped glass cutter x 2 (German made, not Chinese), well-oiled press-button flick-knife (Israeli Army), scissors (Swiss), Blue-Tac (well warmed against the body) short circuit clamp (American) and lastly an excellent pair of night goggles taken from a Syrian insurgent who had stolen them from a dead Yankee soldier boy after a roadside bombing in Baghdad.

Taking out the crossbow, he pulled up the wings to full stretch. Carefully lifting out his drum of thin ultra-strong wire and connecting it, he put the drum under his right armpit. Taking four small steps back, just enough to get the correct angle and not enough to be seen by anyone in the adjacent tenement, with dead-eye accuracy he shot his bolt. Flying between two chimney pots, upon roof impact its five 'star-clamp' fingers sprung out and locked.

He just loved the sound those cable connecting clips made as they sprung around your belt. The feel of those American ultra-friction gloves around the cable gave a sense of real security. With one foot on the wall, he pulled. Up, up, like taking a walk in the park, in under a minute he'd pull-climbed himself up the gable end to the top of the four storey tenement. Settling down, he slipped on his infra-red night goggles and let his eyes adjust to the way the world should look. Immediately he had his target in sight.

As expected, the officer's info was reliable. At this time of night, only a few lights were on around the big Drug Squad briefing room on the third floor but otherwise, all appeared exactly as he expected.

'OK McCauley, here we go.'

Carefully taking out the most important piece of gear he had with him - the grabber - he kissed it before fitting its rubber 'gloves'.

Leaning against the chimney stack for stability, he

had the roof ridge of 'A' Division Police HQ in his cross hairs. Taking aim, he fired. In a split second and in absolute silence, the roof of 'A' Division Police HQ and Colour Sergeant Jim McCauley were directly connected.

His only piece of kit untested in battle was a pair of hand operated American 'bike pedal' wire rollers. But several tests in the deep woods behind the Pentland Hills earned them a five-star rating from Colour Sergeant Jim McCauley on TestYourKit.com.

Within a few seconds Sgt McCauley stood on the window ledge looking into the fifth floor office of Commander Terry Imrie.

His watch confirmed that it had been only seven minutes since he'd left the Sheep's Heid Inn.

Gaining a few seconds from the ease with which the window latch slipped, once inside he set to work. Only the top right hand drawer of Commander Imrie's desk required a few seconds persuasion to open. And there it was.

In a manila folder marked in bold red print 'PRIVATE - Ongoing Investigation - HMA v McLane' was his target. Taking a careful look, there was no doubt; this was what the officer wanted: the signed original Forensic Science Report from Professor Neuberger's Lab about the DNA contained in a sample of purple lipstick found on Lord Aldounhill.

Climbing carefully back out onto the ledge he couldn't resist a wave to the web-camera he knew would be somewhere in the room.

The Trial

Chapter 30

Madam Fiscal closed her email and lifted an unusually heavy bundle out of the printer, laid it on the desk and opened her office door. Catching Sheila's eye, she nodded as a sign to come in.

'Anything this morning Sheila?'

'No Ma'am. I was hoping that MI6 might have more on the boat but …'

'It's alright Sheila. There's a conference in the Crown Office at 3 p.m. today, which I shall be attending. I think we're getting ready to serve the Indictment.'

The very mention of 'we' serving the McLane Indictment sent a shiver through the Senior Assistant.

'So Sheila, is it ready?'

'Yes. It's on my screen ready for your approval.'

Picking up the bundle, Sheila McManus ran her thumb across the six hundred and ninety two pages.

'I'm afraid I had to use your name Ma'am, and our budget but I'm so pleased this came in on time.

'That's fine Sheila. It'll be worth it.'

Outside The Lord Advocate's Chambers the other three attendees barely acknowledged the Fiscal's arrival. Holding a fine bone china cup of tea with the saucer sitting on top of the cup, his little finger lifted to a right angle, the Solicitor-General cracked a smile: 'He's on the phone with the Prime Minister. Shouldn't be a tick.'

Opening the door, his lordship's private secretary gestured the group to go in. Laying closed on his desk, the McLane file gave no hint of where this meeting was going. Peering over his pince-nez spectacles the Lord Advocate got straight to the point.

'The McLane case. The basics gentlemen. I just don't think they're sound enough. I'd say it's shaky at best. Plus - if it goes wrong - there's the danger of adverse effects on other cases.'

Stating his view so bluntly, was a clear sign that the Lord Advocate was inviting challengers to his proposition. Positions now had to be taken. With him or against him.

The Crown Solicitor, technically a civil servant with life tenure, made the first move. But he was predictably treading very safe ground: 'I have always agreed with you Sir. It is a circumstantial case at best. No direct evidence links McLane to the body … to Lord Aldounhill. If this case went the wrong way …'

'Yes, you've hit the nail on the head. That's the real fear. So? Home Depute?'

'Well I agree Sir. It will in all probability be me who prosecutes this case in court. I don't shy away from it. Not a bit of it. But our legal position has to be faced. Circumstantial cases sometimes stick and sometimes …'

'Yes.'

Opening his hands and raising an eyebrow, Lord Caruthers turned to his Number 2, the Solicitor General. Placing his right hand firmly on the table, the Sol-Gen leaned in.

'Well I disagree, Sir. It's not all bad news. We're hoping to hear soon from MI6 about this ship we think Mularkey keeps on or around the Costa-del-Sol. He is *very* close to McLane and any criminality there rubs over onto McLane. We're fairly sure there's been …'

'My good fellow, that takes us nowhere *near* murder of Lord Aldounhill, damn it.'

Calmly taking a sip of tea, the Sol-Gen had seen his boss in this mood before.

'Of course not Sir. But turning the tables, we think his defence will be alibi. He seems to be sticking to being at home with his wife at the time of the murder. Officers have now tried twice to take a formal statement from the wife, Joanne McLane, but to no avail. However, *if* she gives evidence then they don't think she'll be a very good witness. The woman is a bag of nerves. If she makes a mistake or is so nervous that she appears to be hiding something, then she *could* do him more harm than good. We all know the old adage that has hung many an accused man – never put a lie in an alibi.'

'No. No. No. We're scraping around and if we do that in court, it will stick out like a dog's ...'

Lord Caruthers was half way to his feet when the PF coughed.

'Yes? Do you have something to ...'

'Sir, we now have something more. If I may ...?'

'Alright. Get on ... What is it?'

'Sir I agree about the association with Mularkey. His son's second appeal has just been refused.'

'My good woman! Is that what you have? *We* know about these decisions before you. Do I have to ask again? How in God's name does that take us forward with a charge of murder? Will someone please give me a *damned* answer to that question?'

'Actually, when I said there was more I meant *direct* evidence against McLane. Sir.'

When she pulled the thick court transcript from her bag and dropped it heavily onto the Lord Advocate's desk, the meeting had suddenly became hers for the taking.

The Trial

'I took the liberty of ordering a copy, on my budget, of the official transcript from the audio recordings of the trial during which Lord Aldounhill held him in Contempt of Court.'

'But the European Court of Human Rights had that. For his compensation claim. Surely, I don't see how …'

'Yes Sir. With great respect Sir, the European Court of Human Rights had the transcript of the pertinent *parts* of the verbal exchanges between Lord Aldounhill and McLane. They examined the passages where McLane complained that Lord Aldounhill was passing notes to the prosecutor and him returning them during McLane's examination of an important witness for the defence.'

'So? We know all that.'

'Ah yes, Sir. But I ordered a transcript of the *entire* trial. It just arrived this morning. Delays, I'm afraid, Sir. Financial and … Anyway, I was interested more in what was said *after* McLane was convicted and being led away. The tape itself is not absolutely clear because the voice was now turned away from addressing the court in the normal way. But if one listens very carefully then one can just detect what the typist wrote. The direct quote is 'I'll see you in Hell ya' bastard'

Widening his eyes Lord Caruthers sat down:

'Really? Well Well Well. We already had a motive, if a shaky one, but now we have a direct threat. A *related* death threat. Hhmmm. Yes. Better. Better indeed.'

'Oh and there's something else, Sir'

'Pray do tell, my good woman.'

'I investigated the police duty roster for that day. It took a little time but I now have a sworn statement from the police officer who led McLane away from court and down to the cells. He will testify that once downstairs and in his cell, he saw McLane punch the wall and heard him utter a death threat to Lord Aldounhill under his breath.'

Dropping his cup loudly into its saucer, the Solicitor-General spluttered: '*Really*! That's fantastic news ...'

Catching his eye, the PF continued, making sure she took the credit for this latest discovery: 'I've marked the pages in yellow highlight ...'

Lord Caruthers put on his glasses and pulled the transcript closer. But in only a few moments, his initial flush seemed to be waning: 'Well, of course mutterings are one thing. But whether the jury wouldn't just accept a defence version that, in those heated circumstances, he would actually carry out such a threat - I don't know. Hmm. So *maybe* we're back to ...'

The Trial

Sensing his apprehension the Fiscal leaned forward, rather too boldly for the liking of the Crown Office high command: 'I hadn't actually finished, Sir. I've questioned the officer myself and he will testify that in all his 27 years of locking people up in police cells, he never heard a man so determined. He says McLane had a certain look in his eyes, like that of several other murderers he's known. He could be a very good witness. It's direct evidence of a death threat. If we structure the evidence as leading up to that point, we know juries and the press prefer something substantial on which to hook their ...'

Holding up his hand, Her Majesty's Advocate had heard enough. To nods of agreement around the table, he announced: 'Yes. Oh yes. This *is* different. Very well. Let's hit him. Serve the McLane Indictment. Do it today!'

~~~0~~~

Chapter 31

In the Faculty's plush consultation suites situated down the Royal Mile slightly away from Parliament House, Garrad Fitzgerald, solicitor, and his counsel Mr Duncan McIntyre QC, sat waiting for their client.

The sound from across the corridor of McLane retching up the dregs of the trouble he'd been carrying in his stomach these past days, weeks and months were being heard around the building.

'Poor bastard. Still, he's borne a heavy load with dignity. I'll say that for him. The Faculty's split down the middle about whether he ...'

Pushing open the heavy door, McLane interrupted his QC: 'Sorry about this. I'm sure you're coming to that bit Duncan.'

The man upon whose shoulders would rest the presentation of the defence in court remained unflapped: 'I am. But only if you're sure you're feeling alright Brogan. I'd like to go on.'

Wiping his lips and nodding his thanks to Garrad for a glass of water, McLane drew himself up: 'I'm fine. Please do.'

From the side of his mouth Mr McIntyre QC squeezed out his next remarks: 'There are of course no

Previous Convictions attached to this Indictment and the main names on the prosecution witness list betray the fact that they have a largely circumstantial case. Garrad, I don't know if you've shown Brogan the initial Exhibits Schedule?

'Naw. No' yet. Because of that thing ye' were sayin'.'

'What?' What thing? Garrard … What's ...?'

McIntyre tapped the consultation table with just enough force to bring his client's attention back to its proper place, and resumed: 'Brogan. You ask *me* your questions. OK? Now what Garrad's talking about is an item that's not yet on the list. It's only been mentioned as a possibility at this stage. Garrad, have you got our expert lined up to examine it?'

'What? Why should we need an expert?'

'Brogan! How many times? You've not been told because this Exhibit might be the subject of a government Ministerial Certificate. Now that's not certain, I've only just had the word myself. So calm down. Alright?'

'Calm? Fucking calm!'

'*Quiet*!' Brogan, this has to be done *my* way. Please. You're not thinking like an Advocate, man. You can't be. You're a man charged with murder and *you* are the client – and *only* the client. Do we *understand* each other?'

'Sorry Duncan. We do. Of course Duncan. So why am I even here?'

McIntyre looked McLane in the eyes and to emphasise how right he was, shook his head: 'You're here for the usual reason Brogan. To provide me with your formal instructions to do whatever I decide I will do. I know you don't like it, but there it is. Alright?'

'Yes Duncan. You're in charge of *all* legal matters.'

'Good. Now, we don't even have pathological proof of murder yet. Though, of course, that's not imperative for guilt to be established. So, let's get to pre-trial Discovery and Disclosure. The Crown Office list seems a wee bitty light to me. Garrad, remind them that I said it's for me to decide what's relevant for the proper preparation and presentation of the defence. OK? Not the bloody Crown Office! Get busy on that. They're slippery as ...'

'I've already knocked back their offer to agree some things as uncontroversial.'

'Good. Now, I want to turn to the Arrest and Search Warrants. Garrad?'

'They're dead on. There was no way they'd make a mistake wi' them in a case as … well, in this case.'

'Right. Well that leaves just one last thing.'

Looking each other squarely in the eyes, QC and client knew what was coming.

'Brogan, I need hardly ask you this, but …'

McLane slapped both hands on the table, stood tall and took a moment. Looking straight into the face of his learned friend he burst out the words he was longing to say: 'No, Duncan. I did *not* murder Lord Aldounhill. I have never seen him socially nor have I ever been in his house.'

'Good. Thanks Brogan. I just needed to hear you say that. I can assure you I will defend that position with all of my skill and experience.'

Bumping the table with his fist, McIntyre drew the Indictment closer to him. Twisting his Mont-Blanc pen he wrote on the last page:

'On behalf of the above named accused person, Mr Brogan McLane, Advocate in the High Court of Scotland, I Duncan McIntyre QC, hereby enter his plea of NOT GUILTY to the Indictment; and without prejudice to his whole rights and pleas at his trial hereby give Notice of a Special Defence of Alibi; namely that at the approximate time of the death of Lord Aldounhill, the said Brogan

McLane was at home with his wife; and secondly, I give Notice that a second Special Defence of Incrimination of Another Person may be entered.'

McLane's heart pounded as he watched.

Signing the parchment '*Duncan McIntyre QC*' with all the authority of his long distinguished career, McIntyre slapped the signed Indictment into Garrad Fitzgerald's chest.

'Here. Take this to the Principal Clerk of the High Court with my compliments and tell him we're ready for Trial.'

~~~0~~~

End of Part 4

~ The Trial ~

Part 5

Chapter 32

Dropping her bio-tag into her handbag and stepping out into the Edinburgh night, Professor Nadia Suilleman left her Lab. It was unusual for her to be first away and that had been noticed. All afternoon the staff thought she'd been somehow distant. Something about her visitor after lunch had unsettled her. Turning half away from the lashing rain and pressing the bag close with her elbow, she looked in vain for a taxi. But as the evening Grassmarket traffic trundled by, a decision had to be made. She could walk home in 15 minutes.

She took the steps at High School Yards two at a time. Turning into Chambers Street, she turned her head away from the towering Crown Office at the end of the street; resisting its silent influence.

In the Atrium of her building, shaking the rain off her coat and hat, she smiled and nodded as others did the same; but looked away, slightly embarrassed as they crowded into their communal lift and she got into hers.

Carefully placing her bag on her study desk she

removed its contents. Exactly six minutes later, 'Ping' announced that dinner could be removed. Sitting at one end of the long glass table, she ate but hardly tasted a thing. Then, with the plates in the bin and looking out over the grassy Meadows Park below, she knelt to pray: seeking divine help in the most sensitive case of her career. Conversations with her father came resounding back, as did those with former teachers and senior colleagues. But nothing helped.

The pressure had come just before lunch. And all afternoon it built. The self-penned Note from the Solicitor General for Scotland contained only a few words:

'Dear Prof S. Sending round additional materials re Lord Aldounhill as per list. Please supply Supplementary Report by close of play tomorrow if poss. Yours, Andrew.'

Light, cheery and as presumptuous as it could be. Regardless of the science, they wanted their murder weapon and had gone to the trouble of sending the PF's Senior Assistant to deliver it.

Pressing the folded list into her dinner table, a glance revealed that the contents matched. Much as she hoped there would be, there was no opportunity to send it back for correction of some error or ambiguity. Two small clear plastic click-shut boxes, a file of x-rays, another of dental records and a copy of her initial post-mortem report. Did they think she might have lost hers?

In her study, sliding two samples into a sort of 'cat's cradle' hanging inside a strong thin chromium grid, she lined up the cross-hairs on her screen. Clicking 'Begin Scans' four tiny cameras began a ballet around the samples. On her screen, four new sets of data accumulated beside four stacks of established numbers and Greek symbols. In under ten seconds the perfect little performance ended, exactly where it began. Then she ran it again. Then tried it with three cameras. And with only two. Each set of data blinked white on black. To within an average of six microns both ways the samples of broken champagne flute sent round by the Sol Gen matched the data from Lord Aldounhill's neck.

She'd seen such a late sample appear only once before and knew – or thought she knew – of a Lab outside London, near Heathrow airport she thought, which could 'supply' such things. A Lithuanian doctoral student had once mentioned this place casually over lunch. His father was in the Foreign Ministry when they broke away from Russia and he was told about this place – just for future reference.

Professor Suilleman looked out of the window at the rain playing around the lights on Middle Meadow Walk, trying to banish thoughts of spies and counter-intelligence helping law enforcement here in the UK. *Surely it couldn't be true! Not here. Here Brogan McLane - a good man with a practise in international child abduction law - was about to stand trial for the murder of a Parliament House judge. Surely, in this case of all cases, justice would be scrupulously done. Would it not?*

As the printer chugged out the results she carefully removed these new samples and cupped them in her latex-gloved hand. She tried not to listen to rumours but Professional Edinburgh is a small place and people talked. At dinners. Awards. Meetings. Lord Aldounhill had plenty of enemies in life. It was said he dined alone in Parliament House. His only daughter hated him – with good reason – and his ex-wife also despised him. And now in death came the final ignominy; his only friends were the two little samples of glass lying in the hand of Edinburgh University's Regius Professor of Forensic Pathology.

Squinting, drawing, calculating and even getting up to perform the act of approach on human scale. There could be no doubt. On this data, accident and self-infliction could now be ruled out.

The Trial

It was with a heavy heart that Nadia Suilleman opened a new document and headed it:

Her Majesty's Advocate -v- Brogan McLane

Supplementary Forensic Report : Data on murder weapon.

Chapter 33

In the back of a taxi coming from the Consultation, Brogan McLane stared out of the steamed-up window at the city's festive lights reflecting in the virgin snow - deep and crisp and even.

McLane hesitated before putting his key in the front door. Since their last big argument, he'd mentally prepared for separate chairs in separate rooms and another silent night.

Closing the door as quietly as he could, as expected, there was no welcoming call. As days had turned to weeks and months, a draining downward pull had deflated their spirits, their mental state and, it seemed, even the very bricks and mortar of their home. Each was just trying to keep at bay their own horror of what injustice might do to their future. But it was hard. Down in the pits of their stomachs and closing around their minds tighter than any shipyard vice, that downward pull felt bitter cold around the heart and weighed on their minds harder than anything life had ever thrown at them.

In the kitchen, the lights above the stove twinkled in the polished black metal. From the radio, barely audible, a woman warbled in a language McLane didn't recognise. A broken plate and food lay strewn on the floor. Trying every room off the hallway, there was no sign of her.

Unsure of which tone to use, he called: 'Jo. Joanne, where are you? Jo are you in?'

No reply came. Quickly checking the garden, he called upstairs but again got no response.

'This makes no sense. The car's there. Her keys are there.'

Yes, it's her keys. No, he wasn't mistaken. But where was her phone? Her phone. She never went anywhere without it. He'd yelled at her so many times for not taking it that she now took it automatically. She knew he was at the Consultation. She'd sort of nodded that she'd be there when he got back. Where in God's name was she?

Bounding upstairs two at a time, McLane called her name. Nothing. Bursting open the en-suite bathroom doors he looked in the shower, immediately cursing himself for being so stupid – '*I can't hear the water. She's not going to be in the shower*'. His breath now erratic and his hands beginning to shake, he heard a noise. Like a whimper.

The duvet cover had moved. Taking as deep a breath as he could manage, McLane edged around the bed and put his hand on the cover.

'She's underneath. Her head is under the cover.

She can't bear that. She panics when her head's covered. But she's breathing. Thank God.'

He slipped a hand underneath. To his complete surprise Jo was fully clothed. But he couldn't look. He couldn't lift that duvet. Then her whimpers became sobs; heart-wrenching and throat bursting sobs that shook her entire frame.

Pulling away from his touch, Joanne curled up in a tight ball, rocking and moaning. Swallowing hard and his hands shaking, McLane laid both hands softly on top of the mound. Even through the quilted material he felt her trembling. His beloved wife had locked herself down. Adjusting to straighten his back, he rammed both arms under the bundle; dragging then lifting.

'No! No! Put me down. Put me …' she demanded.

Ignoring her muffled demands, he steeled his back, arms and legs. Gripping her even more tightly, he whispered into the duvet: 'Jo, God in heaven knows, I will fix this. I know this is all my fault. Look what I've done to you. My beautiful wife. My darling we *will* cope. I *won't* go down for this. I promise.'

The Trial

Chapter 34

Its usual damp, smelly self, Bridge Street hosted only a couple of hooded teenagers sloping past a closed-down convenience-shop doorway. They didn't even sense the big man in the shadows of the kitchen and bathroom warehouse and he couldn't have cared less where they were going; to a small-time drug deal or some cheap whore's flat high up in the nearby concrete flats. It didn't matter.

The seconds ticked up to 7 pm. But there was still no BMW. Then a dark-coloured delivery van pulled up; flicking its side lights on and off, just once. Crossing the street, Commander Imrie jumped nimbly in the back door. In the dark, in an old winged armchair sat Big Joe Mularkey.

'Evenin' Commander.'

'Joe.'

As his eyes adjusted, he saw two more big chairs. Sitting in silence only McLane's familiar outline gave a clue who he was. McLane's quiet demeanour put Imrie slightly on edge.

'So guys. What's on your mind?'

Speaking through the darkness, McLane sounded slow and deflated: 'Well, we've got this idea and we wondered what you'd think of it.'

'OK. But before you go any further guys, I should tell you … there's been a few developments.'

'Such as?'

'Since our last meeting you can't know … well I *suppose* you can't know … the forensic Pathologist has now issued a Supplementary Report certifying the cause of Aldounhill's death as murder. She's the best in the country. So if your expert even ...'

'I know. We'd look like idiots. So … do you have any details?'

'Yeah. She's now certifying that she's matched the break in the champagne flute *exactly* to the angle, line and depth of the cut in Aldounhill's neck. Down to a few microns. Can you believe these scientists? Anyway, she's now saying that the insertion of the glass, sorry, flute, couldn't have been accidental. That only a person could have inserted it in the way it did the damage.'

Without batting an eyelid at this body blow, McLane moved things along.

'Well if she says so, there's no point in ... Hmm. Any more about the lipstick?'

'That's a puzzle. We know the Glasgow guy, professor Sir Isaac Neuberger says that there's no sign of you Brogan, in the lipstick.'

'Right. We're lining up our own expert to ...'

Imrie interrupted with a tap on the back of McLane's hand: 'I'm sorry Brogan. We're *now* being told that the sample is too corrupted to get an accurate lift for identification purposes.'

Dropping his head, McLane took a deep breath and punched himself on the thigh: 'Fuck. So we've got *no* chance of Incriminating the person who wore the ... Fuck!. Somebody's trying to leave the back door open. Implying in court ... The bastards don't have to say a word. Just *imply* it was me who was wearing that lipstick. Christ, that could crucify me at trial.'

With frustration oozing out of his very breath, Big Joe leaned forward, put his elbows on his knees and spread his hands: 'Let - me - get - this - straight Commander. The lipstick is definitely on the glass thing?'

'Yes.'

'But the Crown Office scientists can't - or won't - say who was wearing it, right?'

'That's right. Because they say it's too badly damaged to lift a DNA Sample.'

'But ah thought this Neuberger guy eliminated Brogan. Right?'

'He did. But here's the thing … they're ditching that report. They prefer to rely on professor Suilleman's Supplementary Report. I'm sure you've seen it many a time before Brogan. The Crown Office has infinite resources. They just hunt around till they find a report they like and stick it to you in front of the jury. Sorry to be so blunt.'

Trying to get back in the game, McLane pressed his forehead: 'But wait a minute. Let me … it's just all insinuation. Right? I mean there's no actual DNA of mine on the fucking stuff.'

'Brogan. Easy man. Easy. Of course not. Your QC should be able to bat that straight out of court. You know that.'

'Well in a perfect world. Yes. But what if they …'

'Brogan. Hear this. I think the Crown Office is looking more and more desperate. All this fannying about with 'first it's a good sample and now it's too corrupted' leads *me* further away from *you*. Get me?'

Being more open in front of a stranger than he'd ever been Big Joe shook his head: 'Jesus Brogan. This science stuff is gettin' deeper man. Ah don't like it.'

McLane held his nerve in the face of a tactical defeat and grasped at another straw: 'You mentioned something about a napkin. From the canal ...?'

'Sorry Brogan, but that's been destroyed. Somebody sent it straight to the incinerator.'

'But it should've been bagged and marked and … sent to the ...'

'I know. But somebody called McManus in the Fiscal's office marked it as a health and safety hazard. Bullshit of course, but there it is.'

In the back of Tucker's van, while morale hit the floor, devastation was waiting its turn to kick Brogan McLane when he was down.

'And, I'm sorry to say Brogan, there's more. A set of keys was also found in the canal. Near the napkin.'

Coming back to his senses, Big Joe tried to see ahead: 'So are these car keys, house keys? Whit?'

'House keys, I'm told. Now, they should've gone with everything else straight to the evidence room in the station. But I don't think they ever got there. There's no log, no reference. Nothing. I think the PF somehow got her claws into those keys. They just disappeared.'

Imrie's words were now coming like bullets to McLane's mind. Each disappointment felt like a nail driving into his head and even through the grinding of his teeth, Brogan McLane seemed to hear Lord Aldounhill laughing from beyond the grave.

'Aw Fuck. FUCK FUCK FUCK. I'm goin' down for this. Eh Joe?'

But girding himself for a new fight against a shimmering enemy, Big Joe blurted out: 'You're gawin' doon for fuck all. You're a fuckin' innocent man.'

Too distraught to go any further, McLane dropped his head into his hands: 'Oh Christ. All the effort. All the work. All the worry. All over before the trial begins.'

Punching McLane on the shoulder, Big Joe wouldn't have it: 'Nuthin's over. Shut up. D'you hear me?' Nuthin's over.'

In an air of deep gloom all three knew that Defence Central wouldn't be able to fix this. This was trouble. Then Imrie remembered something else.

'Oh there is another wee thing.'

'Oh no more man! For fuck sake NO MORE!' shouted McLane.

'Wait. Brogan. This is … well, it's not bad news. It's something definitely worth following up. But it'll have to be you guys. I can't get involved. I can only …'

Spitting out his words, Big Joe demanded: 'Whit? *Whit* is it?'

'The other night there was a break-in. Not a

normal housebreaking. *My* office in A Division HQ was broken into.'

His eyebrows going as high as they could, McLane looked incredulous. 'What? You *must* be joking. Seriously?'

Big Joe slumped back into his chair. 'Jesus II. Surely *that's* never happened before?'

Interjecting, McLane held his hand out as though to give Terry Imrie a chance to finish.

'It has actually Joe.'

'That's right Brogan. It happened about 20 years ago during the Magic Circle investigation. The one where rent boys from London could describe the insides of Scottish judges' houses.'

Allowing a few seconds for everyone to think back, Imrie let the magnitude of this development sink in: 'Well anyway. This guy was amazing. Right at the start of this investigation … sorry Brogan … I had our young IT guy fit a webcam in my office linked to his computer. 24 hour surveillance. Well, as I say, whoever this guy was, he was very *very* good. He must be Army or ex-Army. Maybe even foreign. No civilian is this good. He only *walked* up the side of the tenement building opposite A Division HQ, wire-crawled himself over to our roof - directly above my office, let himself in and raked through my desk looking for something.'

'Did he get it?'

'Oh he got it alright. He must have known exactly what he was after because he only took the signed original of professor Neuberger's DNA report and left behind a copy of professor Suilleman's initial report which was lying right underneath it. That's why I think he's Army. He obeyed his orders to the letter. No less and no more. Exactly to the letter. Somebody is covering their tracks. Correction. Somebody is obliterating their tracks.'

Impressed at this level of execution, Big Joe acknowledged: 'Jeez, that's amazing. It hits us hard, but an amazing job.'

'Well, since the break-in my team have been brought in, one by one, and told that before they send *anything* up to me, they send everything for approval to the same wee lassie in the PF's office who pulled the health and safety trick. A Sheila McManus. Well my lads are having none of it of course. It's *all* being run by me before it goes to her. So I can keep you informed.'

Correcting an obvious assumption, Big Joe was back on form. 'As far as you *know*, they're running everything through you?'

'Yes, of course. As far as I know. My point Brogan is this; forces we know about and forces we don't know about are going through your life with a fine tooth comb. They're following your wife. They know when she visits her doctor and where she has coffee afterwards. They're really going for it Brogan. They obviously hope this will all be too much for her in court and she won't support your defence of alibi.'

Big Joe didn't follow.

'But shouldn't you be able to …?'

'No he can't Joe. Because he's not talking about his own team, are you?'

'No, he's right. It's not my lads Joe. It's MI5 I'm afraid.'

The mere mention of Military Intelligence dug like raining gravel onto an open wound. Grinding back to Advocate mode McLane came back to the agenda.

'Well, we … I'm … we're getting a kicking, no doubt about that. But we've had a wee idea. We think we should be going to the papers.'

Horrified, Terry Imrie's mouth fell open wide: 'The newspapers? Are you kidding? I think that's the craziest idea I've ever heard. Brogan are you in agreement with this?'

'Oh Joe doesn't mean Hold The Front Page or anything. We were thinking more of a trade-off. Any information they can give us before the trial in exchange for an exclusive - either way - after it. That can't hurt me. Right?'

'I *really* don't know. It's entirely up to you Brogan. Just keep my name …'

'Oh, you've no need to worry on that score. And you know it. Right?'

'Aye. I do. But the papers? You're a good man Brogan. And I don't want to see you go down for this. But the papers are a two edged sword. You know that. I mean to say … it's your life. Do what you must.'

Chapter 35

The heavy knock at the door after 10 on a Sunday night sent her long hair spinning around her neck.

Moving the heavy curtain just a fraction, Louise Bishop peeked out. There stood a man in a hat and coat with his back to the door. His hands were in his coat pockets and his polished shoes reflected the light above the door. He wasn't a neighbour or another reporter and definitely not a salesman.

With her phone in her hand and securing the door chain, she called: 'Who's there?'

'It's Brogan McLane, Miss Bishop. Could I please have a minute of your time?'

Stepping back, the sound of that name sent a little shiver down her back. If he'd come to the office, she'd have received him very publicly. Taken him to her desk the long way round.

'Jeez. Brogan McLane my door! Why? And how does he know where I live?

'Who? Sorry.'

'It's Brogan McLane. I'm alone, I promise. I mean no harm. I'm sorry it's late. I'd just like to talk with you in private. Please.'

She'd only heard his voice once, on television, but

it did sound like him. Checking again, she remembered. The hat. His broad black brimmer. All their library pictures showed him wearing it. That Irish hat was his trademark. It was him.

Releasing the chain but putting her hip against the door, she asked: 'What do you want? How did you know where I …?'

'*Please* firstly let me apologise Miss Bishop. For the lateness of the hour and the surprise. I'm really sorry to bother you and I wouldn't, only, well … you know. May I come in please?'

Outside the High Court he always flashed his broadest smile for the cameras - win or lose, he'd seen justice done. But here, in her doorway, his face pale and drawn, he was obviously a man in need, not a threat. Pulling the door wide open, she invited the most infamous lawyer in Scotland through her tiny hallway and into her living room.

'Come in. Go through.'

Watching McLane settle into her sofa, there rose a sense that her career was about to mature. All the big Editors agreed that the arcane world of Parliament House and the ways of the Judges was long overdue for a good exposé.

If found Guilty, it would of course be a huge story.

However, if found Not Guilty, then the spotlight would fall on the other side of the courts – on the High Court Judges and the way things were done in Parliament House. So anything to do with this had the potential to be her second prize-winning story; maybe even a book. The only thing she couldn't figure out was what he wanted. Whatever it was, one decision had already formed in her mind: '*Call Mackie before agreeing to anything.*'

Pointing through to the open-plan kitchen, she broke the ice: 'Can I get you something?'

'I'm fine thanks. No. Actually, I'm not fine. I see you're eating. Maybe I shouldn't have … I'm sorry, but would you have a dram in the house? I wouldn't ordinarily ask but this is difficult.'

'Yes. I do. In fact I'll join you. It's not every night I get …'

Pouring 'three fingers' of Bowmore's finest into two cheap chain-store tumblers, she handed one to McLane.

'Thanks. That's kind of you.'

She watched him down his whisky in two swallows. *'Hmm, the stories are true.'*

Through half a mouthful of lasagne, she opened

with an innocuous remark: 'You seem a bit shaken Mr McLane. I hope you don't mind me saying so.'

'God; *Mr* McLane. That feels good. It makes me sound like an Advocate again. Or somebody talking to my father. But please call me Brogan.'

'I'd rather keep it to Mr McLane, at least till I've, you know, got into this a wee bit. Would you like another dram? There's some left. Help yourself.'

'Thanks. I will. And please, don't let me interrupt your dinner.'

'You're a wee bit too late for that, Mr McLane. I'll just eat and you talk. Is that ok with you?'

'Sure. As you please.'

Pouring another big dram, McLane looked around the room. In pride of place above the fireplace sat a silver framed picture of an older woman, Louise's double; obviously her mother. But no father. And no sign of a boyfriend either. Too many books crammed into a modern storage shelf ruined the design. Through on the kitchen table sat a laptop, its tiny built-in camera facing the sofa.

Pointing over her shoulder he asked: 'Is that on?'

'It is. Do you think I'm daft? I've got Brogan McLane in my house. He's charged with murder and I live alone. Oh I'm so sorry I didn't mean to be so blunt. It's just …'

'No. It's alright. I know what you meant. I meant the web camera?'

'So did I.'

Cracking their respective smiles, Louise Bishop scraped her plate clean.

Sitting back down into the big dent he'd already made in the sofa cushions, he opened his coat and seemed to relax. She'd never seen him speak in court but everybody who had said his commanding voice projected to the rafters without shouting. Tonight that voice was soft, rounded and warm, like the whisky. And just for a second, Louise wondered what that voice would sound like whispering into a girl's ear on the pillow.

Each being a little more comfortable now, they talked across each other, at cross purposes.

'I'm here because …' 'Wait a minute. I want to know how you knew where I lived.'

'That's easy. I had you followed home from work.' 'But I don't come home straight from work.' 'I know that.'

Dropping his head by way of apology was just enough politeness to calm Louise Bishop's shallow breathing.

'I'm not here to harm you. If you have the *slightest* inclination that I have then I'll leave right now. With a promise that you will never see me, or anybody who's helping me again. I promise you Miss Bishop, I'm not here …'

Something in his voice and quiet manner soothed her, and she found herself saying:

'OK. I believe you. Thousands wouldn't, but I do. Coming here can't have been easy for you. The case must be incredibly rough on you. And you're polite. I like that.'

'Thanks. Really, I haven't been around a lot of kindness lately. Well, not like this, if you know what I mean?'

'I don't Mr McLane but anyway, you were saying you were here because …'

'Yes. I think we can help each other. I'm not asking you to do anything illegal. Right now I'm not asking you to do anything at all. I just ask that you hear me out. Is that OK?'

'Like I said, you talk, I listen.'

'The first thing I want to say is that I did not murder Lord Aldounhill. And, I don't know who did. True, we had some history, but so have plenty of others. Some of them were at his funeral. Not a popular man, was Lord

Aldounhill. The question is 'Who did murder him?' I have strong reason to believe that the Crown Office isn't interested in answering that question with any accuracy or honesty.'

'Whoa. Are you saying the Crown is deliberately *perverting* the course of …'

'I'm not saying anything right now. And I'm sure you won't ask me to reveal my source. It's been done before in high profile cases. They have their man and they're going for a circumstantial case against him - me. What I can say is that the police are being sidetracked. Hampered even. Evidence which points away from my guilt is going astray. Well frankly, it's being stolen.'

'What? When was that? If you can you prove … We'd run that for sure if … '

'Easy Miss Bishop. I'm just telling you that when this is all over for me, it *could* be just beginning for you. But I'll need something in exchange.'

'Wait a minute Mr McLane. You're the one who came out with the fact that evidence is being stolen. So I need to know how you know that. Before I go any …'

'OK. I did. I won't say yet which piece, but the evidence I'm talking about was stolen from a certain high-ranking officer's desk.'

'I didn't know that. Nobody ran that. Who? … When was ...?'

'I can't tell you any of that right now. Though believe me when I say that I *do* know that to be true. Please, hear me out Miss Bishop'

Laying down her whisky, Louise Bishop listened carefully as McLane patiently talked in detail about what he knew and what he didn't know. With McLane now in Advocate mode, Louise responded with 'reporter's replies': nothing at all. He was raising point after point and balancing them on his open hands as though he was in front of the Scottish High Court bench.

Tucking her bare feet under herself, she sat straight up. What was becoming clear was how *little* he seemed to know about Lord Aldounhill's life and, more to the point, his death. His points were all legal. Nothing about the facts. This guy seemed *not* to know the kind of things that Lord Aldounhill's murderer would know. And one thing in particular; putting up her hand to stop him she asked: 'Are you here because I was at Professor Suilleman's post mortem examination of Aldounhill's body?'

Genuinely surprised, for a second McLane was stopped in his tracks. 'Whoa! No. I didn't even know you were there. How did you manage that?'

'I slipped in along with some Edinburgh University medical students. I saw Commander Imrie there. When he gave me his seat I thought my game was up. But he didn't seem to know who I was, so I got away with it.'

'Well I can see I came to the right place, Miss Bishop.'

'Please, call me Louise, OK?'

'Fine. So do we have a deal Louise?'

He offered his hand but she resisted the impulse to take it: 'We might be able to help each other out. You towards an acquittal and me towards the next rung or two up the ladder. But I'll have to call someone first. My Editor.'

'I understand. I expected that. It's just that time might be of the essence, if you know what I mean.'

Shoving her hair behind her ears, she picked up the phone. Nodding to McLane that she was connected, she relayed the whole events of the last half hour to her well-known Editor, Johnnie Pryde Mackie.

'Yes, he came alone. Well he's sitting on my sofa alone. No, I haven't promised him *anything*. I haven't made any suggestions, or proposals. Yes Mackie, as a matter of fact I *have* just listened. He's right here. Shall I put him on?'

Handing over the phone, it took under two minutes of no-nonsense exchanges before Mackie approved a deal whereby the Glasgow Daily Tribune shared their information with the defence and provided the support of Louise Bishop to McLane until the end of his trial: in exchange for the exclusive rights to his story, if acquitted.

'We have a deal Mr Mackie. Yes. And goodnight to you.'

Louise felt the same tremble of excitement she had when the announcement came out. 'And the Winner is …Louise Bishop for …'

All the tension she'd felt when opening the door now fell away like so much snow from a dyke. 'So. You're *mine* now, are you?'

'Till the end of the trial. Yes.'

McLane rose to leave but Louise Bishop had one last question: 'Why just to the end of the trial?'

'Because if I'm acquitted you get my whole story. If I'm convicted, nobody will want to know me.'

'Right. I suppose so. My God how do you live with this?'

Lifting his hat and stepping out into the hallway, Louise followed: 'I didn't know whether to trust you or not. You know … when you came to the door.'

'Well you can. Many thanks for your … and the whisky.'

'Look, as we're now partners, there is something …I wonder if you know about the …'

'What? What? Tell me.'

'Do you know about the call to our office?'

'I know a *few* things, but …'

'Mr McLane. Don't try to kid me. I'm young but I'm an award winning reporter. OK? So, if this is going to work, we'll have to trust each other. Right?'

Nodding by way of apology for an old habit, McLane warmed to his newest ally.

'Now. I don't think you know about the call to our night desk. About Aldounhill. The night he died.'

'The what? You're … *Tell* me. For the love of *God*, woman. Tell me.'

Gripping her by the elbows, in an instant he'd become a different man. His anger palpable. His desperation just below the surface showed in the darkening colour of his face.

'Stop it! Stop it! Let me go.'

Flinging both hands up to his face and opening his mouth as wide as it would go, McLane apologised: 'Oh

God in heaven. I'm so sorry. Forgive me. Please.'

'For God's sake. Brogan, calm down. Please.'

Instinctively, Louise Bishop took a couple of steps back into the living room, into shot of the webcam. But the look on McLane's face remained that of a desperate man. Not a violent one.

'Yes. Somebody called our night desk the night Aldounhill died. I was on duty, but I was here in Glasgow, so it took me about 50 minutes to get to Edinburgh.'

'Jesus Christ. Have you *any* idea how important that is? What did the caller *say*?'

'All we know is that it was a man's voice. Cultured. Refined. Definitely well educated. We played it around. No-one in the office recognised it.'

'And ...'

'He gave us Aldounhill's address and said that if we 'arrived there quickly' we'd get pictures of high ranking people leaving Aldounhill's house after a Transvestite sex-party. He was trying to expose Aldounhill. We've no doubt about that.'

Feeling light-headed, McLane held onto the stair banister. Steadying him, she took him back to the sofa.

'The Edinburgh photo-journo we use got there first on his motorcycle. But there was only one light on in the house. So he didn't think there was a party going on or anything worth his while. One of the outer front double-doors was ajar but he needed to keep his distance. He tried to peek in a few windows using a long lens, but most of the ground floor windows were shuttered up for the night. He even climbed a tree, but he really didn't see anything.'

'A tree? So he could've left fibres, or a shoe … Did you say motorcycle? Have the police interviewed …?'

'Don't worry. He's a war photographer really. Very savvy. He left nothing. Rest assured on that. Anyway, I was racing over the motorway. We tried to trace the phone number through a few friends we have. But we couldn't trace it. And this is the weird bit. The call was made on a secure network. The phone call didn't triangulate like regular calls. It was part of some other network. Something like senior police or SIS, high up in the government or MI5. Something like that.'

Chapter 36

Tucker Queen sat alone in his alcove, hunched over the racing section of the Saturday paper, ignoring the yells and screams of celebration and disappointment aimed in equal measure at the Calton Bar's new TV. Putting down three pints, McLane and Big Joe sat down beside him.

'Any joy yet Tuck?'

'Any minute now Brogie. Ah like 'is style. This is called a 3/1 favourite.'

'Are you *sure* it's from our new friend?'

Checking through his figures with the point of his pencil and putting the results into an App in his iPhone, Tucker looked up.

'Yip. I'm pretty sure this message is two things. A GPS location and the letter D. Capital D. See. Ye write the names o' these two horses, then count back three letters frae the first, two frae the second and one frae the third. That's the 3to1 bit. Dae that till ye get to the end. Then ye give each letter ye've calculated its number in the alphabet and write them oot in sequence. Ye put the sequence intae a computer that can show ye GPS and hey presto! Horse names become a pinpoint location. I've checked it three times an' it a' fits Jim Dandy, Brogan. Plus look. The best odds are on 'D'.

The Trial

Big Joe Mularkey furled his brow at the scribblings on Tucker's paper: 'But are we sure it's frae him?'

Leaning in, McLane ran his finger down the careful calculations: 'I'd say it is. You have to wonder, who else would send this through Tucker? We've been getting a right kicking lately. I hope to God this helps.'

Big Joe looked at the screen. It was all gobbledegook: 'OK I follow that. So, Brogie. Assumin' ye'r right Tuck, just exactly where is this pinpoint location?'

Chapter 37

Tucker's information came with a guarantee. This 'hotel' down at the dockside in Edinburgh didn't exist. No name, no sign, no lights, no doorman - who could be seen - just a narrow alleyway beside a solid stone five storey building where men slipped in and out. Big Joe didn't know the place; so it was probably a new venture by the Russians.

'Have we passed it?'

Flashing his eyes up the street at a man who'd stopped a car, walked back and slipped up an alley, McLane whispered: 'I don't think so. No. I think that's a hit.'

Nodding in silent agreement, Big Joe parked crossed the street. In a doorway that hadn't seen a lock for many a long year, they waited.

In under four minutes a tall, well-dressed, silver-haired man walking just a little too quickly for his own comfort, exited the alley, pulled up his collar and crossed the street making straight for his Jaguar.

As he put his fingers under the door handle, something seemed to engulf the man's entire frame, causing him to squeal like a girl. Reaching from behind

Big Joe grabbed his keys. Spinning him and pressing the stunned man against the car, Big Joe clamped the man's mouth shut and looked him right in the eyes.

'Have you jist come from the Tranny Hotel?

'Whumthfukr …?'

Tightening his grip on the frightened man's wrist, Big Joe spoke to him very firmly: 'It would be very unwise of you to lie tae us. We're not polis and we're not the slightest bit interested in you. We just need to know if the Tranny Hotel is up that alley. A simple nod or a shake will be enough.'

'MmmHmmm'

Big Joe opened the car door and bundled the guy in; sure that McLane was out of sight. Pushing the trembling man's face into the leather wheel, Big Joe announced the end of the audition: 'Thanks. Don't call us. We've got your number. If you're lyin' we'll call you.'

From the street, the painted-out windows and rusty padlock on its steel shutter gave the building a look of being disused. Leading the way slowly down the alley Big Joe counted 23 strides. Three paces behind him, McLane counted the same. At the end, a stinking brick wall and a low unlit black steel door with a slot welcomed guests to the Tranny Hotel.

Lifting his eyes up to the right, McLane spotted a tiny blinking green light. Attached to a cable running up the building, a little black webcam had just announced the hotel's latest guests to Reception. Knocking only once, Big Joe waited until a shaft of light lit his face.

A strong Russian accent barked: 'Show me money.'

Holding up a wad of fake notes thick enough to be two grand, upon hearing three iron bolts slide back, hitting their buffers, McLane pressed his phone. Fifty miles away in the Calton Bar, three men breathed more easily.

Inside, a row of expensive outdoor shoes lay in line. The carefully dimmed lighting over pale luxurious carpets wafted an air worthy of any Five Star Hotel in the city. But the similarity ended there. Here there was something *in* the air. That lingering fragrance around perfumery counters when too many women have sprayed themselves with samples.

To the sound of the doorman slamming the three bolts back into their locks a man in a hand-made suit and silk tie put out his hand.

'First time here gentlemen?'

Big Joe reached into his leather coat for his cigar case, giving nothing away: 'You come highly recommended.'

'I see. Well it's Lipstick Night as I'm sure you know. Is there anybody in particular you came to see tonight?'

Big Joe Mularkey could feel the doorman's eyes burrowing into the back of his head: 'We do have somebody in mind'

'Well it's entirely up to the player if he wants to play with both of you. Their names are on the doors. Enjoy.'

Leaving them standing beside each other, the man turned and disappeared into a tiny office. No-one asked them for money. Neither could quite work out the deal. From a large leather sofa up against a wall, they began to observe. Almost immediately a pencil-slim boy about 6 feet tall with pink-blonde shaggy hair glided over; wearing only a see-through Sarong and ballet pumps.

'Drinks gentlemen?'

Instinctively Big Joe Mularkey ordered: 'Two very large single malt whiskies son. No ice.'

'£40 please.'

Dropping four crisp 20s from his wad onto the tray, Big Joe told the boy to keep the change. Within a minute he was back; setting out linen napkins, four tiny rolls of sushi and two three finger drams.

'Thanks. Keep them comin' son.'

Giving Big Joe a broad girlish smile, the boy winked his understanding. Big Joe's first ally in this place had just been bought.

On their second dram, a man came out of a room on the half-landing beside them, blowing a kiss inside before closing the door. It was what he did next that put all the pieces in place. He put the door-key back in the lock – on the outside. Nodding their understanding to each other, Big Joe waved his empty glass at their new-found young friend.

The players paid for their room; highly no doubt. The visitors bought very expensive drinks and they didn't stay long. Some people were known to each other. Others were guarding their privacy. It was basically open-night.

What happened after a punter chose a room, went in and locked the door was entirely up to those in the room. High turnover, high profit, nothing done in public, zero-cost, word-of-mouth publicity and everything legal; except perhaps the tax evasion and the small matter of brothel-keeping. Not a bad business model. Not bad at all.

Downing their last drams in one, McLane took up position near the tiny office while Big Joe went to the top of the stairs to begin. In his dark charcoal suit and open-neck white shirt he looked more like security than a punter. The doors weren't numbered. Instead each door bore a little metal holder screwed to it at eye level in which a business card could be inserted for the duration of the occupancy. The names were obviously fictional but slowly passing along the corridor, more in hope than expectation, Big Joe trusted he would know the one he was looking for when he found it. A few men leaving rooms looked at the floor and hurried past.

But as he reached the far end of the lower corridor he began to doubt Tucker's analysis; until he spotted it. A card reading 'Darling D'. According to Tucker, the name of the first horse in the message was an anagram of a boy's name: Darren.

Big Joe passed the room twice before stopping. Stepping into view at the opposite end of the corridor, McLane had his back. Like a soldier under command, Joe put his hands behind his back and spread his feet; the sign to McLane that he'd hit the target. McLane did the same, as his signal back, and the two men did their final checks. No witnesses, no cameras, no sounds. Good.

Using his sleeve, Big Joe removed the key and turned the handle. Inside, he closed the door with his elbow, locked it and looked around. A wide circular bed draped in black and a blood-red velvet love-seat dominated the room. Mirrors were everywhere. Too many mirrors for Joe's liking. Checking around for cameras he stopped himself.

'Naw. Cameras are unlikely. These high-class punters would never accept cameras. Plus they provide evidence of all that untaxed money. Hah. No chance.'

Slowly walking around, passing his eyes over the delicate glassware, a beautiful set of pencil drawings and two hand-carved incense burners, he figured there could be no mistake. Business must be very good. What troubled him was the absence of Darling D. Then a voice called from the en-suite bathroom.

'I'll be right with you sweetie - have a drink - I'm just changing.'

Remaining silent, Big Joe tilted his head. Just inside the bathroom door he spotted a beautiful face in a mirror. Below, but for her white silk stockings and a tattoo of a pink flamingo, her lightly tanned body was naked. Taking his opportunity, Joe pulled a camera from his pocket and took aim. Half expecting it, she flashed her eyes, pouted her lips, tightened her buttocks and lifted onto the balls of her feet. Flash! Big Joe took Exhibit No1 for the Defence.

A few minutes later she emerged as Darling D! What a stunner! Tall, nearly as tall as himself. Slim with fabulous long strawberry blonde hair and beautifully made-up. A delicate little red lace Basque perfectly framed her body. Disarmed, for several seconds Big Joe slid off mission. Her casual super-sexy manner was doing what no man in Glasgow had ever done: netting Big Joe Mularkey in one sweeping gesture. She didn't walk, she prowled towards her prey in delicate red high-heeled shoes, her long slim legs in white silk stockings with broad hold-ups. Holding his gaze, in the centre of this incredible creature her tiny white satin panties barely concealed that 'She' carried a weapon more deadly in this room than the .38 in the back of Joe's waistband.

Holding up two lipsticks the way a child would, she asked: 'Which colour would you like sweetie? I think the Chanel red. Deeper, don't you think?'

Not allowing him to answer, D blew a kiss to her client, who stood nodding like a dog in a car.

'Good choice sweetie. I'll just pop back in here to put it on. Better light, don't you agree?'

Big Joe tore his eyes away, trying to remember why he was there and scanned the room. On a light-oak chest he noticed a silver picture frame. In it the 'Menu' set out the Services available and their corresponding rates. 'Darling D' started at 30 minutes, fully dressed and would blow your mind for £200. To touch her started at £250 and everything you wanted was available (maximum time 1 hour) for £500. No credit cards, no checks, just cash.

Re-appearing 'Darling D' approached, slowly and purposefully, eyes wide open, putting one step directly in front of the other.

'So? What can I do for you tonight darling?'

Taking out his wallet Big Joe put ten £50 notes on the silver tray beside the frame.

'Yeah. I'll need a wee bit of your time tonight. Whit dae Ah call you?'

She picked up the notes, deftly counting them in one hand before slipping them into a slot in the wall.

'D' is fine. That's one hour of the complete service. We're going to have *such* fun!'

With a broad grin that included more embarrassment than he realised, Big Joe stammered: 'Ehm, come 'ere'

Gliding over, Darling D pulled him by the hand towards the bed. Running her hands over his big strong face, she pouted her lips.

'Let's start with a kiss. You *do* like to kiss, don't you?'

She pulled off his jacket, pushed him flat onto the bed and got astride his tree-hard body. Her intoxicating perfume filled the space between them. It had been a while, a long while since he and Molly … oooah, the softness of her fingertip touch … stirred Joe in a way he'd forgotten. Closing his eyes and breathing deeply Joe took her whole weight on his pelvis. God. Her beauty. Her touch. Oh SO Fabulous. Molly had been sexually switched off for over a year …their boy's trial and all the injustice was … Ooohhh, in Darling D's hands all thoughts of fidelity floated away.

Feeling her tiny bottom begin to massage the rock in his trousers, Big Joe lay flat on his back, swimming in her pool of delicious sexuality. Grabbing the back of D's neck, he pulled her down and kissed her. Hard on the mouth. Responding, 'D' reached around, her long fingers gently pulling down his zipper; reaching in she caressed the tops of the thighs. Pulling her delicious lips away, with a broad smile D whispered: 'I'm going to *blow* you away sweetie. Just wait and see.'

As she fell in to kiss him again, Joe snapped back on mission and made his move. With mouths clamped to each other he shoved both her arms behind her back, swung her around and with his whole weight, pinned her to the bed. Pulling a nylon cable-tie from his belt loop, he slipped it around D's wrists, pulling hard.

D's squealing only filled Joe's mouth. Eye to eye Joe lay on top of her for a count of ten. Then with his free hand he stuffed a handful of bed-sheet into her mouth.

Pulling out his phone and hitting #1 he muttered: 'Your witness Brogie.'

Out in Reception, McLane casually hung up and

made his way to the room.

Still pinned down tight under Big Joe's 275 pounds, Darren Walker shivered in utter terror. Fearing for his life, there was only one thing this could be. This had to be connected to Aldounhill. Questions solidified in his freezing mind: was this giant a friend of Aldounhill's looking for revenge? Or sent by someone else to recover money? Whatever this was, this guy could snuff him out; right here, right now; the inside of this room would be the last place he'd ever see.

With his whole body shivering in white fear, Darling D wet himself, soaking the silk sheet below. Adjusting his knees away from the wet patch, Big Joe pulled him round to face McLane.

Keeping his hand over most of his face, McLane took a very deep breath: 'What's your name?'

Pulling the sheet out of Darren's mouth to let him answer made no difference. Too scared to utter a syllable, the young man peed again. The decision having been made for him, Big Joe had no choice.

'Oh fuck, he's pished himsel' again.'

Big Joe pulled Darren to his feet and dragged him

into the bathroom: 'Get that gear off, wash your face and get dressed.'

'Please. We'll never get out. Please. They've got guns. Please.'

Big Joe jabbed his finger into the boy's face, making certain he wasn't playing at this like some demanding parent: 'Jist do as ah tell ye. Right?'

'Please. There's a safe. I've got money. Please. You'll never get ... '

Pulling the .38 from his belt, Big Joe shoved it between Darling D's teeth. His purple face saying more than words. Almost touching D's lip, his trigger finger was going white.

'Stop fuckin' pleadin' wi' me. Fuck wi' me this night an' you could die son. Hav you got that?'

Watching Darren transform back into a boy; pulling off his wig, scrubbing roughly at his make-up, removing his eyelashes and dropping his tiny panties to the floor with an unconscious wiggle of his hips, Big Joe had never seen such a thing and probably would never see its like again. In the corner of the bathroom he spotted an unopened bottle of Bowmore single malt and picked it up.

The Trial

'Here. Open it. Drink some.'

Glugging down mouthful after mouthful, Darren shook as he handed the bottle back. Grabbing it, Big Joe slugged down well past the top of the label. Filling the bathroom with his huge whisky breath, Big Joe sat for a second. Eyeing each other, Darren fidgeted with make-up brushes, trying to figure out what this would be. Still terrified but trying not to annoy this man, only one thing was obvious. Lying wasn't an option. Not to this man. That would be dangerous. Mortally dangerous. Whatever he wanted, Darren was about to provide it.

Darren sat on the end of the bed, pulled on his socks, bent over and stared at the floor.

Through his fear, Darren heard only every alternate word from the man giving him instructions. But there was something ... something about the way the man asked his questions. Something that reminded him of Latin class at school. That purposeful, step-by-step approach leading inevitably to a conclusion.

'It's Darren Walker. Yes. I am. Yes. I get it. You're *not* connected to ... Aldounhill. Uh huh ...Yeah, I do. Mostly London. Yes. Sometimes in Edinburgh. Especially now that this place is ...Right. I have, Yes. Of course I'm scared. I *have* seen my share of … I know he is … I *get* it … My life depends on …Yeah – Just a min – I … I …

At the mention of being alive or dead in the next five minutes, Darren vomited onto the snow-white carpet.

Grabbing the boy by the hair, Big Joe pulled him back upright: 'Speak to the man.'

Trying not to vomit again, Darren continued: 'Yeah. Sorry about …The first time? Some man … in a good hotel sauna in London - to service a friend - a Scottish judge he said. We met in London. We got on alright. Nothing special. He seemed OK and he paid well.'

With Big Joe standing over him, Darren sounded to McLane like a boy in Confession. Nevertheless, every word he said was being recorded for later checking by the guys over at Defence Central.

'Go on son.'

'Then the visits up to Scotland started. I wanted to fly, showing off I suppose. But he insisted I take the train. Never the plane. Once in Edinburgh it was always black cabs but always from different spots. At first I got off down the road a bit from his house. Then I couldn't be bothered with the walk.'

'How were you dressed? In the taxi I mean.'

'Oh straight. I usually had a bag, cos there was always a theme.'

'A what?'

'A theme. You know. One night it was schoolboys, another it was TVs. Different themes, different people. He paid well. My first really good money. I didn't know them all.'

'How often? At his house?'

'Oh, it got to be about once a week. Yes. The TV nights were about once a week.'

Pacing around the room, the man had taken on the air of a lawyer. The way you see them on TV: 'OK. Now. One last thing. When was the last time you *saw* Lord Aldounhill?'

'I showed up for a TV night. I was a bit late. The train was late. I let myself in. I had a set of keys.

'Keys?'

Yes, I …'

'Have you still got them?'

'No. I dumped them.'

'We know about the canal. Is that where you dumped the glass in the napkin?'

'You *know* about that? How did ... ? Yeah. Sorry. In the canal. I don't know. I was scared. I really wasn't thinking all that straight.'

'Son, you're not answering my question. Don't make the mistake that because you've told me a story we're now best friends. All this will be checked. So when was the last time you ...?'

'Oh God sorry. It was a while ... you know ... after he die ... after he was ...I don't really remember. Maybe a week or something.'

Crashing into the side of his head, the full force of Big Joe's flat hand smacked Darren across the bed onto the floor. With one huge hand around the neck, Big Joe silenced Darren's squeals. Pulling him up off the floor, he flung Darren onto the bed.

'That kiddo, was just a wee love bite. Now *don't* lie tae us again. Right?'

'Yes. Yes. I'm sorry. I'm not ... I'm confused.'

With blood oozing from his face where Big Joe's

wedding ring had crashed into his cheek bone, Darren stared at the man who was obviously running this.

'Now listen. You were hit because you lied. The police had long since sealed the house a week after he died. Now answer my question son.'

'Maybe it was a couple of days. I … really can't think …'

'Well, you're going to have to think. That was just a taste of what can happen. Do you understa …'

'I *found* him. I just … kind of …*found* him lying there.'

McLane shot a jumble of legal questions through his mind. Would McIntyre run a defence of Incrimination of Another Person when that other person could well be lying? Such witnesses often spontaneously invent a story in the witness box. This boy was savvy. Was it worth the risk? Juries who are confused always convict. They don't like being lied to. They don't like being used.

'So you found him. Dead?'

'Oh yes. Without a doubt.'

'Who else was there?'

'No-one. I was alone. It was weird. The house

should have been full, but it was empty.'

'Who *should* have been there?'

'The usual crowd. I know most of them by their femme names.'

'Such as?'

'Well the guy who had first introduced me to Lord Aldounhill. He wasn't always there but when he came he always brought very good champagne and French cheese.'

'What's his name?'

'Do I really have to … I mean he's …'

One glance at Big Joe answered the question and Darren spat out the name. 'His femme name is Winnie but he's *Sir*. Sir Aubrey. Sir Aubrey Winstanley actually.'

'What's his thing?'

'Nothing. He'd arrive. Drink good champagne. Join in a bit. That's it.'

'Son, I don't believe that. I think you're making this up. So, let's you and me play a wee game. OK? This game is called If I Think You're Lying To Me Again I Tell That Guy To Do His Thing.'

'Honest. I promise. Sorry. Really. There was one

Tranny he liked but I don't know her name. Honest. I never asked. I don't. Ask I mean. Well there's one thing Winnie did do.

'What?'

'It's nothing. He mostly liked to watch. But he'd be in …'

'What was it? I need to know what it was.'

'He never dressed but he did wear lipstick.'

'Lipstick? Is that all?'

'No. He was dressed. I don't mean dressed as a Tranny. Just straight.'

Pulling Darren's hair, Big Joe pressed his head into the bed and put the .38 to his eye: 'There's a good boy. Tell the man about the lipstick son. Every fuckin' word.'

'It was … oh please. Don't kill me. *Please. Don't.* It was … horrible on him. Always the same… mess. I think there was some of … on the …'

'The *what*? Come on. Out with it.'

'The … the glass. The champagne glass.'

'OK son. Good boy. You're doing fine.'

'Better. Yes. McIntyre might incriminate this Sir

Aubrey Winstanley. But not yet.'

'Tell me son; I'm guessing he always wore the same colour lipstick. Right?'

'Yes. Always.'

'But I want *you* to tell *me*. What colour?'

'It was purple. Always purple.'

Big Joe Mularkey let him go, pulled the gun away and slotted it back into his rear waistband. He paced around the room, clenching and unclenching his fist. Confused, Darren watched his every step.

'And the others?'

'Oh, yeah. Well, Terri, …'

At the sound of the name, Big Joe spluttered out a mouthful of Bowmore: 'Terry? Terry who?'

'Yeah. Terri. She was always there. Short little fat guy. English. Always sweating. Really yucky.'

'Fat? Short. English! Right OK. And the others?'

'Well Jenny was usually there. Penelope – he had a thing about a TV character called Penelope something … Pitstop. Is that right? I don't know it.'

'Anybody else?'

'A few. I don't know … some would always show up, others only sometimes …'

'Tell me this. Were you the only boy. I mean young person?'

'There was supposed to be another boy. That night. But he …'

'Name?'

'Erm, Giles. I only know him as Giles. Really nice boy. I started to get him work. He's from Edinburgh but he'd run away. He was doing OK in London and I spotted him. He was late. No. I tell a lie. Sorry. He wasn't coming. That was it. He was being taken to Paris. By a client. I said it was fine. He'd never done anything for me in Edinburgh before. I remember. It was his first time coming back. He took a bit of persuading. But he was just coming up for the night and straight back to London – until he got the better offer. The Paris gig. That was it. Definitely. Honest.'

'Did Aldounhill know him?'

'No. Defo he didn't. I'd filled him in a bit on the phone. Told him Giles was originally from Edinburgh. Good family, that sort of thing. He was cool with it.'

'OK son. You are now going to leave with this

man, You'll …'

'Leave? But I *can't*! There's no way I can just walk …'

'I'll deal with all that. Now you *will* leave with this man, take him to where you live, give him …'

'Whoa. I *can't*. You don't understand. I live in London and I can't just …'

'I don't give a fuck if you live on the moon! You will take him to your address. You'll give him your passport and all other papers in your house with your name on them and if you're lucky, he might not shoot you. Have you *got* that?'

Chapter 38

'London St Pancras: International Central Holding Unit' read the sign leading to three linked leaking PortaCabins around the back of a high brick wall.

An Eastern European civilian guard holding a clipboard, wearing a cheap uniform and shoes which hadn't seen polish since the day they were bought, long ago and far away, hovered around the entrance. Getting his first 'client' of the day, he demanded: 'Show me Pass.'

Looking him square in the eye, in uniform for his visit to London, Commander Imrie just looked this underling in the eyes, saying nothing. Stepping aside, the guard left Imrie dismayed at the lack of procedure around this place.

Inside, a smart-looking young woman officer stood to salute. In return Imrie just gave her a broad smile. 'Good morning. Do you have the file?'

The young officer handed Imrie a file showing pictures and a printed interim report. She tilted her head to the left: 'He's at the bottom of that corridor. Take as long as you need Sir. I haven't filed anything yet.'

Opening the door, Commander Imrie towered over a boy sitting in the only seat in the middle of a tiny windowless room. Glancing at his interviewee, the boy seemed transfixed as he picked at a thread in his cuff. Producing a neatly folded pink silk handkerchief the boy turned away before blowing his nose. That little gesture of politeness revealed an upbringing very far from the usual mule: dragged up in a sink estate, occasionally attending a concrete school with gun control and life lived in parental poverty.

No. This kid was posh. Very posh.

Commander Imrie walked round behind him, pretending to read the file. He was being cagey, unsure about how well connected this kid might be: 'What's your name son?'

The boy pulled hard on the thread, saying nothing.

'Well, that's alright. I already know your name. So let's move on. You've been arrested on suspicion of Passport crime and other, even more serious crimes. But I've flown down here because I'm principally concerned with another matter. The death of a Scottish judge. Are you with me so far?'

'Yes, but I don't know anything about the death of Lord Aldounhill except what I've read.'

'Hmm. Lord Aldounhill. OK. Well, nonetheless, I am cautioning you that you are not obliged to say anything, but anything you do say may be noted and later used in evidence against you at your trial. Do you understand the formal Caution?'

'**Trial**? What …? I haven't done …'

'Just a yes or no son, is all I need at this stage. '

The boy swallowed hard and dug his nails into his sleeve. He'd gone white in the face: 'Yes. Sir. I mean I think I …'

'I need a Yes or No.'

'Yes.'

'OK. Let me begin by saying that I'm not interested in the crimes committed by the man you went to Paris with. And, I know all about Darren. He's being interviewed., erm, *elsewhere*.'

At the mention of Darren the boy's eyes widened and he bit his lip. It was a common enough sign of getting ready to resist police questioning and one which Commander Imrie had seen dozens of times. Cracking a smile, he thought he might break his own record for getting to the stage of compliance.

'Look kid. I can take you up to Edinburgh with me or we can do this here. Take your pick.'

The very idea of his mother opening the door to police, bringing him back after all that had happened; No.

Not that wasn't happening.

Staring at the floor, the boy asked as quietly as a church mouse: 'Can we do it here?'

'OK. That's fine Giles. Would you like some coffee?'

While waiting for the coffee, Imrie eased up a gear into; 'Getting To Know You'.

Now almost keen to unburden himself, the boy quietly began: Heriot's School where he played chess, not rugby. Scoring very highly in the Oxbridge University Prelim Exams. Head of Classics said he was a prime candidate for Cambridge and then the Civil or Diplomatic Service. Just like his father. But all wasn't well at home. Far from it. His parents fought angrily and latterly they didn't sleep in the same bedroom. And the teasing at school about his long blonde curls and girlie looks. He'd even been roughed up a few times. So he'd run away. To London.

'What did they argue about? Your parents.'

'Me, sometimes. But mostly it was about Dad. Going out. You know?'

'Well I *think* I know Giles. But put me in the picture here eh?'

'It was nearly always about Dad going to Allan's

house. You know.'

'Allan?' Who's Allan?'

'Allan Coatbridge.'

'I'm sorry Giles, you've lost me.'

'Maybe you just know him as *Lord* Aldounhill. That's his judicial title.'

'Ah yes. I do remember that. But you say *Lord* like you don't think he deserved it.'

'He bloody didn't. *Lord* Aldounhill. It even sounds common. His *real* name is Allan Coatbridge. He *was* my Dad's best friend. Dad helped him tons, but I suppose you know about that.'

'I don't actually know about that. Tell me about it.'

'Will you let me go? I mean without any trouble? When this is over.'

'You'll have to speak to others about that. Right now I'm going to ask you a question. And, if you answer me truthfully, that will be a big plus for you. Have you *ever* been to Lord Aldounhill's house?'

'Yes. But only when I was a child. Oh, do you mean his new house?'

'I mean the one he lived in recently. Where he was found dead.'

'No. I've never been there. I don't even know where it is.'

'Alright. Tell me this. Had you made *any* arrangement to be there around the time he died?'

'*No*. I've …'

Wagging his finger, Imrie pressed his lips together, spitting out his words: 'Bad Giles. Very bad. I know that to be a lie. I'm *very* reliably informed that you made a call to Darren, the day or two days after Aldounhill died. Saying that you were going to Paris and wouldn't be at the sex party that night in Edinburgh.'

'*What*? Darren? Darren from …? Look, I swear I'm not lying. I *did* call Darren about going to Paris but I did *not* know the gig was at Allan Coatbridge's house. His new house. If I'd known that I'd have been sick.'

'But you made the arrangement with Darren about a week before …'

'Darren only gave me an address. I swear to you.'

Standing bolt upright and punching his right fist into his left palm, Giles' new demeanour would have convinced any jury.

'Sit down Giles. Take me through this.'

Remaining standing, Giles opened his hands and looked Imrie right in the eye: 'I was to go up by train and take a taxi from the street, not the station. I swear. My God! That was Allan Coatbridge's house? Oh Christ, my father might've been there. Oh God. He'll *kill* me. If I'd turned up and he was there. Oh my …'

Giles burst into tears and dropped into the chair. Commander Imrie had seen it all before. Reaching out, gripping the boy's shoulder, he looked at his watch. In just over quarter of an hour, trust had been established. His new record.

'That's quite a coincidence. But I'll accept it for the moment. Tell me more about your father and Allan Coatbridge.'

Closing the file and putting it under his arm, Imrie leaned against the thin wall, crossed his feet and listened.

'Well, when Allan Coatbridge was applying to become a judge in the High Court, my dad helped him. My parents fought about it and my mother said he'd regret it. Dad shouted at her and told her it was none of her business. She cried and shouted back that there were far too many things going on that were none of her business these days and that he was moving into the guest rooms. About three days after that I ran away, to my aunt in London. But mother came and brought me home. But with dad in the guest suite and mum always in tears, as soon as I had passed my Oxbridge Prelims I ran away again. I had my own money, from Grandmama, and stayed with a friend in London for a bit. I don't suppose you approve of …'

'Giles, please. I'm really not here to judge you, son. And I don't want to destroy a promising young man's university career if I can help it. But was there something? Did something happen, something in particular, that caused you to run away the second time?'

'I suppose there was. Looking back … I suppose so.'

'I can tell it's painful Giles, but I do need to know. Take your time.'

Pulling back his shoulders, running his hair behind his ears and stretching his palms hard down into his thighs, Giles steeled himself to do something he'd long desired. Clicking his pen, Commander Imrie prepared to jot down the endgame.

'Well I'd gone up to my father's rooms to ask about something. Latin prose, I remember. He was on his mobile. My father's worked in Parliament House since he left the Army. He was then Private Secretary to the Lord Justice General of Scotland. I heard him talking about sending only one name to The Queen for approval. *The Name* it's called. The only one who should be the next

Judge. I only heard one side of the conversation. But it sounded basically a done deal. He was telling the LJG that only one candidate met all of the criteria and that he was sure the Queen would approve him. So the LJG agreed to send Allan Coatbridge's name.'

'But Giles, you were only …'

'I was old enough to understand. There was definitely some deal being done. Anyway, I'm glad he's dead now.'

'So your father helped Lord Aldounhill become a Judge. If, as you say, there was a deal being done, then your father must have been expecting something in return.'

'Oh I think he was expecting the same back. You know, when his time came.'

'I see. Quite a big deal then.'

'Oh Mr … whatever your name is … let me be *very* clear. Allan Coatbridge reneged on the deal. My father never became a Judge and had to settle for some Admin crap. And my father doesn't mess about. He's old Army. Lord … I mean *Allan* Coatbridge couldn't fight his way out of a wet paper bag. My father would wait his chance …'

'Just be *very* careful what you say there Giles. I'll be looking into that line of enquiry in due course. But right now I'm going to take a formal statement from you. Just what you've been telling me. We'll leave everything else out of this for now. Alright son?'

'Yeah. Thanks. Where do we …?'

Opening the file, Imrie took a few sheets of Edinburgh 'A' Division paper from his inside pocket and slipped them under a paper clip: 'I want to start with your full name. But before I do, I need to ask if you've ever come across the name McLane. Mr Brogan McLane. He's an Advo … he works in Parliament House too.'

Looking as genuinely quizzical as any suspect he'd ever seen, this boy obviously hadn't ever heard the name. Shaking his head, Giles opened his hands and just said; 'Nope. Never.'

Trying not to show any relief in his expression, Commander Imrie drew breath and asked again: 'Good. OK. Your full name is?'

'It's Giles Aubrey Hilary Winstanley, the Third.'

Chapter 39

In his trusty old Land Rover, in a parking spot on the grassy side of Edinburgh's leafy Inverleith Park Circus, Sergeant McCauley checked his watch against the BBC sounding 11.00 pm. He'd checked it every quarter hour since sundown. And every quarter hour, in his top pocket he fingered an acceptance letter from GlobalOps4U.com in Iraq.

When Sir Aubrey Winstanley paid for the last job and asked about body-guarding, Sgt McCauley saluted proudly and accepted on the spot. The officer hadn't exactly looked frightened, just rattled. Anyway, it was a pleasure to get away from doped-up pop-stars and jumped-up businessmen.

The officer knew the drill and kept rigidly to it. He left home for the Office of the Advocate General for Scotland in Parliament House at exactly 8.45 am. and drove the 2.1 miles to his parking spot. With his entire day now spent inside Parliament House, that allowed time for sleep back in the officer's greenhouse.

Sir Aubrey didn't leave Parliament House until Sgt McCauley sent the 'return all-clear' text message. They'd agreed the officer could drive, with himself following, either to the Edinburgh Old Club for dinner then home or directly home and microwave the ready meals Sgt McCauley had bought in. Nowhere else. Absolutely nothing else was to come onto their radar. Not until the McLane trial was over.

Tonight only a matter of hours remained till that trial started, then, it was anyone's guess as to how long it would take to end. Trials are like that.

Sgt McCauley had double checked. Back door bolted. Check. All windows and tall wooden shutters secure. Check. All 20 glass milk bottles filled with fully-charged car battery acid sitting on window ledges ready to crash onto anyone who tripped either of the criss-cross wires in the back garden. Check. He'd listened as inside Sir Aubrey barred and bolted the double front doors and padlocked the newly fitted full-breadth heavy steel latch. The only key now safely hung on a ring attached to Sgt McCauley's belt loop.

He'd asked Sir Aubrey if he could install a baby-monitor connecting the house to the Land Rover but the look he'd got in response said that was out of the question.

At precisely 11.30 pm. the second floor bedroom light on the front left side of the house went on, then off, then on again and remained on. Seeing the sign through the crack left in the shutters, Sgt McCauley relaxed knowing Sir Aubrey was on his way to bed on the third floor at the back of the house. With the whole front of the house in view, he turned the radio up a little in his headphones and settled down for the night.

By 11.49 pm. not a single light shone in the terrace of stone-built Edinburgh grandeur forming the Circus around one side of Inverleith Park; except the dim shaft coming through a crack in the shutters of number 21.

Scanning the Terrace with his night goggles, the sodium street lights were all in perfect working order, casting their orange glow around the circus. All was quiet.

Next door to the sleeping Sir Aubrey, in number 23, Lady Hume-Mansfield, now 87 years old, offered more tea and Madeira cake to the officers who, at just before 9 am. that morning, had shown her their credentials and asked politely if she would assist the police in a surveillance operation. Drug deals, they said, were occurring in the private park, right in front of her house, late at night. They gave her a phone number of their 'Control' to call for verification. Once she'd verified them and declined Control's offer to cover her expenses of tea and sandwiches for the officers, Lady Hume-Mansfield felt pleased to assist. Although well-mannered, these middle-aged policemen seemed just like the rough types she'd seen on television. Just what the public needed to match these ruffians who dealt these dreadful drugs nowadays. As both officers politely refused more tea, Lady Hume-Mansfield wished them every success before bidding them goodnight.

A little over half an hour later, with Lady Hume-Mansfield sound asleep in her ground floor front bedroom, one of the officers unclipped the only telephone in the house from its socket. The other checked the front and back door bolts. Softly climbing the stairs to the top of the house, they used an old wooden chair from the children's playroom to gain enough height to lift the access hatch into the roof space.

Once up, they switched on the bare hanging light bulb, quickly getting into their black nylon coveralls and balaclava masks. Motioning only by hand the two men tip-toed across the roof beams to the dividing wall between numbers 23 and 21. The next piece of information they needed had been double checked in the back of the Calton Bar and, as the men reached the back wall of the house, they found their information to be dead on. In Victorian times the builders always left just enough space between the stone wall and the wooden soffitt boards holding the roof slates for a burly roof Slater to squeeze through.

Careful examination of the original house plans put them in exactly the right spot. Standing facing each other on two stout roof beams above the back of number 21 they attached exactly 13 feet of the strongest elastic rope to their waists, fixed the ends to a stout cross beam above and nodded approval that there was easily enough space to allow them both through. Clutching each other around the chest and jumping as high as they could, their combined weight sent them crashing through the ornate plastered ceiling below, landing right on the bed where Sir Aubrey Winstanley lay sleeping. The Arab's right boot accidentally knocking him straight out.

Standing frozen like cartoon characters, they did a quick audio-visual check for anything that might have broadcast their arrival. A few seconds of silence brought confirmation that they were alone. Drawing his 0.38, Big Joe picked up Sir Aubrey's clothes, glasses and mobile, dropped them down the stairwell and listened. Satisfied that their arrival had not been broadcast, he went to work.

The Arab pulled Sir Aubrey up to a sitting position, shoved in a gag-ball and dragged the hard rubber strap over his head. Tightly tying Sir Aubrey's wrists to each bedpost the target was ready for interrogation. Flinging a ceramic basin-full of night-cold Edinburgh tap water over him, brought Sir Aubrey abruptly round.

In his terror, Sir Aubrey pulled on the ropes and tried to scream. He couldn't help but let his bowels move, filling the small room with the warm reek of fresh shit. Bending right into Sir Aubrey's face, Big Joe Mularkey whispered: 'Good evening Sir Aubrey. We want a wee word wi' you.'

In a pool of his own mess, with his neck hurting like hell and one eye swelling closed, in the side of his chest a sharp pain stabbed at his heart. But all that was as nothing. For the first time in his life, Sir Aubrey Winstanley DSO and Bar, felt the white hot terror of those about to die.

Leaning into his face, Big Joe spoke very softly. 'Let's start with our mutual friend, Lord Aldounhill, shall we? Now, he's going to remove that ball. Alright? And you know what happens next if you make even the slightest sound, don't ye?'

Sir Aubrey forced a long blink, signalling his understanding.

The Arab ripped out the gab ball and slid it silently under the pillow. Big Joe Mularkey opened the bedroom door wide and everyone listened. Down through the stairwell, Big Joe could see the light on under the second floor front bedroom and mentally praised The Arab who, a few nights before, from his vantage point up a tree in the centre of the park, had spotted Sgt McCauley and timed the signal. His plan for scamming the elderly next door neighbour had been used before. But reliable information in the Calton Bar from an old retired roofer about the way the roofs of these traditional Edinburgh circuses were built put the seal on their plan.

Pacing from side to side at the bottom of the bed, it had been a few years since Big Joe had interrogated anybody: the last one being on board Neraida 2, but he hadn't lost his touch: 'Now. Let's see here. You've been covering your tracks since you left some purple lipstick on a champagne flute that was found sticking into the neck of Lord Aldounhill. You won't dispute that, I'm sure.'

Sir Aubrey blinked again. Taking that as an affirmative response Big Joe nodded back in appreciation.

'Thank you. *You* are good. No, correction Sir Aubrey. You are *very* good. It's not everybody who could reach that guy you have outside in the Land Rover; far less order him to pick a Report right out of a senior officer's desk in Edinburgh 'A' Division. Very good. But you have a tiny wee problem, Sir Aubrey. Right?'

Bowing his whole head, neck and shoulders, still trying to figure out his captor, Sir Aubrey embraced his pain and tried to think beyond it. If caught and convicted for this break-in and kidnapping, these bastards would do at least 20 years. If there was a link to McLane, he'd do 20 years too. Unlike Sgt McCauley, his captors probably weren't being paid for this work. So what *could* be motivating them?

Then he got it.

The indignity of slipping in his own excrement didn't really bother him. That would pass. Tied in the crucifix position, Sir Aubrey concentrated for a moment; then he got it. He recognised something he hadn't seen for many years. Volunteers.

But why? Only one answer made sense. This man owed Brogan McLane his life.

Big Joe continued: 'Now. I figure that if you'd murdered Lord Aldounhill, you would've used the few days before he was found to do a professional job. Probably paid yer man out there to clean the house from top to bottom. Done a better job of getting rid of the murder weapon. At the very least, he'd have been planting decoys all over the place to provide you with defences in court. So, let's just say that after a wee visit to London recently, I'm swithering about whether you killed our dear friend Lord Aldounhill or not. But if ye' didn't, I think you know who did. Correct?'

Stony-faced Sir Aubrey closed his eyes, more to deal with his pain than answer the question.

'Now, I think you *will* help me tonight because otherwise for the rest of your life, you'll not get a minute's sleep.'

Trying to nod, the pain was excruciating. So Sir Aubrey did what he could; took a deep breath and blinked, giving nothing away. But at the sight of Big Joe clenching his fist, through phlegm and blood in his nose he mustered enough breath to say: 'I don't know …who killed him. I really … don't.'

'Ha! Ye'r ballsy, I'll give ye that Sir Aubrey. From that insignia on yer arm, I see ye were 2 Para. Captain? No, Major. Around the border country. Armagh, probably. Right?'

Nodding and screwing his eyes to absorb sweat, Sir Aubrey confirmed his name and rank.

Just in case the good Sir Aubrey was getting the wrong idea, The Arab showed him there was no sign of becoming pals. Yanking Sir Aubrey's head back by the hair, he shoved the gag-ball back in. Coming under fire,

Sir Aubrey's broken ribs immediately responded; shooting automatic pain to every nerve ending in his body. Producing a long flick-knife, The Arab gave Big Joe a nod. The feel of Big Joe's thumb on his left eyeball sent a white fear to the centre of Sir Aubrey's stomach. This could mean only one thing: a big question was coming and the slightest perception of a lie would mean losing that eye. Presenting the point of the blade to Sir Aubrey's eye, Big Joe calmly asked again:

'Now, I'm gonnie remove that gag and you *will* tell me what I need to know.'

As Big Joe dragged the elastic strap over his head, Sir Aubrey spat out two teeth: Now, *Sir* Aubrey. *Who* did ye say murdered Aldounhill?'

Shivering in fear, incapable of answering, Sir Aubrey passed out.

Both men looked at each other and Big Joe scratched his head. 'Aw, fuck it. What noo?' asked the Arab.

'Yer a' right, man. Ah didn'ae really expect an answer. No' immediately. But Ah'm sure one will be forthcomin'. Shortly. Right now we're just dancin'.'

'Dancin'?'

'Aye. The old time 'Interrogation Waltz': two

steps forward and wan back. He'll know it well.'

A quick whiff from a phial of Ammonium Carbonate brought a flicker of the eyes and a painful cough. Holding up Sir Aubrey's eyelids, Big Joe looked deep into his prisoner's eyes.

Wheezing from his freezing cold lungs, Sir Aubrey tried to count the time since their arrival. Several minutes, he figured, and that was well outside the boundary. If they intended to kill him, he'd now be dead. Leading with the right foot, Sir Aubrey gave evasion one more try: 'I really can't help you. I wish I could... but ...'

Gripping Sir Aubrey by his wispy hair, Big Joe bounced his head off the back of the wooden bed: 'Now, now, Sir Aubrey. If you think we'd kill you right here in Edinburgh for all your pals up in Parliament House to come after us, you're very much mistaken. See, this gentleman here is gonnie show you somethin'. Ah suggest you watch very carefully.'

Pulling a phone from a case on his belt The Arab held the screen a few inches from Sir Aubrey's face. At first the location wasn't clear and the sound was just noisy machinery in the background. Then a naked man, hog tied and crying, came into shot, being lowered by a crane into the picture. Holding out his hand to stop the load swinging, a tall burly masked man stepped forward stapling a copy of the Spanish newspaper 'El Mundo' to the prisoner's belly. Panning-out, down in the Hold of a ship, two men wearing black cover-alls and ski-masks stood ready beside a hydraulic car-crushing machine. As the crane lowered him further, screaming for his life the man disappeared through the broken windscreen of a small rusty French car. One of the masked men shouted a bleeped-out question but got no discernible reply.

Drop!

After less than 15 seconds in the crusher, hoisted up by the crane came a cube of metal which had been car and man. As the cube swung lightly on the crane, a message addressed to the dead man's brother scrolled across the screen. Panning up, the bright half moon showed a lovely starry night down on the Med as the cube dropped over the starboard side, splashing into the sea.

Slotting the camera back into its case, The Arab's eyes betrayed a smile below his mask. Tapping Sir Aubrey on the cheek, The Arab was *dying* to tell him he'd love to do the same to him, but kept to what operational security demanded. No voice ID of the second man.

Sir Aubrey fought back rising vomit, closed his eyes and began: 'Our Father, who art in Heaven, …'

Interrupting, Big Joe recognised the old sign of surrender: 'Would ye' like a wee drop of water there Sir Aubrey?'

As Sir Aubrey drank, The Arab pulled the sodden stinking bedding from under Sir Aubrey, flinging the bundle in the corner.

'In yer own time, Sir Aubrey. More water?'

Refusing with a shake of the head, half breathing and half crying, Sir Aubrey Winstanley, spitting clots of blood and lumps of vomit, began to save his own life: 'The lipstick is mine. You'll know that.'

Matter-of-factly, Big Joe asked: 'Were you *there* the night he died?'

'I must have … I was there … shortly before he died. But please, whatever you do tonight, … know this: *I* didn't kill him. His death … *might* have been an accident. (cough cough) Have you thought of that?'

Pulling the 0.38 from his belt, Big Joe cocked the hammer and stuck the gun to the side of Sir Aubrey's head: 'Sir Aubrey. Don't fuck me about. I know all about Professor Suilleman's supplementary report. Now ...'

'Yes. Sorry. Sorry. I *was* there that night. I was furious. Because … well my son … Giles ..'

'Oh aye. Little Giles Winstanley. You'll be pleased

315

to hear that he's under police witness protection. And he's back in Edinburgh.'

'Witness pro …? Why?'

'That's for us to know. Go on.'

'What? There's no need for … Please. It's not his fault. My wife and I … we had blazing rows. About me, well … you know. Giles heard a lot of them. About me going out … to Allan's … to Aldounhill's parties. She knew of course … about my … predilection. It hadn't bothered her. Then it did.'

'And Giles?'

Unable to answer, his humiliation now complete, Sir Aubrey retched in emotional and physical agony. Lifting his head and slapping him hard, for the first time, Big Joe betrayed anger: 'Shut the fuck up! You're a disgrace man. Answer me!'

Swallowing hard and lifting his eyes, Sir Aubrey wished he could salute a better man: 'We had a rule. An unwritten one. No boys. I mean no under-age boys. Consenting men only. That way … we had the law on our side; not one we could shout about from … But it was there … in the background. No police raids. Not like the old days.'

'Who is 'we' Sir Aubrey?'

Sir Aubrey counted his missing teeth with his tongue and spluttered: 'The usual lot. Some I knew, some I didn't want to know. I usually insisted they leave if I didn't know enough of them. It was usually Penelope, Amanda, Jen …'

'I need *real* names, Sir Aubrey. You understand.'

A note of resentment crept into Sir Aubrey's tone at the disapproval being shown of how he'd lived most of his adult life.

'Of course. Alright.'

Through his searing pain Sir Aubrey pulled on the ties holding his aching arms, pleading with The Arab.

'Could you?'

His flick knife opening as though it was part of his hand, The Arab cut the ties.

Taking a moment to allow the blood back into his hands, Sir Aubrey went on: 'There was always Nicholas Lloyd-Weatherby, that's Penelope. He named himself after his niece. He dressed like her, spoke like her – everything.'

'Address?'

Sir Aubrey shook his head, moving away a little from the centre of the bed where his bowels had moved: 'I've absolutely no idea where he lives but since the news broke I think he's been abroad. He has a yacht, 'The

Penelope', of course. In Cannes, I think. Near Cannes. Amanda is a bit of local rough trade. Allan would occasionally bring someone like that. Then there's Jenny. She's a bad lot … a tart if ever …'

'Names Sir Aubrey. *Real* names. Where do we find these …?'

'I've no idea where to find him. Some farm somewhere is all I know. He does motorcycle racing .. or allows a club to use it. Something like that. Sorry.'

'Tell me more about the last time you saw Aldounhill alive.'

'I'd arrived with my usual champagne and cheese for supper. There were three or four others there. I shooed them away to the kitchen and sat with Allan.'

'Who?'

'Allan Coatbridge. Lord Aldounhill.'

'Oh right, aye.'

'He was full of beans. Excited. Telling me about some teenage boy that Darren, his latest fixer, was sending up to arrive later that night. He kept looking at the time. Some local boy was coming back up from London. I asked about him and when he gave me the description I was nearly sick. He described *my* Giles. I was fairly sure he was gay, but I wasn't certain. I didn't want to think about it.

But then Allan mentioned the boy's first name and that did it. I exploded. He hadn't seen my Giles for years. Ten years maybe. So he didn't connect us.'

'Go on.'

'We had been drinking champagne. Not the crap he usually drank. The bottle I brought. He was standing by the fire, warming himself.'

'Why? The house has central heating.'

'Yes. But he was naked. He was always naked at his supper parties.'

'Did you spike his drink with Rohypnol so that he'd be out of it when Giles arrived?'

'How could you possibly know …? That hasn't been released.'

Shoving the 0.38 harder into Sir Aubrey's temple, Big Joe left the impression of the barrel on Sir Aubrey's skin.

'Yes. Of course. I always took some to his house. It *was* a little dangerous. But I don't know when he drank it, or even *if* he drank it at all.'

'How long after that did you leave?'

'I don't know. I was last to leave his house. That much I do know. I also know I did *not* murder him, so - and I don't care what that Professor says - it *must* have

319

been an accident. Maybe he was drinking from my glass, the drug took effect and he fell into the fireplace, breaking the glass and it stuck in his neck. I don't know.'

Until that moment The Arab had kept strictly to Big Joe's OpSec. But the tone of Sir Aubrey's voice telling this tall tale was too much. Losing his temper The Arab swung his fist straight into Sir Aubrey's face: 'Ya lyin' bastard.'

Landing a full-force uppercut that broke Sir Aubrey's nose, The Arab immediately pulled back by way of apology to Big Joe. Looking at the perfect red arc the blood had made on the wall and the crumpled heap beside the bed, Big Joe hoped Sir Aubrey wasn't dead.

'For fuck sake man. Will you leave this to me?'

'Ach the bastard's lyin'.'

Staring at each other, Big Joe broke the ice: 'Ah know Arab Ah know. But this is only the fuckin' dance man. *Just* the dance. He's only tryin' tae … Is he ...?'

'Naw, he's alive. But he's out cold.'

Another basin-full of cold water and Sir Aubrey was back under interrogation. Pacing slowly around the bed, Big Joe could have been McLane's senior counsel in court.

'Well now; Sir Aubrey. We know perfectly well that the Professor says it *wasn't* suicide *or* accident. Because it *couldn't* have been those things. The *angle* of penetration and breakage *pattern* of the glass didn't fit with either suicide or accident. So *no*, Sir Aubrey. Lord Aldounhill *was* murdered. We know that and you know that. And now we know you were last to see him. Right?'

Drenched in blood, Sir Aubrey looked like a man close to his own death. A man at the end of the dance.

'I swear by Almighty … On my son's … I didn't kill him. It wasn't me.'

Pondering his options, Big Joe took a decision. Pulling on the rope ladder hanging from the roof beams the two men took a last look at Sir Aubrey Winstanley.

'We'll it's been a pleasure to do business wi' ye Sir Aubrey. For the moment Ah'm goin' to accept what you've told me. But before we take our leave, there is one last thing. It was *you* who phoned the Glasgow Tribune that night, correct?'

Clutching his ribs, Sir Aubrey forced a tiny shake of his head.

No-one saw the two shadows leave Inverleith Park Circus by Lady Hume-Mansfield's back garden. Speeding along the back road towards Glasgow, they waited twenty miles before calling Brogan McLane.

'Yeah. Ops is aw' good news. Nae casualties an' nae mistakes. We left him alive. Even admittin' certain things. There's confirmation of what the boy Giles told our friend. So good news for your Defence of Incrimination.

'Any bad news?'

'Aye. Sorry, but very little else has been learned. He did the Rohypnol. We got a few fanny names but Ah don't think they'll go far in court. We think he was last to leave but he's still our pop-up fur the murder. Brogie I'm fairly sure he didn'ae do it.'

'What? Really? Oh fuck. '

More than a few seconds of silence passed before McLane asked the question he knew would imply they'd done a less than professional job. But he had to ask: Did you take him …?'

'Oh aye. Ah took him *right* to the brink Brogan. He was sure he was a dead man.'

'OK. So we have him reneging on the deal with Aldounhill … sending his name to the Queen, that's number one. And now secondly, we have Aldounhill exploiting the son, Giles. Good. So the pot's boiling for a couple of years about not supporting him to be a Judge, and the thing with the son Giles is the last straw. A fantastic motive. That's brilliant work big man. Brilliant.'

'Thanks Brogie. Oh, an' somethin' else. The phone call to the paper. He said he didn'ae make it - Ah didn'ae believe that.'

'OK my man. I owe you.'

'Aw naw ye don't. I'll owe *you* Brogie. For ever.'

Chapter 40

Touching his grey top hat, the concierge of the Gersman Hotel saluted its most famous guest; the man everyone in Glasgow called 'The Greatest Living Advocate'.

Gliding over, the Manager apologised: 'Good afternoon Sir. We weren't expecting you today, until Mr …'

'No. I don't see him. Where is he?'

'Mr McLane asked if he could wait downstairs, Sir.'

Near the basement fire door, alone at a small round table, McLane sat drumming his fingers.

'Hello Brogan. You *know* we're not supposed to meet like this. So what's so important?'

Pulling out five sheets of typed paper, McLane slapped them down: 'This came by motorcycle a couple of hours ago. It's not even on the Crown Office 'Received List' yet.

'You've got me here to look at a witness statement? What are *you* doing with a …? We shouldn't really be alone together never mind looking at this.'

'Please Duncan. It's my lifeline. You're the first to see it.'

'I don't know Brogan. It's all a bit cloak and dagger for my liking. What does it say?'

'It's a solid motive for murdering Lord Aldounhill and a definite legal basis for lodging a defence of Incrimination of Another Person.'

'*What*? At *this* late … Your bloody *trial* starts on Monday morning. *Who* in God's name are we incriminating?'

~~~o~~~

End of Part 5

Part 6

Chapter 41

Striding hand in hand, up over Castle Terrace and down the Royal Mile towards Parliament House, ignoring the cameras fixed to motorcycles and straggling journalists all asking the same questions, Brogan and Joanne McLane focused on what lay ahead. But turning into West Parliament Square, they bowed their heads as a flash hundreds of times brighter than daylight illuminated them for all the world to see.

They made the perfect picture. He in his usual black coat and broad black brimmer. Mrs McLane wearing a scarlet ankle-length coat and black court shoes. Her thick blonde hair blew back in the morning wind; they said, like Boadicea. Their locked hands and stern faces masked their torment but their unmistakable love and devotion to each other looked unshaken.

As they crossed Parliament Square, Brogan's phone rang. Looking skywards above St Giles Cathedral Spire, McLane pressed the phone to his ear as the media got everything they wanted.

'Hello Brogan. It's to be Court 9. The old oak

court. But there's still nae word as to who's presidin'. We've got the Motion to Incriminate ready to lodge at the Bar o' the Court. McIntyre thinks it'll be tricky. This late an' all that.'

McLane stopped and smiled straight into the cameras: 'Of course. That's fine. As expected. Good.'

Closing the phone, McLane gave the baying pack their quote: 'Excellent. Bring it on.'

But beneath their bravery lay the less than happy facts: patchy sleep, an early morning argument tearfully made-up, three visits each to the toilet before leaving the house and one last thing. Mentioned in the car just before parking, Joanne laid down her law. 'Trust your lawyers and don't dare end up representing yourself.'

Outside Parliament House in the cold, the waiting lines of ghoulish spectators hoping for Gallery passes was three-deep.

In Parliament Hall, Queen's Macer Jimmy Robertson, carrying the wig and robes of Lord Marchion, slowed his pace. Passing Brogan McLane he dropped his eyes to the ermine and silk bundle in his arms. Taking the hint, McLane followed Jimmy's finger poking through the thick ermine to the label bearing the name of his judge.

Before hurrying on, Jimmy silently mouthed: 'Good luck, Sir'.

Inside Court 9 through high stained-glass windows, shafts of sunlight flashed across polished leather-bound books behind the judge's chair, lighting the old oak court from heaven above.

Entering through the two sets of sturdy old swing doors at his usual composed pace, Duncan McIntyre QC took his seat at the leather-topped table - 14 feet long and 6 feet wide - below the judge and to the left in the 'Well of the Court'. Opposite, on the judge's right, sat the 'Advocate Depute' - the old name for the Lord Advocate's Deputy in a trial. The Clerk busying himself immediately below the judge's chair nodded a welcome to both. While their juniors' checked the tidy bundles of carefully indexed papers, both counsel ignored the public filing along the solid old wooden benches. Closing his eyes, McIntyre went through an old habit: rehearsing his first move.

Jimmy Robertson appeared through 'the wee panel' – an almost invisible door in the oak panelling; his mere appearance being the signal to everyone in a wig that the Judge was ready.

It was time to summon Brogan McLane to his trial.

Standing outside the door of the court and facing

towards Parliament Hall, Jimmy Robertson cleared his throat, touched the button on his microphone which sent his voice to every office and down every corridor in Parliament House: 'In the matter of Her Majesty's Advocate against Brogan McLane. Lord Marchion presiding. Court 9. The trial of Brogan McLane. Court 9.'

McLane marched quickly to the front of the Court, taking his place between two police officers in the Dock. As per time immemorial, the impeccably uniformed officers wore white gloves as a symbol of their purity. Their black ebony batons drawn, laying on their thighs. Even if upon hearing a guilty verdict the crowd rose up, they wouldn't flinch. Their sole function being to protect the judge from the menace in the Dock.

With counsel assembled and the accused in the Dock, for several minutes the whole court sat in absolute silence. Waiting. Sitting still as stone staring at the judge's empty, tall, carved-oak and red buttoned-leather seat, McLane let his mind drift to the dozens of trials he'd conducted for the defence in this Court; sitting exactly where Duncan McIntyre QC was sitting now.

Holding the carved lions on either side of the judge's chair, Jimmy Robertson called '**Cou-ou-rt**' signifying the entrance of Lord Marchion.

McLane did his legal duty and stood to attention for his judge's entrance, but couldn't look the judge in the face. He could see nothing but the blood-red crosses woven into the judge's white silk robe. To keep his fraying nerves at bay, McLane stared down at his shoes, giving the false impression of bowing to his betters.

Rising with the usual thundering shuffle made by 100 or so members of the public, the press corps and nosy Parliament House worker-bees, respect to justice was duly paid.

His lordship couldn't have moved any slower. Once eventually seated he had issues. Were his spectacles polished? Was his ink well filled? Did he have two sharpened red pencils at the ready? Was his evidence notebook opened at the correct page? Was his crystal glass filled with his approved brand of water?

At last, as his lordship signalled to his clerk that he was ready, everyone could be seated.

The clerk of court remained standing and cleared his throat. In a loud, clear voice, ostensibly to the whole world his well-practised voice resonated to the back of the court: 'I Call The Diet of Her Majesty's Advocate against Brogan McLane.'

Then softly, looking into the chest of the accused

man in the Dock, he asked: 'Are you Brogan McLane?'

Instinctively McLane stood, replying clearly in a voice betraying nothing of what he was feeling or thinking: 'I am.'

'Please remain standing, Sir, while I read the Indictment.'

Between the uniformed officers McLane didn't need to listen to the clerk. With the exception of the name, he'd heard charges like these so many times he could recite them in his sleep.

'In the name and authority of Lord Caruthers, Her Majesty's Advocate in Scotland. Brogan McLane, having identified yourself, the charges against you are that sometime between the night of Friday the 6th of November and Tuesday 10th November, in Year 68 of Her Majesty's Sovereign Reign, at a precise time and date being to the Crown unknown, you did (1) break into the home of Lord Aldounhill, or at least enter thereat uninvited, (2) within the said home of Lord Aldounhill you did cause damage to property belonging to the said Lord Aldounhill, namely breakage of two champagne flutes, (3) cause fear and alarm to other good people, occupants therein, the names and other details of the said other occupants being to the Crown presently unknown, (4) you did obstruct the course of justice by removing evidence from the scene of your crimes, namely to gather the said broken champagne flutes and a set of keys which you later deposited in the Edinburgh canal in an attempt to hide your guilt, and lastly, (5) you did murder Lord Aldounhill. Brogan McLane how do you plead? Guilty or Not Guilty?'

As expected Duncan McIntyre stood to interrupt in his usual resounding voice: 'My Lord. I appear on behalf of the accused and tender a plea of Not Guilty to the entire Indictment.'

With a look of resignation, Lord Marchion noted the plea: 'Ladies and gentlemen, you have heard Mr McIntyre on behalf of the accused man, Brogan McLane, tender his plea of Not Guilty. We shall now require to impanel a jury to reach a verdict in this case.'

One by one, as the clerk randomly picked a slip with a name on it, their names were called; the 15 people of Edinburgh who would judge the Advocate on trial, Brogan McLane.

With the 15 jurors chosen, Lord Marchion addressed them: 'Ladies and gentlemen. You have now been lawfully selected to serve as the jury in this trial. There is under consideration the most serious of crimes.

The charge is murder – and murder of no less a person than a judge of this High Court, Lord Aldounhill. A great man, ladies and gentlemen. Who was brutally murdered, as you shall discover. But we won't begin until you have had time to remove your coats etcetera and make yourselves comfortable. So please, ladies and gentlemen, follow the lady who has appeared by your jury box. Meanwhile the 20 of you who were not chosen are free to go, with the court's thanks for your attendance.'

As the last Juror filed out and the oak door to the Jury Room thudded closed, silence once again returned to court 9. Looking over his spectacles at the Writ headed 'Motion on Behalf of the Accused', Lord Marchion pushed it aside with his sleeve. 'Mr McIntyre. Is this Motion absolutely necessary? Can't we just get on?'

'I regret not, my Lord. This is a murder trial and I am required by law and my own ethical standards to pursue every possible …'

'Yes. Yes. Very well. If I must hear it. What is it?'

'I seek to introduce a Special Defence of Incrimination, my Lord. The name of the incriminee was made known to my learned friend the Advocate Depute as soon as possible. So in presenting this Motion I create no ambush.'

'What is the basis of this Motion Mr McIntyre?'

'My Lord, that the named person was in the home of Lord Aldounhill when he died. That he also had a motive to …'

'Sorry Mr McIntyre, you mean when Lord Aldounhill was murdered.'

'That has not yet been established by law, my Lord. So I therefore cast my submission in the neutral form of 'when he died.'

'Very well. Go on.'

'There is evidence that the DNA of the incriminee was found within some lipstick. On a champagne flute discovered by the police and a smear on the neck of the deceased, to be precise. My client is charged with breakage and removal of two champagne …'

'I'm sorry. Did you say lipstick, Mr McIntyre?'

'I did my Lord.'

'Do you suggest that Lord Aldounhill was murdered by a woman?'

'No my Lord, by a man.'

'How extraordinary. And has this person been lawfully summoned to give evidence, Mr McIntyre?'

'Yes, my Lord. But he was adamant he would not speak to anyone from the defence side. No-one at all. And furthermore, quite recently a *motive* for murder has been established and accordingly I must …'

'Mr McIntyre, the name of the incriminee is thoroughly extraordinary. I therefore will not, I repeat *not*, allow it to be mentioned by you, or anyone else in public. Do you understand me?

'Well, I will probably require to …'

With a flash of real anger, Lord Marchion crushed what he saw as disobedience: 'You will do as I *say* Mr McIntyre and *only* as I say. Is that clear? If and *only* if I allow this Motion to succeed, will you be able to mention that name out loud. Do you understand me?'

'Yes. Thoroughly my Lord.'

'Now, you are telling me that … this person has not been interviewed by the defence?'

'No, he hasn't my Lord. And that is quite contrary to law. He is adamant that he won't speak to the defence. However, he is a crucial defence witness. My Lord, I have several case precedents to cite in support of my Motion.'

'So I see. That will take time and this court is eager if not anxious to proceed. But if you must, then get on with it.'

Whilst the Jury drank coffee and read the morning papers, out in court 9 the next hour and a half saw

McIntyre citing case after case of the European Court of Human Rights supporting such Motions. But throughout this expert oration, Lord Marchion didn't even raise his pen to take notes.

'Well, time is now pressing. I shan't rule of course until I hear what the Crown has to say. Mr Depute, do you oppose this Motion?'

As Duncan McIntyre sat down, with timing as tight as children on a see-saw, the learned Depute rose, unnecessarily bowed to his Lordship and opened: 'My Lord, I *do* oppose this motion. None of these precedents makes any difference to this *particular* trial. Although as my learned friend has said, this matter is not unknown to the Crown, it came *extremely* late in the day. The Motion, in my submission, has no substance. The defence have lodged no scientific report about this DNA or this mystery champagne flute. And, as to whether this person was even ever in the home of Lord Aldounhill, I cannot say. But I doubt it. One thing I can say is that the person whom the defence now seek to incriminate, a most highly respected member of the ... of the community, was attacked in his home just two nights ago. He was brutally assaulted in an attempt to murder him. I very much regret to say that he's now in hospital where he has undergone extensive medical procedures. He is in no physical or mental condition to give evidence. However, as I say, in my submission there is nothing for him to give evidence about. Now, if there is any other matter with which I can assist the court, I will …'

Having noted every word of what the Depute had to say, Lord Marchion skimmed his notes; making sure it was all there: 'Hmm. Thank you very much Mr Depute. I am particularly concerned that such a so-called 'central witness' has been the subject of attempted murder. Hmm. No. There's nothing of substance in this Motion and I therefore have no hesitation in refusing it. And, before you ask me Mr McIntyre, leave to appeal that decision is denied. My grounds are firstly that the person incriminated is in hospital after suffering an attempt to murder him and so cannot possibly defend himself. Then there is the importance of proceeding with this trial expeditiously in all fairness to the accused man; not to mention the entire lack of legal substance in the Motion in the first place. Now, bring back the jury and let's get on with this wretched trial.'

Chapter 42

Lord Marchion touched his pencils, adjusted his cushion and studiously ignored the Advocate sitting in the Dock.

With the 'Good 15' settled into the Jury Box, Lord Marchion smiled down upon the Advocate Depute: 'Now Mr Depute, please call your first witness.'

'My first witness is Constable James Thomas Delaney, an officer in these courts.'

Standing rigid in the witness box at just the right angle to meet his Lordship's command, officer Delaney placed his left hand squarely on the bible, raised his right hand to God and his Judge and took the solemn oath: 'I James Thomas Delaney, swear by Almighty God, that the evidence I shall give, shall be the truth, the whole truth and nothing but the truth, as I shall answer to God on the Great Day of Judgement.'

The Advocate Depute began by taking officer Delaney through his age, many years of service in the Edinburgh police force, his two commendations for gallantry and general pride in serving the community. Then he got down to business.

'Let me take you back three years: to the trial in this very courtroom of one Terence Scott for rape and murder. On the last day of that trial, were you serving as a

Dock officer?'

'I was.'

'How did that trial end?'

'Well it didn't end, Sir.'

'What do you mean?'

'The trial collapsed, Sir. It was Mr McLane's fault, he …'

'Slowly, officer. His Lordship is writing down your evidence.'

'Thank you Advocate Depute' offered Lord Marchion with a smile towards the Depute. Then turning sideways he added: 'Of course some of the jury may also be writing this down and we must give them every opportunity.'

'Yes my Lord. Officer can you say why the trial collapsed?'

Bowing to Lord Marchion, officer Delaney began again: 'Yes Sir. The defence Advocate, Mr Brogan McLane lost his temper with the Judge, Lord Aldounhill …'

'Yes, officer. One important point, can you just tell the court if the person you are talking about is in court today? Take your time and look around.'

'Of course Sir. Mr McLane is sitting between the

two officers in the Dock, Sir.'

'Thank you. Do continue.'

'Well Sir, he accused Lord Aldounhill of conducting ... I don't know how to say it Sir, ... private correspondence ... sending wee notes between you, Sir.'

'Officer Delaney, you included a reference to *me* in your evidence. Please explain that to the ladies and gentlemen of the Jury.'

'Well Sir, you were the prosecutor in that case and Lord Aldounhill was the judge. Mr McLane said ... well more burst out really ... that you and Lord Aldounhill were sending each other notes, Sir.

'Notes?'

'Yes, Sir. *Billy-dues* he called them. I think he meant, you know, like wee love letters, Sir. He said no-one was listening to his cross-examination of my colleague, Sir. Officer Collins.'

'Yes, officer Delaney. And what did Lord Aldounhill do about that outburst?'

'He sentenced Mr McLane to a month in prison, for contempt of court, Sir.'

'And did you take Mr McLane down to the cells?

'I did Sir. He shouted something. A name. Keepou, Keepriou. Something like that. But Lord Aldounhill wouldn't have it, Sir. Oh he .. Mr McLane I mean …he went wild, Sir. On the way down he was ragin' an' shouting about Lord Aldounhill being in a Magic Circle; something like that Sir, I'm not sure what else.'

'Do you know what he meant by Magic Circle, officer?'

'Sir, no Sir. I've never heard of such a thing.'

'Could the name Mr McLane shouted have been Kypriannou?'

'That could be it, Sir. A case name. In the European Court of Human Right …'

'Thank you officer. And when you got to the cells. Did Mr McLane calm down?'

'No Sir. When I released the cuffs he swung a punch straight at the wall, about face height and shouted, he would "get that bastard … or … see that bastard Aldounhill. See him in Hell, Sir."

'Did he hit the wall?

'Oh yes, Sir. Twice. Hard Sir.'

'Have you heard the common expression 'get' before, officer?'

'Oh many times, Sir. It means to attack or do harm, Sir.'

'Thank you officer Delaney, no further questions.'

Lord Marchion paused for a few moments, allowing the jury to write down officer Delaney's evidence, then nodded approval to McIntyre to begin cross-examination.

McIntyre floated to his feet, but waited. He looked to the high ceiling, then waited some more. With the jury staring as one at his client, he waited again. McLane looked a forlorn figure; hands clasped, trying to heed the advice McIntyre gave to every client - Don't under any circumstances look at the jury. Look straight ahead or up. Never down.

Then, as McIntyre dropped his pen onto his bundle of papers, the wind began to blow the other way.

'Officer Delaney, during the trial of Terence Scott, on the subject of these 'communications' between the learned Advocate Depute and Lord Aldounhill, you may be surprised to hear that there is no dispute between the Depute and myself that certain notes *were* passed at the point in the trial where Mr McLane 'interrupted' proceedings. Now, you just testified that *Mr McLane* called these notes *Billy-dues.* Do you remember calling them that?'

'If you say so, Sir.'

'Well I don't give the evidence. You do. Now do

you remember calling these notes *Billy-dues* or shall I have your testimony read back to you?'

'I think I recall, Sir. I'll take your word for it, Sir.'

'His Lordship's Macer will now put agreed Exhibit 23 in front of you.'

Officer Delaney tried a glance to the Advocate Depute; but had no luck. He tried Lord Marchion; again no luck. This hadn't been mentioned at his prep and as the Exhibit was being handed to him, officer Delaney even tried Jimmy Robertson for a clue of what was to come; no luck again.

'Do you recognize the Exhibit as a Scottish courts administration transcript of the incomplete trial of Terence Scott?

'Yes, Sir.'

'Please flick to three pages from the end. Now do you see the exchange between the Advocate, that's Mr McLane, and Lord Aldounhill beginning?'

'I do, Sir.'

As officer Delaney fumbled with the Exhibit, Jimmy Robertson distributed copies to the jury, making officer Delaney even more uncomfortable.

'Three pages from the end. Take your time officer. Just show the court where the term *Billet-doux* or anything like it appears, please.'

With his finger following the typed lines, Officer Delaney slowly began reading. Those on the jury quicker than others were way ahead of this game. Only Lord Marchion kept his copy closed.

McIntyre let sufficient time pass in silence, then asked: 'Well, we're waiting. Can you show us please?'

'I can't find it, Sir.'

Spinning and looking the Jury in the eyes McIntyre asked: 'Is that because it's not *there*?'

'I don't know, Sir.'

Officer Delaney shifted uncomfortably from foot to foot in the witness box, pressed his lips together and prepared for what was to come.

'And this quote. The one about seeing Lord Aldounhill in Hell. Where is that?'

'As I said Sir. It was all jumbled. He was shouting a lot.'

'Oh no doubt. But the truth is he was shouting at *you*. Correct?'

'No Sir.'

'For spitting on him as you flung him into the cell.'

'I would never do such a thing, Sir. That would be

strictly against …'

'Against regulations?'

'Yes Sir.'

'Do you see where the typist has just written the words 'See you in Hell?'

'Yes Sir'

'And do you see the time-line on that transcript?'

Fumbling, officer Delaney looked back a few pages and then around the court for support.

'Can't you see it officer? This transcript is one of the first in these courts to have a time-line.'

'Oh yes, Sir. I didn't know what that was.'

'And can you see just at page 762, line 34?'

'Yes I see that line.'

'Please read it for us.'

'It says 'Cell door closing.'

'And that's right before the rather jumbled words about Hell, correct?'

'I … I suppose so.'

'So, do you want to revise your evidence about 'seeing Lord Aldounhill in Hell?'

'I don't rightly know Sir. I'm a bit confused now.'

'Very well. Let's leave that point and turn to the matter of Mr McLane shouting in the corridors on the way *down* to the cells. Were you leading Mr McLane away in handcuffs?'

'Yes'

'And, in accordance with police regulations, did you have one hand on the rigid bar between the cuffs allowing you a free hand as you led him down to the cells?'

'Yes'

'So you obviously opened the door, The 'wee panel' as we call it, with the other hand?'

'Yes'

'Can you explain why no-one else in a packed courtroom – this very courtroom – heard this shouting?'

'No, Sir. *I* heard it.'

'And can you explain why if Mr McLane had shouted anything it was not picked up on the tape recording machine from which the transcript you have in your hand was compiled?'

'No. Maybe the typist didn't think it was worth …'

'Ah! Of course there is a typist but there are also microphones. Do you see that there are sundry words, which the typist has helpfully transcribed from the tape recording, at the very end of the Exhibit'

'Yes'

'And do you accept that the transcript goes from the last words of Lord Aldounhill to the words of the unknown officers downstairs?

'Yes, I suppose so.'

'And do you therefore accept that anything shouted by Mr McLane must have been in between these entries?'

'Again, I suppose so.'

'So the only explanation for the shouting – which only you seem to have heard – being missing, is that the typist decided, on her own, to omit those crucial parts which would fit in between Lord Aldounhill and the other unknown voices. Is that right?'

'I don't know.'

'Of course not. Let us turn now to this punching of the wall business which you say you saw. You testified that Mr McLane punched the wall twice and hard? How hard?'

'Not very hard, Sir.'

'But according to you, he swung two punches – hard, at face height and swore he'd *get* Lord Aldounhill.'

'Yes, Sir.'

'Can you explain why, again as a matter of routine

procedure, when the prison doctor saw Mr McLane only five hours later, he recorded no mark on his knuckles or other part of his hands?'

'That would be a medical matter, Sir?'

'Ah yes officer, but also a *jury* matter. Now, would you say that during your long police service, you've become well acquainted with standard procedures?'

'Of course, Sir.'

'Than why didn't you record on Mr McLane's door sheet that he'd punched a wall – twice and hard - and may need medical attention?'

'I ... I ... I ... don't rightly ...'

'Of course not. Now let's turn back to the subject of *Billet-doux*. Were you or were you not also on duty in the High Court of Criminal Appeal three months ago when the appeal of Brenda Curry, a lawyer, was being heard?'

'I don't remember.'

'You don't? *Really*? Her appeal was heard here in Parliament House. Along the corridor in Court 3. Mr McLane and Lord Jamieson, who is the Lord Justice General of Scotland were discussing the actions of Miss Curry during a trial in a lower court and whether those actions amounted to contempt of court. The judge in the lower court claimed that Miss Brenda Curry was in contempt for failing to concentrate on the evidence against her client. According to the judge, she was passing little love letters to her boyfriend, one police constable Michael Visceglia, who happened to be the police officer on door duty. At her appeal, you sat beside her as a Dock officer, in your white gloves. Are you saying you don't remember the case?

'I do now. Aye right. Sorry.'

'And throughout the appeal, what were the love letters in that case called by Mr McLane and the Lord Justice General?'

'I don't reca …'

Duncan McIntyre could feel the jury's obvious frustration and turned up the heat: 'Officer Delaney, do you *really* want to *join* the deep ranks of those we've been discussing who've been convicted of contempt?'

'*That* is *not* a matter for you, Mr McIntyre.' Looking over his pince-nez, Lord Marchion gave McIntyre a cold stare: 'You will confine yourself to asking questions of the witness, who has been doing his best to assist you. Now please remember the courtesy to be extended to *every* witness Mr McIntyre, or it may be *you* who requires the warning. Do I make myself clear?'

With more of a nod than a bow, McIntyre

continued: 'Officer Delaney. Do you recall what the love letters in that appeal were called.'

Scanning the court Delaney looked for anyone who might be able to give him the slightest hint of what the PF's preferred answer might be. But he found himself alone. Sweating a little he gripped the bar of the witness box. Staring down at his hands, he recalled his wife's warning before leaving home – 'Whatever happens, don't ruin yourself. There's nothing in this for us. The PF is using you, isn't she? Retirement *and* our pension aren't far away. So keep that in mind Jamie.'

For the first time since he stepped up to the witness box, officer Delaney told the truth. 'They called them *Billy-dues* Sir.'

'Yes. Thank you. They did. Now I must warn you officer, you're on very thin ice. So here's my question: 'Did you fabricate that fancy term in your evidence in this trial because you heard it in the Brenda Curry appeal case, or did someone during the preparation of this prosecution *plant* that exotic term, knowing it would stick in the minds of the Jury?'

'DON'T ANSWER THAT OFFICER!' Every head in the court spun, looking up at Lord Marchion.

'Officer Delaney, I consider that you are being led

into territory that is quite improper. You have given your evidence to the Advocate Depute very squarely and with great dignity, if I may say so. This, ... this ... trickery, has no place here, and Mr McIntyre should know better. You are dismissed with the court's grateful thanks officer.'

McIntyre looked with a shrug at the Jury and sat down.

With his mouth dry and sweating visibly officer Delaney stepped down from the witness box a very different figure from the confident man who'd entered it.

Lord Marchion was an old hand at feigning neutrality, so his face gave nothing away. Turning to the Jury, his voice on the recording the essence of balance and temperance, he offered his fatherly assistance: 'Ladies and gentlemen. It's been a full day, what with your initial selection and the unwarranted wait during, eherm, I hesitate to say, legal argument. We've also dealt with administrative matters and then latterly evidence from officer Delaney. So I think that's enough for today. You should not discuss the case with anyone. It's only in the early stages. I shall rise now and see you all tomorrow morning at ...'

'My Lord! I must ...'

Glowering at McIntyre, his eyes bulging and fists

clenched, Lord Marchion spluttered: 'How DARE you interrupt me whilst I am addressing the Jury. I have a good mind to hold *you* …'

My Lord. I regret to remind the court that *before* the court rises, there is the usual important matter which your lordship *must* deal with. I require an opportunity to address the court *outwith* the presence of the Jur …'

'Oh that! Very well, Bail is continued.'

'Ladies and gentlemen, please be in your places at 10 O'clock tomorrow. I bid you all good day.'

In the press gallery, their headline read: 'Advocate on Trial lucky to get Bail'

Chapter 43

The dull tramp of policemen's footsteps pounding all day, unchallenged, in and out of the old oak court saw the Jury progressively slump down into their seats. Despite Jimmy Robertson keeping them busy showing this Exhibit and that, and Lord Marchion becoming more and more keen to get through these 'plod' and into the scientific evidence against the accused, in truth the day was bog standard second-trial-day stuff.

'I was the duty desk officer when the call came in, Sir … I swear by Almighty God that the evidence I shall …Yes Sir, I am a Scenes of Crimes Officer with Edinburgh Police 'A' Division … Yes, Sir, this Exhibit is a series of photos I took of Lord Aldounhill lying dead … I have 29 years of service, Sir … I assisted in sealing Lord Aldounhill's house, Sir … As we can see on the video Sir … Yes, I was ordered by Commander Imrie to … No Sir, the street cameras around Mansionhouse Place right down to Gorgie Road gave up nothing we could work on … We picked up a few people taking taxis but we couldn't find them all … I typed up and completed that statement … I did give her tea … Her name is Miss Mary McCracken, Sir … I swear by Almighty God … That is my signature against this police individual ID Tag, Sir … I swear by …

I stood on front door duty outside Lord Aldounhill's house for six hours, Sir. No-one entered who didn't have ID, Sir … I stood on back door duty at Lord Aldounhill's … I solemnly and truly declare upon my honour that the evidence I shall … I went door-to-door, Sir making enquiries about … Yes Sir, I lifted a partial boot-print from Lord Aldounhill's garden. I'd say a motorcycle boot. But it was wet and it sort of fell apart … We've put together a full print using the manufacturers' template. You can see where we've done that. We eliminated all police officers' prints and the only gardener … I swear by Almighty … I contacted everyone who'd sold anything to Lord Aldounhill. Yes, Sir, I went through all of the receipts … Yes, Sir, those are my work sheets, Sir … I didn't Sir, No. … Along with constable Cameron, I seized this item as a Production in Evidence, Sir, … I was on mobile patrol duty with my colleague constable Davidson when we got a radio call … erm, I don't Sir, may I refer to my notebook? … to attend at the Edinburgh canal where evidence was found in the form of … No Sir, no-one could have interfered with it, Sir. Yes Sir, I did seal that evidence bag. Yes, I presented my statement to Sergeant Terrence Connolly for corroboration, Sir … I was in the back of a patrol car with a suspect in another matter at the time, Sir ... I have completed the relevant training in police community liaison, Sir. I tried to contact Mrs, sorry, Lady Aldounhill, Sir. Just after the Report, Sir. No I couldn't find her after the funeral, Sir. I sent my report to Commander Imrie, Sir. No I have never been told any such thing by the PF's Office, Sir. I happened to be on duty when ...'

Chapter 44

Settling into his chair and smiling over to the jury, Lord Marchion bowed his head to one side.

'Good morning ladies and gentlemen. I trust you are all well. Now, I regret to say that before you begin to hear today's evidence, I have another legal matter to resolve. I'm not told in advance what these matters are. All I can say is that, subject to any *defence* objection, this may take some time. But we'll just have to wait and see.'

The Advocate Depute fingered the corners of his Motion paper for the umpteenth time but couldn't make the bundle any more square. Listening for the click of the closing door leading down the corridor to the Jury Room, he checked again with his Junior; the Motion was properly lodged on time and in the correct form. The terms of the Motion were reasonable and supported by rulings in the Supreme Court of …

'Now, Advocate Depute. I believe this is your Motion.'

Leaping to his feet, the AD forgot to bow. 'Yes, my Lord. It is. My Lord, the court ought to Order the sealing of Crown Office Exhibit number 1, the book of police Scenes of Crime photographs of Lord Aldounhill lying … lying dead; and that seal not be broken for a period of 50 years; it NOT being in the public interest to have these revealed.'

'I see Mr Depute. Well I certainly found these photographs rather gruesome and I don't suppose there is anything to be gained from … hmmm … let me hear what the defence has to say.'

'Mr McIntyre, I suppose you have again prepared a long list of European Court cases to put to me in support of your objection. How long? Might this take?'

The Greatest Living Advocate rose to his feet knowing he'd discussed the point with his client the night before. But now in the cold light of morning, he could feel the eyes of everyone behind him in the back of the court focusing on his next move: 'My Lord, having consulted with my client, Mr McLane, I am pleased to say that we have no objection to the Motion.'

Chapter 45

Fat Jackie switched off the TV in the Canteen and waved goodnight to the last of the day-shift lads before lumbering along the corridor to his locker. Checking over his shoulder, he lifted out a rucksack, slammed the door and checked his watch. Exactly 15 minutes before the Deputy Chief Constable was due back from his dinner up in Edinburgh Castle. Plenty of time.

Turning the corridor security camera onto the Station's only 'Rule 41 Suicide' that night, he padded along the cell block. A few grasping hands up to no good got a crack from his night stick.

By carefully massaging the times of arrest and processing at the station, cell No2 contained three prisoners, whilst No 3 opposite contained only one. Sliding the peeper and simultaneously unlocking the door, he quietly entered Cell No 3: 'Mr McLane, Sir. Are ye' awake?'

'Hmmm? ... What?'

'Sorry to wake yi' Sir. Ah've brought ye a wee drop o' the wife's chicken soup. An' her fresh bread. A few chocolate biscuits an' a few drams in a plastic bottle. But ye'll need to pish in the boattle in the moarnin' to mask the smell. A'right, Sir?'

McLane got up onto his elbow and shook Fat Jackie by the hand: 'Jackie. Are you sure this is not going to get you into any trouble?'

'Naw, Naw, ye'r a' right, Sir. She sends her best to ye. Oh by the way. She's been on the phone. *Your* wife, like. No' mine.'

That brought the first crack of a smile to McLane's face for days: 'I thought that Jackie. When was …'

'She wanted tae know if she could visit. But as you know Sir, its legal only at this …'

'That's alright Jackie. I know the rule.'

'Och Sir, Ah wazn'ae goin' to let *that* get in ma way. Ah've written the visit on a spare sheet an' slipped it intae the page. So nuthin's in the book, like. Ah'll put her doon as a legal visitor. Ah've used her maiden name, if that's a'right, Sir?'

'You're a star Jackie. An absolute star.'

'The only thing is, Ah couldn'i slip her in till Sunday moarnin'. We've got the Deputy Chief on this weekend. Daein' hiz 'Ah'm still wan o' the lads routine.' Ah've left the visit time blank an' Ah'll fill it in to suit ma'sel when she's left.'

Drinking the soup, McLane dribbled and scooped some off his chin.

'Wow Jackie. No kiddin' man, this soup's fantastic. But are you sure it's …'

'Don't worry aboot me Sir. There's hardly a soul in the station. Upstairs is empty, except for young Coutts. Ah know he's takin' the Sergeant's exams but he's surrounded himsel up there wi' tons o' papers; goin' back years. We've had an Advocates' Library van bringin' him stuff. Anywaey, … Jesus! Ah've just noticed yer hand Sir. Yi've been bleedin. Should a get yi' a doactor?'

'No. Jackie. I'm alright. It's just …'

'Whit happened? Ah mean, Ah put yi in here yersel' so nuthin' like this could … Whit happened?'

'Nothing Jackie. Really. I was a wee bit … you know, earlier. When the judge refused to continue my Bail over the weekend, I was … well, I got angry and I punched the wall. Hard. Twice.'

Chapter 46

'McLANE TRIAL: ADVOCATE STREETS AHEAD BUT BAIL WITHDRAWN' bawled the Sunday front page headlines. Photos of Duncan McIntyre Q.C. leaving the High Court, resplendent in frock coat and tilted hat vied with a shadowy figure snapped through the window of a moving prison van.

The back six pages brimmed with comment about Scotland's latest defeat at the hands of New Zealand in Murrayfield Rugby Stadium. The city's two big events on everyone's lips. Over Arthur's Seat Hill the heavy rain echoed Scotland's defeat. In The Old Town, both sides' supporters staggered up and down the Royal Mile; beer-soaked kilts and royal blue rugby jerseys signed and swapped, until next time.

All was quiet on the Eastern Front.

At just before 8 am. on the sleepy edge of the city, a well-dressed gentleman behind the wheel of a brand-new Bentley Continental pressed a button; automatically opening two tall iron gates. Purring through the leafy suburbs, it took him less than ten minutes to reach Morton House Private Hospital.

As the hospital's automatic gates closed behind the Bentley, no doorman ticked his list. No Receptionist signed him in. The only evidence of this morning's visit was the the sound of crunching gravel.

Waiting at the top of the driveway, a young man about 21 in a hand-made suit, checked his tie and pulled down his cuffs. As the Bentley came to rest he opened the driver's door.

'Good morning my Lord.'

'It's just Sir when I'm off the bench. You haven't begun to read law yet, I suppose.'

'No Sir. Next year.'

'Splendid. Do come and see me when you begin.'

'Thank you very much Sir. I most certainly will.'

Looking around, Lord Marchion checked that no buildings or windows overlooked this side of the hospital: 'How is your father? He's now the … Finance Director …Is that right?'

'Yes, My … Sir. He's Group European Financial Director. I think they have 37 hospitals now.'

'He was always good with numbers, your father. We knew each other in the Army, you know. And the

Lochies of course.'

'Yes, Sir. He has a photo of you together in uniform. In his study.'

'I hope coming out on a Sunday morning didn't put you to too much trouble. But I just needed to see the poor old ...'

'None at all, Sir. It's my pleasure. Just up these stairs I'm afraid, Sir.'

Pushing a door marked 'No Admittance – Strictly Emergency Exit Only' the young man stood aside: 'Sir Aubrey's private room is the only one on this floor, Sir. And I'll be locking the door behind us.'

'Splendid. I suppose you know about this ruthless attack, hmm? How is the poor old chap?'

Chapter 47

After the Saturday night crowds and busy traffic, as it had for centuries, solid and stately Morningside Parish Church began to wake from slumber. Awake to the sound of the faithful. Morningside night life belongs to the Belhaven Brewery but its Sunday mornings still belong to God Almighty.

Waiting in her mother's old car, Madam Fiscal - or plain Marjorie Millbank as she was in church - carefully eyed each passing parishioner. Waving once or twice, she fussed with her handbag when others passed. All through childhood there'd been Sunday School. Then Pathfinders, the Girls Guildry and the day she became 21, a warm welcome to the Thursday Prayer Group. Her whole life spent going through old oak doors to church.

But this morning, getting ready for church seemed a chore: Taking breakfast up to mother, then almost not leaving the house, picturing her father's pew, now occupied by that new Elder. Her father's prayers and advice were now long forgotten by church committees, but his Christian influence lingered on in his only daughter. Pacing the hallway, the dining room and the library, all attempts to push away thoughts of what her father might have said about all this failed. Just bearing up under the weary weight of preparation for the trial of Brogan McLane, Marjorie Millbank spiritually prepared herself for what was about to happen in Court 3 of Parliament House the following morning.

Wearing no make-up, a brown hat, plain tweed coat and beige court shoes, Madam Fiscal stepped out into the street. While locking the car, the first bells began: 10 minutes until the Minister's Procession. The Sunday School would already be in the front pews. Fidgeting with hymn sheets and giggling. Teachers would be telling off the usual troublesome ones. But no Millbank would be among them.

She just couldn't do it. Getting back into the old worn-out car, she clasped her hands, closed her eyes and began: *Our Father, who art in Heaven, Hallowed be thy name. Thy Kingdom come. Give us each day our daily bread and Forgive us our trespasses as we forgive those who trespass against us ...'*

Chapter 48

'Chicken soup, chocolate biscuits and *whisky*?'

'I know. He's a real star. Did you have to sign in?'

'No. He brought me in through the car park. I don't think anyone saw me.'

'Jo. I've been thinking. It's all I do in here. I *really* don't think you should ...'

'But Brogie, I can *do* it. I've been practising. Walking from the back bedroom to the living room. As though I've been called ...'

'Oh God. *No.* Jo, I thought you understood this. Look my darling. I know you can't think this through, you can only feel it. But remember what you've been told. I've told you and the lawyers have told you. If you give the slightest impression you've been coached or that you're lying, it'll be a disast ...'

'But Brogan. I *have* to. You know. I know. That night. Brogan, I may be the only person in the world who knows the truth ... If it all went ... I could never ...'

Taking her hands across the divide between his slab and her metal chair, Brogan squeezed her fingertips; the way they did when they made up: 'Jo. You're not getting this. If you gave evidence, and they *didn't* believe you ... Eh? What about that? You'd be thinking it was all your fault. I know you. You'd blame yourself for the rest of your ...'

'I *might*. But I don't care. Brogan I *have* to ...'

'No. Stop. Jo. You *would*. So you definitely shouldn't. In law, a wife can't be compelled to testify against her husband. I've seen wives *demolished* by ... God, even by mediocre counsel.'

'But Brogan, you're ... steamrollering me. You said you'd never do ...'

'But Jo, if you *don't* give evidence, then you can sit in court while I give mine. We'd be able to see each other. Jo, I need you to be in there with me. Not outside for two days in a witness holding room.'

'Well ... how would it work? I mean ...'

'It'll just be me, with the Jury looking between you and me, then Professor Neuberger to say it was that bastard Winstanley's lipstick on the champagne flute and that's it. That's how we get our incrimination in by the back door.'

'But what happens if ...'

'When the evidence is all over, it's time for the Jury speeches. We can rely on McIntyre to persuade the Jury that in a ... in a *very circumstantial* case ... with clear contrary evidence on our side ... that there's reasonable doubt of guilt and therefore they *must* acquit.'

'Oh Brogie, you make it sound so easy. What if you're …'

'Cm'ere. McIntyre's the best. If anyone can do it, he can.'

Squeezing his wife with all his strength, McLane didn't hear the peep-hole open. But recognising a woman in tears on her husband's shoulder, Fat Jackie shut it and waited a few minutes.

'That's her away, Sir. I've written the visit up the way I said. She's down as a legal. '

'Thanks Jackie. That was amazing of you. I *really* owe you. I mean, if I get out …'

'Oh you will Sir. Mr McIntyre is the best and anyway, you're an inno …Well, let's just hope, eh? Oh by the way, I wanted to show you this.'

Pulling a crumpled photocopy of a European Arrest Warrant from his back pocket, Jackie opened it, flattening it on the slab: 'There's nae known first name. But it was the last name and the nickname Ah recognised. Ma brother's a polis in Glasgow an' … well, everybuddy in the polis has heard Big Joe's nickname 'First Prize'. But a European Warrant? They must be awfy serious aboot nickin' him. They say he's been out of Glasgow since Sir Aubrey Winstanley was ... Ah've heard fae ma brother, aboot when you two were younger an' that ... Before you Called to the Bar in Parliament Hoose.'

'I've known him all my life Jackie. But I haven't seen him in ... oh ...'

'Ah've aye waanteed to know, Sir. How did he get that name? Ah mean, if ye' know.'

'Oh I do know Jackie. But this is for you and you alone.'

'Ye' can rely on me, Sir. No' a word tae oanybuddy.'

'Well, when we were young, in the East End, Glasgow I mean ... we were both card dealers. He'd been dealing for his father, Cloudy Mularkey since he was little more than a child.'

'Ah've heard the name 'Cloudy' but no' fur years ... How ...?'

'He was six feet seven. He and his wife had two sets of twins. He was some man. Well, on the older twins' 14th birthday Sean got slashed from ear to mouth on one side of his face in a knife-fight he couldn't possibly win. He might've died ... No, actually I'm sure he *would've* died if I ...'

'*You* were there, Sir?'

'Yeah. I was the dealer. If I hadn't jumped in.

'So you saved his twin brother's life, Sir?'

'I did Jackie. I saved Sean Mularkey's life. It was a crying shame. Sean's had to carry that scar his whole life; plus the name 'Second Prize'. It wasn't his fault. He was outnumbered and the guys were *much* older …'

'But if Sean was called Second Prize, how did Joe get the name First …?'

'Big Joe tracked every one of those guys down. Five of them. One by one. And every one now carries identical scars on *both* sides of their faces. And one's in a wheelchair.'

'My God. Ah've *seen* that guy. Scars on *both* sides an' in a wheelchair …'

'Right. That's why Joe's called First Prize.'

'Waow. So if he's left Glasgow, where do you think …?'

McLane gave Jackie that look reserved by fathers when a child asks the impossible: 'Jackie! Is there any more of that soup?'

The Trial

Chapter 49

Two heart attacks notwithstanding, Lord Marchion couldn't break the habits formed so long ago at boarding school in Perthshire. Breaking another slice of white bread to mop up the remains of three fried eggs, two black blood sausages, mushrooms, tomato and bacon, his lordship laid back.

'Can't sit on the bench on an empty stomach Jimmy. My father used to have a fry-up every morning, in this room.'

Pointing to the newly-installed television, his lordship dabbed his mouth. 'Oh I say, that's her!'

Joanne McLane's face remained stony as she pushed through the gaggle of Press and TV, resplendent in her scarlet coat and black boots.

'Yes m'lord. Would you like me to put the sound up?'

'Yes. Yes. What's the word Jimmy? Will she be giving evidence? I say, what fun if she does, eh?'

'I haven't heard yet m'lord. But I'll know as soon as I see which door she takes.'

Wiping his mouth, Lord Marchion kept a close eye on the screen: 'She's coming right up Jimmy. It's the public entrance. Look! Look!'

Turning on the top step, Joanne McLane swept her hair behind her ears and straightened her shoulders. The arc-lights brightened her strawberry blonde hair showing it at its best on television. But the same lights picked up lines across her forehead, which hadn't been there the last time. 'Mrs McLane. Mrs McLane. Will you be giving evidence today Mrs McLane?' 'Will you stand by your husband if he's convicted Mrs McLane?' 'Is he sticking to Alibi? Over here please Mrs McLane. This way please Mrs McLane.'

With all the dignity she could muster, Joanne McLane cleared her throat: 'My husband and I have every faith in Scottish justice. He's an innocent man and we're sure that will be established. Thank you.'

Lord Marchion wiped his mouth, letting out a snort into the remains of his tea: 'Oh feisty. Feisty. Well, let's get cracking Jimmy. Where's my wig? Work to do. Work I say.'

Around Parliament House the word was out. Today Duncan McIntyre Q.C. would open the case for the defence. Returning to wait in the cold, the line again three abreast, stretched even further than for the opening of the trial. In court 9, the packed polished-oak benches got so full the spectator on each end could only sit on one cheek.

'Cou-ou-rt'

Settled in his chair, Lord Marchion took a second, allowing the last Juror to drag her eyes away from that scarlet coat and look his way.

'Now, Advocate Depute. What say you?'

With red court tape still tied tightly around his bundles of papers, every face under a wig knew what was coming. 'My Lord, I now formally Close the Case for the Crown.'

'Thank you Advocate Depute. Now, Mr McIntyre, I don't imagine you have any …'

'Oh but I do my Lord. So once again, …'

'Oh dear, how tiresome. Well I suppose you are entitled … Ladies and gentlemen, I'm so sorry to have to say yet again, that a legal matter has arisen and you'll have to retire to … Well you know the routine by now. Thank you all.'

Well practised, the Jury filed out; and in under a minute the Press had their headline.

'My Lord, the Crown evidence having been completed, in my submission my client has No Case To Answer.'

'What? I had hoped you'd have more …'

'My Lord, it is quite normal for this …'

'But Mr McIntyre, you know as well as anyone that the legal test for a No Case To Answer motion is whether, *taken at its highest*, the Crown evidence is *incapable* of being interpreted by the Jury as demonstrating the guilt of the accused person.'

'I do, of course know that but …'

'Then where can you *possibly* be going with this motion Mr McIntyre? The Crown has led strong evidence of guilt, has it not? The motive, the punching of the walls and swearing in the cell to murder Lord Aldounhill. They don't need to prove opportunity any more, so isn't that enough to convict? Many a person has been convicted on less.'

'Of course they have. But my Lord the safeguard against wrongful conviction has always been that the trial judge should have regard to … my Lord there is another test. Not the numerical amount of evidence but the *quality* of the Crown evidence.'

Leaning heavily into his hand, Lord Marchion closed his eyes. 'Didn't that go out with the Ark, Mr McIntyre?'

'Oh no, my Lord. Far from it.'

'Well, of course defence counsel always used to say that.'

'If I could just begin my …'

'Look. Supposing you're correct and there is some remaining legal test of quality and not quantity. Isn't that a matter of discretion for me to judge?'

'It is my Lord and that is why I say …'

'Oh No! No. No. No. I'm afraid not Mr McIntyre. Your No-Case-To-Answer motion is denied. Now Macer, let's have the jury back in their places.'

Dropping his head, Duncan McIntyre flung his pen onto the desk, turned to McLane and shrugged his shoulders.

As the Jury filed back into their places, Joanne McLane's face told them that whatever had occurred in their absence, it wasn't good for the defence. 'Now, Mr McIntyre. Are you offering a defence?'

With obvious pride, McIntyre's voice rang in the rafters: 'Yes. I call the first witness for the defence, my client Brogan McLane.'

John Mayer

Chapter 50

Parliament House held its breath. Over the centuries its Advocates had suffered from the slings and arrows aimed by lesser men at those who dare stand tall and be of independent mind. Baron Erskine in the 18th century. The great John Inglis in the 19th. But never had the College of Justice in Scotland seated in dear old Parliament House seen anything like this.

Opening the Dock, Jimmy Robertson stood to attention in absolute silence as Mr Brogan McLane, Advocate of the Scottish Bar, rose from his seat, looked round at his wife and stepped up into the witness stand.

Lord Marchion looking straight past McLane as he raised his right hand, his ermine sleeve falling to reveal a tattoo from his army days.

'I Swear By Almighty God.' 'I Swear By Almighty God.'

'That the evidence I shall give.' 'That the evidence I shall give.'

'Shall be the truth. The whole truth' 'Shall be the truth. The whole truth''

'And nothing but the truth.' 'And nothing but the truth.'

'So help me God.' 'So help me God.'

376

All eyes locked on the sworn witness. With their pens gripped and poised, everyone in a wig got ready for battle to commence. A mere flicker of Lord Marchion's' eyes was McIntyre's permission to begin.

Leaning one hand gently on the Jury box, McIntyre paused, then rang the rafters: 'Brogan McLane, I have but one question for you: Did you kill Lord Aldounhill?'

Gripping the witness stand with both hands, McLane resounded: '**No**. I did **not**.'

With a solemn nod of thanks to his client, McIntyre turned to the Advocate Depute.

'Your witness.'

~~~**0**~~~

Chapter 51

Jumping to his feet and pointing straight across the court at Brogan McLane the Advocate Depute shouted: 'Liar.'

Slamming his fist into the desk, McIntyre too jumped to his feet: 'Objection!'

Lord Marchion let out a long breath. His enquiry was the height of politeness: 'Yes Mr McIntyre? Is there something amiss?'

'That wasn't a question. That's what's amiss. It was a bald, unsupported statement. He knows perfectly well he's required by law to keep strictly to questioning and not shout insults at the witness.'

'Over-ruled Mr McIntyre. It was an implied question. Do continue Mr Depute.'

Reaching for his pre-prepared list of questions, the Advocate Depute sensed he was already on thin ice. Should the case ever see the inside of the Criminal Appeal Court just along the corridor in court 3, he'd need an explanation. Dropping the list back onto the table, he took time to think. Several jurors tapped their pencils. One picked his fingernail and another caught his first glimpse down the blouse of the woman sitting next to him.

'Mr McLane how do you explain the evidence against you? Have you got anything to say about the threat

378

you made against Lord Aldounhill?'

'I haven't really. I've never seen such a spurious case against anyone in all my …'

Lord Marchion narrowed his eyes, taking pains not to sound angry on the recording that might one day see the inside of the Appeal Court along the corridor: 'Mr McLane! Surely I do not need to remind you that you are not the Advocate in this case; you're the accused. Now answer the question.'

McLane feigned a bow which gave him a few seconds to gather his thoughts: 'I'm sorry my lord. My answer is that I've never been in Lord Aldounhill's house and there's no evidence that I have been. I've never met him socially and there's no evidence that I have. I didn't kill him and despite the lack of ... I was at home with my wife when you, sorry, when Professor Suilleman says he was killed.'

Half leaning and half sitting on the back of his chair the Advocate Depute relaxed. 'Well so you say. But I take it you don't deny making the threat to kill him?'

'I most certainly do deny it. When he sent me to a cell for doing my job in court - while he *and you* were passing notes to each other - I was furious. Of course I was. Any counsel worthy of the name would've been. So that rules you out!'

Lord Marchion jumped in to the rescue: 'Mr McIntyre you really must *not* make personal remarks about the learned Advocate Depute. He is a public servant and you are on Oath. Now, do you understand me?'

'Of course. I apologise to the Jury for giving irrelevant evidence. It won't happen again, my Lord.'

Quietly now, more assured of his success, the Depute persisted: 'Well, Mr McLane, do you have an answer?'

'No I don't. Because you don't have a case for me to answer. If this wasn't so serious it would be pathetic.'

'Please answer the ...'

'Oh give it up! You had to *push* Professor Suilleman to say there even *was* a murder. Her first report was equivocal ...'

'That's not an answer to my question Mr ...'

'Ah shut it. It took his lordship here to rescue you. It took *seven* questions before she ...'

'Mr McLane! Please! You're on very thin ice.' barked Lord Marchion.

'Before she'd say that the angle of cutting the Carotid artery *suggested* murder rather than suicide or accident.'

'Well, suddenly you're an expert in everything.'

'No. Just that your case fell apart several days ago and you know it!'

'That's quite enough, Mr McLane. The learned Advocate Depute is quite properly … you will answer his questions as becomes a Member of Faculty. Or I will …'

'I apologise my Lord. The stress has been … It's been …'

'Yes. I do understand stress you know. Now. Do continue Mr Depute.'

'Mr McLane, we've heard about the partial motorcycle boot print. You ride a motorcycle, don't you? And the description of the motorcyclist with the false plates going from Glasgow to Edinburgh and back fits the timing of death and your physical description. Correct?'

McLane began to feel the old rush he got when racing over solid ground after his prey: 'Nope. None of it. Prove it. Go on. Prove it was me and I'll accept it. Go on.'

'You left your boot print in Lord Aldounhill's garden. Didn't you?'

'Again. Do I actually have to remind a Deputy of the Lord Advocate? This *is* a court of law. Prove it. Go ahead. Prove it.'

The Advocate Depute had nothing else and

resorted to the last kick of a tired ball: 'You killed him out of twisted revenge for holding you in contempt of court. Didn't you? Admit it. Didn't you?'

'That's ridiculous! I admit nothing of the kind. Again, I say. Prove it. You *can't.*'

'You've … You've heard all the scientific evidence against you. How do you explain the …'

McLane positively smirked towards the jury: 'Oh give it a rest. Yes. I heard it. Such as it was. So did the jury. Professor Suilleman's final position became - after his lordship pushed her - that she didn't think a person could insert such a thing as a champagne flute at that angle and depth into their own neck. So what? That only rules out accident. But it takes you nowhere against me and you *know* it.'

The rest of the day deteriorated into the Depute singing his old song: 'Oh yes you did.' and McLane calmly replying 'Oh no I didn't'.

Some of the jury doodled on their clipboard sheets. Some listened to the busking piper out on the Royal Mile and the juror in the front row concentrated on the view deep down that stretched white blouse; but none wrote down any of the evidence elucidated by the learned Advocate Depute.

Chapter 52

Sitting together in the dreary witness room, Professor Sir Isaac Neuberger and Professor Nadia Suilleman tap-tap-tapped their respective files and tried studiously to avoid each other's gaze.

Looking again at his watch, it was Neuberger who spoke first.

'You'd think that since there's been criminal trials since at least Egyptian times, they'd find a better way to take our evidence than this; what?'

Nodding, Professor Suilleman agreed. 'I suppose so. They must know what they're …'

'Must? Must? There's no Must about it. Dithering on all day. We both have better things to be getting on … My Lab assistant says they're more interested in what looks good on television. My white hair. Your sallow skin. 30-second interviews. Silliness. Silliness I say!'

The loud click of a big brass door handle turning, spun him around.

'Professor Neuberger?'

'The same. And you are?'

383

'Robertson. Queen's Macer. We're ready for you now, Sir. Please follow me.'

Standing tall, the Professor pulled down his red waistcoat, buttoned his tweed jacket and bowed in thanks; the way he did to servitors the world over.

In the witness box, providing the court with his qualifications and expertise, he flung his head this way and that, recalling the dates of his two Doctoral Degrees, his many Fellowships, how many Honorary Doctorates he'd been given and the names of certain eminent scientists whom he'd taught: all the while his white hair swirling like clouds around his head.

With his folder perched on the tiny ledge of the witness stand, he opened it and slipped on his glasses. McIntyre ran through Exhibit numbers and dates of compilation. When just about to ask the Professor to turn to the detail of his Report, the Depute floated to his feet. Looking over his glasses, Lord Marchion was the very essence of politeness.

'One moment please Professor. A legal matter seems to have arisen.'

'Ah Legal. Yes my Lord. Should I leave the stand my Lord?'

'No please remain for the moment. I'll hear the Advocate Depute.'

'Now, Mr Depute. Are you objecting to something?'

'I may well be my Lord. But I shall need to make a few enquiries before finalising my position. If I may?'

Shaking his head more for the benefit of the Jury than his client, McIntyre sat down.

'Yes, Mr Depute. Please continue.'

'Excuse me Professor Neuberger, but what is that you have in front of you?'

'It's a copy of my Report on this case. The DNA in the lipstick. My methodology. It's ...'

Raising his hand politely Lord Marchion interrupted: 'Professor, I am so sorry but I think I know what's coming ...'

'If you're worried about it being a copy, the original disappeared mysteriously from my ...'

'Please Professor. Say no more until I've ruled ...'

'But I assure you, this is an *exact* copy of ...'

Staring the good professor down, Lord Marchion

raised his hand: 'Professor please! I'm sorry but having only proceeded so very little with your evidence, I shall have to ask you to return to the witness room for a moment. I am so terribly sorry about this.'

As he left, to the amusement of the jury, the Professor swirled his clouds once more as he followed Jimmy Robertson.

Lord Marchion apologised to the jury: 'And ladies and gentlemen, you too I'm afraid. So sorry once more.'

The press had their pencils ready to fill fresh pages. But Lord Marchion had other ideas: 'Macer, please open the doors. For the avoidance of doubt, because the reputation of an eminent scientist may possibly come into question, I am ruling that, in the public interest, these legal submissions will be heard *in camera*. Clear the court.'

Pushing back his chair, McIntyre got ready.

'Now, Mr Depute, what is your objection to the evidence from this witness?'

'My Lord, my objection comes in two parts. The first is that the Professor's report seems not to be original - a 'copy' he said - and that accordingly violates our 'best evidence rule'. Put another way, my Lord, the witness must use the best source for his evidence. Not the second or third best. My second point is that if this evidence is designed to put in the minds of the jury that someone other than the accused in the Dock murdered Lord Aldounhill, then it can have no bearing on the case. Your Lordship has ruled, and emphatically if I may say so, that the defence of Incrimination of Another is irrelevant because the defence cannot produce that person to speak in court.'

'Thank you Mr Depute. I see your objection clearly. Now Mr McIntyre, what do you have to say in reply?'

McIntyre opened with the eyes of his client burrowing into the back of his head: 'I would open by saying that the Depute must have x-ray vision because he seems to know what's in the Professor's report without the Professor saying a word in evidence about it. I can only wonder at how that situation arose. Also, this is scientific evidence. I've called this expert witness to explain two things to the Jury. Firstly, *how* he extracted certain DNA from the lipstick on the champagne flute and, Secondly, that the only DNA he found in it did *not* belong to Brogan McLane. He can do that, with, or without, holding a report in his hands. He could give evidence from memory, if need be.'

'Hmmm. Difficult. I don't know. I think in all fairness to you and Mr McLane, I'll retire to consider this. Thank you gentlemen.'

'Cou-ou-rt.'

After kicking off his buckled shoes and hanging up his wig, Lord Marchion picked up the morning edition of the London Times and got comfortable in his club chair: 'Mr Robertson. Is Lord Glen-Chivas in Parliament House at the moment?'

'Yes m'lord. Sitting in court 5, this morning. A bankruptcy Hearing I think.'

'Good. Get word to him please. Adjourn his case. I need a word. In here.'

'Lord Glen-Chivas, m'lord'

'Thank you Jimmy. Show him in. We'll bolt the door from this side.'

Still in wig and gown, Lord Glen-Chivas gave Jimmy a broad smile as he entered the chambers of a boyhood friend and fellow Lochie: 'Trouble old boy?'

'Not exactly. Just a tactical problem.'

Chivvie helped himself to whisky: 'Ah. How to avoid the Appeal Court. Correct? What's McIntyre's position?'

Setting out the legal submissions, Lord Marchion poured himself tea and offered shortbread: 'So Chivie. What do you think?'

'Well, old boy, my trick is always to find an absolute. Something favouring the Depute that's unshakeably correct. Start there old boy. What've we got?'

'Well, McIntyre has made a solid point, but I think the Depute hit the nail on the head with the first part of his objection. If the Neuberger report is 'second hand' as it seems to be, then ...'

'Oh. And it is. Didn't you tell me at lunch yesterday that there's absolutely no doubt that whatever he's brought to court, it can't be the original.'

'Quite. Excellent work, eh? My nephew did well there. Now, I can rule the second-hand report to be inadmissible. But where does that take me?'

'Well, if this batty Professor is allowed to give *any* evidence for the defence, he'll be thrown back on his recollections.'

'Yes. And when that happens, the Depute can object on the grounds that the evidence being given is not truly expert evidence at all. It's unreliable and can't be cross-examined because it's all over the place. Perhaps even guesswork.'

'Precisely old boy.'

'So the Jury hears nothing about any canals, lipstick, Aubrey's DNA. None of it.'

'No. And all you've done is keep second-hand evidence from being given. The law is squarely with you there, old boy. So McIntyre would get nowhere in the Appeal Court. Quite elegant really, wouldn't you say? But what will you tell the jury? When they don't see the Professor return.'

'Tell? The jury? Bugger them.'

The Trial

Chapter 53

Old Jimmy Robertson hovered in the morning light beneath the South Window in Parliament Hall, keeping an eye on the front door; hoping the media would keep to their usual routine - pictures of Joanne walking down the Royal Mile and Brogan stepping out of a prison wagon.

The folded pink slip in his hand bore the signature of the Principal Clerk of Justiciary. It had come down with a pinned copy of an Interlocutor of their Lordships. But the Lords who'd signed this interlocutor weren't those in Parliament House. This missive had come from Her Majesty's Privy Council sitting in Number 1 Downing Street in London.

Hoping the news hadn't leaked out of Parliament House was like hoping the morning tide wouldn't rise. But for the sake of that poor woman coming through the doors into Parliament Hall and her husband, Jimmy hoped nonetheless.

As she passed under the clock in the box corridor on her way round to Court 9, Joanne McLane kept her head down, only acknowledging the occasional 'Hello' or 'Keep your chin up' from passing Advocates.

Sitting alone in the Dock, McLane looked a very

sorry figure. Taking a chance with procedure, Jimmy Robertson approached the prisoner, the pink slip still in his hand. Checking for the third time that no-one in a wig was close by, old Jimmy leaned in: 'Sir. I'm sorry but there's been a bit of a development. I'm sorry to be the one to bring this to you.'

As he spoke the calm expression on McLane's face told Jimmy that somehow the prisoner must have heard the news which he himself received only that morning: 'You're a good man Jimmy, but it's alright. I've known about this since last night.'

'I don't think it was scheduled, Sir. I'm sure Mr McIntyre had no choice in the matter.'

'I *know* he didn't. It's OK Jimmy. It's a blow, but I'm ready. You can tell Lord Marchion I won't be whining to stop the trial.'

As the jurors filed into their places, they noticed. Having watched these actors on the High Court stage for over a week, it was immediately obvious that one of the leading players in the case of Her Majesty's Advocate against Brogan McLane was missing.

With everything to his satisfaction on the bench, Lord Marchion turned to address them: 'Good morning ladies and gentlemen. Now you will have noticed that Mr

McIntyre and his team are no longer with us. That is because they have been required by law to address a higher court in London. It's a rare occurrence but this kind of thing can happen. Now, in these unusual circumstances my immediate inclination is, in all fairness to Mr McLane, to halt the trial. But he has intimated through channels to me that he doesn't wish me to do that. He will go on by representing himself. Further, ladies and gentlemen, he has indicated that he wishes to call no further witnesses. That means the part of the trial in which you hear evidence is over and it is now time for you to hear closing speeches before taking my directions in law and reaching your verdict. The Advocate Depute will address you first so that, in all fairness, the closing words you hear will be those of Mr McLane.'

'Mr Depute. In your own time.'

With a deep bow, the Depute rose to make the traditionally short prosecution speech.

"Ladies and gentlemen, the Crown brings this prosecution purely in the public interest. And in a murder trial the public interest demands that there be no distractions from that charge.

Accordingly, ladies and gentlemen, I invite you to take your red pens through the minor charges leaving only the charge of murder. The burden of proof is on the Crown and it remains on the Crown throughout any criminal trial. Well, with one exception. That arises where the Crown puts some evidence before the jury which in pointing to the guilt of the accused is so compelling that it naturally calls for an equally compelling rebuttal. We have a technical name for such a thing, but I hope you see what I mean without further explanation.

Now, ladies and gentlemen, you heard Professor Suilleman testify that the breakage of the champagne flute was at the correct angle for the glass to be a murder weapon. Well, let me correct that. When pressed, she said it was probably *the* murder weapon. Why? Because the chances of any other thing being an identical match were too remote. She showed you photographs of the cut in the Carotid artery, the circular bruising on Lord Aldounhill's neck which gave her a diameter and entry point of the weapon. It all fitted with *that* glass being the murder weapon. And, then there was the partial boot-print. You may have noticed at the time, but I am entitled to mention it now, that Mr McIntyre - very properly I may say - did not try to contradict the evidence that his client, Mr McLane, does or did once, ride such a vehicle and would own boots which would make a print like this. Added to that, there was the video evidence of the motorcyclist with false plates riding to Edinburgh before the time of death of Lord Aldounhill and back again after the time of death. As I say, Mr McLane rides - or has ridden - such a thing. Ladies and gentlemen, *none* of that has been rebutted. Absolutely *none* of it. So, I hope that you can begin to piece together the outline of a circle. Indeed, a circle around Mr McLane.

Then there's Mr McLane's motive. Other people will of course live near Mr McLane and some of them will have motorcycles and the required garments. But that's where they can be eliminated. Only Mr McLane had history with Lord Aldounhill. Mr McLane didn't deny that. You might call it 'bad blood'.

Now. Mr McIntyre did his professional job by blaming the court typist who hadn't recorded something she had no duty to record. Obviously a desperate attempt to deflect attention, was it not? It's of no importance in this case that Mr McLane's fingerprints were not found in Lord Aldounhill's house. Criminals are often clever. They cover their cowardly tracks and this case is no exception. There was *no* other evidence, far less *compelling* evidence, that the crime was committed by someone else. Nothing to connect the crime with anyone else. No DNA or other -

well I hesitate to call it - 'fancy evidence'.

No, ladies and gentlemen, this is a simple case. A very important and socially disturbing one, but surely simple enough to decide. The standard of proof to convict is the well-known one – "beyond reasonable doubt". Ladies and gentlemen, there is *no* reason to doubt the Crown evidence. Accordingly, it is your *duty* to convict. You should not be swayed by emotion or feelings of sympathy for anyone, even Mrs McLane who, I noticed, sat in court catching everyone's eye.

Her beauty or her wardrobe are none of your concern. Your sworn duty is to weigh the evidence and only the evidence. And if the evidence points to guilt, as I say it clearly does, then you *must* convict. Ladies and gentlemen, this case has been a trying time for all of us. But with your guilty verdict, it will soon be over. And with that, ladies and gentlemen, I bid you good day."

Bowing before the Jury, before retaking his seat, the Advocate Depute glanced at Joanne McLane. His clever reference had done just enough to mock her only purpose; to support her husband to the end.

The Trial

Chapter 54

Lord Marchion seemed to take more time than usual to ensure his water glass was full and his pencils were properly arranged. It was an old move and one that was completely unchallengeable; letting the Crown speech sink in to the minds of the jury. Turning with a modest smile towards the jury, he'd become almost grandfatherly in his care to see justice done.

'Thank you Mr Depute. Now, Mr McLane, do you wish to make a speech to the Jury, or are you happy for your case to speak for itself?'

Snapping to his feet, McLane announced: 'Of course I do. I've been sitting waiting here for ... Sorry my Lord. Yes.'

'Very well. Ladies and gentlemen, prisoners are not usually allowed to approach you. Anything they say is usually said from the Dock. But this is a special case and I have no reason to suspect that you are in any danger. So in all fairness, I have allowed Mr McLane to approach you.'

'Mr McLane. In your own time.'

Mouthing thanks to Jimmy Robertson for opening the Dock, taking those ten steps towards the jury, McLane passed into a zone. The nerves and doubts of the night before dropped to the floor, trampled by the fearless

Advocate within. All his best moves charged back to his mind on winged horses: What moved juries to convict? Lies and Sleight of Hand. What compelled them to acquit? Honesty and bravery in defence.

'Build Brogan. Build your speech. Build it so strong and so high they can't convict. Now, son of Agnes McLane, go to work.'

Taking a deep bow, McLane stood tall and straight resting both hands on the rail in front of the jury box. Absolute silence reigned in court 9 as the wigless Mr McLane, Advocate, looked every juror in turn straight in the eyes.

"Ladies and Gentlemen, it is now my great privilege to address you directly. I say privilege because in these courts until 1893, the defence wasn't allowed to say anything. That's right, nothing at all. Murder trials, like this one, took an hour or so to complete. There was no such thing as a defence speech because there was no such thing as a defence. It was only after pressure from other European justice systems that we in Scotland changed our criminal law to allow the defence to speak. We were shamed into allowing a defence. That may, here in the 21st century, strike you as grossly unfair. But it's true. These days we have the European Convention on Human Rights which is there to protect us – yes, you and me – from the tyranny of unfairness imposed by the state. But ladies and gentlemen, I can assure you, that around this old High Court, that Convention is thought to be like the Chinese Emperors of old; 'omnipotent but far away'.

I want now to remind you of the most important thing in this trial. I see you're all keen to hear what I think that might be. Well, actually it's not what I think it is that makes it important. It's the Oath you took at the beginning of this trial. Whilst the surroundings were new to you and you were just getting used to the idea of being chosen for the jury, you were asked to say something you may only have said once before in your life. Those words were in response to the clerk of court reading the oath to you and asking if you would respond with the words 'I do.' which I noticed you all did.

Ladies and gentlemen, you - and only you - are the judges of the facts of this case. Yes, I said 'judges'. Every one of you. But although your ordinary task is judicial, your ultimate task is ethical.

I am pleading with you now to bear something in mind as you deliberate on my client's … sorry, of course I mean *my* case: it's not only power that corrupts. Weakness corrupts too. Weak people become cynical and see no point in engaging with the powerful. This leads to two separate ways of life; an 'us and them' society. Two sets of standards. We can't have that in the Scottish High Court. No. What I ask you for is neutrality. In reaching your verdict, you must do the *right* thing, not just the expected thing.

If you are not true to that oath, we may as well demolish these magnificent courts. Tear down these ornate plaster ceilings and carry away the stones; one by one.'

Some lifted their eyes to the details of angels in the plaster. Others drew deep breaths at the idea of justice being torn down. One woman wrung her hands, perhaps showing that someone close to her had passed this way before. McLane was beginning to spin his web and it was working. It always did. Gripping the bar of the jury box, he continued:

'It is your integrity that keeps these tall stone walls up, keeps the glass in the windows and the winds of tyranny from blowing through. Your personal integrity is far more important than the mere fabric of Parliament House. You give *vital* meaning to the billions of words printed in the law books in the Advocates' Library and *you* give reassurance to the public who rely on you to be fair to their sons and daughters, husbands and wives, friends and enemies – yes enemies – who come through these doors for one purpose and one alone. That purpose is Justice.'

Leaning over the rail, in a stage whisper, McLane emphasised his point.

'Ladies and gentlemen, if it cannot be said that everyone - absolutely everyone - who comes through these courts gets a fair trial, then no-one in our ancient and dearly loved little country can hold their head up high when they say that only the guilty are punished by the power of the law.'

The motherly white haired woman who throughout the evidence made copious notes, dabbed her eye.

'Now within your oath there are several elements. Firstly, there's you. You the person. Then there's truth. That's an absolute and cannot be varied according to preference or prejudice. Truth is truth. Then there's God. Well, we don't ask if you believe in God, so you can substitute the words 'my own conscience' for God. We ask that you be true to yourself and all that you hold dear. Then we ask you to deliver a verdict. Not to waste your time and ours, but to deliberate upon the evidence and deliver. There is no time limit on your deliberations but I would give you this caveat as we near the end of the trial – if you are arguing and debating, then there *must* be doubt.

If there is doubt then the law demands that you give the man on trial – me – the benefit of that doubt. Ladies and gentlemen, what it comes to is this; when you are sitting in the Dock on trial before his Lordship, what represents justice is not the grandeur of this old court, not his Lordship's finery nor the Depute's privileged position. It's you!

Nodding along with him, McLane had no doubt that his Jury understood the point.

'Now ladies and gentlemen, I want to turn to the charge. The only charge left for your verdict is that of murder. The wilful taking of another person's life. Note, the wilful taking. Not accidental or unintentional, but willing. Ladies and gentlemen, my first serious question to you is 'where is the evidence of my willingly taking the life of Lord Aldounhill? Where?

Can you really accept that some professional incident about a case, just one of many around Parliament House, so long in the past is a motive for murder? Of course not. That is a leap too far. So I say this to you; You have no starting point in this case. Without a motive, you have to ask – Why would this man, a man of good character, an Advocate, a married man – why would he murder a judge? You may well ask, but the evidence you've heard provides no answer.'

Noting his well-made point, several of the Jury looked him in the eyes, nodding their agreement.

'Now I wish to turn to the evidence of the boot-print. The *partial* print. Do you doubt that evidence? *Why* was more of the print not produced in court? Answer: 'It fell apart'. Well, without it, you cannot be sure that on the rest of the print, wherever it may be, there weren't *non*-matches demonstrating with certainty that, although there are these 'points of reference' in one part of the print, the remaining 'points of reference' clearly point to the *whole* print as belonging to someone else? Did you get the truth, the whole truth and nothing but the truth in that chapter of the evidence? Of course you didn't.

Ladies and gentlemen, I was cross examined at very long length. If you accept my evidence that, at the time Lord Aldounhill died, I was at home with my wife then that is the end of the case. The end. You would be *bound* to deliver a verdict of Not Guilty.

Now ladies and gentlemen, this was not a public inquiry. That may strike you as odd, even wrong, but these proceedings were not designed to inquire into and discover the truth. In fact, this is no kind of inquiry. What you have sat through is a trial. An adversarial trial on the Crown evidence as to whether they have proved beyond reasonable doubt that at the time and place stated in the only remaining charge, I murdered Lord Aldounhill.

Now, we are in the field of human affairs where no system is or can be perfect. Accordingly no-one expects 100% perfection. Not from the court, not from the prosecutor and not from you. But the test for conviction in this court is nevertheless very high. Let me give you an example. Imagine you were not trying me but were about to buy a house, or thinking about marriage, or divorce or planning to have children. Possibly beginning a business or investing in a company with all your savings. Something in your own lives that is of the utmost importance to your future. Then ask yourself, *on the evidence in this case*, would you buy the house, start the business or invest your whole life's savings? *Your whole future?* On this evidence? Or do you have a doubt about some aspect, maybe more than one aspect, of the Crown evidence? If you hesitate to answer that question then the Crown case against me fails the test of getting beyond reasonable doubt. In that event you *must* acquit by returning a verdict of Not Guilty.

Now lastly, ladies and gentlemen, I want to reflect on some history before making an extremely important point. Scottish Law is based on Roman Law. The ancient Romans had a phrase which still resounds today, particularly here in Parliament House. That phrase is 'Corruptio optimi pessima'. It means that corruption of the best is the worst that can happen. You may recall ladies and gentlemen, that phrase was the spark which lit Vaclev Havel's revolution against those living in what he called a 'contaminated environment'. Whoever else may be living that way, I will have none of it. There should be no contamination in Parliament House!

That brings me to another great historical figure. An American. When I mention the phrase 'A House Divided Against Itself Will Not Stand' you will know that I mean none other than Abraham Lincoln.

I mention his famous phrase for I have one last request to make of you. It's an extremely rare, if not unique request.

I want nothing less than a *unanimous* verdict from you. One way or the other. No compromises. Only if you **all** believe the Crown has failed in this shambolic prosecution will I accept your verdict of Not Guilty. In other words, I will accept no less than a unanimous acquittal.

Ladies and gentlemen, there is only one sentence

allowed by law for those convicted of murder: Life imprisonment. I now rest my life - and that of my wife - in your hands.'

Chapter 55

Shifting awkwardly on his six-feet-long concrete slab bed, his belt and shoes removed, Brogan McLane stared straight ahead at the heavy grey-green steel door of Holding Cell No10 in the sub-basement of Parliament House.

From down the cold stone corridor came the clink of iron keys hitting steel. Then the walls resounded to the slamming of a heavy door. With each sound of jailers' keys in old locks, people called by numbers and the smells of human waste, fresh and stale, one question ran around and around in the mind of Brogan McLane: Is this your life now?

Standing up. Sitting down. Biting his lip. Turning round. Turning in the tiny cell. Clenching his fist and wanting with all his heart to punch the wall, his voice almost inaudible, even to himself, regret oozed out of every pore. *'Hhmmm. Big man in court there Brogan. Yeahhhh. Big Advocate. Unanimous verdict. One for the books was that. Oh yeah! They'll be talking about that in the dining rooms and university halls for a long time. Oh yeah. Big man. Big mistake.'*

Leaning his forehead onto the painted walls, his

mind teased and tortured him. *'What more could've been done? What else could Big Joe Mularkey do? The lawyers? And Jo. God in high heaven. Jo.'*

Reaching his arms over his head, McLane pulled his hair: *'I've told her. I've eaten plenty of shit in my life. But not her. Move on. That's the trick. I can do this. But you, move on. Begin to get yourself into a place where you can move on. A life punctuated by prison visits? No. Don't do that. To be alive and yet never to hold each other again. Jesus God in Heaven. Help me.'*

He didn't hear the footsteps but he heard the squeak of the heavy door hinges. Turning, he feared the worst: The Verdict. Already?

But leaning only half way in, the screw seemed too relaxed.

'Visitor for you Mr McLane.'

'Eh? Me? But my jury's out, so … nobody can …The Scottish Prisoners Act says that until there's a verdict, I must be kept in solitary ...'

Behind the turnkey, a voice in the corridor finished his quote: 'With one exception. You *can* be visited by police officers on duty.'

Looking out past the screw, there stood

the familiar figure of Commander Terry Imrie:
'Hello Brogan.'

Flashing his eyes at a rank he so rarely saw, the turnkey was unsure what to do: 'Sir. Do you want me to …?'

'Thanks, there's no need. Lock me in. I'll be fine. I'll give you a knock.'

Imrie said nothing until they both heard the slam of the steel door at the end of the corridor. Both men looked right at each other.

'Terry. Man. You shouldn't *be* here. Christ man. You could get into all *sorts* … I mean, right now I'm legally radioactive, so I have to ask: *Why* are you here?'

'Don't you worry about me. This visit isn't officially happening. I want to ask you a few questions. Is that alright?'

'Ha! A few questions? You're a bit late for that. Are you not?'

'Yeah. Maybe.'

Imrie perched himself on the slab beside McLane and looked him in the eye. Then he put out his hand; but McLane hesitated: 'Brogan. Man. Take my hand. Trust me. I haven't closed this investigation. Not by a long way. I said from the start I didn't think you did this murder. And I still believe that. Now, will you answer me a few things?'

Heaving a sigh, McLane couldn't see the point. Looking apologetically at Imrie, McLane took his hand. Gripping each other, their old trust remained.

'Aye, OK. What?'

'This partial boot-print. It's bothering me. There's something not right about that.'

'You're telling me! That's *the* most circumstantial evidence I've ... '

'I know Brogan. I was on my way here, just this morning, when my young uniform - Coutts - approached me in the corridor. Just out of camera range. So I figured that whatever it was, it was to be on the hush-hush. And it was.'

'It's too late for that ...'

'Hold on. Now, I need a straight answer. I've seen you – not for a while now – true enough - on your big ... what is it? A Honda something. In the boots and all the leather gear.'

'It's a Pan European. 1100 cc of superb Japanese engineering. Everybody's seen me on it.'

'Brogan man. I need a straight answer, and quick. Have you *ever* been to Aldounhill's house? Ever?'

Stunned by this late question, McLane got up

paced the tiny cell. '*What was the point of the question?*'

But Imrie persisted. 'What about after Faculty dinners in Parliament Hall? Years ago maybe.'

Turning slowly, not wanting to get ahead of this, McLane looked at Imrie: 'No. No way Terry. No way under the sun. Impossible. What's all this about?'

'Good. I'm glad. You see, when we got that boot print, it came in as a Field Report. Useless in court. We all know that. But that and the traffic video and the so-called motive. I agree - it's the most circumstantial case imaginable. It would never get past even the most dopey Crown Counsel. So how did it end up becoming central in your trial?'

'Ha! I wish I knew.

'Me too. So I've been - well not me, but young Coutts has been digging around.'

'Are you telling me …?'

'*All* I'm telling you at the moment is I have phoned the PF's office … that lassie Sheila McManus, for an explanation about how a Field Report came to be an Exhibit in the High Court and I got a stone wall 10 feet high. Three times in the last two hours. So, as far as I'm concerned, the jury might be out, but this investigation is far from over. Good luck Brogan.'

After shaking hands as firmly as he ever had, Commander Imrie kicked the steel door.

On his way out, he saw no-one. He signed nothing and no camera recorded the visit. Vaulting the stairs two at a time, Imrie quietly opened the side corridor door leading through to Parliament Hall. Standing quietly at the end of the corridor, Jimmy Robertson gave a nod. On his way past their eyes met but nothing was said. Only very occasionally can anything happen in Parliament House which is done in absolute secrecy.

As both men saluted each other, each knew that this was one of those times.

Chapter 56

Snapping down the handle of the Squad Room door, 'A' Division's Duty Sergeant always enjoyed these occasions. In full dress uniform he stepped up onto the podium, a large manila envelope in his hand. Proudly casting his eyes over the whole shift, he broke the seal and opened it.

'Four officers from 'A' Division took this year's Sergeant's Examinations in Police Procedures and Practice, Legal Knowledge and the new one, Human Rights Procedures. I am pleased to say that ... three of you passed.'

Half-hearted, muted applause recognised the disappointment of one hard-working colleague who'd have to wait another year. But which one?

'Dear God, some of you will *never* make detective. I said three passed because they did. But you, Coutts, *you* passed with Distinction. Top of the Year. 'A' Division does it again. Get up here Sergeant Coutts.'

Jumping to their feet, whooping and skirling, bloody mayhem burst through the windows and walls. Whistling and yelling, the whole squad applauded as Sergeant Coutts accepted his stripes and held them high.

Commander Imrie shook his hand and leaned in to his new Sergeant's ear: 'Brilliant Coutts. Well done. Did you get anywhere?'

'Yeeeaaahhh! Thanks guys … woah, Ya Beauty! Sorry Sir. What was that?'

'Did you get …? Never mind. My office, ten minutes. Sorry to spoil the party, but …'

'Oh no Sir. I know. Ten minutes. Your office. Yes, Sir.'

The noise of the celebrations below merely dimmed as Sgt Coutts closed Imrie's door.

'Come in Coutts. Come in. I got wind of the results yesterday. I thought you'd like to have this.'

On the desk, a gift wrapped present, about the size of a shoebox, bore a tag: Sergeant Graeme Coutts, Edinburgh 'A' Division Police HQ.

'For me? Thank you, Sir. Thanks a lot.'

Tearing open the paper, inside Coutts could see brass. Bright shining brass. Lifting out his present, he held a pair of First World War binoculars.

'Ehm, thanks Sir. I don't often use binoculars but …'

'They're not for using. They were given to me by my Chief Inspector when I made Sergeant. They're for sitting on your desk: reminding you that the best police work is done taking the long view.'

'Thank you very much Sir. I'll treasure …'

'There's no need. You've earned them. Just keep in mind what they tell you. Now, for the last few nights, you've had van loads of boxes sent round from Parliament House and I see you're eating into my budget like a beaver through a log. So, what did I get for my money?'

'Oh, yes Sir. Sorry but I had to use your name to get the stuff from Parliament House … and I'm afraid I had to use most of the squad budget for all the Admin. But I think it's been …'

'Oh Christ. Thinking like a senior officer already. Just tell me man. How did you get on?'

'Oh, quite well, I think Sir. I was watching the DVD from Lord Aldounhill's desk when I drifted away from what was happening on the screen onto those Aldounhill would have trusted being in his house. That gave me an idea.'

'Go on.'

'Well Sir, I went through *every* case McLane has ever been in. Since day one, when he Called to the Bar. It was tedious …'

'And?'

'Well, while I was noting and cross-checking the

415

names of everybody else who acted in the same cases, I remembered something I learned in police college.'

'Uh huh. About?'

'Ministerial Certificates, Sir. To lock away the photos of Lord Aldounhill. They require a Law Officer of State's signature.'

'Usually they do. But actually any Crown Counsel can do it for him. What's your point?'

'Well Sir, I had a look at the Exhibit and ...'

'How did you get your hands on a High Court Exhibit during the trial?'

'You don't really want to know Sir. But you did once tell me that old Jimmy Robertson could do most things around Parliament House, Sir. So I ...'

'Coutts! Stop. I *don't* want to know! Just tell me what you came up with.'

I checked the signature on the Certificate. And it rung a bell from a name on my list of other counsel; in McLane's old cases. So I cross checked and there it was. The same name. Then I had to spend some real money I'm afraid Sir.'

'How much? Never mind. Go on.'

'I ordered copies of all invoices sent to 'A' Division in the last six months.'

'What? That must have cost a bloody fortune!'

'I think it was worth it Sir. I only found what I was looking for late last night. And with the exam results coming out today …'

'Yes. Yes. So what was worth it?'

'I found an invoice from the PF's office to us for reimbursement of work done in London. Their computer budget programme automatically identifies the arresting officers and spits out …'

'London? *I* have to approve of anything for us outside of Scotland. What did you…?'

'That's the thing Sir. It stood out a mile because the money was astronomical. The invoice was for work done to an Exhibit. It's all cloak and dagger - phoney company names and …'

'Oh Christ. This gets worse. And?'

'I checked the PF's Reference and it turned out to be Sheila McManus.'

'Her? She's …'

'Yes, Sir. The PF's point woman on the McLane case.'

'So? Where does that take us?'

'Well it was the work done, Sir. "Extension to boot-print" it said – not 'on' a boot-print – 'to' a boot-print.'

'The bastards.'

'But Sir, that's not the killer punch. It's the signature authorising the work. Look who it is. The same signature as the Ministerial Certificate about the pictures of Lord Aldounhill. *And* I think I've found a motive for why McLane's been set up.'

'Jesus Christ Almighty. Coutts, we might be too late. Call Parliament House right now. Find out if McLane's jury is back yet.'

'Who would know that?'

Putting his phone to his ear, Coutts provided his own answer: 'Jimmy Robertson.'

The Trial

Chapter 57

Jimmy Robertson ignored his own mobile tinkling inside his locker and prised his new Parliament House issue phone from its clip on his belt. Peering at the screen, it read merely: 'LJG Now'. Downing the last of his tea, Jimmy flung on his gown and got up there.

'You beeped me my Lord.'

'Do we *have* to call it that? Can't we keep to summoned?'

'Of course my Lord. Is it …?'

'No. It's this. Come here. See. I had my intern do it for me. Look at these lists.'

Pointing with the nib of an old wooden handled pen he'd had since school, the Lord Justice General stabbed the newly-installed computer screen.

'Oh m'Lord. I don't think it's good for them to be stabbed wi' the nibs o' pens.'

'But I've got it Jimmy. See?'

'I do m'Lord. But what can *anyone* do at *this* late …?'

On the screen two lists showed one name highlighted in red.

'I asked my intern to check the list of McLane's jury with the latest list of Lochies. I suspected Jimmy.

419

Right from the start, I suspected. And there he is. A bloody plant. On McLane's jury.'

'Plant is right m'Lord. Usually the Keeper of the Rolls of Court would, ehm …'

'Weed them out Jimmy, is what he does. Lochies don't do civic duty. Civic duty is done for them. Well, I've got'choo my lad. Now, any sign of a verdict Jimmy?'

'I'm told any minute now, my Lord. They're just finalising the …'

'Right. Get my kit Jimmy.'

'Yes m'Lord.'

~~~0~~~

Chapter 58

Kneeling on the cold stone floor, Brogan McLane clasped his hands and lowered his head. The pressure of stone slab through suit trousers hurt his knees. Trying not to breathe the stale air in the cell, he listened. But the walls being so thick and so far below ground ensured that no sound from the world above gave the prisoner any clue of whether life remained up there or not. Down here was the end.

'Dear God, please take care of her. I've failed, I know. But it's not her fault. If I've ever ...'

Cutting through his prayer came the unmistakable sound of a turnkey's tread and his jangling keys getting louder as they approached the cell. This had to be it.

As the key slammed into the big steel lock Brogan McLane pressed his eyes tighter.

'Goodbye my darling.'

'That's your verdict Mr McLane. Time to go.'

Handcuffed between two officers, McLane and his Dock-guard squeezed through the narrow double doors into Court 9. All around the court a ring of officers in white gloves blocked out the oak panelling.

With McLane seated and the lock on the Dock gate double-checked, the clerk of court rose to give the public his usual warning: no matter what happened, keep absolutely silent or be arrested for contempt.

Filing back one by one into their places the jury settled, all looking at the floor or fidgeting with brooches or ties. Court 9 quietened to a heavy hush. Setting the tempo for what lay ahead, the loud tick of the round clock mounted on the Gallery dragged time forward. Slow. Dead slow. A minute went by, then two. Crushed into the second row the Press and a sketch artist sat at the ready; a special Motion to televise the verdict having been refused by the Appeal Court.

Brogan McLane couldn't see her but he could feel her presence. His darling, there in the back row, probably in that red coat he loved to see her wear. Reminding him that there is a world beyond Parliament House: where laughter and fun remain; where human contact is felt and love is made. Where no-one is on trial.

Standing to attention at the end of the bench, Jimmy Robertson waited for the knock; his signal that the judge is ready to come on the bench. The Clerk laid out the verdict paper. Flashing on his screen, the two verdicts 'Guilty' and 'Not Guilty' vied for attention. Underneath flashed the only sentence allowed by law for murder: Life Imprisonment.

The Trial

Outside Parliament House a special police security team reversed an empty Scottish Prisons van into West Parliament Square. The specially erected press gallery groaned under the weight of TV cameras, dishes, cables and presenters making sure their hair looked just right, their teeth sparkled and their mic levels suited the sounds of their own voices. Everyone was exactly where they were supposed to be. Everyone, but the judge. Waiting.

'Co-ou-rt' drew the assembled mass to their feet. Keeping his head bowed, McLane heard the Golden Mace being clasped and Lord Marchion's chair being dragged out; but only when the Clerk announced 'I Call the Diet of Her Majesty's Advocate against Brogan McLane. Please be seated Mr McLane' did McLane lift his eyes.

Shocked, his mouth went dry. He tugged on the handcuffs, trying to rub his eyes, which brought a quick 'snap' back to waist level from the guards. Reeling, McLane slumped down into his seat. As both officers hauled him back up, he stood not in front of Lord Marchion. Presiding over the court was the Lord Justice General himself, old Lord Jamieson.

Once settled the Lord Justice General turned to the jury. Taking an inordinate time to descend into the Well of the Court, Jimmy Robertson tried to catch McLane's eye. But too far removed from reality, McLane couldn't see him.

'Ladies and gentlemen, who speaks for you?' asked Lord Jamieson.

Standing, the Foreman held the verdict sheet up to her chin.

'Madam Foreman, Have you reached a verdict?'

'We have my Lord. We found it very diffic …'

Pushing his hand out as far as it would go, the Lord Justice General stopped Madam Foreman: 'Please. Go no further at this stage Madam Foreman. I just need to know what that verdict is. Thank you. Now, have you reached a verdict upon which you are all agreed?'

'Well, yes. We …'

'Thank you. Please announce your verdict.'

Clearing her throat the Foreman looked at the trembling man in the Dock and then through the crowd at his wife. Returning her stare to the judge, the paper shaking in her hands, she attempted to return the verdict of the jury. 'It's … It's … It's Guilty.'

En-mass the court gasped. A woman in the lower public gallery screamed at a bundle of blonde hair and red coat crumpling into her lap. Instinctively, two officers lifted the rag doll in a red coat, carefully laying her out on the polished parquet floor.

Springing to his feet, trying to jump the Dock, McLane dragged the two handcuffed officers from their seats. Instantly twisting his arms in the tiny Dock space, they pinned him down. With a knee in his back and his face pressed to the floor, McLane could see two things; the feet of dozens of people and that bright red coat, horizontal on the parquet floor of Court 9.

'**Co-ou-rt**' shouted Jimmy Robertson; his undignified yell hardly heard as Lord Jamieson briskly left the bench.

Throwing up his hands, the Clerk of Court took charge: 'Order. Order. I'll have the court cleared. Order! Is that woman alright? Take her to the medical room.'

Drawing their night sticks, issuing warnings and standing hard by the end of each row, the police took control of both lower and upper public galleries. Giving the Clerk a nod indicating that he had control, the Sergeant at Arms called for a wagon; just in case.

'Now. Order. Quiet! I will *not* allow that to happen again. Anyone, and I mean *anyone* who makes a disturbance when his lordship comes back on the bench, will be dealt with immediately and *very* severely. Does everyone understand me? Alright. Macer, bring back his lordship.'

Back on the Bench, speaking very softly, Lord Jamieson again addressed the Jury.

'Madam Foreman, please rise. I am speaking to you but I am addressing the whole court, including the Jury. Now, at the end of the speeches to the Jury in this trial it was brought to my attention, rather too late for anything to be done at the time, that Mr McLane invited the jury to judge him *unanimously*. As a matter of law, that should not have been allowed because Mr McLane had no legal authority to do such a thing. In other circumstances I am certain he would have known much better. But these are unusual circumstances, ladies and gentlemen; very unusual indeed.

Now, in Parliament House an illegal verdict will not stand. Not while I preside over it. Therefore, what I am about to do is rectify the mistake made by Lord Marchio ... the judge who presided over this trial. However, in order to do that, I require you Madam Foreman to assist me.

Now, I am going to ask you to do a simple addition sum. Is that clear? I see by your nod that you understand my directions so far. Now, please take your time with my next request. We want no further errors in this trial. Fear not, Madam Foreman, all I am asking you to do is check your ballots and count the votes for Guilty and those for Not Guilty.'

Swallowing hard the Foreman seemed rooted to the spot. Everyone but the man in the Dock and his guards, stared at this woman, nervously biting her bottom lip. Raising his eyebrows, Lord Jamieson hurried her along.

'My Lord, I know those numbers without referring to the ballots. I did it three times before … when we were voting.'

'I see. Very well. You are fifteen in total. Please tell me the number for Guilty.'

'2 my Lord.'

'And for Not Guilty?'

'13 my Lord.'

Bursting into tears, Brogan McLane fell back, lifting his sobbing eyes in thanks.

Allowing a moment for the accused to compose himself, through McLane's final sniffles Lord Jamieson smiled at the Foreman: 'Thank you Madam Foreman. The Clerk of Court will now record your proper verdict. Please be seated whilst that is being done. My Clerk will ask you to rise again to confirm the verdict once it is recorded.'

Dutifully deleting the box marked 'Mandatory Sentence – Life Imprisonment' the Clerk wrote the final Interlocutor for signature.

'Madam Foreman, please rise. Is your verdict now correctly recorded as follows: "In the trial of Her Majesty's Advocate against Brogan McLane, the Jury, having been allowed to consider an illegal procedure before deliberation and return of an illegal verdict and now having been corrected by the Lord Justice General, Lord Jamieson, now presiding, having by a majority of 13 to 2 voted truthfully for a verdict of Not Guilty: now by due Direction of the Court, formally return the said verdict of Not Guilty. Madam Foreman, is that an accurate reflection of your verdict?'

'It is.'

'Then please be seated. Thank you.'

Bowing from his seat, Lord Jamieson had one more thing to do.

'I will add my personal thanks Madam Foreman. But please remain seated while I undertake a legal matter.'

Handing up the Final Interlocutor, the Clerk put his finger to a line. Dipping his nib into fresh ink, Lord Jamieson signed it, ascribing the words only he, as Lord

Justice General of Scotland was empowered to write: Jamieson *Ius Praesandum Dominorum.* Blowing the ink dry, Lord Jamieson looked down at McLane.

Drying the nib of his old school pen he slipped it back into his waistcoat pocket.

Once written, no-one could appeal the Interlocutor. By law, no lower judge could disagree with it. To even try would simply be met with the plea that the highest Judge in the land had ruled: 'I Preside over all laws and Judges and bind them all to my Final word.'

'Now, ladies and gentlemen, your verdict and my approval of it, has been duly recorded. No doubt this has been a most distressing case for you. Indeed for all of us. I am therefore happy to release you from Jury duty, not only from this case but jury service for the remainder of your lives. Thank you once again for your most valuable contribution to our system of criminal justice. But please wait in your places for the moment.'

With a fatherly glint in his eye, Lord Jamieson looked down at the prisoner: 'Now, Mr McLane. Please rise.'

Unlocking their handcuffs, the officers remained seated as McLane stood to attention.

'Mr McLane, you have stood trial in the highest

court in Scotland on the charge of murdering Lord Aldounhill; and been acquitted by a jury of your peers. I now free you of that charge for evermore. Mr McLane the court wishes you well. Open the Dock. He's free to go.'

End of Part 6

The Trial

Part 7

Chapter 59

Closing the medical room door, hand in hand Brogan and Joanne McLane marched along the corridor. Rejoicing in the sound of their own footsteps; walking to freedom.

Waiting at the top of the stairs, outside Court 9 Jimmy Robertson stood ready: 'Lord Jamieson has ordered all press and public out of Parliament House, so you'll no' be bothered wi' that lot oot there till ye'r both good an' ready.'

Touching his gown, Joanne leaned in, giving Jimmy a peck on the cheek: 'Thank you Jimmy. I'm sure you've been …'

'That's quite alright Mrs McLane. You're both very welcome. Sir, can I just say how relieved I am that it's all over?'

'No need Jimmy. None at all.'

'Oh, and this came round on a … well, on a motorcycle actually.'

Handing over a bottle of Dominique Neuville Brut Reserve Particuliere, Jimmy's smile couldn't have been broader.

'Awfy good stuff it looks. So away yeez go an'

431

celebrate. An' Sir, I'm so pleased.'

Through the tiny aged leaded panes the McLanes could just see them. A mere ten yards away. Hundreds of them. Waiting.

Joanne checked her lippie and his collar, getting them ready. McLane sighed and closed his eyes; still seeing the walls of the cell; still listening for the turnkey coming.

'That's your verdict Mr McLane.'

Kissing him softly, Joanne gripped his hand: 'Come on. Let's go.'

'Wait. Grab that champagne.'

'Woah Brogan. *Brogan*! *What* are you doing?'

Scooping his wife up into his arms, Brogan McLane booted open the 500 year old door. Joanne's blonde hair blew in the wind. Holding the champagne high above her head, her unbuttoned red coat billowed as she kicked the sky.

In a thousand flashes, the space between the McLanes and the rest of the world disappeared.

'Mr McLane ...Mrs McLane ... over here ... How does it ...? When will you ...?

Chapter 60

Leading the way up the wide curved staircase, Lady Winstanley whispered: 'Aubrey? These officers wish to show you a film. I can't imagine why. Would you like me to telephone somone?'

'No. No don't. It's alright. Go and see to Giles.'

'Come in. Please. Sit down. Is it surveillance? Have you got a lead on who assaulted me?'

'Well Sir. We have a DVD to show you.'

'They wore masks of course. And only one spoke, I think. No. The other one said something too. Not much. I don't really remember. It was all so, so, well, you know.'

Closing the heavy brocade curtains, Imrie gave Coutts the nod: 'I think we're at cross purposes, Sir Aubrey. We've, let's say, discovered a little movie. Made some time ago. And you, we think, are the star of the show.'

'Me? What can you possibly mean? Oh? But if this isn't this about my attack … What can you want with a film made a long time ago? No. If this is something I made years … decades ago at university…we were all drunk. It was just a joke, a …'

'No Sir. But we can talk about that one later. This DVD was found in a secret compartment. By Sergeant

Coutts here. In a desk. Can you guess, Sir Aubrey, whose desk?'

Jabbing his morphine button, Sir Aubrey coughed again and swallowed hard. 'Secret compartment? I see.'

Having made their opening move, Sir Aubrey had no choice but to counter. 'Look. Is it *Commander* Imrie? Of course. Commander, anything I ever did was amongst consenting adults. So I don't see what you've got that can possibly ...'

'Oh Sir Aubrey. You're clearly not at your best. Maybe it's the morphine, but please, don't try to kid us. We both know you did plenty that's illegal. What you don't perhaps remember is that in this little production you were filmed clearly having ... how would you put it Sergeant?'

'Well Sir, the Indictment will call it unnatural carnal knowledge of a boy who is clearly a minor. Under the new Sexual Offences Scotland Act that attracts a mandatory minimum of 10 years in jail, SIR Aubrey.'

'What? Impossible! I have *never* ... not with boys ... I mean I don't ... I don't deny that I sometimes ...'

'Well let's take a look, shall we? Sergeant.'

Holding the screen close to Sir Aubrey's face, Coutts started the movie. Panning down from an ornate plastered ceiling through an unmistakable chandelier to a marble Adam fireplace, the camera stopped on a rotund man in his 60s wearing only a Venetian carnival eye mask.

Making an involuntary flash of his eyes in Imrie's direction, Sir Aubrey provided confirmation of the first actor in this little drama.

'I see we agree Sir Aubrey. That's obviously Lord Aldounhill. Right?'

Making no visible response, Sir Aubrey peered back at the screen. As the camera panned out, two other naked men came into view; sitting at a table eating grapes and quaffing champagne. One wearing purple lipstick while the other tall and slim, wore pink underwear. Only when the camera panned lower did a beautiful blonde haired boy about 14 or 15 come into view under the table. The whole lettering never became clear, but a reasonable inference could be drawn that what was stitched into his tiny lacy panties were the words 'Darling D'.

As the action heated up it quickly became obvious to Sir Aubrey that he couldn't be positively identified. Every man shown wore a mask, and never did the camera show a whole body. But one thing could be proved beyond reasonable doubt. That large ornate room, especially that chandelier, was clearly identifiable.

After a couple of minutes, Sir Aubrey sank back into his pillows, waving Coutts' hand away.

'Clever Commander. Clever, I agree.'

Coughing through his pain, Sir Aubrey managed a wry smile at Imrie: 'You can't *prove* I'm in this movie, can you? But one of the men is wearing purple lipstick, so you can *suspect* I'm in it. And if you can do that, you can arrest me on suspicion of serious sexual crimes involving under-age boys. That will ruin my career and probably deny me my pension. Clever. I will deny all, of course, but the accusation would be enough to raise a Civil Service disciplinary hearing or a trial in open court. But I don't think you want to do any of that to me Commander, do you? That's not your objective here, is it?'

'Oh I couldn't *possibly* say Sir Aubrey. I'm just a policeman who has evidence of a serious crime and thinks he has a suspect. That's all. Now, from clever police computer comparisons, we know from Professor Suilleman's report and the shape of the naked man in the centre that he's Lord Aldounhill. We've perhaps even agreed that. Then, apart from the boy, there are two men. Both masked. One is clearly wearing purple lipstick and the other man dressed in ladies' pink underwear. He's the one having the boy over the table and getting Sergeant

436

Coutts' mandatory minimum of 10 years.'

'But Commander, I'm the one known to wear purple.'

'Ah yes, but unless you admit that to a jury and get five years for aiding and abetting, no-one will ever know that. So as I was saying, right now, you're the one getting the 10 years for …'

Snared both ways, Sir Aubrey hadn't felt this vulnerable since that night two weeks before; when he also lay in bed, facing two men who were very good at what they did.

'How can I trust you Commander? You might be playing everyone against the others. It's what I'd do.'

'You'll never know, Sir Aubrey. But if you'd like to try me, on you go. Sgt Coutts here will read you your rights and …'

'You bastard. I took an oath, never to …'

'Don't you *dare* call me that! I don't give a flying fuck about your secret Lochie oath. Name! Now! Or Sergeant Coutts here will arrest you for serious sexual crimes against a minor.'

'You'll never prove the boy's under … He's long gone.'

'Is that medication muddling your brain Sir

Aubrey? To ruin you I don't need to *prove* anything …Name! Now!'

In searing agony, Sir Aubrey jabbed violently at his Morphine button. Imrie let his new Sergeant earn his day's pay. 'I think it only works on a timer, Sir. But if you'd like to be taken to a public hospital in a police car, I could …'

Wearing a stony grey look, Lady Winstanley could take no more.

'Oh for God's sake. How much more of this?'

Pulling the DVD player from Coutts' hand, Lady Winstanley confirmed her suspicion: 'It's him. Of course it's him. It's always bloody him. The man you want is Andrew Spiggot, Commander. He's the …'

'Him? Well, well, well. Thank you. We know perfectly well who *that* is. Thank you *very* much Lady Winstanley.'

Looking suspicious, Coutts beat his boss to the question.

'How can you be so sure?'

'It's him all right. I've seen him dressed like that many times, when we were young. Even at university. And I recognise the room. It's in Aldounhill's house. We've dined there. I heard he made sure the decorators came in a lot. Just in case a moment such as this should ever arise and you'd have nothing on him. But he loved that chandelier. It was his mother's, you know.'

Looking tearily out of the window, Sir Aubrey surrendered. A man relieved, as though searching for a light in the distance.

'At school we were all great friends. All chums together. Until we got up to Parliament House. Then the ambitions took over. First the little gifts to those who brought up the most lucrative cases. Then the drive for promotion. You have no idea what Parliament House is *really* like Commander. None at all. It's been called a nest of vipers, and it is. People will do *anything* for elevation to the Bench. *Anything*. I've seen it so many times.'

'You're getting off the point Sir Aubrey.'

Turning back to face his interrogators, Sir Aubrey found a flicker of strength: 'Ah but I'm not Commander. Andrew stood aside freeing the way for Aldounhill's elevation to the bench. Good man. Good Lochie …The deal was that Aldounhill was to sponsor him for the next slot. But instead of doing the honourable thing, of course Aldounhill reneged. Typical. Little shit. And he began to humiliate Andrew at his parties. Loved it. It got him off. Twisted little …'

Shaking his head and putting up his hand, Imrie stopped him.

'Aahh Sir Aubrey. I see your game. Do you think I can't spot deflection when I see it? I happen to know it was *you* who was up for elevation. So it's *you* who was disappointed. Humiliated. It was *you* who took revenge …'

'Rubbish. *Where* did you get that? This is all on record in Parliament House and in the Palace. You can easily check. It was …'

'No. No. We got this from Giles. I interviewed him myself, in London, quite recently. He seemed very sure …'

'Giles was only a boy at the time. He's simply mistaken. I ...'

Turning his attention to Coutts, Sir Aubrey asked genuinely: 'Do you know that humiliation is the deepest feeling of hurt which humans can experience? It's been the motive for many, many murders. Did they teach you *that* at police college …'

'What they taught me was that if I find someone's DNA on a murder weapon, they're the murderer. So I think you murdered Lord Aldounhill.'

'Me? Oh please! Don't be silly. I haven't... Once

440

upon a time, maybe. But not any more.'

Spluttering and catching his breath, Sir Aubrey raised a bony finger: 'Didn't they also teach you to find out who was last to see the victim alive? Aren't they usually the killer? Sergeant.'

'Well in this nest of vipers, we think you were last to see him.'

Lady Winstanley had had enough: 'Oh for God's sake Aubrey! Can't you just let go of these stupid Lochie loyalties. Look where it's got you. It's all over. You won't be elevated to the bloody post-room after this. Tell him. Tell him everything or I will.'

'What? Tell us what? Lady Winstanley!'

Sinking as low as sheets and pillows would allow, Sir Aubrey croaked. 'I took an oath and I won't break it. Not even in death will I …'

Shaking her head, Lady Winstanley gripped Sir Aubrey's hand: 'You bloody fool. The truth is Commander, Allan Coatbridge took them *all* for fools. He promised everyone in town with a chance at the bench, that if they supported him, he'd make sure they were next in line. He took them all for fools. It's like a sickness, I believe. Ambition in Parliament House Commander, is a sickness.'

Turning to her broken, worn down husband, she

insisted. 'Tell him. Tell him what you know and when this is over, we'll retire. We'll leave Edinburgh … for our house in the Ticino. Tell him Aubrey.'

Her promise penetrating where narcotics couldn't reach, a glimmer came into Sir Aubrey's eyes; the hope of life, a very different life, led in warm sunlight and where this would never again be mentioned.

'It was Andrew. Andrew Spiggot was last to see Aldounhill alive. The night he died … I'm sorry, I'm in a lot of pain. I left the party shouting about telling the papers. So they all scarpered. All except Jenny. There's nothing will scatter a pack of closet Queens quicker than mention of the press. I'd called the newspaper. I didn't want Giles to go through … anything. But Andrew was last out. I'm certain of that. Others *might* verify that. I don't know any more.'

Leaving a bewildered Sir Aubrey Winstanley coughing and jabbing his pain relief button, Coutts flung open the door and the police were gone.

Chapter 61

While some blocked off Chambers Street with patrol cars, a thin blue line of uniformed officers took control of the Crown Office: forbidding any movement inside the building. Both lifts rested in the basement and on every staircase landing stood four burly officers.

Striding down the corridor Imrie and Coutts passed the offices bearing brass plaques leading to the Chambers of Her Majesty's Advocate, only to be disappointed. Giving no hint of his purpose, Imrie tried the handle of the door nearest to the Lord Advocate's Chambers marked Solicitor General for Scotland. Locked.

'Coutts!'

The office door being no match for Sergeant Coutts' rugby prop forward shoulder, he burst through on the second charge.

'Grab that bastard!'

Spinning around, the Solicitor General stared with eyes like a madman. His whirring shredder choked to a standstill, stuffed with half-torn photographs and his laptop lay in smithereens all over the floor.

In his time Coutts had body-slammed hundreds of opponents into touch but never with more satisfaction than this time. The whole floor vibrated as the two men thundered into a cabinet that splintered into matchwood.

Coutts pinned the Solicitor General to the floor face-down and stuck a knee in his back. Holding him by the hair, he snapped on the handcuffs.

Commander Imrie picked up the photos that hadn't made it into the shredder. Standing over his suspect, he administered the formal caution: 'Andrew Spiggot, Solicitor General for Scotland, otherwise known as *Jenny*, I am arresting you for sexual offences against children, perversion of the course of justice i.e. falsifying evidence against Brogan McLane in the High Court and suspicion of the murder of Lord Aldounhill. You are not obliged to say anything but anything you do say will be noted and given in evidence at your trial. Do you understand?'

The Solicitor General was dribbling blood from the gap left by his front tooth as it smashed into the floor. Stoic and resolute, he made no legal reply to the caution and charge. Propping the suspect up against a wall, Coutts wiped his hands and straightened his suit. Swinging a seat backwards between his legs, Commander Imrie began the formal police interview.

'Hello Jenny. Remember me? Mr Plod the Policeman.'

Dripping blood onto his shirt, the Solicitor General

tried to kick a photograph under a cabinet.

'Look at that. Pathetic. Wouldn't you say, Coutts? Pathetic.'

'I would Sir. Yes. I wonder if the suspect is wearing pink under his suit Sir.'

'Oh plenty of time to let the Duty Sergeant organise a strip search at the Station, Coutts. Now Jenny; oh you don't deny you've been calling yourself Jenny for many years, do you?'

Squeezing his eyes tight shut, the Solicitor General winced as Coutts tightened the handcuffs.

'I'll take that as a Yes.'

Producing the photograph taken by Big Joe Mularkey in Darren's hotel bathroom Imrie went to work: 'This is Darren. You might know him as Darling D. Seen him recently?'

Taken from behind, the picture showed the boy's face reflected in the mirror. But the rest was all there. The tall lithe feminine body naked but for a pair of white stockings, that beautiful smile, a very expensive haircut and something else: a tattoo of a pink flamingo, low on his right buttock.

Shaking his head the Solicitor General muttered: 'I don't know any Darrens.'

'So you don't know Darren huh? Note that Sergeant. The suspect's first lie to the police. Let's make that charge number one, shall we?'

The Solicitor General stuck his tongue into the gap in his upper gum and gave Imrie a look of disgust.

'You see, that's a wee bit … how would you people put it? Oh yes, a wee bit tiresome. Darren's being driven to 'A' Division HQ right now and he's already told us he knows you. What was his phrase? Oh yes, 'Up me like a rat up a drainpipe since I was 14.' That ring a bell?'

Getting no reply to the question, Imrie nodded to Coutts to haul him up into a seat: 'Try this other picture. We found this in Lord Aldounhill's desk. See that boy in the picture. The one on the right. He's 15 in this one. We can't see all of his face but there is something we can see very clearly on his bum. Sergeant, what is that we can see?'

'A pink flamingo, Sir.'

'Correct Coutts. And who else can we see in the picture?'

'This suspect Sir.'

'Now' resumed Imrie, 'You're not very well disguised though your long wig and make-up were enough to throw us off your trail for quite a while. Tut-tut. You must have been enjoying yourself and didn't remember to get the picture back. Are you sure you can't remember Darren?'

Through a wince of pain, the Solicitor General for Scotland shook his head.

'Well anyway Solicitor General, we now have plenty of evidence to convict you of serious sexual offences with children. Oh and there's another wee thing. I have a witness who puts you in the frame for Lord Aldounhill's murder. Please don't lie and tell me you have an alibi for the exact time of death. You see, our witness knows you as Jenny. He's known you nearly all your life and he'll testify that you were last to leave Lord Aldounhill's house the night he was murdered. And oh, please do ask me how I know he'll testify.'

Glancing up at Imrie for just half a second, it was a question to which Spiggot already knew the answer.

'I see you already know the answer Solicitor General. We do too, eh Coutts?'

'We do Sir.'

'Because he's saving his own skin. The old ones are the best, eh Coutts?'

'None better, Sir.'

Sitting on the window sill, Imrie looked out over

the Edinburgh skyline: 'You know, right since the start of this investigation I've been asking myself one question - why Brogan McLane? Why him? Plenty of other counsel had run-ins with Lord Aldounhill. So why pick McLane? Where's the connection? Why set him up? Kept me awake at nights that question did. Then I got it. Simple and straightforward. I *just* got it. '

'You're rambling Commander. Rambling on …'

Imrie wagged his index finger and was beginning to enjoy this: 'No. No. The answer is … Coutts?'

'There is no connection between Lord Aldounhill and McLane, Sir.'

'Precisely Coutts. Where *is* the connection Coutts?'

'Between this suspect and McLane, Sir.'

'What? Rubbish. You can't prove a thing like that in …'

'Oh you don't think so? Well try this. The connection is based in 'revenge'. Did I mention that the old ones were the best, Coutts?'

'You did Sir.'

'We all know that every lawyer wins some and loses some. Par for the course, you might say. But you lost a big one didn't you Mr Spiggot? A *very* big one.'

Coughing and spitting out blood, the Solicitor General managed: 'As you say, everyone loses sometimes. It's inevitable.'

'Ah no. I said a big one and I meant it. Nine years ago. The case of Her Majesty's Advocate against Joseph Thomas Mularkey for kidnapping and murder. You were struggling to rise in the Crown Office and that case was your big break. Or correction, it should've been. But at the pre-trial legal debate Mularkey's Advocate demolished your case like a wet cardboard box. The trial never happened and you languished on the lower rungs. If you'd won that, you'd have been Lord Advocate by now. Maybe even elevated to the High Court bench. But after losing such a high profile case, your career rose like unleavened bread. And who beat you?'

Again the Solicitor General glanced up, his grey stony face giving nothing away.

'Big Joe Mularkey's counsel was none other than Mr Brogan McLane, Advocate.'

'Pure speculation ... *cough cough* ... Commander.'

'I agree. In isolation, yes. But then we come to the case of one *Wee* Joe Mularkey. You set Wee Joe up. Purely because his father walked out of the High Court

449

after a legal debate. Jesus, you people make me sick. Now. We've tracked down the two guys who gave evidence for the Crown. We don't know why exactly, but their statements say that if they don't tell the truth, they're rather fearful that they might end up on a wee holiday in the Mediterranean. So they're co-operating fully. What's their defence Coutts?'

'Defence of death by accident, Sir.'

'That's right Coutts. Accidental killing. So they'll tell us all about your wee chats in private rooms while they were languishing on remand in Saughton Prison.'

Biting his lip and shaking now, the Solicitor General tried Coutts rather than Imrie: 'I demand to see a solicitor. I have that right.'

'Shut up. The Commander will decide when this interview is over.'

'But I have rights under the European Convention on Human …'

'Human Rights! You bastard. Don't you dare mention human rights to me. You've wrecked more lives than tongue can tell.'

Sticking up his thumb, Imrie began counting down his fingers: 'Molly Mularkey, Big Joe Mularkey, Brogan McLane, Joanne McLane, wee Joe Mularkey, even …

even that poor soul Marjorie Millbank sitting down there in a patrol car. How many years were you manipulating her? You piece of shit.'

'It's all circumstantial. It'll never …'

From his inside pocket Imrie pulled the Ministerial Certificate produced by the Advocate Depute in Court, crushing it in his fist: 'The signatures! The same signatures. *Yours* you … I should ram these down your fucking throat you bastar …'

Catching his boss's wrist, Coutts again stopped Imrie from going too far. Taking charge, Coutts stepped over the remains of the door. Leaning out into the corridor, he motioned for two uniforms to remove the prisoner.

Still seething, watching from the window as the Solicitor General got into the back of a patrol car, Imrie made a call: 'Brogan, have you seen a telly in the last half hour?'

'Joanne's getting it all on her phone. Well done my man. There's a big drink waiting for you in the Calton Bar. When you're ready.'

'Thanks Brogan. Sounds good. I'll take you up on that. Did you know they were married?'

'Who? Who's married?'

'*Were* married. A long time ago. Spiggot and the

451

Fiscal. Coutts found out. When he matched the notes from your war council with Civil Service lists. Really great work.'

'Married? Jesus, you couldn't make it up.'

'No Brogan, you couldn't. But you can bet your last penny that the next time that pair stand side by side it won't be in a church: it'll be in Parliament House.'

Chapter 62

The concierge touched the rim of his grey top hat and opened the glass door of the Gersman Hotel allowing two young women and a man with only one bag between them to avoid the group of grovelling businessmen blocking the revolving doors.

Swishing to their side, the Bell Captain touched his pencil moustache: 'Good afternoon Miss Bishop. Mr and Mrs McLane have just arrived through the basement. They're up in the Penthouse. Their private lift is this way.'

Welcoming them with outstretched hand, Joanne McLane introduced herself. Pulling the cord of his fluffy white dressing gown, Brogan let the champagne bottle in his hand drop into its silver bucket. As the bottle bobbed back up, Louise just caught the label: Dominique Neuville Brut Reserve Particuliere, a Fontaine.

Blurting out her opening question, all her preparation vaporised. 'Do you always drink that brand?'

With a wink, McLane raised his glass, avoiding giving her a straight answer.

As her photographer ran his cables and the make-up girl took Joanne McLane into the bedroom to change into the outfits agreed for the shoot, Louise sauntered over to the terrace, feigning interest in the skyline. Watching McLane in the floor-to-ceiling glass, as he turned towards the dressing room Louise took her chance.

Sliding the heavy glass terrace doors behind her, Louise Bishop crammed herself into a corner and stabbed her phone: 'Mackie. Mackie it's me. Listen … No … listen. I'm not sure about this. No … listen. It's the champagne. Of course I'm here. They're getting ready. For God's sake man listen to me. The champagne. It's the same … *exactly* the same as the kind found in Aldounhill's house when he was … Mackie. I'm trying to tell you …'

Feeling his heavy hand on her shoulder and shivering in fear, Louise spun round as McLane grabbed the phone. Putting it to his ear, his smile reached from ear to ear: 'You owe me £20 Mackie. I got her! Here, I think she wants to speak to you.'

'You bastards! You absolute bast …'

Laughing loudly, McLane couldn't contain himself: 'Sorry. It was Mackie's idea. To see if you'd get it. I said it might frighten you but he said you were tough-a-plenty. I'm not so sure. But I won't tell anyone, if you won't.'

'Brogan McLane! What a man! Give me a drink of

454

that stuff and let's get started.'

Posing in his suit and broad black brimmer, holding Joanne in her red silk evening gown, McLane's eyes twinkled, lighting up the shoot.

LB: You must be looking forward to going home?

JMcL: Well yes. But not straight away. The house is being re-decorated and a holiday is being finalised – the Caribbean. Brogan likes the music.

Creeping around the room, on the carpet, over the sofa, the photographer clicked and flashed as Louise edged closer and closer to their pain. The horror at nights. The pain of injustice. The drag of uncertainty. The worry about procedure. Their collapses and recoveries. All was told with nothing to hide.

'Well, that's great, I think we've just about …'

The sound of the hotel phone and Brogan's mobile ringing simultaneously sent Louise's meter into overload. Leaning over the arm of the sofa McLane grabbed the phone.

'Sorry. It's my Chambers Clerk in Parliament House. Won't be a sec.' he apologised.

Striding around the vast room, holding the phone tight to his ear, McLane's left fist began to clench. Taking out a little digital camera, the photographer sensed a moment.

Suddenly and without warning, McLane shouted like a flare zooming into the sky: 'What? A TRIAL? NO chance. Absolutely **fucking no chance!** I don't care a **fuck** about the Rules of Faculty … **No!** … Are you listening to me? I'm **NOT** doing it and that's that. Got it?'

Throwing down the phone, everyone in the room waited while McLane downed a big gulp of champagne and caught his breath.

Touching her 'Record' button, Louise Bishop plucked up enough reporter in her to ask: 'I heard the word 'Trial'. Brogan. Would you mind telling me? Who's your client?'

Chapter 63

At well over 100 mph The Gersmen Hotel Jaguar flashed by everything on the M8 motorway in a blur. Weaving through Edinburgh, McLane's phone showed eight unanswered messages from Big Joe Mularkey, three from Joanne and one from the Dean of the Faculty of Advocates.

Slamming the door, Brogan McLane marched into 'A' Division Police HQ: 'Where is the bastard Jackie. I'll fucking do the bastard a ...'

Flinging up the old oak counter-flap, Fat Jackie did his best to avert the crime about to happen: 'Oh my God, Sir. Please ... Mr McLane! you have to sign ... Sir you canny go down there till you've ...'

Blocking the cell corridor door, Fat Jackie panted, trying to keep McLane from grabbing the big set of iron cell keys hanging on his belt. The sound of a siren and the banging of a few more doors did the trick and McLane calmed down: 'Sorry Jackie. It's just ... I don't want to get you into any trouble.'

'Ye'r a'right Sir. There's just a few officers in the station.

Giving the three officers who'd appeared a wave, Fat Jackie took the last of the heat out of the situation: 'It's a' right lads. No problem.' saw them turn and resume their duties elsewhere. But wiping is brow, he now had to deal with a very delicate matter.

'Sir. Ye'll need tae see my prisoner. But ye'll still have to sign in. I'm doin' this visit by the book.'

McLane tried to regulate his breathing: 'OK Jackie. Sorry. Where is he?'

Going sheepish, Fat Jackie couldn't look McLane in the eye: 'He's in 3 Sir. We thought … we never thought...'

Slapping Fat Jackie's shoulder, McLane saw the irony: 'No, you're right enough. I didn't expect to be back so quickly myself. Right. I'm ready. Give me the sheet.'

Signing his name with a flourish, McLane gathered his wits for the Consultation of a lifetime: 'OK. I'm in. Now, let me see my client.'

McLane leaned against the wall of Cell 3, staring down his client, thinking: '*No soup for you.*'

'Well?'

Andrew Spiggot sat crouched on the cold stone slab, with one hand over his mouth, which had stopped bleeding. Turning to his defence counsel, he gave a wry smile before carefully saying: 'You can't get out of representing me you know. Try it. Go ahead and you'll be struck off.'

McLane kept his gaze on his client, trying to keep from recalling all the horror of battling those sneaky little thoughts which had crept into his mind by day, and the terror of the nightmares by night; all suffered on that same slab: 'I'm well aware of that. That's the only reason I'm here.'

'You're fully and properly instructed to act in my defence. Through your Clerk in Parliament House. Fees paid up front, so you can't get out of it.'

'I'm giving your money to charity. If you think I'd touch a penny of it, you're … So, anyway. The charges; sexual molestation of minors, perversion of the course of justice and murder. OK. So? Got a defence have we?'

'Oh I'll have one, to all charges. And I'll have you.'

Pushing out his chest and clenching his fist, McLane wanted to pummel the bastard into the floor. The time would be worth it. But one more thought shot to mind like an arrow – the sight of that red coat on the floor of court 9. Pulling back, he teased this pathetic figure of a man: 'Is that some sort of threat?'

'Oh no. Not a threat. A promise dear boy. A promise.'

'What are you talking about? How can you possibly think you'll get off?'

'Bungled. Bungled by Maiden Help. That's what went wrong. If I'd done this myself, it would be you who'd have gone down for it all.'

Losing his last piece of composure, McLane flung himself screeching like a wounded banshee onto the Solicitor General. Springing up from the slab, Spiggot got a hand around McLane's throat. Tripping him up, McLane got Spiggot down, his head pressed up against the slab. With a knee on his arm, McLane drew back to take a punch.

'IN! EVERYBUDDY IN.' shouted Fat Jackie, opening the cell door.

Three officers flung themselves into Cell 3 thudding down on its occupants. All three grabbed McLane, tripping Fat Jackie and sending him crashing to the floor.

'Get him out o' here. Out! Do yooz hear me? Now!'

Dragging McLane along the corridor, the cell door inadvertently left open, the Solicitor General for Scotland shouted after them: '**You can't get out!** You're properly instructed to defend me at trial. You'll *have* to do it. The

Dean of Faculty knows that. I know it and *you* know it. And *all* the privileges apply. Face it. There's no way out McLane. I won't go down for anything!'

John Mayer

Chapter 64

Pulling down another box carton of files from a wobbly metal shelf, Sergeant Coutts' eyes skimmed the dates. In descending order, they flashed by. Shoving his thumb in, he stopped.

'*Gotcha.*'

He flicked through manilla folders, old sellotaped Exhibit envelopes and bundles of stapled photocopies. Nothing.

Lifting the next carton onto his impromptu desk, he got the same result. Carton after carton filled with stuff no-one would ever see again. Then it came to him. It might still be with Forensics.

Slapping the dust from his suit trousers, he lifted a phone on the wall: 'Jackie? It's me. Can you buzz me into the Inactive Forensics Store?'

'Oh hello Graeme. As it's you. Aye, bit only fur a wee minute.'

'And Jackie. Put this down on Commander Imrie's authority, will you?'

'Oooh, Ah shouldn'ae withoot askin' … Bit as it's you ….'

Opening the box marked Her Majesty's Advocate -

v- Brogan McLane, Coutts lifted out an opaque click-shut plastic folder and pressed the lock with his thumb. Holding a single sheet up to the light, his eyes widened.

Knocking on Imrie's door, Coutts waited.

'Enter'

'Ah Coutts. Come in. I've been going through this whole bloody mess of files that bitch Millbank left behind. It's a pain in the bloody arse if you ask me.'

'Yes, Sir. I've had much the same idea. But I went through Sheila McManus' files and I've had another idea.'

'Sit down; if you can find a seat.'

'Thank you Sir. I won't. I have more to do. I'm afraid I've had to use your name Sir. I just thought I'd come up and show you these.'

'That looks like an Inactive Forensics File, I hope its properly signed out to… Why are you wearing latex gloves?'

'Well it's not exactly signed for, Sir. Not yet. I'm …I wanted to show you two things. They may not be connected, but I think they are.'

'Show me. What've you got?'

Opening the plastic file, Coutts took out two single sheets of paper and laid them side by side on Imrie's desk.

'You see, Sir, I've been going back to basics. Taking the long view, you might say. And two things struck me as being ... well, as possibly being connected. So I've opened our Field Files from Aldounhill's house, from the day we got there, and I've ...'

'Hold it Coutts. Why are you looking at Field reports?'

'Sir, there's something that throughout all our investigations I've never ... Sir, I've never found a *pattern*. Something that locks solidly together with something else. It's all been smoke and mirrors, so to speak. Sir, look at the date on this letter.'

Putting on his glasses, Imrie lifted a blank sheet of paper, folded it and used it to turn the letter round. Headed Procurator Fiscal for Edinburgh, it was addressed to someone Imrie knew well.

'So? We know about that.'

'Sir, this would have arrived only *two days* before the death of Lord Aldounhill. And it's not the first. Sir, it's the accumulation of ... Well, Sir, maybe I'm wrong but maybe there's a ...'

'Hmm possibly. What else have you got?'

'Sir, this is the original Field report of the boot print, about size 12 or 13 we think. Lifted from the flower bed at Lord Aldounhill's house. All of ours and a gardener's have been reliably eliminated. I gave a guy a call. A guy I play rugby with. He works down in Central Forensics. But he's not very long out of university and he's only at Lower Scientific Executive level, so there's no way Forensics will stand by his opinion.'

'How much did this cost? Another bloody invoice. Oh alright. OK. And?'

'Sir, in his opinion the print was made by a big man who leans over on his left foot as he walks. Possibly due to an ankle bone injury when much younger. They did their pre-trial tests but you'll recall, Sir, they certified this partial-print as being unreliable.'

'I do. It was something and nothing. We didn't know the age of the print, we didn't have a comparator to Exhibit. From our point of view there was nowhere else to go with that …'

'Yes. Also, it was too degraded to get a plaster cast. Something to do with moisture levels and big birds, like seagulls, landing on the imprint. Sir, I think whoever left print this might be …'

'Wait a minute. Leans over? To his left? Oh Christ Coutts.'

Walking round behind his desk, Imrie looked out

over Arthur's Seat Hill.

'What is it, Sir? Do you think …?'

Spinning round, Coutts had never seen Imrie so serious: 'What I think Coutts, is that we *do* have enough evidence to convict Spiggot of the sexual crimes and certainly enough for perversion of the course of justice. But we *don't* have enough to convict Spiggot for murder.'

'Then because it's a murder trial all the minor charges would be dropped at the end of the trial …'

'Precisely. Brogan McLane will stir these points up at trial in the High Court like your granny's soup. He'll spin the jury around till they don't know whose name is on which piece of evidence. Doubt? They'll be eating reasonable doubt out of his hand for their bloody lunch.'

'Is he that good?'

'Good? If McLane's got the bit between his teeth, he'll win this trial. Spiggot's sure to walk free.'

'Then no-one will *ever* be convicted of Aldounhill's murder. Fuck me gently!'

Clenching both fists, Imrie pressed down into his desk: 'Fear not Coutts. We're short of vital evidence. But I think I might - just might - know where to find it. Are you due at rugby training tonight?'

Chapter 65

Springing into life with one pulse to her solenoid the big cat purred. Clicking-in to the wired waiting dock, the GPS lit up, filling the double garage with her scary-bright electronic glow.

Up through second into third. Careful of her speed in the city streets, she passed the motorway sign to 'The East: Berwick and The South' on the other side. Whistling like the wind down the on-ramp and up into top, man and machine slipped effortlessly through the damp night air.

Revolving slowly the GPS pages showed 'Glasgow city centre – wide view' 'South Side – wide view' Then his leafy third location – pinpoint.

'Gotcha.'

Watching from a new set of binoculars, parked by the side wall of a mansion house and garden, the driver eased around in his seat. Checking his Google Earth print-out showing pathways, the garage and escape routes, he lowered the window and listened. Babbling in the darkness, fast running and wide, the stream at the back of the house marked the boundary.

Unpicking the lock in the side gate in under ten seconds sent a wave of pride through his chest. Those

467

years in Army Special Ops had never left him: *'The old training never dies'*. Keeping close to the perimeter wall, he listened but heard no dogs. He waited - but no security lights detected his presence.

At the back of the garage he scanned the electric door frequency. Dead-in domestic range. No problem. Pressing the green button, the crack of that first lift split the silence. Dropping onto the balls of his feet he touched the driveway with his knuckles, just for balance. Five. Ten. Twenty seconds. Nothing.

Inside the garage she lay tilted to one side. Cold, with her eyes shut. All of her proud chrome and steel asleep. Calculating that the torchlight wouldn't be seen from the house, he flashed around. Nothing. Then there, hanging on the wall. There were his helmet and leathers. But no boots.

Where? Where could these be? In the garden tools cabinet? No. By the oil cans? No. Not in his car? Surely not? No. Where? Gotcha! Under the tarpaulin. Gotcha!

With the torch beam tight on the bench, he shoved his arm down inside the left boot, spraying the sole with silicone. Laying the boot sideways on the workbench, he pulled out a plain sheet of tissue paper and stretched it tight. Pressing the sole down into the tissue, he counted.

The Trial

One Two Three Four Five. Done.

All the way back to Edinburgh, he hoped against hope it wouldn't be a match. *'It can't be … Surely not. Not after all that's happened. What if it is? Dump it or don't dump it? No. No. Do your duty. Take the long view. By itself, it's not conclusive. Take the long view.'*

Going up in the 'A' division lift, Imrie's heart pounded. Stepping out, he took a minute and went to the lavatory. Splashing water on his face, he stood looking into the mirror, letting it drip off his chin: *'OK Commander. Time to find out.'*

Opening his office door, to his surprise, there on his desk lay a bottle of Lagavulin Islay 16 year old, 20 cans of beer and five bottles of Irn Bru.

'What the hell's this Coutts? A party?'

'No Sir. But we are on our way to one. If we could just get on?'

'Christ. Is that what you take to parties these days? Can I come? I could use a …'

'Sorry Sir. You wouldn't like the music and well, Mrs Imrie might have something to say to you in the morning. Can we just …?'

'Fair enough. Here. I did it with the silicone. Five seconds, just as you advised. Worked a treat.'

Taking the tissue and laying it on a neon light box, Coutts' Lower Scientific Executive level friend overlayed the print with a thin film of electronic pathways. Connecting a reader to ten tiny plugs, he waited. Millions of numbers flashed as one. But within seconds the lowly Scientific Officer made his first official report.

'That's a perfect match, Sir. And it will be incontrovertible evidence at trial. Cast iron. So, Sir, can we go now?'

The Trial

Chapter 66

Hand-scrawled on the back door of the Calton Bar, a sign just said 'Shut'. But the noise from inside was deafening. In the bar, so many people wanted to sing, they were chalking their names in a list on the wall. The old rule applied: 'one singer, one song' until the choruses of course, when every voice in the place stretched to its deepest sinew. These were the sounds of Defence Central celebrating its win in the historic case of Her Majesty's Advocate versus Brogan McLane.

On door duty, Tucker Queen thought he recognised the tall shadow passing the barred stained glass window in the alley. Unbolting the back door he opened it a crack, flashed his eyes up the alley and kept a wooden wedge jammed under the door: 'Oh it's yourself Commander. Nice to see you again.'

'And you Tucker. Would you like to see my Search Warrant?'

'Search Warr … Whit?'

'It's OK Tucker I'm very much alone on this enquiry.'

Inside, taking off his coat, Imrie counted more than twenty women in the bar. That was unusual. But on this special occasion even children had been brought to pay respect to the main man. A night like this comes once in a lifetime and every man, woman and child in the place knew that.

Standing at the bar, Brogan McLane - the man of the hour - and Big Joe Mularkey raised their glasses with a swarthy looking man whose name Imrie didn't know. Making his way through the crowd he spotted Louise Bishop and Joanne McLane, giggling like schoolgirls among a group of women. Deep in conversation, Imrie figured Miss Bishop was collecting background for her book about the case. Catching his eye, Joanne McLean mouthed a silent '*Thanks for coming.*'

As Imrie leaned on the bar, the swarthy man with no name melted away. Whiskies galore bought for McLane stretched along the bar for a yard and a half. So many that Lenny the barman had put name-tags under each one.

Offering his hand, McLane beamed like a man back from the dead: 'HELLO Commander. Thanks a million for everything. I really mean it. I can't tell you how it feels to have been on the other side and come back.'

Shaking hands, Imrie beamed: 'You're very welcome Brogan. It's great to see you cleared and with a smile on your face. It's all over Edinburgh about your formal instructions from that slimeball Spiggot. Do you *have* to take the case. I mean, *can* you take it?'

'Oh the Dean's already made it clear. I've got no choice. I'm Andrew Spiggot's Advocate at trial and that's that.'

'*Christ* man, Parliament House breaks me up. You don't need me to tell you; the Lochies will be swarming like flies on shit to protect him.'

'Oh yeah. Well, he should walk away. The Crown won't have enough for murder. And when all the other charges are dropped for the jury's final consideration ...Ah well ... that's the way it goes.'

'If he does walk away Brogan, that would be a tragedy. I mean even with you defending ...'

'Oh Commander, you know as well as I do, stranger things have happened in Parliament House.'

'Stranger things indeed, Brogan.'

'Well aye. That would be a bastard. But, what can I say? Right now I'm half drunk and my head's all over the place, but ... tell me straight. Do you disagree? I mean do you think you *actually* have a legal sufficiency of evidence against him for murder?'

Narrowing his eyes Big Joe Mularkey said nothing, but watched closely as McLane drunkenly waved to more people who'd bought him drink and shook hands with people passing through, who didn't seem to want to catch Imrie's eye.

'No. Not really.'

Drunkenly throwing up his hands, McLane swayed: 'Right. And until something changes I can't see me changing my legal opinion.'

Giving Big Joe a flash of one eye, Imrie squeezed out: 'Look Brogan, I know I'm maybe a bit of a damper on the party. I partly came tonight because I've got some *new* evidence.'

'But the sexual stuff will all stick anyway, so you don't need any more.'

Just waiting his time, Big Joe slipped his arm through McLane's, getting ready to put several men between Imrie and his future in Parliament House. To Big Joe, it came as no surprise to hear Imrie say: 'No. Brogan, I mean the murder.'

'Hey big man! Great tae see yi' out!' interrupted the latest arrival who himself had been a guest of Her Majesty until only an hour before. Reaching over a shoulder, McLane slapped the guy's hand as he melted into the crowd.

'Sorry. *What* did you say? Did you say the

murder?'

Feeling the weight of half a dozen pairs of eyes on him, Imrie took another step in his investigation: 'Yes. I did. As I was saying Brogan. I get the feeling I'm close to a breakthrough. Right Joe?'

Swaying a little, McLane dropped his shoulders, dropped his bottom lip and dropped his guard: 'What? Joe? How would *he* know about your breakthr …? What the **fuck** do you mean?'

Big Joe Mularkey broadened himself as Commander Imrie reached into his inside jacket pocket. Standing hard square up to each other, neither breathed. Signalling to his boss from the back of the bar, Tucker joined the tips of his thumbs and held out his index fingers: making the sign for W. For Warrant!

Thirty nine men stopped singing. The women stopped laughing and behind Imrie the Arab got ready. Behind the bar, with the toe of his shoe Lenny lifted the brass ring of the basement hatch.

Looking Big Joe straight in the eye, Imrie brought out two sheets of folded paper. To a collective sigh of relief, everyone in the bar spotted immediately that these weren't a Warrant. These were court Exhibits.

Opening them out, Imrie laid them side by side on

the bar. One a full footprint from a boot. Slightly more worn on the left than the right. The other a partial print showing identical wear. On its own, not enough to prove anything in court. But with it's comparator and the supporting evidence of officers, the partial print lifted from Lord Aldounhill's garden became deadly evidence.

Drawing big breaths, McLane desperately tried to clear his drunken mind. Swaying uncertainly. Burping. Staring at Big Joe Mularkey.

Raising his glass, Big Joe broke into a broad smile: 'Vital evidence indeed, Commander. Precisely whit you need to convict. Well done. Whit gave you the idea?'

Taking a step away, barging into people behind, McLane screwed up his face, trying to reconcile being Andrew Spiggot's legal counsel and the suspect's oldest friend.

Putting a steadying hand on McLane's shoulder, in the hush that had befallen the festivities, Imrie reassured him: 'Fear not Brogan. When I said I didn't think it was you *or* Big Joe here who murdered Aldounhill, I meant it. But I think Joe has known a thing or two about this case all along that he's kept to himself. Am I right Joe?'

Raising his glass, Big Joe Mularkey played along: 'You are Commander. An' ye' still haven't answered my question. Whit gave you the idea?'

Holding on to the brass rail at the bar with both hands, McLane shook his head. Turning to Big Joe, he looked bewildered: '*All along*? Joe? What the …?'

Slapping a friendly hand on McLane's back, every man in the bar sensed that Imrie didn't have the air of an officer about to make an arrest.

'Don't worry Brogan. All is well. Joe isn't my suspect. Isn't that right Joe?'

'Aye. Dead right, Commander.'

Leaning on the bar, Big Joe's wink ordered the Arab to stand down. His suntan down on the Med would have to wait till another time. Lenny dropped the hatch ring back into its slot. Clinking whisky glasses, the three drank heartily. As the whisky went down, so the tension eased among those men who would do absolutely anything for Brogan McLane.

Big Joe pulled McLane in to listen and in a soft voice designed for an audience of only three, Imrie put his cards on the table: 'The first uniforms on the scene found a boot-print in the garden and took a Field Impression with some kitchen paper. Normal procedure. We tried to match it with a muddy mess in the hallway coat room, but got no joy. We almost immediately eliminated Aldounhill himself and his old gardener and you Brogan when Forensics checked all your boots and shoes. Again, all routine. Now, Forensics didn't have a perfect comparator to match anything, so I dumped that line of enquiry. And the whole line of inquiry didn't really go anywhere until it became a dot in a circle during your trial. I thought putting such a wide circle in front of a jury was a desperate thing to do, and I was right. But I digress. Recently, my Sergeant made a connection between two things. A limp and a letter.'

Coughing out enough whisky fumes to burn down the pub, McLane misheard: 'Limpna *what*?'

Whispering into McLane's ear, Big Joe Mularkey corrected his blood brother: 'He said *limp* Brogan. He meant my limp.'

Nodding at the dawn of understanding crossing McLane's face, Imrie took another confident step: 'Yes. I did. Oh, and I've been meaning to ask Joe – How *is* your ankle these days? Still get stiff when you ride the bike?'

Big Joe Mularkey raised his glass in salute: 'It's fine Commander. You were sayin'?'

But before Imrie could draw breath, McLane saw the point: 'His *ankle*? Now hold it right there Commander. Are you saying Joe's *been* to Aldounhill's house? I can't believe that.'

But as the two heads nodded in unison, McLane steadied himself on the Bar. 'He has.'

Turning and standing right in front of Big Joe, McLane was somewhere back in his boyhood East End.

'Do your worst. If you want him, ye'll have to come through me and ten men in this bar!'

'Brogan. You're drunk, man. Ah'm fine. Hear him out.'

But through a haze, McLane held on to Advocate mode: '**Joe**! I'm warning you. This is dangerous ground. Don't you say another word. He could be …'

'It's alright Brogan. Calm doon. The Commander here isn'ae wired. He's been brushed three times between the door and here.'

'Correct Joe. I'm not wired. Nice work by the way. Can I continue Brogan?'

'Sorry. I'm steamin' drunk … aye, what were ye sayin'?'

Leaning McLane against the bar, Big Joe signalled for cold water and somebody to get Joanne.

'So Commander, yuv now matched yur *partial* print at the scene. Whit's the letter aboot?'

'It was something in the Correspondence file kept by the Fiscal's senior assistant, Sheila McManus. Two dates, only a couple of days apart. I didn't connect them at first. Brogan, you've just been to hell and back, plus as you say your absolutely steamin' drunk, so you may not remember. But Joe and his wife received a letter just two days before Aldounhill was murdered. Right Joe?'

'Correct Commander.'

'OK. A letter?' burped McLane.

'Yes, bluntly telling them that Wee Joe's second appeal against conviction in Lord Aldounhill's court for murder, had been refused. That must have been awful for you Joe. And your wife of course.'

'Aye. It wiz like the ground just opened an' swallied her, Mr Imrie. It might be the death o' her yet.'

Having to speak out loud about the injustice done to his son, Big Joe's steel doors opened up. Tears welled and he choked on his words. But two very large whiskies in rapid succession put that right.

Back to taking charge of his purpose at this party, Imrie let his next words out loudly for all to hear: 'Now, you're not the kind of man who could just let that go. Are you Joe?'

Grabbing Joe's lapels, his face so close that their breath mingled, McLane tendered a formal caution to the man he thought of as his other half: 'For Christ's sake Joe!

Shut the fuck up. What are you doing? Jesus man. Don't tell me you weren't just *at* Aldounhill's house. No. Please. Joe! Were you *in* it?'

Big Joe Mularkey made no reply. Other than the one written all over his face.

Taking a turn at calming the tension, Imrie accepted a glass of cold water from Lenny, shoving it into Brogan's hand.

'Look, Brogan. Tonight you're celebrating. And with the best of reasons. So be sure of one thing. If I'd come here to make an arrest, the wagons would be full by now. So please. Let Joe do us both a favour. Now Joe, can I have it from the beginning?'

Looking around his beloved Calton Bar, Big Joe Mularkey downed a welcome cold beer, swayed and began: 'The night effter we got the letter, Ah went through to Edinburgh. Tucker got me the address. Ah would've gone straight there. But Molly was oot her mind wi' despair. Anyway, Ah got word that Aldounhill was staeyin' at 'is club in London that night. Bit the followin' day we found out that his cleaners had sent a shirt up tol Parliament House. Starched fur court the next day. So Ah figured he'd be at hame that night.'

McLane drew a deep breath: '*Please* tell me you

481

didn't go in the BMW? There's CCTV everywhere.'

'Brogan please. Ahm no' daft. Ah went oan the motorcycle. Wi' mah hookie plates oan. Oh, sorry Commander.'

Brushing that aside, Imrie raised his glass to another job well done.

'Ah got there aboot half 12. Quarter to wan in the moarnin'. Somethin' like that. An' parked behind some road work signs. There wur big trees coverin' the street lights right up baith sides. It was *really* dark. Ah watched the hoose for a bit frae just inside the driveway gate an' saw lights on in the room wi' the chandelier. An' the kitchen next to it. But then the kitchen light went oot an' Ah wondered if the wee bastard was on his ain. Ah couldn'ae hear anythin'. Bit there was four fancy cars parked on the drive. Nae music. Nothin' like that. So Ah got closer. The drive was gravelled, so Ah was hopin' Ah wouldn'ae leave prints. But Ah got a surprise. Ah heard a voice frae behind the front door an' Ah hid to duck away intae the bushes.'

McLane again raised his hand, but Imrie re-assured him with a tap on the arm.

'That's where we got the print. The uniforms covered it with a plastic dome, but it had already been badly damaged. As you can see, the heel's obliterated; trampled by a big bird, would you believe? Talk about bad luck? Forensics were tearing their hair out. That seagull saved you in court Brogan. Go on Joe.'

'Well, it was men's voices Ah heard behin' the door, but it was a wummin who left. At least Ah thought it was a wummin.'

Interrupting, Imrie wanted more to go on for the formal interview in the Station they all knew would follow: 'Help me here Joe. How tall was she? Wearing what?'

'Well the one who ran oot first was definitely oor new friend Sir Aubrey Winstanley. Ah was only a few feet away an' a bright security light came on when the door opened. So Ah got a real good look. He was wearin' a man's suit but nae shoes. He did huv a pair o' high heels in his hand. He was oan his mobile to somebuddy. Ah watched him jump intae wan o' the cars in the driveway an' he was oaff. Ah mean, he really floored it.'

Raising his index finger to his mouth, Imrie coughed. It was all the reminder Joe needed.

'Oh aye. An' of course he was wearin' somethin' that could be of some importance in a trial.'

Spluttering his water down his suit, McLane widened his eyes: 'For Christ's sake! Joe! It wasn't …?'

483

'It *was* Brogan, aye. Lipstick. Purple lipstick. So him Ah'd know anywhere. Ah didnae see the other yin till a wee bit later. She was aboot six feet tall Ah think. A slim wummin. Really skinny Ah remember. Werrin' a pink Bra thing wi' white stockins under a shawl thing. An' high heels. Masses o' long blonde hair tae.'

Producing the photograph of the not-very-well disguised Solicitor General from his inside jacket pocket Commander Imrie let both men see it: 'Like this?'

To McLane it was as though his hearing had been switched off. The bar went silent and he stood rooted to the spot. Now there were two Imries, two Lennys behind the bar and dozens of glasses in front of him.

Holding McLane around the shoulder, Big Joe continued: 'Aye. That's her. Ah mean him. Whutever it is. That's the wan who was shouting the odds at Aldounhill. Deffo. That's her. The argument must have started between them a' in the hoose when Winstanley fund oot that the star prize fur the followin' night was his wee boy bein' brought up frae London.'

Conscious that a jury of his peers were now listening carefully, McLane wanted the record straight. Widening his eyes and standing up straight, he nearly sounded like Mr Brogan McLane, Advocate in Parliament

House: 'Let's just be clear Joe. It was the Solicitor General who was shouting. Right?'

'Oh aye. Deffo. Winstanley left. An' only aboot five minutes later another bunch left tae. Aboot five o' them Ah think. A' werrin wummen's clothes. They a' piled right intae a brand-new Bentley Continental parked on the drive an' they were off. But this wummin person staeyed. She was shoutin' stuff like: Do you think I believe *you*? After you shafted me with the Palace? I should've killed you for that, you lying bastard. *This* is the *last* time. I swear it. You've always preferred her. I don't know why I listened to you. It was aw' stuff like that. She soundeed awfy drunk.'

Slipping deeper into Advocate mode for the Jury behind them, McLane asked : 'How can you be so sure Joe?'

'Because Ah saw her. Well, him. Winstanley was off in the car but he'd left the front door open. That's when Ah slipped in. Ah heard the voices. Angry voices upsterrs. So Ah ducked behind an open door in the hallway. Intae a coat room place. Plenty o' Barbours, an' like, hikin' boots an' aw' that. Ah just made it before the voices on the landin' got louder. The wummin ran right doon the stairs. Tae within' a couple a' feet frae me. She wiz wrappin' a

485

shawl thing roon aboot hersel'. Aldounhill was naked at the top o' the stairs. Ah could see his bare feet an' the lower bits o' his legs. The wummin was callin' Aldounhill a' the cheap low-lifes under the sun and sayin' she was gonnie ruin 'im. Aldounhill was shoutin' back but the wummin was kind o' spittin' oot the words sayin' he wid be 'out' in under ten minutes. She was wavin' a phone aboot, saying Winstanley had phoned the papers. Aldounhill screamed back that neither o' them had the guts. An' that was their problem. "Nae guts", he said. He was shoutin' that it took guts tae sit on the High Court bench an' they didnae have them. It was a proper cat-fight. But the wummin left an' it a' went quiet. She slammed the front door but it sort o' bounced open again. So ah waited. Quite a long while. Jist to be sure. Aboot ten minutes. Then Ah heard a motorcycle ootside.'

Nodding in agreement Imrie and McLane said as one: 'Probably Louise Bishop's photographer.'

'Aw ah heard was somebuddy prowlin' aboot. But they got nothin'. Anyway, Ah was in this coat room place wi' the door just ajar.

Both knowing the evidential significance of this moment at trial, McLane and Imrie leaned in closer. The jury would be underlining (1) Lord Aldounhill being alive at the top of the stairs when (2) both Winstanley and 'Jenny' Spiggot had left while (3) Big Joe Mularkey remained.

Downing the last of his water, McLane took the initiative: 'Are you absolutely sure about the sequence Joe?'

'Dead sure man. Ah got a real good look at him when he got tae the bottom o' the stairs. Ah'll never forget him. Anyway, Ah was just aboot to come oot when the front door opened again. Ah only just got the door shut, well ajar, before the same wummin came in. Ah say wummin, but ye know whit Ah mean. It was the same person who'd left after the lot in the Bentley. But wi' the blonde wig aff. The same gear on, the stockins, shoes; everything but the wig.'

'Did you see the face at that time Joe?'

'Naw. No' right away. Ah just remember gettin' back behind the door, an' bein' a bit confused aboot the back o' a man's head passin' me an' thinkin' that his bum was really like a wummin's. He ran up the stairs two or three at a time an' shouted somethin' aboot this being the last time. This is your last … minute or your last breath. Somethin' like that. It was *definitely* threatening. If there's wan thing Ah know when ah hear it, it's a threat.

Then Ah heard the thud. That must huv been Aldounhill hittin' the flair. An' then Ah heard glass smashin'. Mibbe it was the smash then the thud. Ah don't really remember. Then there was silence an' the guy came back doon the stairs. He didnae run or anything, he just sort o' swaggered. But Ah saw him at the boattum o' the stairs Mr Imrie. Clear as day. This time he was real careful to shut the front door wi' his shawl. Very quiet, he was. The whole thing only took a minute. Ah listened again fur a wee while an' then Ah took oaf ma' boots in the coat room an' went up the stairs. Ah looked in a few rooms, naturally no' touchin' anythin', an' then Ah went intae the room wi' the chandelier.

Taking a moment to down another four-finger dram, Joe continued his testimony to a now silent Calton Bar: 'The wee bastard was lyin' there. Naked like a cheap whore. He didnae recognise me of course. The champagne glass was sticking oot 'is neck an' his blood was oozin' intae the flairboards. All Ah can remember was that Ah waanted tae murder the wee bastard. Ah *so* SO waanted tae be the wan that did it. Fur mah boy. Fur mah wife. Fur masel'. Fur everybuddy lyin' in the jail who shouldnae be there. But Ah froze. Ah remember Ah waanteed tae piss oan him but then Ah thought o' you Brogan. Tellin' me aboot DNA an' shit. So Ah didnae. Ah just stood there watchin' 'im. He coughed a wee bit an' struggled tae look up at me. But Ah knew he wiz dyin'. Boys, Ah'm tellin' ye Ah *enjoyed* it. Ah stood there an' *really* enjoyed it. Watchin' that bastard die. He kind o' reached oot tae me but Ah didn'ae flinch. Ah just watched him die. Ah loved every second o' it. But as soon as he died Ah knew Ah hid tae skip. Ah waanted tae trash his posh hoose an' his chandelier but Ah knew Ah was better aff getting' the hell oot o' there. Ah hud ma memory an' Ah waz the wan who passed final sentence. Ah can pass that oan tae ma boy. That's his inheritance. Me. Big Joe Mularkey. Ah'm the only wan who saw Aldounhill die and that's enough fur me. Fur now.'

Gripping Joe's hair at the back, McLane pulled them forehead to forehead: 'My God Joe.' Why didn't you *tell* me man?'

Stepping in, Imrie settled the point: 'Brogan. Easy man. He couldn't. Just *think* about it for a second. If Joe had told that story when you were on trial, who would've believed him? Nobody. They'd have said he was covering for you. Setting up a smokescreen. Plus, he ran the risk of not only sinking you, but himself too by admitting to being at the scene of the murder. Right Joe?'

'Correct again Commander.'

Turning to the crowd with all the depth in his eyes that a lifetime's friendship brings, Big Joe continued: 'Brogan. You *always* told me never tae chase the game. You always say, that when you're swimmin' wi' legal sharks, ye should never make yer move too soon. If Ah had told you, Ah don't know how this widd've played oot. Ma way, we could try tae find the murderer an' get you aff; plus keep ma fresh evidence fur your appeal, right?'

Widening his eyes, Imrie corroborated Big Joe: 'Brogan. You must agree. Surely he's right.'

Seeing the point, McLane flickered his eyes in recognition.

Now tying up loose ends, Imrie stuck to business: 'So Joe, you're certain about the ID of Spiggot?'

'Absolutely Mr Imrie. 100%. But whit aboot the illegal entry charge? How duz that pan oot?'

'You'll be given absolute immunity from prosecution because you'll be a Crown witness against Spiggot. In fact you'll be the *star* prosecution witness at his trial in Parliament House.'

At that announcement, the air around the three men lightened and McLane was once again the man with the broadest smile in Glasgow.

The Trial

Imrie raised his glass: 'So Brogan, you're still Spiggot's defence counsel. Having heard the best evidence for the prosecution, are you sticking to your considered legal Opinion?'

The whole bar roared with laughter as McLane pulled on his lapel, playing counsel: 'Rubbish Mr Mularkey. I put it to you that you weren't there at all!'

Playing along, Imrie bellowed: 'Please have in front of you Prosecution Exhibit No 1, a 100% certain boot print. Mr Mularkey, do you recognise that?'

To more raucous laughter the whole bar raised their glasses. With the last detail settled and McLane still in mild shock, a swinging lamp caught some old stained glass, flickering a rainbow light across the crowd. The light reminded McLane of the Great South Window in Parliament House and he wondered if this was the kind of justice King James the Fifth had in mind in 1532 when he inaugurated a High Court and appointed a Lord Advocate to prosecute criminals in Scotland. For the moment it didn't really matter.

Hand upon hand fell on the bar, sending a signal that a dark cloud had lifted. And that maybe, just maybe, the time to see some real justice coming out of Edinburgh was coming. Wee Joe's latest appeal would be the first test of that.

On a nod from Tucker Queen, Lenny the barman clanged the bell.

Standing taller than any other man in the bar, Big Joe Mularkey scanned them all. With every eye on him and the only sound the deep breathing from those who had just stopped dancing, Big Joe became emotional and this time he let it show; a significant moment in itself.

Grabbing a full glass of whisky, Big Joe raised it to his full arm's length. Calling in his steady commanding voice, he silenced the Calton Bar: 'Friends and neebors, please be upstandin' an' charge your glasses for the man o' the hour. Tae the finest lawyer in the land an' mah auldest pal. Our man in Parliament House, Scottish Advocate Brogan McLane!'

The End.

Author's note to the reader:

I want to express my deepest thanks to you for reading my first novel. I hope it was an enjoyable read.

Of course, the life-blood of any Amazon Kindle author is 'reviews'. So I would be deeply obliged for your review.

As a thanks for that, I'm happy to include below the first few pages of the second novel in the Parliament House Books series entitled The Order.

However, before release of the second novel - called The Order - you could read a Prequel to Brogan McLane's crusading efforts in Parliament House. The prequel is called 'The Cross – How blood brothers died and rose again.'

If you'd like to read the Prequel, just email me at johnmayerauthor@gmail.com and I'll send you a copy. You have my absolute assurance that I'll never sell, pass-on or otherwise do anything with your email address which is in any way dodgy, distasteful or illegal. I'll keep it to myself. Happy reading of The Parliament House Books.

John Mayer

Sneak Peek

at

The Order

The Parliament House Books

Book Two

~ The Order ~

Prologue : Africa, oh Africa.

Splitting the air between the tree that speaks and the tree that doesn't, the Blue Head soldiers' trucks smashed straight through their village; shattering the silent dawn and scattering the feeding BiriBiri birds and the screeching monkeys in their high tree tops. The wind stopped supporting the sky and millions of rain stones fired down, pelting the women and children.

From the hut her grandfather built long ago, delirious with rage and still half-drunk, Senga staggered out screaming and distraught. Pulling out her hair and stretching her throat drum tight, she screamed a call up into the big trees. For death to tear out her soul. For animals to drink the blood she no longer needed. Spinning and screaming, in her breathless empty blackness, she collapsed into the out-ditch.

Truck after truck's big wheels narrowly missed her straggling legs, drenching her in cold red mud.

From their sewing canopy, the bread-grinding stone and the new mud-brick water store, a dozen clicking women ran towards their sister. But none dared touch her for fear that what had struck her, might strike them too. Hopping from foot to foot around Senga's wretched soul they screeched, watching Senga lose her tortured mind.

Falling quiet, the women averted their children's eyes from the lifeless body in the ditch.

The men kept away; over in the new red-brick Hall, pretending to be in council. Some said they'd seen it coming, and knew: but all agreed that since the arrival of Monsieur Combot, nothing could be done. Taken by the rhythm of the truth, along with Senga's children, the old ways were gone.

John Mayer

The Order

Part One

Article 1.1 ~ The Order

To the sound of good brogues on parquet flooring, Brogan McLane QC strode across a darkened Parliament Hall, where only a dozen pencil lights shone down onto the white marble heads of judges long dead. With his white shirt sleeves rolled up and his silk bow tie loosened, McLane glanced over at the King's clock striking 10:15pm. The Evening Servitor had been hesitant to interrupt him and only coughed into his hand about someone at the front door... who wasn't a Member of Faculty.

In the darkened Atrium, through the narrow faded panes in the old double doors, it wasn't at all clear who this might be. Just someone tall, wearing polished Oxford brogues and a good raincoat. As he opened the wide double-doors the man turned, and there stood the last person McLane expected to see: 'Well I never! Commander Imrie as I live and breathe. What can I do for you at this late hour?'

'Hello Brogan. Nice to see you again. I'm sorry if this is ...but everyone else is at ...'

'The Big Wig Ball. I know. No, it's OK. The night servitor looked like it might be urgent. Come away in Terry. The library's empty.'

Pressing down a row of six old brass-ball switches, McLane flooded The Law Room: the inner sanctum of legal research in Parliament House. Two wide crystal chandeliers twinkled in the iron railing of the surrounding gallery and reflected in the polished brass inkwells in front of every Senior Counsel's desk. Pulling out a half-round wooden armchair, McLane nodded that it was OK to sit.

Perched on the edge of his seat, Imrie's face fell from a forced half-smile down to grim.

McLane got right down to business: 'What? I mean … what is it Terry? You look awful, *if* you don't mind me saying so.'

His guest wrung his hands and couldn't look McLane in the eye: 'I need an Order, Brogan. There is an international child abduction element. And the intel is all MI5 background stuff.'

McLane cleared a space on his desk: 'An Order? Man, it must be statutory if you can't sign it yourself.'

From the briefcase on his knees, Commander

Imrie pulled a bundle of field reports two inches thick and dumped it on the old oak desk in front of McLane.

Picking up the bundle, McLane flicked through the first three pages. 'MmHmm. Diamond smuggling, international child abduction, money laundering, import duty evasion and ... what?'

'A charge under the Maritime Security Act 1976.'

'What's *that* doing in amongst diamond ...?'

'The eh ... The people we're looking at are ... well, we tracked them escaping to sea from a port in North Africa and right now they're in UK waters without proper safety certificates. As we speak the ship is steaming up the west coast. So time *is* of the essence.'

McLane knew Imrie of old. He was the toughest and fairest police officer imaginable. All this hesitance and wringing of hands just wasn't like him. Flicking to the back page, McLane was getting a sense of why Imrie needed his services when his eye fell on the name of the suspect. He froze in his chair. Ticking at the wall, the big grandfather clock marked this moment in McLane's mind as a day of reckoning. *'WHAT? How could he? It's just not ... He'd never in a million ... Well, I don't suppose he'd ever ... I've seen him ... Christ, I've seen him do some ...*

But this?'

In the reverential silence of that legal sanctum, the two lawmen stared into each other's stony faces. The moment had come. University professors mention them but no-one ever expects the moment to actually arrive. Yet here it was.

With a croak in his voice and looking around the empty library, McLane could only whisper. 'But ... Neraida 2? Terry, that ship belongs to ...'

'I'm really sorry Brogan. But everyone else is at ...'

Letting the bundle go limp in his hand, McLane finished Imrie's sentence: 'The Big Wig Ball. Yes, you said. But this is surely ... I mean, Neraida 2 belongs to Big Joe Mularkey. Terry, how could ...? Did you say MI5? This is *way* too much of a coincidence.'

'Click' went the top of Imrie's ball-point pen, and it was his turn to interject: 'Brogan, I'm afraid it's not. Look, tonight, please ... just do your duty as a QC. You're the only name available, or I wouldn't be here. I don't have to tell you, the list of qualified people to sign one of these Orders is laid out in statute. You're named as the expert in international child abduction. I've got the evidence and every ...'

'Everyone else is at the Ball and I'm Cinderella. The last name available.'

'Actually I was going to say that every second counts.'

Imrie double-clicked his pen and looked McLane in the eye: 'Brogan, take my advice and just do your legal duty. If you're satisfied that our field reports reveal reasonable suspicion that diamond smuggling and international child abduction has or is now taking place in UK waters, then you are duty bound to ...'

McLane's chest felt tight and his breathing became quite erratic. Raising his eyes to the ornate plastered ceiling, McLane swallowed and took a moment. Surely not? His oldest friend. His best man. His protector during all that trouble two years ago. Surely not?

Edging forward to the point of almost falling off his seat, Imrie pushed his point: 'Brogan, please. I wouldn't be asking *you* if the intel wasn't ... well, *overwhelming*. I've got the *entire* serious crime squad standing by. Four helicopters, every armed officer available and I've even requisitioned three bloody speedboats. Brogan, I know he's your ...'

McLane shook his head, and with a wave refused

Imrie's pen. Dropping his chin into his chest, he succumbed: 'Alright. Yes. OK. But I'd prefer to write it with this.'

The fountain pen his wife gave him upon Calling to the Bar was lying next to his inkwell. As McLane dipped the nib in his inkwell, Imrie thought he detected a nervous twitch in his hand. But when McLane straightened the Warrant Sheet and began to write, his hand was as solid as a rock:

Given under my hand within Parliament House :

I, the undersigned, being a legally nominated person for the purposes of the Hague Convention against international child abduction; and having been presented with sufficient credible information to warrant the granting of powers to arrest the ship 'Neraida 2' and those persons controlling her on board or from afar, I now Grant all such lawful power and Order such arrest.

Brogan McLane, Queen's Counsel.

29612025R00276

Printed in Great Britain
by Amazon